CONTENTS

HAYTI

Sor Lucrezia di Marchionni, a Florentine nun, leads a mission to Hayti, Spain's first American colony, two decades after its 'discovery' by Christopher Columbus. But she also has a secret assignment – to find out if the passage through to Asia depicted on a world map published by the German cartographer Martin Waldseemüller actually exists. On the island, she meets up with Fray Hugo de Montenegro, a Dominican monk who has been there for several years and has been collecting accounts of Spanish atrocities. Their investigations bring them into contact with Taíno freedom fighters and their allies, escaped African slaves who had been imported to work on the new sugar plantations, as well as to the attention of the brutal colonial authorities. The story unfolds against the background of the horrors of the Spanish Conquest of the Americas, the destruction of its original peoples, the commencement of the Atlantic slave trade and the beginnings of globalisation with the foundation of the Spanish Empire.

HAYTI

A NOVEL

KURTIS SUNDAY

ꟼ

Cover images: Waldseemüller World Map of 1507;
and Cuban red macaw, also called the Hispaniolan macaw,
by John Gerrard Keulemans, 1907.

The island of Hayti, as it appears in these pages, is a dark fictional place. The events that occurred on the real Hayti during the last decade of the 15th century and the early decades of the 16th century, and subsequently, are among the most horrific in the annals of human history. A true description of those events is beyond the scope of any fictional account.

Preface to this edition

Hayti is probably the first work of fiction written in a European language in the New World, set in the New World, and which has the invasion of the New World by the Old World as its central theme.

The original manuscript, with its rather unwieldy title, *A True History of Depredations Committed by Those Who Call Themselves Christians in the Newly Discovered Islands of the New World, Penned by a Sister of the Order of the Hieronymites and a Brother of the Order of the Preachers, with Accounts of Heathen Practices*, came to light in Granada in 1904. The first printed edition, bearing the title *Hayti*, appeared twenty years later; the wheels within wheels of the world of book publishing ground as slowly then as they do now, it seems. Its dust jacket claims that the original manuscript had actually been unearthed in France, found among the papers of an unnamed Napoleonic officer who had come across it in the archives of the Inquisition in Madrid during the Peninsular War, sometime in the first decade of the 18th century – a plausible account, but no further details or evidence for this was offered. The original manuscript is now lost again, quite possibly destroyed during the Spanish Civil War.

The book, in its present form, consists of two intertwining narratives, both purporting to be actual accounts rather than fictions, though this is nowhere explicitly stated. The primary narrative is by Sor Lucrezia di Marchionni, a Hieronymite nun who supposedly led a mission in Santo Domingo on Hispaniola, Spain's first American colony, in around the year 1510, two decades after its 'discovery' by Christopher Columbus – or Don Cristóbal Colón as he is referred to in her account. The second narrative – originally intended to be only a commentary on Lucrezia di Marchionni's but which became much more – was written by Fray Hugo de Montenegro, a Dominican monk, while crossing the Atlantic on his return to Spain. The original manuscript, the dust cover of the first edition claims, was written in Castilian, Italian and at times even in Latin, its authors (fictional though they may be) being fluent to varying degrees in all three languages, though what parts of the text were originally in which language is not very discernible; nor is the language in which the protagonists were speaking always clearly indicated.

The first edition was in Catalan, published by Florian Books, a small semi-academic anarchist-leaning press, in 1924 in Barcelona, a decade before the Spanish Civil War. A Spanish (Castilian) edition, a translation of the Catalan edition, only appeared in 1969, in Mexico. The first English-language edition was published in London by the left-leaning Tilsiter Press in 1939, just before the outbreak of World War Two. It included the historical notes, reprinted in this edition, by Christian Neufeld, a German historian who fought with the International Brigade on the Republican side in the Spanish Civil War. How and why Christian Neufeld came to write the historical notes is unknown. Spanish America was not his field. His only known works are two short monographs: *Peter Gaiß, the Struggle for Dignity*, an account of a peasants' revolt in Southern Germany just before the Reformation; and *The Brethren of the Free Spirit, Revolt, Mysticism and Ideology*, an account of a pantheistic revolutionary Christian movement in the Middle Ages which was suppressed by the Inquisition. Perhaps, while in Barcelona, he had some contact with Florian Books, perhaps even brought the Catalan edition to the notice of Tilsiter Books through an English acquaintance in the International Brigade. One can only speculate.

At a cursory glance, *Hayti* appears to be a bona fide historical document, but it is undoubtedly a work of 'fiction' – the word 'fiction' I have put in inverted commas for reasons which Neufeld explains in his historical notes. Traditionally, the first work of fiction thought to be conceived and written in the Americas, in Santo Domingo, is Fernández de Oviedo's *Libro del muy esforado e inencible caballero Don Claribalte (Book of the very striving and invincible caballero Don Claribalte)*, published in Valencia in 1519; though Oviedo is best known for his *La general y natural historia de las Indias*, a book which Bartolomé de las Casas said "contains as many lies as pages". An apologist for the

Conquest, Oviedo was appointed master overseer of the annual gold smelting at Santo Domingo in 1514. *Hayti* – in which Oviedo makes the briefest of appearances, being mentioned twice – may actually predate Oviedo's romance, in its conception if not its completion, but it is impossible to prove that it does so. The first book written in a European language in the Americas is Ramón Pané's *An Account of the Antiquities of the Indians*, a very sketchy report written at Columbus's behest on the religion, myths and customs of the Taíno, the original inhabitants of Hispaniola; the true authorship of which, some scholars suggest, should in fact by rights go to his interpreter Guaticabanú, or Diego Colón II as he is referred to in *Hayti*, because Pané, on his own admission, did not actually speak all the Haytian languages, and often only wrote down what Guaticabanú related to him.

Alison Owens
Dept. of Hispanic Studies
University of Wales
Wales, UK

Translator's note

This edition of Hayti is both a translation of the original Catalan edition published by Florian Books in Barcelona in 1924 and an edited reproduction of the English translation published by Tilsiter Press in 1939, the latter being itself translated directly from the Catalan edition (translator unknown); though I have also referred to the 1969 Mexico City translation on occasion. I have endeavoured to keep the original texture of the 1939 English edition. In the 1924 Catalan translation, the names of places and ships were often translated into Catalan; and in the later English edition, they were translated into English; I have followed the same practice. At times, I have also retained anglicised versions of Spanish names as they appeared in the 1939 Tilsiter Press edition, though that would not normally be the practice today; for example, the Apostolic Nuncio Bernaldo Buil is referred to as Bernaldo Boyle (as he is in Washington Irving's 1828 Columbus biography). I have not anglicised or translated Taíno words except where it would tax the reader unduly.

Katherine Ireland
Aberystwyth, Wales, 2017

ONE

An Account of the Indian Countries Discovered by the Admiral Don Cristóbal Colón, in the Hand of Sor Lucrezia di Marchionni, a Sister of the Order of the Hieronymites, Santo Domingo, the Spanish Island.

Life abounds here. Never have I laid eyes upon such fecundity. It is what they call the rainy season now but every now and again the rain ceases and the grey clouds part and the sun appears – never for very long, but long enough to give one an impression of its reputed ferocity at these latitudes – and everything becomes suddenly bright and lustrous and glistens; and the world fleetingly appears as it perhaps appeared, newly created and glorious, to our first parents. And I look with a sort of childish wonder on it all: the verdant grass and palm trees in our nunnery garden, the flowers so delicate and colourful, the white mist enveloping the hills to the north of us, and the glittering surface of the sea in the bay.

It took twenty-eight days for our armada – six caravels, three large square-rigged carracks and a nao – to reach the Fortunate Isles, apparently longer than is usually the case. There, after picking up fresh water, wood and additional victuals, we were joined by another three vessels and in their company set off on the principal part of our journey, the longer crossing of the Oceanus Occidentalis. It took us another forty-four days, and nights, to reach the Antilles, to give these islands their proper and ancient name. The swiftest crossing ever achieved, I was told, is two and a half weeks. Officially, thirty to forty or so ships a year make the voyage now, usually in smaller armadas. How many make the voyage 'unofficially' it is impossible to know.

The sheer discomfort and tediousness of an ocean voyage is scarcely imaginable to those who only know solid land. Images in books and paintings give the impression that a ship is akin to a floating citadel. In fact, it is more akin to a floating farmyard, and smells like one. Our ship, *The Valiant Crusader*, a caravel, the swiftest type of vessel ever to sail upon the seas our captain assured us, was a hundred feet long and twenty or so feet wide at the middle, larger than usual for its type. And in this cramped space, above deck and below deck, all of the numerous and sundry items necessary for the sustenance of life, which we normally take for granted on land, needed to be carried: from cheese to thread to salt; and livestock, squealing pigs in our case; a flock of chickens had the run of the deck. No small number of passengers and seamen sickened on the voyage across.

We also carried a half-dozen neighing horses and a pack of war dogs. The former, lest they break their legs from the incessant rolling of the ship, were hung in slings from the timbers below deck for the entire duration of the voyage, though they were exercised on deck as regularly as weather permitted, which was often enough. Every morning their droppings were gathered up and cast overboard. Their fodder and water, needless to say, needed to be transported too. The war dogs, thirteen vicious Irish wolfhounds and mastiffs the size of half-grown heifers, were kept at the stern, as the rear of the vessel is called, in cages under the so-called quarterdeck. They were exercised on deck every day, straining at their leashes and muzzled. Once a week a squealing pig was slaughtered to provide them with the raw meat they needed. One of the bitches gave birth to a litter on the fourth week out.

However, a good captain attempts to keeps his ship clean, both above and below, inside and out; and one of the common sailor's main tasks is to skivvy and scrub endlessly, forever heaving buckets of seawater up out of the ocean. This substance, poisonous to drink, is so different to fresh water that it barely deserves the name of water. Clothes washed in it slowly rot. Impregnated with salt, it coats and dries out one's skin but one has no choice but to wash with it. The barrels of fresh water we were carrying – though after a week or so at sea to call it 'fresh' is somewhat of a misnomer – were far too precious to be wasted on ablutions.

The ship's 'kitchen' – an iron pot hung over an open fire in a box filled with sand and surrounded by a screen to shelter it from the wind – was situated at the bow, as far away as possible from the gun powder and armaments stored at the stern. Our meals consisted of two hot, or rather warm pottages a day, served just after noon and at dusk. The principal nutrient these contained was either meat, salted bacon or beef for the main part, bony and gristly, or more commonly fish – we carried salted cod, and salted barrelled sardines – filled out with rice, chickpeas, lentils and other beans, and flavoured with garlic. Officers and passengers had the privilege of their own utensils. The crew helped themselves from a common wooden bowl. We ate this pottage with so-called ship's bread, a sort of twice-baked biscuit; it is hard and unpalatable, and capable of lasting a year if kept dry, I was told, but was reasonably edible when dipped in the pottage. However, retaining cooked food in one's stomach is a near impossibility in the early days of a sea voyage, even for not a small number of seasoned sailors, some of whom were wretchedly sick. During the calmish days we enjoyed, and there were many, the sailors managed to catch some fishes which, freshly cooked, were a welcome addition to our diet. The wine, despite strict rationing, lasted only four weeks. Needless to say, no small quantity of firewood, which had to be kept dry, was also part of our cargo. Fire aboard ship is every seaman's nightmare; so when the weather was bad, which was not often, we had to do with cold fare, which, it must be said, was often superior to the hot. This consisted mainly of ship's bread dipped in watered Jerez wine and meagre rations of almonds, a few olives, oil of the same, molasses, and honey and goat cheese which we'd picked up on the Fortunate Isles – a very superior cheese it must be said.

Officers and passengers were lodged beneath the quarterdeck in cubicles little bigger than a confessional. Only our captain had one room – or cabin, as seamen say – to himself; it was furnished with a miniature and roughly carpentered escritoire at which he kept his log, made his navigational calculations and noted discrepancies in his sea maps. These portolano charts, as they are called, show only coastlines, islands and ports, and are criss-crossed with compass-rose lines to indicate the relative positions of these to one another; all inland features such as cities, mountains and rivers are omitted. Two of these cubicles – or berths as the seaman calls them – were allocated to us. We slept in net beds, called 'hamacas', hung from the timbers of the deck above; these remain motionless while the ship rolls, and are thus effective against the nausea; during the day they are rolled up and stored. They are an Indian contrivance, and surprisingly comfortable when one gets used to them, so it was possible to sleep reasonably well – when the dogs directly below us in their cages suffered us to. At times the fearsome creatures whined and barked incessantly through the night, their chilling howls echoing over the ocean as we sailed otherwise silently through the starry darkness.

The crew, of which there were over two dozen, and the twenty soldiers, passed the hours of darkness as best they could in any corner they could find on the packed deck or in the hay store. Our captain said they would be able to buy their own hamacas when they arrived in the islands and sleep in them on the way back when the ship would most likely be less jam-packed. The performance of one's necessaries in such a confined space is barely possible in a decent manner, and a ship is more a man's world than any monastery; but for modesty's sake, arrangements were made for us which it would hardly be appropriate to describe in any detail.

The hazards of the voyage are always on one's mind, especially the terrific possibility of simply getting lost in the endless watery vastness. Our captain laughed when I once voiced fears of this and said his compass and the Pole Star would see us through, God willing. The methods the navigator uses to find his way are several. He needs to be able to determine both his latitude and longitude if he is to sail with any degree of certitude. It was instructive to see these methods being used in practice, and in part explained, but I am now too excited and full of new impressions of this country to rally the concentration necessary to provide you with an adequate description.

Then there are the dangers of hidden reefs, storms, running into land at night or in fog, the predations of mercifully rare leviathans and kraken, and pirates, though our captain reassured me the latter do not venture so far from land. To preserve us from all this multitude of dangers and to keep our spirits up, a Salve Regina was recited by the entire assembly of officers, passengers and crew on deck every evening, at Vespers, just before the sun descended into the endless horizon ahead of us – a practice, I was told, also followed by Don Cristóbal on the ships he commanded. On Sundays and Holy Days, both during the first leg of our voyage and after we had left the Fortunate Isles, our three Franciscans took turns to celebrate mass.

At times – and the one thing one has no shortage of aboard ship is time – I took to wondering what worldly passions drive men to brave these dangers and tolerate such discomforts. Spiritual passions I can understand; for what hardships, pains and tribulations, often self-inflicted or not avoided when they could have been, have not spiritual men and women down the ages endured to mortify the flesh and glimpse eternal beatitude, not to mention the mortal agonies countless martyrs have willingly suffered for our faith. But to endure such privation and misery for worldly things? I sometimes wonder if those of us who have taken vows of poverty and chastity underestimate the strength of the worldly passions, trivialise them even.

Our captain laughed when I once asked him what drove him to risk such dangers, to ply the wet desert, as he calls it. We were on the quarterdeck, at night, making good speed on the shimmering, spectral and seemingly infinite expanse of the waters. In the moonlight, it was hard to tell what manner of laugh it was. He often laughed at my questions.

"A sober captain can grow rich from his cargos," he said, "or, if lucky, by some act of gallantry or daring or discovery find himself favoured." He is a man of relatively modest origins, like most of his calling. "Or maybe I was simply born with much salt in my blood," he added, laughing again

"And your men?" I ventured. "And the soldiers?"

"The world's flotsam and jetsam," he said, pausing for a moment to think. "Gold, and all they believe it can buy. Visions of finding the Gold Land, El Dorado, the Holy Grail – the ilusión indiana." Below us, on the lower deck, a caballero and one of the Franciscans – they were little more than ghostly shadows in the moonlight – were conversing at the rail. "Some search for material gold. Others search for spiritual gold," he added. I was about to object to the thoughtless comparison but then he laughed again and said something about the wind and how the moon in a clear sky was the seafarer's truest friend. "Our light in the darkness," he called it.

A day or two later, as we transversed the mar de baga, the so-called seaweed sea, one of the sailors caught a shark, a repulsive creature near enough the size of a man. It thrashed and flounced about the deck, snapping at the air with a mouthful of teeth so ferocious that one could not help thinking that the beast was some sort of demon made flesh. The soldiers sliced off its fin and its tail with their swords, inducing the creature to even further frenzies of agony and ferocity, before finally hefting it over the side with their halberds to a chorus of loud cheers – seamen will eat such sea monsters only if faced with starvation. For men who are accustomed to a life of action, days, nay weeks, of enforced idleness aboard ship must be unbearably monotonous. Their craving for distraction is understandable. And indeed, after this minor adventure, spirits on board were noticeably lighter for the rest of the day.

We sighted land at dusk on Saint Cyril's Day and such was our desire for it that it seemed for a moment that it was no less than the Garden of Eden itself which our sea-weary eyes were catching a glimpse of. But since it was a moonlit night, we sailed on, hugging the ghostly coast. The next morning it began to rain.

When we sighted Santo Domingo, we raised the red and gold standard of Castile, and sailed triumphantly into the harbour and dropped anchor in its flat, rain-sprinkled, brown waters. The bells of a whitewashed church – perched on a rain-drenched hill, under a grey and low-hanging sky – rang out to announce our arrival and to give thanks for our safe passage.

"Can you smell it?" our captain asked me as we waited on deck in the rain to be ferried to the quayside. And there was indeed a strange and noticeable smell in the air. I had been so preoccupied with the unfamiliar sights and sounds that I had not noticed it. It – 'smell' is perhaps too weak a word but I know of no other – is hard to describe; it was of earth and warmth, decay and fecundity, and quite distinct, sharp even, like a whiff of some vague musty spice. It seemed to be announcing that we were now, finally, indeed truly somewhere else.

"It is the smell of Asia," he explained. "In a few hours or so you will no longer notice it."

Rowing boats carved from massive tree trunks, called 'canoas', capable of holding twenty men, rowed by Indians and captained by Spaniards and Black Ladinos – as we call our Castilian Africans – ferried us ashore through the rain, where yet more Indians waited to unload our chattels and our armada's invalids on their makeshift litters. And so eventually we stood on solid land again, knelt, gave thanks and kissed the ground of this new land. The good Fray Pedro, instantly recognisable in the black and white habit of the Dominican Preachers, was waiting to welcome us. The gentlemen from the customs house cast a cursory glance over out chattels before allowing us on our way. As Fray Pedro led us to what is to be our nunnery, the unloading of the ships had begun, the barrels of Fugger quicksilver first – they were the last item of cargo to be loaded in Cadiz, the priceless metal corrodes the toughest wood and needed to be decanted quickly.

Thus, my dear Balthazar, ends my first proper entry in this report, and my mission – in both senses of that word – finally begins. Not knowing if any sort of paper would be available here, I purchased a dozen and a half quires in Cadiz before our departure, along with a quantity of ink and a supply of the best swan quills.

Ж

Here begins Fray Hugo de Montenegro's commentary – also a narrative – on Sor Lucrezia di Marchionni's 'Account', which he wrote sailing back from the Indies to Spain. It has been printed here in a different typeface for the facilitation of the reader.

If only God had willed that this journey were as pleasant! We have been two weeks at sea now, at first sailing north, and then a few days ago turning east towards Christendom – I nearly wrote 'home' but I have been so long on Hayti – or was rather ... Shall I ever return there again? During those two weeks, the *Incarnation* has heaved and swayed and bounced relentlessly on an endless grey sea under an unremittingly bleak and sunless sky. I have lost count of the number of times I have had to scramble to the pot in my cupboard – my 'cabin' is no larger than a cupboard – and disgorge into it most of the little of what I have been able to eat; or when my stomach is empty, retch and retch. Or have had to rush to vomit into the sea, or attempt to, for the heaving and swaying means that most of what I throw up merely streaks down the side of the hull. For the most I have been reduced to lying in my hamaca, attempting to keep as much nourishment in my stomach as is necessary to maintain life, with only the creaking timbers of the ship and Savonarola's dumb macaw for company. The sole exception to this lying in despair and wishing that this seasickness would simply stop – as it does, quite suddenly, they say, and did on my voyage out – is that I have made it a point of honour each day, at least once, to haul myself out onto the deck, my beloved prayer book or beads in hand, to say my offices. At other times I say my prayers lying in my hamaca. I find great comfort in the familiar words. They lull me back to my childhood days, to the purity of my childhood faith, to a time when to my child's eyes angels were almost materially visible. My prayers are my only antidote to the perpetual state of disgust I find myself in, disgust at the excretions of my body and the sea itself. However, there has been some slight improvement in my condition today, which has enabled me to take the opportunity to begin to read this document, which has been my intention since it came into my possession. I have had to break the seal, unavoidable but necessary, for there is much at stake, and I feel duty-bound to ensure that the good Sor Lucrezia di Marchionni's account of conditions on Hayti, and her description of the events which led to my banishment from that island, is true and complete in its essentials.

TWO

The Indians are a golden-brown complexioned race, not unlike the Guanche natives of the Fortunate Isles. Many of them are finely proportioned creatures blessed with pleasing, if odd, countenances. They have a somewhat delicate, even fragile, air about them. They have long proud noses, which in some are almost beak-shaped. The foreheads of many – the more striking of them – slant backwards to an exaggerated degree, which in the most extreme cases gives their heads an oval, egg-like shape. This effect, I am informed, is achieved by binding the cranium in infancy between two boards, one pressing against the forehead, the other against the rear of the skull, and leaving the infant in that painful and dangerous condition for several days. This peculiar deformation, combined with the timid pride which with they carry themselves, lends them an unexpected if strange, nobility of bearing. Their eyes are invariably a dark brown. Both men and women have jet-black curl-less hair, usually worn long by both sexes, mane-like, though many of the men shave the front of their skulls; indeed, it has a texture vaguely similar to that of a horse's mane, the finest thoroughbred's mane, for it is not coarse, at least not to look at, and at times seems to shimmer like the oily feathers of a starling. All the men are utterly beardless, having at most the trace of a moustache like that of a youth approaching manhood. Both sexes paint their faces, mainly with red ochre, but also with white and black pigments. Many also have markings and designs engraved on their faces and all over their bodies; I have been told that the symbols indicate rank and family. Their principal vice is sloth, not greed, Fray Montenegro tells me.

It has been raining almost without interruption since our arrival.

Santo Domingo, like all ports, is a manly place, the rhythm of its rude masculine life punctuated by the coming and going of ships. Every few days the sails of another ship appear on the rain-drenched horizon, as if out of nowhere, and the sails of other ships disappear into the same vastness and another uncertain voyage across the Oceanus Occidentalis or to the other Indian countries. At any one time, there are at least half a dozen vessels lying at anchor in the harbour.

The original settlement was founded by Bartolomé Colón, Don

Cristóbal's brother, in '96 and was on the other side of the Río Ozama, whose mouth forms the bay. He named it New Isabela in memory of Isabela, the unsuccessful settlement which his father had attempted a few years earlier on the north coast of the island; which, I am told, now lies completely deserted, inhabited by feral pigs and mosquitoes, and some say haunted by the ghosts of those who came to grief there. It had little fresh water and was exposed to the so-called hurucans, storms so fierce that there is no word in Latin or Castilian for them. But New Isabela fared little better. It was also ravaged by a hurucan and the spot suffered plagues of ants. So Nicolás de Ovando, the then Governor, in its stead, ordered the building of Santo Domingo on this side of the bay. That was about ten years or so ago.

The city now contains several thousand souls. Most of the buildings are whitewashed and are all laid out in a most orderly manner; the straight and perpetually muddy streets – though I am assured that constant rain is not typical for this time of the year – run more or less parallel to one another. There are several squares, the largest and central one being called the Plaza de Armas. Many of the building plots are in the process of being built upon, including the one on which the cathedral will stand; but other plots are still vacant. Warehouses, many of them half-built, and taverns, at the back of which cheap seafarers' lodgings are to be had, line the quayside. The chandlers do a roaring trade. I'm told that the price for maritime fixtures and fittings can be five or six times what is in Seville or Cadiz. Gangs of Indians, overseen by their Castilian or Black Ladino foremen, spend their days loading and unloading cargoes – there is a lot of coastal and island-to-island trade – or patiently going to and fro laden with hods of bricks and tiles from the kilns in the woods to the north.

The Governor's current residence, called the Castle in the local parlance, because that is what it looks like and is, is as impressive as many a like building in Christendom. Construction of a new residence, or the Palace as everyone calls it, is underway; the ground floor and the colonnaded frontage are near completion. Like the Castle, it too will be surrounded by an extensive garden, and work has already begun on that. A garrison of soldiers lodged in a barracks a stone's throw from the Castle, opposite the sturdy powder house, is responsible for upholding the peace and maintaining good order in the settlement; though at times, I have been told, they cause as much disorder as they are charged to prevent. The Hospital de San Nicolás de Bari, constructed and decorated in a strange mixture of Gothic and Mozarabic styles, is another imposing building; in fact, many of the buildings would not look out of place in Andalusia. It is said that Ovando was inspired to commission the building of the Hospital when he saw the devotion with which a Black Ladino woman was caring for the sick under the most miserable circumstances and decided that a suitable building was required for that charitable purpose. Of the private dwellings, the large tile-roofed house of the Genoese Grimaldis, the richest merchants here, is the most imposing. There are even the beginnings of a seminary – currently a collection of buildings no grander than our nunnery – where a Dominican Doctor of Theology and a Franciscan Doctor of Canon Law read to less than a dozen young men of their respective orders, as well as teaching Castilian, grammar, Latin and theology to some of the sons of Indian notables. But above all Santo Domingo is a port. Concepción de la Vega, situated in the Vega Real, the island's large and long central gorge, where much gold is refined, is reputed to be even a rougher place.

At times I am given to dizzy flights of enthusiasm for the novelty of all I behold. The plants, the trees, the bushes and the grasses are as different to those in Christendom as is summer from winter. Yet they are also familiar in an odd and somewhat disquieting manner. And some days I am haunted by a sense of melancholia, a flattening of the spirit. Life abounds here, but so too does decay, the one feeding upon the other.

During our first few evenings, while sitting on the sheltered porch of our humble but sufficiently comfortable nunnery, enveloped in the humid tropical darkness of the nights of this place – which are filled with bats, of which there seems to be an inordinate number here, and the sounds of strange frogs and toads and other strange creatures – I have often had the peculiar feeling that there were presences about, hovering just out of sight.

"Our local incubi and succubae," Fray Montenegro says. The good Preacher is responsible for us settling in here and arranged the lease on our house. Our mentor and confessor, a big man, he has been here for many years, alone, Fray Pedro and the other Dominican Preachers having arrived only about a year or so ago. "Remnants of the demons that the Haytians used to worship, and still do in the hills," he says. "The warlocks or wizards, the so-called bohiques – and there are still a few left – used to conjure them up." He insists on calling the island by its old heathen appellation of 'Hayti' or 'Ayti' and the Indians 'Haytians';

though they also, he tells me, call themselves the 'Taíno', which means good or noble.

He smokes – that's what it's called – a local herb called 'tabaco'. The large leaves of the plant are rolled tightly up into a tube called a 'cigar', which is lit at one end and sucked at the other, and the smoke is drawn into the back of the throat for a few moments before being blown out again. Mist-like, it is vaguely bluish in colour. The aroma is difficult to describe. It evokes something of the richness, the languor, the strangeness and the promise of the island. And, he says, it keeps the mosquitoes at bay.

"I sometimes sense the demons in hills," he says. "It's as if they are refusing to be banished. They will disappear in time. But there are other dangers."

When I asked him what, all he said, rather cryptically, was: "Poisonous serpents lurk in our verdant woods, as in all Edens."

Everything is perpetually damp and clammy, our clothes, our bed linen. Even the paper on which I write these lines has soaked up the tepid vapours in the air and to write clear crisp letters is impossible. Getting wet is unavoidable but an hour later one's clothes are dry again, or damp rather, for nothing ever dries out properly. Our bed linen and habits, we have been told, unless we wash and air them once a week, will become infested with fungi and rot just from lying unattended in their chests. We hang them in the open air under the shelter of the overhanging roof, but they only half dry out.

I have resumed my spiritual exercises.

Today, finally, taking advantage of a brief respite in the rains, we made our way through the muddy streets of Santo Domingo – and through a herd of pigs being driven to the twice-weekly market on the Plaza de Armas – to present our credentials at the Castle. The Alcalde Mayor's secretary, who introduced himself as Sebastián Ramírez, a tall elderly man, probably a morisco – a morisco is a converted Moor or the descendant of one – near as dark as a Black Ladino, escorted us personally to the Alcalde Mayor's bureau, the most impressive room I have seen here yet. The furniture is of the finest. Two splendid paintings, one of the Virgin and one of the Catholic Monarchs of the Spains, hang on opposite walls. And there is a large exquisitely painted globe on a stand beside the Alcalde's rather gigantic caoba-wood writing table.

Rudolfo Jesus de Paz, a small man, dark-haired, going grey,

moustached and goateed, and unexpectedly finely dressed in matching dark blue jacket, hosen, slops and codpiece, at first gave the impression of being taken aback somewhat at our unannounced appearance. He vaguely reminded me of a Russian I once met in Venice. In fact, the resemblance was striking. He was counting money when we were ushered into his presence – stacks of silver Joachimthalers, a Fugger coin I was somewhat surprised to see here, so far from Habsburg lands. I suppose it is not that often that he receives nuns in full habit, lined up in front of him like soldiers on parade, accompanied by their rather stern-looking, if diminutive, Mother Superior. True to the time-honoured manner of officials, he took his time looking over our letter of introduction from the Casa de la Contratación de las Indias before speaking.

"The Florentine Marchionni, the illustrious bankers?" he asked.

"The Genoa branch," I corrected him.

Finally, satisfied that our documents were bona fide, he laid the stern mask of officialdom aside and donning that of the caballero, and with a considerable if not an excessive display of chivalrousness, insisted that I introduce all of my beatas to him one by one. Each curtseyed to him each in her turn as I did so, saying a laudatory few words about each, while he for his part beamed at each in turn, with a trifle too much gallantry – but perhaps he is at an age when men find all young women fair. Then he gave us a small impromptu speech welcoming us to the island, praising our religious zeal and expressing the hope – "nay, the certainty" – that our presence would prove "salutary", after which he finally invited me to sit and retreated behind his writing table again.

"Communication with our beloved fatherland is erratic," thus his surprise, his not expecting us, he explained. "But a pleasant surprise," he assured me. "Very much a man's world here I'm sure you've noticed. Sadly deprived of the feminine influence I'm afraid. The manners of men, sadly, deteriorate somewhat in the absence of Christian ladies."

He is not quite a lower class man, but I doubt if he would have risen to the elevated position he enjoys here if he had been in the Crown's service in the Spains. More than a bit of the peacock about him, if the truth be told; but it is uncharitable to pass judgment on a man because of the circumstances of his birth.

"The Spanish Island is a heathen place," he continued. "I have studied the people and their tongue ..." – Fray Montenegro tells me he can speak it well – "... and I can assure you it is a very heathen place indeed. But we do what we can. I myself have been here going on eight years now. I haven't been back to Castile since. Bit of a slave to duty, bit of a workhorse, I suppose. But there have been improvements in my time and I hope my presence here has played a humble part in implementing them. The Indians have been pacified." The recent wars with the Indians are known as the Wars of Pacification or simply the Pacifications. "A new time has been born. And we have some excellent tailors now, not as good as in Seville of course, but ..." Then, mid-speech, he suddenly stood up and did a slow turn with arms outstretched – like a Florentine ballerina doing a pirouette. It took me more than a moment to realise it was to show off his finery. "Not bad, I'm sure you'll agree," he said as he sat down again. "Appearance is important, I always say." I stifled a giggle.

"This will be a fine city someday," he continued. "It's laid out according to the latest Italian ideas, you know, straight lines, the geometry of perfect forms. The previous Governor was an avid admirer of Vitruvius. They say Alexander laid out Alexandria in a like manner. We're a diocese now too. A long-promised bishop is on the way, could be here by the year's end. The walls will soon be completed. Our masons are as busy as bees on the new cathedral. Someday our humble seminary will become a fully-fledged university. And, of course, your school for the education of young girls will be a most welcome and edifying addition to our Christian colony. Many of the settlers, and most cannot afford to have spouses from Castile, have daughters of mixed blood – 'mestizos' we call them – who would greatly benefit from a decent Christian education. And the daughters of the nitaíno – that's the local aristocracy, if you can call them that – require it even more if they are to make half-decent wives for Christians. But I fear you will not find it an easy task. It's the devil even to even learn your well-born redskin to sit on a bench and eat from a table."

He then went on to say that "things are a bit up in the air at the moment, administratively speaking" with His Excellentissimo the Governor being on a tour of all the other Castilian possessions.

"In Spain, the world looks one way," he then continued, but in a different tone. The formalities were done, so to speak, and now he was going to give me some confidential advice. Or at least that was the impression he wanted to give me. "Here, well ... things are different, very different at times, a different world, a new world some say. Things from afar appear one way, but up-close ... A man on a ship sees an island and he imagines that in most respects it will be like the land he has left. How can he think otherwise? But when he steps ashore ... explores, and attempts to make a living there, he finds out that it is not at all what he had imagined from the deck of his ship. That's the way I see it anyway. And I'm sure that after you have been here a while ... I suppose what I'm saying is that we have our peculiarities. Of course, you'll need some time to familiarise yourself with our particular circumstances here, what I sometimes call the peculiarities of the tropics, as will no doubt your charming sisters."

He beamed at my cares standing mutely in a row behind me.

"The good Fray Montenegro ...," he went on, obviously wanting to tell me something he considered of some import but not quite sure which words to choose, "we all love him dearly of course, an admirable missionary, absolutely devoted to the people ... but, well, he does allow his enthusiasm for his flock to cloud his judgement at times somewhat. But perhaps Castile will send us more nuns. Monks, especially the Preachers, can be quite set in their ways. The nobler sex, I find, can be less demanding, more understanding."

He looked at me obviously expecting some sign that I had understood, but I merely nodded.

"And," he added, "Granada and Seville are a long way away, half a world away."

Then, seemingly satisfied with that, he began talking about the rain.

The remainder of our conversation consisted of chit-chat for the most part. Before he escorted me personally to the courtyard, my charges trailing dutifully in single file behind me, he made a point of saying that should any little "problema" arise, "no matter how seemingly trivial", I should consider the gates of the Castle and the doors to his bureau always open. "In the interregnum," he said, "that is the expression, I believe. While His Excellentissimo is on his grand tour. Well, anyway, I'm – how shall I put it? – sort of in charge of the shop. Not officially, not quite de jure, rather de ..." He searched for the word.

"De facto," I suggested.

"Yes. Quite," he beamed at me. "That's it. De facto."

My cares behaved impeccably throughout, not a giggle nor a squeak out of them. On the muddy way back to our nunnery, we purchased some earthenware plates at the market. They were of Haytian manufacture and well made, and in the Castilian style.

The rains started again shortly afterwards.

Ж

I try and imagine the scene above. Lucrezia di Marchionni
is a small creature, no higher than a young boy, as skinny
as a rake; 'not a pick on her' as the saying goes. All her
charges, whom she manages with an iron will, tower over
her by at least a foot, and the Sor Hildegard, who is a big
woman in both height and girth, by near enough to a foot
and a half. Her first impression of the Alcalde Mayor was
obviously of a harmless man whose only vice was vanity. If
only that were the case, then Hayti would be a less
unhappy isle. Rudolfo Jesus de Paz arrived a year or so
after Isabela had died and is typical of that generation of
officials, and like all of them, with no exception that I know
of, is a greedy, puffed-up, vain, devious and crafty man with
a face for all occasions, who takes an impassionate
pleasure in ordering cruel and violent acts. How such men
can claim to be Christians will forever elude me! They laugh
about the cruelties they committed during the years of the
Pacifications – and still commit – the way naughty
schoolboys snigger over the pranks they have played on
their masters and fellows.

My seasickness is gone, as if it never was.

THREE

We awoke this morning to azure skies. The sun has come out. And with it the birds, who possess every imaginable colour of the rainbow: glittering greens, blazing yellows, all the shades of blue, the brightest purples, the deepest blacks and the purest whites. The colours on a master painter's palette are but a pale reflection of the colours that the hand of God has painted these creatures. And butterflies, flocks of them, arrayed in an even greater range of sumptuous raiment, fluttering over the paradisiacal greenery of our garden. The mystic, granted a fleeting glimpse of beatitude in a divine vision, can hardly see anything more glorious. There must be creatures like these in paradise, I am sure of it. We have washed our habits and our linen and hung them in the sun to dry, and laid out our prayer books on a table on the patio that they might do likewise.

The Spanish Island is the largest of the Antilles – with the exception of the island called Cuba, or Cubagua, which is reputed to be larger. It is perhaps about the size of the Kingdom of Naples or of Portugal, with a total circumference of about six hundred Latin miles. The land is exceedingly fertile and there is an abundance of fruits and vegetables that are unknown in Christendom. There is probably little that would not grow here. The sugarcane plant grows better here, I am told, than in any other country. Most of the numerous other islands of the Antillean Sea, sometimes called the Caniba Sea after the Canibas that plagued these islands before the Wars of Pacification, are also inhabited, though more sparsely.

The accounts related to me of the early days of the conquest of these islands are conflicting and unclear. Fray Montenegro says that to form a true picture of that history one would need the keys to the jealously guarded archives of the Casa de la Contratación; and that even then he doubted that much of the truth of it could be discovered, as not all was recorded and many of the accounts sent to Castile were written by men more concerned in furthering their own names and interests than recounting the truth of their deeds. Fray Montenegro, I fear, at times, takes a rather less than charitable view of most of his compatriots.

When Don Cristóbal Colón claimed the island in the name of

the Catholic Monarchs, it contained five heathen kingdoms or 'cacicazgos': Higüey, Maguá, Maguana, Marién and Jaragua, all of about equal size, each ruled by its own 'cacique', the Haytian word for 'prince' or 'king'. A great prince, a cacique of caciques or a king of kings, is known as a 'guamiquina'; though, oddly, only lower caciques had the power of life and death over the pueblos they ruled. A queen or a princess is known as a 'cacica'. All these lords and their families belong to the noble class, the 'nitaíno'. All the rest are known as 'naboria', a class, Fray Montenegro tells me, more akin to city men in Christendom – rather than to countrymen – in the freedoms they enjoy. There is no lower class among them. That, at least, it is how it used to be.

Don Cristóbal Colón's reputation is as tarnished here as it is in the Spains. The mention of his name, or 'the Admiral' as he is often simply called here, or 'the Pharaoh' by the more disparaging, is usually met with some scathing comment. Once, on the quayside, I overheard him being cursed in language I do not wish to repeat, and described as both a fool and a knave who should have been thrown overboard, 'chains and all', when he was being ferried back to Granada to stand trial. But generally, the colonists seem reluctant to go into the specifics of his alleged folly or knavery. I think Fray Montenegro actually met him once. He almost invariably refers to him as 'the Pharaoh' but in a manner which suggests he wants one to believe, while not actually saying so, that it was more than a passing acquaintance.

The Indians, or the Haytians as Fray Montenegro calls them, make up, as one may expect, the greater part of the inhabitants. Fray Montenegro describes them as "a most tender and effeminate people". Though I have also been told that they are prone to unpredictable outbursts of gratuitous violence and faithlessness.

He says: "They possess few if any goods, and those they do possess they do not seem overly attached to. They are as parsimonious in their diet as an eremite of old in the desert of Egypt. A family makes do with in a week with what the average Spaniard consumes in a day. The man who sleeps in a hamaca counts himself prosperous and happy, and if he has not that, he is happy sleeping on a mat. Before our coming they wore nothing but ornaments or at the very most a cotton skirt concealing their pudenda from public sight; no son or daughter of Eve is ever absolutely without some sense of shame, or a rudimentary sense of good and evil, however how slight. Though like the Moor, they do have has an unhealthy obsession with hygiene, with the bodily, and think nothing of washing themselves publicly in streams and ponds. They are nowadays forbidden to go naked in towns. Beyond their lack of knowledge and understanding of the principles of the Catholic faith, there's nothing wanting in them to prevent them acquiring eternal beatitude. But they need to be preached to in a manner suited to their intellects and way of thinking. I've seen them suck in the rudiments of the faith as a man dying of thirst would suck up water; and when they receive the sacraments they do so with an extreme of zeal and fervour I've rarely seen in a born Christian."

These, of course, are not the exact words he actually spoke – though at times, when he is relating such things, he does speak as if he is composing an official report – but rather the sense of them with, I admit, some poetic liberties taken on my part. Transcribing any man's speech word for word, complete with the 'ums' and 'ahs', false starts and all the rest, would produce dubious grammar and make tedious reading. He likes to talk – he finds little educated company here – and is proving an excellent informant regarding what you called "the secrets of the new world".

My own humble observations: The Indians possess a natural anxiousness to please and a natural, and at times excessive shyness. It is as if they seem determined to keep some part of themselves hidden, which can give the impression that they lack something, something essential; which in turn, lends their way of being, their manners and movements, a vaguely unreal quality. It is almost as if they exist in the world in a different, a less substantial way that we do; not that that can be, for they are surely as much flesh and blood as I myself. At times, this feeling gives rise to the strange and no doubt sinful thought that they are a different category of being, almost not wholly men. The attitude of the Castilians to them is, more often than not, it pains me to write, rather haughty. They refer to the common people among them as 'redskins' because of the ochre many of them paint their faces and their bodies with.

I have not yet succeeded in organising our life here according to the rule of our order, which as you know, dear Balthazar, consists of work in the mornings, from Prime to Sext, with afternoons, from None to about an hour before Vespers, devoted to prayer, contemplation and study. Though we have now begun to prepare two school rooms. I have also decided to have tiles baked for the nunnery roof. Fray Montenegro has recommended a master-tile maker by the name of Alfredo Castro, who has several kilns in the woods just outside the city, some for tiles and two so-called Moorish kilns for pots and the like. He came here on one of the original seventeen ships and is perhaps the Christian who has been here the longest time. Montenegro refers to him as an "old roldanista".

It appears that in the early years there were two factions on the island, the followers of Don Cristóbal known as the colombistas, and the roldanistas, the followers of Francisco Roldán, a caballero from Andalusia. When I asked Fray Montenegro in what things Don Cristóbal and this Roldán disagreed, he said, rather dismissively, that they differed only in as much as the right hand of the devil differs from his left. He was reluctant to say more beyond that Roldán had drowned in the armada sunk by the 1502 hurucan, (the one that destroyed New Isabela and led to the founding of Santo Domingo), along with Don Cristóbal's successor, Bobadilla, and a rebellious cacique by the name of Guarionex being sent to Granada for trial. A nugget of pure gold the size of a loaf of bread, the legendary so-called pepita de oro, was also lost.

There is a sugar mill near Castro's kilns which I have had the opportunity to see in operation. A true hive of industry. But time presses. I shall describe its workings later.

I no longer notice the 'smell of Asia' that the captain of our caravel referred to. But I can't remember exactly when I ceased to notice it.

Ж

Yes, I knew Don Cristóbal Colón, the Pharaoh of the Ocean Sea etcetera etcetera, or rather met him once. It was but a passing acquaintance. But we oft reveal more of ourselves to strangers than those alongside whom we wander haphazardly, day by day, through this vale of tears. One can live in company with a brother monk for a decade and in the end know nothing essential of the man; but spend a few hours with a man on the road, partake of a single supper together, share with him a room and a bed and in that fleeting time get a portrait of his character tenfold deeper than that which his spouse of twenty long years might have. And what priest has not heard in the limbo-like darkness of the confessional complete strangers reveal aspects of their souls which they normally keep buried in the crypts of their imaginations?

Our brief meeting took place shortly after his return from his fourth and final voyage. He was on his way to La

Rábida, the Franciscan Monastery near Palos de la
Frontera. He had spent much time there during his early
years in Spain, and had gleaned much from its extensive
library – ten thousand volumes, they say; the number of
books in the Indies can be counted in their hundreds, but I
digress – and its collection of maps, and learnt astronomy
from the monks. It had also become his custom, between
voyages, to don the Franciscan habit and spend some time
in retreat from the world in order to purify his soul by
prayer and fasting, and perform penance – and of the latter,
he was much in need.

The inclement weather of that year had caused him to
interrupt his pilgrimage to La Rábida and spend a few days
at our monastery at Salamanca. I was in the chapel,
offering up a prayer for some special intention. I was a
young man then and believed that prayer was merely a
supplication to fulfil one's selfish wishes, and those wishes
one has convinced oneself are selfless, as if one were a
saint. In the cold December light shining faintly through
the panes of the church windows, I noticed a figure in the
grey sackcloth of a Franciscan habit prostrate on the
flagstone floor before the altar. But for his head of long-
grown white hair – they say in his youth it was a fiery red –
I would have taken him for a brother monk. Just as I had
finished my prayer, he suddenly rose with more agility that
one would expect from a man so stricken in years, crossed
himself and made his way down the aisle as I, my prayer
done, was about to leave my pew. As he passed me our eyes
met for an instant and I suddenly heard myself blurting
out, "What was it like?", and felt myself immediately blush
at what was an impropriety bordering on insolence. But he
stopped and looked at me – his eyes were blue – and
appeared to think for a moment. He was older than I had
expected and carried that unmistakable chastened look,
which I have since learnt to recognise, of a man aware that
the time remaining before he stands before his Maker can
be counted in months rather than years. He knew he was
not long for the world of the flesh. Yet the embers of the
passions that must have driven him to do what he had
done were still smouldering in his blue eyes, bloodshot from
the passage of the years.

"A dream," he said, but then hesitated, as if he had
belatedly noticed that he had misunderstood my question.

For a moment I had the uncanny feeling that he was
going to stretch out his hand and actually touch me, as if to
make sure I was not some species of phantom.

"Oh, you mean India ...," he said then, in the manner of a

man speaking to himself. "It was like the Garden, Brother. No, it was the Garden. When I saw it first ... Oh, the beauty of it, the birds, the flowers, the trees ... I remember I didn't even have the words to describe it. But then I forgot. But I can see it now again. Knowledge comes slowly, so slowly. And I wasn't a young man. I sailed to the edge of the world in search of it ... to the edge of the known world. They thought I was mad, you know, the scholars and the doctors, the learned men ... But the Queen, she had faith, she believed in me. I thought it would be a ruin, weeds everywhere, everything gone to seed, its walls heaps of rubble, like the alcazárs of the Romans, but ..."

He paused, lost in thought again. A confused old man, I thought for a moment, but then he came to life again.

"There are riches beyond imagination," he continued. "Gold, pearls, silver, spices, precious stones, land tenfold more bountiful than in any part of Christendom. Rhubarb grows wild as if it were a common flower, and mastic trees, or so I thought then. I could have liberated Jerusalem with the profits of it but men robbed me, robbed me of what was mine as surely as if they had waylaid me in an alleyway. And now I am a poor man, a pauper. Like Christ. They had me brought me back in chains. I still have them you know, those chains. I'll never see it again now. My time has come, and very soon my poor immortal soul ..." He cast a wistful glance at the image of Our Suffering Saviour on the cross above the altar. "Souls, millions of souls in darkness, countless millions, yet to be brought to Him. That is the great task now." He then made to go but hesitated and turned back to me. "You are young. India needs fishers of men. There are souls to be saved. I was nothing and I went ... and soon I will be nothing again. You are young, you could ... India needs men of God ... All men must be baptised before He comes again."

And then – I still don't know to this day quite what possessed me – but before I knew it I was on my knees before him, kissing his old man's hands. But he lifted me to my feet and bade me come to myself, embraced me and asked me to pray for him, before limping down the aisle and out through the chapel doors, leaving me suddenly filled with a sense of vocation, filled to the over-brimming ... I was ordained a few months later and applied to the Mission to the Indies. So doth the Lord use the Devil for His own ends.

FOUR

Much of what the Strassburg map depicts is considered common knowledge here, but much would also be contested.

The large landmass to the south is usually called simply tierra firme by the settlers here, or sometimes the Parrot Land because of the vast number of these strange birds found there; when they speak of the 'new world' it is generally only this landmass that they are referring to, for they consider it too far south and west to be part of Asia. None call it America, though it is generally accepted that the Genoese Americus Vespucci was the first to map its jungle coasts and mangrove swamps. Waldseemüller claims, in one of the inscriptions on the map, that Vespucci actually was the first to discover it, though some here say its first discoverer was Don Cristóbal on his third voyage. That was the voyage in the course of which he discovered Trinity Island – the Blessed Trinity was always close to his heart – and other coasts which he mistakenly believed were islands but were in fact that of part tierra firme subsequently christened Little Venice by Vespucci – he found a town there built on wooden posts in a lagoon. Pedro Alvares Cabral, who landed further south, also thought it was an island, though a vast one, christening it the Island of the True Cross; he planted a wooden cross two dozen feet high on its shores as a symbol of his claiming it for Portugal. Vespucci was one of the navigators on this voyage and it was he who was given the honour of returning to Lisbon with tidings of the discovery. Much of this vast country lies to the east of His Holiness Alexander VI's line, in that part of the globe His Holiness gifted to the Portuguese, so Spanish ships only sail those waters in the greatest secrecy. The natives are said to wear Moorish turbans, engage in unnatural practices which they consider natural, be much given to drunkenness and, unlike the inhabitants of Hayti, to possess slaves. Their women are said to be as fierce as the men and engage in war willingly. The islands depicted off its northern coasts, more or less directly south of the Spanish Island, are the source of blemish-free pearls.

The northern landmass depicted on the map is commonly believed to be either some Asian peninsula, an Indian archipelago, or a large island off the coast of the Realm of the Great Khan.

There are numerous and contradictory reports and speculations as to whether both of these vast countries join together to form a single landmass. Some say that the only way further west is to sail around them, either at their southern and northern extremities, as depicted on the map, if that is possible. But others claim there may indeed be a passage between them through to Cipango and the Realm of the Great Khan, as also depicted on the map. The possible extent of the Southern Ocean which purportedly lies somewhere further west is also hotly debated.

"The Pharaoh searched for the passage on his fourth voyage," Montenegro told me yesterday evening. "He was so confident of finding it that he even had a letter from Isabela and Ferdinand to Vasco da Gama, whom he was apparently hoping to meet up with in India, as well as one to the Great Khan himself. He landed at various places but could never be quite sure if he was on islands or an uninterrupted landmass. Too many impenetrable mangrove swamps. When he returned he swore on all the saints he'd rediscovered Solomon's Ophir and Ptolemy's Aurea Chersonsee. The Coast of Riches, he christened it. Though he did find gold, quite a lot of it, they say. For all his faults, it must be said he understood the winds and the tides and ocean currents like perhaps none before him. Getting here was one thing, sailing back to Christendom was another. And he did both. They say he could even smell the onset of hurucans, that he was able to read the subtle changes in the air and the light and the colours and forms of the clouds that take place in the days leading up to one, as if he were a Haytian himself. He said that the inhabitants of one of the places at which he had landed told him there was another sea, as big as the Oceanus Occidentalis, nine days march through the jungle to the west. Others have searched for a way further west since, officially and no doubt unofficially. A couple or so years ago, an expedition by Francisco Pinzón and Solís – they had two ships, called the *Magdalena* and the *San Benito* if I remember right – tried again, exploring along the coast north of where the Pharaoh had sailed, but they did not find the passage either. Explorations constantly take place, but the captains guard their secrets from each other more jealously than bickering fishwives. The official accounts – for what they're worth – disappear into the archives of the Casa de la Contratación. A cacique once told me they see their world as a collection of islands between two great seas. So maybe there is a passage. But I think half the time they just tell us what they think we want to hear.

"Settling tierra firme has not been as easy as settling Hayti. The

Indians there are more ferocious, their arrows more poisonous, and they have long bamboo pipes out of which they blow poisoned darts just as deadly as any poisonous arrow. But there are two colonies there now, the Vice-royalties of Golden Castile and of New Andalusia, and a city, Santa María la Antigua del Darién."

As regards the other question which the Monsignori of the Congregation were anxious to have unprejudiced observations upon – namely how the possession of islands so far from Christendom can be so extraordinarily profitable to a Christian prince ... I remember your words precisely: "The King of the Spains sends ships halfway across the world. Everything has to be brought across an unimaginably vast ocean in ships eighty feet long and fifteen feet wide: grain, seeds, horses, cows, pigs, blacksmiths, carpenters, monks, mercenaries and God knows what else. It's a two-month voyage. A tenth of the crews, if not more, die on the way across; and they say more than a quarter of the settlers don't make it through their first year. At least one in ten ships – if not one in five – are lost. Yet the ships keep being sent out. Ferdinand the Catholic may have the welfare of the antipodean heathen at heart but he's not a man to throw his ducats down the privy. It's taken years to colonise the Spanish Island, but now the seemingly mad enterprise appears to be paying for itself, indeed turning hefty profits, even though some say the island itself possesses no great amounts of gold and silver. Or is the Spanish Island a mere bridgehead to even richer lands further to the west which, if Americus Vespucci is to be believed, are vast?" And who better than a banker's daughter to investigate such secrets, you said. Then you spoke of the "secrets of the new world", its natural wealth, latitudes and longitudes; and how I was to seek out a prince of the people and enquire into the customs of the people and into how deeply our holy faith is taking root among the inhabitants of these islands.

At present Fray Montenegro, as you will no doubt at this stage have gathered, is my only substantial informant. The colonists, with only a few of whom I have made polite acquaintance, have little interest in matters beyond their immediate concerns and are at times, I suspect, wary of newcomers, and especially of inquisitive ecclesiastics, even if female. And even at times, I sense that Fray Montenegro, honest soul that he is, perhaps does not reveal all that he knows, not that I suspect that there is any falsehood in what he says. But in the next few weeks, I shall endeavour to inquire further, reflect and gather my thoughts, and reach some considered conclusions.

Loud flashes of lightning filled the heavens just after the sun set this evening, illuminating the hills and the dark waters of the bay with a cold blue light. A little later it began to rain again. I can hear it pounding the roof and the vegetation as I write.

Ж

Robbery and plunder. That is how it is all so extraordinarily profitable to a Christian prince! To describe it as otherwise is to mince words. The depredations of the Castilians are naught but that. Tear away the veil of learned rhetoric and slippery excuses and justifications and that is what it comes down to. Robbery, plunder, murder, and rape. It cannot be justified by any moral scheme that has ever existed among any nation at any time or place.

Ж

The Indian womanservant who translates for Fray Montenegro at what he calls his Haytian masses, the masses he says for the Indians, came over shortly after Sext on an errand and was waiting for me in the room I use for my administrative duties, keeping the account books and such. Her name is Felicitas. She is fine-boned like most of her race, of about my height, her jet-black long-flowing hair beginning to grey in streaks.

After she had delivered her message, I made to dismiss her, fully expecting her to curtsey and to leave – Haytians are polite and humble to a fault in the presence of their betters – but she seemed reluctant to do so. She simply stood there like some fidgeting schoolgirl trying to muster up the courage to request some special favour or confess some trifling but embarrassing misdemeanour. But when she eventually did speak, I was taken aback more than a mite by what she said.

"Doña Sor Lucrezia," she said. "Why didn't God make the earth flat?"

"Because ...," I began, but suddenly, and in retrospect understandably, I was lost for words. But thinking it was perhaps merely a silly question I asked her: "Do your people believe the earth is round?"

"Oh, yes," she said, "we do now. If God had made the earth flat, Colón's ships would simply have sailed over the edge and the Christ Men would not have found us." The Indians have a habit of misspeaking many words and are infuriatingly resistant to correction.

Still more than somewhat bemused and no wiser as to the intent of her amusing inquiry, I was tempted to say that perhaps that was one reason why God had not made the world flat. But something, a feeling I could not quite put my finger on, held me back.

Ж

The drunk Serrano had regained consciousness at about this time. The workings of fate? But his condition was so grave that Fray Pedro bade me to come to the infirmary to see the state he was in with my own eyes.

"The good ship *Trinity*," he was repeating to himself over and over again, barely aware of our presence, if at all, and laughing to himself. It was a laugh without mirth, the disjointed laughter of a madman, his alcohol-poisoned mind obviously inhabited by all manner of those demons which possess the mad.

"I have exorcised him," Fray Pedro told me. "But it's possible the demons have damaged his mind beyond repair. If that's the case, there's nothing to be done. We can only hope. Perhaps he will regain some measure of reason over time."

"The *Trinity*," I said to myself.

"Is it a real ship?" Fray Pedro asked.

"Yes," I told him. "Very real, or at least it was. It disappeared at sea a few years back."

However, several days later Serrano did regain his senses and we were able to question him.

Ж

The idols of the Indians are called 'zemis', and there was once a great number of them, each man and woman – in the time before our coming – possessing as much as ten of the things. They fashion them out of various materials – such as wood, earthenware and stone – but most of them are ugly cotton dolls, soiled from pawing, in a variety of hideous forms and of different sizes. One of the duties of the Preachers is to collect those that remain and destroy them, a difficult task; for the Indians are very superstitious and stubbornly attached to them, and not easily persuaded that these figurines are the likenesses of demons.

This afternoon the monks were burning several dozens of these zemis in a bonfire at the bottom of their garden, sprinkling them with holy water before casting them into the flames. The earthenware ones they were simply smashing. Montenegro was officiating.

"They also use them for necromancy," he explained to me. "The dead, they believe, can tell the future and help them cast spells and do various acts of black magic."

He then showed me a strange tray or bowl-like sculpture, intricately carved from what looked like caoba wood, with mysterious tube-like protuberances at either end.

"It's a sniffing tray," he said. "They make an intoxicating powder called cohoba from a bean, a so-called magic bean, which they place in here in the centre and sniff it through these tubes until they're utterly senseless. They believe that in that state, when all their faculties of reason have been utterly extinguished, they can communicate with their dead and with demonic forces. Like drunks possessed by devils. They call it sniffing the dust of the stars. They also make cotton likenesses of those who have offended them, or who they imagine have offended him, and keep them in their caneys and stab and beat them when the mood takes them in order to harm the man it is supposed to be a likeness of." 'Caney' is an Indian word for a dwelling. "There is a great commonality in the methods of witchcraft from culture to culture, even though the outward appearances of it can diverge considerably from one place to another. The substantia of it and the accidentia of it, I suppose you could call it."

He then muttered a few half-audible words of banishment in Latin, sprinkled some holy water on the evil contraption and threw it into the fire, and I found myself crossing myself.

"Perhaps nothing in the world is more purely evil than witchcraft," I said.

"Except perhaps those who would try and convince us that it does not exist," he said.

On his return to the Spains after the discovery of these islands, Don Cristóbal was given seventeen ships and licence to come back here and trade with the various kingdoms at that time existing here. Though some say he had in fact rediscovered these islands rather, believing that they were known to the Ancients as the Hesperides, thus called because they belonged to an ancient king of the Spains called Herperus, who reigned more than a thousand years before the birth of Our Saviour.

The expedition consisted of over a thousand men and some small number of women, as well as the Apostolic Nuncio,

Bernaldo Boyle, accompanied by twelve Franciscans, bearing a
Papal Bull instructing him to provide for the spiritual needs of the
colony and bring the Word of God to the Indians. The ships
carried trade goods: large quantities of Venetian glass beads,
brass rings, toys, trinkets and those small bells falconers attach to
the feet of their hawks – for particularly in regard to the latter he
had discovered on his first voyage that the Haytians, being a
child-like people, took a great delight in baubles – as well as
other items.

Only Don Cristóbal himself was licensed to carry out trade and
every transaction was to be attended by a royal accountant and
recorded in order that neither Crown nor Indian be cheated. Most
of the settlers, being paid a stipend by the United Crown, were
royal employees. They included masons, brickmakers and
carpenters to construct the settlement, miners and smelters,
blacksmiths and armourers, artisans and guildsmen of all kinds,
men at arms to provide for its protection, and a physician. And
there were many farmers, supplied with seeds and the cuttings of
numerous crops, and pigs, and goats and sheep. Some of those of
rank even brought their spouses with them.

A Hieronymite priest, a 'humble friar' as he was reputedly
wont to call himself, a Fray Ramón Pané, was also among them,
his mission to learn the tongue of the Indians and write an
account of their religion, customs and antiquities in order that
they could be more efficiently catechised. Don Cristóbal had
brought the converso Luis de Torres with him as a translator on
his first voyage – he spoke Arabic as well as Hebrew, Aramaic
and Chaldean – but his skills had proved of little use. Fray Pedro
has told me that he has a copy of Pané's account and has offered
it to me to read and transcribe if I wish.

All were enjoined by royal decree to treat the peoples of the
Spanish Island "very well and lovingly and to refrain from
causing them any harm". The Crown's reward from this venture
was to be one fifth of the value of products brought back, the
royal quinto as it is called, be it gold or spices or precious stones,
with no account being made for expenses incurred in the
procuring of those products. For this purpose, a royal factoría was
to be built and this was done at Isabela, as well as a church and
house for Don Cristóbal; as was a Moorish water wheel to grind
the wheat they'd brought with them. But today, as I have said,
that settlement lies in ruins.

*

Gold is by all accounts the chief source of the wealth of this place. I have it from two sources that as much as two hundred and fifty thousand pesos' worth of gold can be shipped back to Castille in a year. In the beginning, I have been told, the Indians were more or less ignorant of the true value of the metal. In their childlike innocence, they considered it a mere decorative thing, of no intrinsic worth in itself, of use only for pretty vanities such as earrings, nose rings, bracelets, badges and the like. Though they have now learnt from us Christians that it is the most valuable of material things.

The metal is both panned for and mined in the hills around Concepción and some very large nuggets have been found. For many years gold dust was also collected as a tax or a tribute, a practice instituted by the Admiral, paid by those who had accepted the lordship and protection of the Catholic Monarchs. But this practice has since been discontinued. Silver ornaments have been found on the island of Cuba, perhaps originating from some place on tierra firme, for no silver is found on the Spanish Island or on Cuba itself. There seem to be no precious stones except, of course, for the pearls which are found in the waters off some of the other islands and the coasts of tierra firme. It was once believed that the island would be a rich source of copper but only modest quantities have been found. John the Baptist's Island is also reputed to be rich in gold. More I have not yet been able to find out.

I recall the first time you showed me the gold of what you called this 'mundus novus'. I'm sure you remember too. How, after showing me Cardinal Riario's near-completed and wonderful Palazzo della Cancelleria, you brought me to San Maria Maggiore, one of Rome's most magnificent houses of God. High up on scaffolding a group of craftsmen was gilding the ceiling. The gold leafing they were using, you told me, had been rolled and beaten from some of the gold Don Cristóbal returned to the Spains with in 1492. And how later we talked of other occurrences of that eventful year: the conquest of Granada, and of how the Jews expelled by the Catholic Monarchs had been offered refuge in the Papal States ... But it grows late. Hard to believe that that was on the other side of the world.

Ж

And if the people led by their caciques – who in their turn had been led by ruses, lures and threats to make oaths of loyalty and submission, the meanings of which they could not possibly have understood – failed to produce their bells of gold dust and cotton bales, what punishments did the Pharaoh and his cronies mete out? They cut off their hands! Twenty-three men bore witness to his brutality at his trial.

ж

It is no easy task to put a figure on the number of settlers here. A thousand perhaps reside in Santo Domingo but because of the number of Haytian servants of all sorts and labourers, the size of the city is such that one could at first glance believe that it houses four or five times that number. Perhaps on the whole of the Spanish Island there is a total of five thousand Christians, with a little less than that number living on John the Baptist's (Boriquen on the German map) and Xaymaca (Iamiaca on the same) and the other smaller islands, with another two thousand or so on Cuba (Isabella Insula), and a few thousand more on tierra firme, mainly at Santa María la Antigua del Darién.

A few have been here, on the Spanish Island, since the beginning, having come over on Don Cristóbal's second voyage; none of those who were left here on the first voyage survived. Many others came on later voyages and have been here many years now, and every time a ship casts anchor in the harbour more arrive. Some settle here, others end up on the other islands or make their way to tierra firme. But many also leave, and in the past, I have been told, there were quite large exoduses of disillusioned adventurers. Large numbers succumb to what is called the so-called 'seasoning fever' and find their graves here.

It is a deceptive land, at times a balmy island aired by the freshest sea breezes, at others hot, fetid and deadly; though those that get sick and survive are reputedly the more robust for it. But every year the numbers of Spaniards of all types increase, and many so-called mestizo children are born from unions between Castilians and Indians. A small few, including our current absent Governor, have brought their wives; these can be seen in their Spanish finery on Sundays or on market days being carried around on their litter-chairs, the less prosperous by their Indian servants, the more prosperous by their Black Ladino or even Guanche servants from the Fortunate Isles.

*

There is much that the settlers require that is not produced here, still. His Majesty may receive his quinto, and much else besides, from licences and the sale of privileges and monopolies, but that leaves much money in the purses and strong boxes of no small number of settlers, though not all by any means.

Those that do make fortunes – men of rank for the most part, but not always – dispatch their profits to the Spains where they purchase lands and wives and court favours, and pay off their debts there, for many have borrowed heavily to finance their enterprises here. But much of their money also goes to pay for the importation of those necessities required for the execution of their various schemes and businesses, such as quicksilver, armaments and gunpowder, indeed any item that cannot be manufactured here; as well as horses, sheep and cattle, and jackasses for the breeding of mules. Then there are what one could consider luxuries, though many a colonist might call them cultural necessities, which need to be carried across: Jerez wine immediately comes to mind, as well as fabrics of many sorts, fashionable clothes and berets. There is also a bustling trade in objects of devotion such as statues, rosary beads and holy pictures.

All these imported items cost five times or more than they would in the Spains, and vast profits can be made. But, as I have said, not all men here are rich, and many fall further into debt – above and beyond the debts they have incurred to make the voyage in their first place – and are to all intents and purposes stranded here. And the converso money lenders – and most usurers here, as in the Spains, are New Christians – though willing to lend them money, are naturally unwilling to lend them sums large enough that would enable them to return to Christendom and escape their clutches. The Jew, it seems, finds it far easier to abjure his religion than his usury.

Besides taking its quinto, the Crown levies taxes and duties on all that enters and leaves, and on many other activities, as is its ancient right and custom; and in addition, the Crown also receives all ecclesiastical tithes, in recompense for which it has undertaken to see to the catechisation of the Indians and the building and maintenance of the churches.

The caballeros, the soldiers and mercenaries are greatly devoted to the Virgin Mary. All of them, without exception, wear silver and brass medals embossed with her image, and some wear badges depicting her on the arms of their tunics. Her holy portrait also adorns their shields. The Castilians here are as greatly devoted to Saint James the Moor Killer as they are in the Spains. His name is their war cry. And, I have been told, they are scrupulous in performing devotions before drawing their swords and shedding any blood.

FIVE

Montenegro has told me a strange and rather gruesome tale, of a shipwreck that occurred several years ago.

"A caravel named the *Trinity*," he told me, "was heading from Santa María la Antigua del Darién, the colony on tierra firme, to Santo Domingo. It was carrying the colony's procurator, accompanied by his legal advisor, a Franciscan priest by the name of Gerónimo Sanchez, and a quantity of gold. In total there were seventeen or so souls on board, including two women. A few days out to sea, they ran aground on a sandbank and were forced to take to an open boat, hoping the winds would take them to Cuba or to Xaymaca. But they ended up drifting for about two weeks. Most of them died of thirst, including the two women. But eventually, the survivors were washed ashore on some island or peninsula several hundreds of Latin miles somewhere north of Golden Castile, where they were taken captive by the local Canibas. Half of them were immediately dragged to a mosque and sacrificed to idols. Slaughtered like animals, their hearts cut out from their living innards, and their remains roasted and eaten at some filthy ritualistic feast."

He paused for a moment, perhaps to allow me time to fully apprehend what he had said. I remember the moment exactly. A waxing moon had appeared above us in the black velvet sky. In these latitudes, the moon, when it is a crescent, hangs on its side, as depicted on the banners of the Turk, rather than in the more upright position familiar to us in Christendom.

"The rest were locked up in cages to be fattened up for the same treatment," he continued, blowing out a mouthful of aromatic tabaco smoke, "but somehow they managed to escape. A year or so ago, two of the survivors, both common sailors, two rogues by the names of Franco Serrano and Carlos Goya, were picked up by a passing ship."

"In all that vastness?" I said.

"It happens," he said. "There is more traffic on the seas than is officially admitted. The authorities are reluctant to grant exploration licences to captains who are likely to turn into potential rivals, claiming anything they discover in their own names rather than on behalf of their lords. The hidalgos and their companies are unruly beasts, loose cannons, unpredictable. The result is that no small numbers of ships undertake secret voyages, and not just Castilian ships, but also Portuguese, English, and Bretons and Normans from Dieppe and Sant-Maloù. God only knows how many of them have fallen afoul of hurucans and ended up on the bottom of the sea. For the most part, accounts of these voyages are mere tales and tales of tales told in the taverns of Santo Domingo, their outlandishness increasing in direct proportion to the amount of chicha and sugar wine consumed."

Chicha is a beer-like drink the Indians brew from the kernels of 'mahiz', a plant which grows to the height of a man and bears heads of kernels (vaguely reassembling the heads of some sorts of grains) but which are the size of small cucumbers. Sugar wine, another if not the favourite beverage of most Christians here, is obtained from fermented sugarcane. Real wine is in short supply and the little there is, for the most part, is reserved for the Holy Sacrament and the tables of the richest men. Beer is unobtainable.

I was about to ask him if he could be sure that these tales of man-eating Indians were not also seamen's tales but he had sensed my incredulity.

"One of the men who was rescued," he said, "his name is Franco Serrano, he told me all this."

"And you believe his account?" I asked. Half the common seamen are convicts from the prisons of Seville and Cadiz, hardly trustworthy.

"The Pharaoh did not believe the Haytians' tales about Caniba raiders and their taste for human flesh," he said. "Not at first anyways. He thought they were referring to Khan-iba, slavers, subjects of the Great Khan, not man-eaters. Until he found human bones in cooking pots and body parts roasting on spits on one of the Caniba islands, and castrated boys being fattened for the pot. They do not eat women."

"Surely ...," I began, intending to say that surely there are limits to human wickedness, but he cut me short.

"If men can imagine something," he said, "they are capable of it. Men eating men, gorging themselves on roasted human flesh as if it were bacon, is imaginable. If you do not believe me, come to the Haytian mass on Sunday, and you can talk to this Serrano yourself."

Much of the above I had already read. What she believed was a theft of her papers that Rudolfo Jesus de Paz had arranged was, in fact, an act that I had initiated. I, of course, intended to return the papers, and had hoped that she would not miss them – but she did, and she writes of it later.

I had no idea what I expected to learn from those pages. Now, of course, I can see that, in some measure at least, it had been the hand of providence that had moved me to arrange to have them borrowed. For now that I have the complete document in front of me, I can see that I would not have acted as I subsequently did if, by mere chance dictated, a different half a dozen pages had found their way into my hands. Everything has a meaning or nothing has. The invisible hand of providence regulates the essentials of our lives, not mere chance, if indeed there is such a thing. Even the Haytians in the unenlightened childhood of their race believed that there is a mysterious design in the unfolding of things, a design that forever remains veiled to us in our mortal earthly state. (And it fills me with a profound disquiet to suspect, and it be surely heresy, that in that ignorant childhood they were happier in their souls than they are now, before we 'Christians' set foot upon their shores.) The Pharaoh was wrong, as he was wrong about much else, about his rhubarb and his mastic, his griffins and his sirens and all the rest, when he said that they had no religion. Yes, they were idolaters, but are we not too, with our love of gold and riches?

If it were not for my learning that her report was eventually destined for some 'Monsignori of the Congregation anxious to have unprejudiced observations', I might even have been left with the impression that she was composing her account of life here merely for her personal amusement and not for any serious purpose; or even perhaps writing a devotional tract. But in one respect, my suspicions had been laid to rest: she had not been spying on me or my brothers. Her ceaseless questions had not been designed to cause me to incriminate myself through my own mouth. Or at least not spying on me in the strictest sense of the word. And I had immediately seen that the Good Lord had delivered into my hands a means of perhaps furthering our cause.

In the beginning, in the years before Fray Pedro arrived with the other brothers, circumstances and fear (which, in essence, is an insufficiency of faith) had conspired against me doing what I knew in my heart was my Christian duty with the vigour that was necessary. Though it is not that I had remained mute. But my first writings to Salamanca I had, in hindsight, worded too far too diplomatically.

In my zeal to see right done at the time I made no copies of what I had sent to Spain. However, I do have a copy of one reply I received – with its seal obviously tampered with. It casts some light on my situation and the attitude of the order in those days:

To Our Brother in Christ, Fray Montenegro, Santo Domingo, the Indies, from Your Servant and Brother in Christ, Francisco de Lillo, Secretary General to the Order of the Preachers of Saint Domingo and the Tribunal del Santo Oficio de la Inquisición, Saint Stephen's, Salamanca.

Pious and sincere greetings. The Master General has bid me acknowledge receipt of and reply to your reports pertaining to your mission among the Indian people and convey his praise of your devotion to the cause of Christ. Both your unconventionally dispatched letters arrived safely, though the seals were slightly damaged, both in a similar manner, from which no doubt you will draw your own conclusions, as we have ours.

Your zeal and concern to carry out your duties, in circumstances which the order, and I myself, are more than aware are difficult and at times with certainty disheartening, do not go unnoted. The mission to the heathen is fraught with dangers, both physical and spiritual, but one must seek to find consolation in the fact that its prosecutors are more often crowned with success that those whose mission is to wean the Mohomedan from his perversity or the unrepentant Jew from his stubbornness. Far from the comforting familiarities of home and hearth and the broader Christian community, like Ruth among the alien corn perhaps, it is only natural that even the most level-headed and determined evangelist feels at times forlorn, and finds the circumstances of his mission less than ideal. The courage that you exercise for God's sake inspires the admiration of many of the younger brothers on this side of the Oceanus Occidentalis.

The situation which you describe in your epistle – most eloquently and movingly, I might add – is grave and worthy of reformation. Men hardened by the violence of battles and campaigns, even Christians, have behaved cruelly and unchivalrously towards the populations of conquered lands since Cain raised his hand against Abel. And it is certainly our role, within the confines of what is practicable, to mitigate their excesses and enjoin all Christian conquerors to greater gentleness and to respect persons and property. The Council at Constance was clear in the matter, as were the late Queen's decrees: the persons and property of pagans are to be respected, they may not be enslaved or have their goods removed from them solely because they are unbaptised.

The Master General has full confidence in your zeal and your ability to carry out your duty with the means currently at your disposal. Your dispositions have been considered with all the gravity they deserve. But there are also specific practicalities which need to be taken into consideration. You cannot be unaware that there are many who wield considerable influence at the Alhambra – the King resides and holds court there most of the year these days, in the old Moorish palace overlooking Granada, as was the case when Isabela was alive – as well as many in the Casa de la Contratación and in ecclesiastical circles who would argue most forcibly against your arguments, and say that they are erroneous in both their factual and theological premises. That is, should those arguments be put to them, which they have not.

The debate as to the nature of the Indian has become more intense since your departure and our arguments, now that the Blessed Isabela is no longer with us, are less in favour. I have even heard one learned doctor, whom I shall not name, describe them as "animals who talk". There are reports even that His Catholic Majesty is considering shipping fair-skinned female slaves across in order to prevent Castilians mixing their blood in marriage or in concubinage with Haytian and other Indian women. He has reputedly described the Indians "as being far from rational creatures, by nature inclined to idleness and vice"; which is not far from saying that the Indian is a homunculus, admittedly one created in nature rather than in an alchemist's retort, but less than fully homos, in short, not descended from Adam. The possible consequences of such a heretical notion taking hold of the minds of men I leave to your imagination. But one thing is sure: it would mean that the Church would have no role at all in the Indian countries beyond ministering to small numbers of colonists.

In addition, the current wars are expensive, like everything else these days. And the more gold that arrives here, the more exorbitant the prices of even the most basic of necessities become, it seems. Wheat was again selling at six hundred marevedís the fanega in early summer. Thus, and understandably, any policy which might interrupt the substantial flow of revenues to the Crown from the Spanish Island is unlikely, at this moment in time, to find any favour in royal ears. You are not the first to express strong opinions on these matters. The temperature of the bathwater has been tested, so to speak. Another monk, not of our order, voiced similar concerns in a most unwise, public and undiplomatic manner, and has been accused of 'besmirching the honour of Spain' – no light accusation. He is now in a remote monastery. Moral and ethical arguments must be tempered by what we observe to be true in the world. However, this is not to say that you should not, exercising the utmost discretion, continue to collect precise statements from the priests, friars and other men of goodwill on conditions in the Indies and on abuses committed against the native inhabitants.

The debate here is vigorous, both on the nature of the Indian and on the moral and legal justifications for what some are calling our new Spanish empire. The Master General and many of like mind take consolation in that. Other nations would not debate at all. Did Rome or Carthage debate such things, they say. Does the Turk? The tide of opinion in Castile ebbs and flows, and may well in time flow in the direction in which we desire it to flow. The sworn and sober statements of witnesses who have seen these things with their own eyes and which you are collecting will strengthen our hand. The official post being not safe, another method will need to be found to ensure their secure delivery, but the details of that we leave confidently in your hands.

Postscriptum: The titular lord bishops of the islands of Cuba and John the Baptist's have received reports that conversos still secretly practice Jewish rites, and even moriscos secretly practising Mohomedanism, and other heretics have settled in the islands and are still doing so, paying large sums for the licences to do so, and to live in a country in which the Holy Office is not currently established. Any intelligence you could provide with regard to this state of affairs would also be received with much appreciation.

I shudder to think of the consequences of the thought that we are not all descended from Adam infecting the minds of the likes of Rudolfo Jesus de Paz and the rest of the Aragonese clique who rule the Indian countries. Of course it was he, I was as certain as one can be, who had been responsible for tampering with my correspondence – his unsubtle way of letting me know he was keeping an eye on me! The Alcalde has eyes and ears everywhere. Half the gardeners and cooks on the island are in his employ. Every word said at the pulpit is noted and reported back to the Castle.

Ж

"The Haytians," Montenegro says, "have a great need of instruction in the letter of God's law, but less need of instruction in the spirit of it. Their world is inhabited by demons and incubi and succubae but they also have a certain faith in and knowledge of a one and true God who is immortal and invisible, a being they call Yócahu Vagua Maórocoti ..." – he wrote the words down for me – "... though they believe his mother was the moon. They also have a concept of the eternal soul, though they have different words for the soul of a living man and the soul of a dead man, which leads to no end of confusion. The spiritual needs of the colonists might be described as quite the opposite, a need of instruction in the spirit of God's law, rather than in the letter of it." He is prone to sarcastic judgements at times, especially with regard to his fellow countrymen.

SIX

Fray Montenegro's Haytian mass, as opposed to the so-called Spanish mass, is distinguishable from the latter only in the composition of the congregation and the fact that the readings and sermons are translated into the native tongue and, as one would expect, treat of themes deemed more appropriate for those new to the faith. He celebrates it in the modest whitewashed stone church whose bells rung out to announce our arrival and to give thanks for our safe passage. The congregation, decked out in their Sunday-best raw cotton robes, and gathered in its cool flagstoned interior, numbered perhaps a hundred. Some of the women carried infants on their backs.

Felicitas translates the sermons. Montenegro does speak the Indian tongue. And holds it in high regard. God, he says, created all tongues when He destroyed the Tower of Babel and scattered men to the ends of the earth, and though He may have elevated some tongues above others, none are the Devil's invention. He says there are in fact three, as dissimilar to each other as German and Portuguese. But if possible, he says, he prefers to use an interpreter when preaching, because he believes the Indians are more receptive to the truth if it is conveyed to them by one who speaks to them in their own accent and is totally familiar with all the native idioms. What follows is an account of his sermon written from memory and thus imperfect, which you may find of interest, for its theological idiosyncrasies if nothing else.

"Many thousands of years ago," he said, preaching from the rude caoba-wood pulpit situated halfway down the aisle, "when God created the first man and the first woman out of the clay of the earth, like any master potter, He was proud of His handiwork and filled with love for it."

He spoke slowly, pausing after each sentence to allow Felicitas, her jet-black hair only barely concealed by her cotton head-covering, to translate his words. The tongue of the Indians has a musical quality at times.

But to continue: "So God made a garden in this part of the world," he said, "in a land called Eden, and put the man and the woman in this garden so that they would be happy." Now that we can reach the east by sailing west, he explained to me later, to say that Eden was in the east would give the false impression that

Eden was in Europe and from whence we came. "It was a perfect garden and all those natural things that give sustenance and pleasure to man grew there in luxuriant abundance: casabes, batatas, mahiz, calabashes, beans, pea-nuts and papaws, pine-apples and avocados, guava, sugar and the essences of tabaco."

Casabe is our daily bread here; it is a turnip-like plant, but can be made into a flour and baked; the juice is poisonous unless boiled; the Haytians call it 'the giver and taker of life'. Batata is another turnip-like vegetable, but very sweet. Pea-nuts are nuts which grow on the ground, not on trees, and are so called because they grow in pods like peas. Pine-apples are so called because they resemble pine-cones; they also grow on the ground. Guava is an apple-like fruit which is also used to make a juice. Avocados grow on trees and are pear-shaped; their flesh is green and succulent, resembling that of no plant grown in Christendom. Calabashes are a type of melon, and come in a variety of colours, shapes and sizes, and the dried-out skins of some are so tough and impermeable as to enable the husk to be used as a water container. The Indians are not great flesh eaters. In fact, the only animal they keep is a small dog which cannot bark, but they keep it not to hunt with or as a pet but to eat. They also eat turtles which grow to a great size here. And hutias, a sort of squirrel that chirps like a bird, lives in the ground and in trees, tastes like rabbit, and which they cook in a pot with honey and wild nuts; at the market they display them in cages, as they do parrots which they catch in nets and also eat. There is also a sort of a giant lizard called an iguana which they also eat. Fish of all sorts abound, including a large fish with legs called a manati which Don Cristóbal mistook for sirens and which tastes like veal and is delicious; it was once reserved for caciques and their families. They season everything with a pepper called axí, which is sharper and fierier than any pepper I have ever tasted and beloved of both Christians and Haytians. Many of these things they 'barbacoa', a method of cooking over a slow fire which the settlers have also taken up. But I digress.

"This first man," he continued, "God named Adam and the first woman He named Eve. They are our first parents, from whom all of us are descended, Haytian and Castilian, cacique and hidalgo, emperor and jester, pope and clown. They went naked like the beasts – even more naked than you yourselves did in the world-before – for not having any knowledge of good and evil, they knew no shame." The 'world-before' is what the Haytians call the time before our coming. "But God also placed in this garden a tree, a very special tree, the Tree of the Knowledge of Good and Evil. He warned Adam and Eve that the fruit of this tree was poisonous, more deadly even than the serpent that dwells in the petals of flowers, and that if they ate of it, they would know good and evil. And death."

At this, there was some commotion, like the sudden confusion triggered off in a nursery when a nursemaid has told a story that stretches the limited understanding of her cares. Felicitas suddenly found herself engaged in a heated conversation with some vocal members of the congregation, of which of course I understood not a syllable. But Montenegro, understanding what it was that was troubling the Indians, raised his hand and bade them be silent.

"God," he said, "made Man and Woman in His own likeness, not in the likeness of the beasts. He gave Man an eternal soul and free will. But free will in a world without temptation would mean naught." But his words did little to soothe his flock and there were renewed confused queries.

"No," he said, not waiting for Felicitas to translate what he knew the Indians were saying to each other. "God does not tempt men to be sinful. He allows us to be tempted – which is different." The commotion slowly died down. "His ways are mysterious. God's love is mysterious. It is beyond human understanding. The tree was put in the garden as a sign of God's trust in Adam and Eve, to give them the choice as to whether they would love Him in return and obey Him, or reject His love and disobey Him. Eat of this fruit, He told them, and you will know sin and be no longer as innocent children, and you will know death. But that was hardly a great temptation, so God also allowed a serpent to enter the garden – one of the fallen angels who had rebelled, the ones I have already told you about, who disguise themselves as zemis, as false gods – a wily serpent with wings, a feathered serpent, who told the woman Eve that if she ate of the fruit of this forbidden tree, she would gain boundless knowledge." He paused to allow Felicitas to translate. "And the woman ate of it," he went on when she had done so," and her spirit became corrupted and the seeds of corruption took root in her body. And she then tempted Adam, who took the fruit from her hands and also ate it. The Devil knows how to tempt Woman. But Woman knows how to tempt Man, better than the Devil himself."

Oddly, Felicitas often seemed to use twice as many words of the Indian tongue to repeat what Montenegro was saying. I thought that this might be because she was obliged to use several words or a phrase to explain what can be conveyed in a single word in Castilian due to the Indian tongue having not as many words as Castilian. But Fray Montenegro assures me it does have as many words. Yet at other times she seemed to explain in a few guttural syllables what he had taken a long sentence to elucidate. But again I digress.

"Now," he continued, "when God saw that the creatures He had created had disobeyed Him and spurned His love, He was filled with anger. For there is no greater sin than to reject the love and bounty of one's Creator. And with a heavy heart He sent another angel, an avenging angel, a cherub, armed with a sword of searing fire, to cast them forever out of that garden, and the Voice of God said unto them: From henceforth, you shall know labour in stony fields and the pains of sickness and childbirth, and know old age and death, and your children and your children's children and their children's children shall know the same, and Man shall rule over Woman for her sin. And to this very day, an angel with a fiery sword stands guard over the garden and will do so till the end of time." There was some further commotion at this point but it passed. "Yes, all of us, Haytian and Castilian, and the black men too, the sons of Ham, and the Jews and the Moors, have been cast out of the garden to know sickness, pain, injustice, labour and death. And this is just. For do not the sons inherit the sins and the debts of their fathers? Can any man or women look into his or her heart and deny that he or she is a sinner? No. The fault is not in God, for is not God perfect? By definition perfect. And is not perfection by definition without any fault?"

Again he paused for Felicitas to translate his words. The good preacher that he is, he times his revelations well.

"But God still loved Man," he continued. "It is the sin in Man He cannot bear, not Man himself, for God is infinitely good and infinite goodness cannot bear evil. So He promised to send a Redeemer who would save Man, as proof of His love and to show Man that amid all the tribulations of earthly existence he could hope that one day, at the end of time, to return to the state he had enjoyed in the garden. And what greater and more generous thing could God do but to send His only begotten Son down to earth to become a man like you and me, to suffer and die like us."

When Felicitas was done translating his words, he remained silent for a moment, giving his congregation time to absorb the import of what he had said.

"Yes, about fifteen hundred years ago," he continued, "in the land of Palestine, far across the Oceanus Occidentalis, the Almighty God, Creator of all things physical and spiritual, sent Our Redeemer Jesus Christ among us to show us the way to salvation. God Himself – for the Son is indivisible from the Father – came among us, became a man, became one of us, lived like a man, suffered like a man, despaired like a man and died like a man. For He did die. He took upon himself even that, the greatest tribulation of Man. The Jews, a stubborn and ungrateful people, a wilfully pig-headed people, handed Him over to the Roman Pontius Pilate in the city of Jerusalem and demanded He be nailed to a cross of wood until He died."

For a moment he held up the simple wooden crucifix he wears, inviting us to gaze upon the simple object and contemplate the mystery of suffering and death, both human and divine, that the Cross symbolises, and ponder upon its meaning.

"Yes, the Son of God died," he said. He spoke with such intensity that for a moment I thought that silent tears were about to well up in his eyes and trickle down his cheeks. "He died for us. And the world was plunged into darkness and zemis walked the streets and alleys of Jerusalem. But on the third day after He had been laid in His tomb, Jesus Christ rose from the dead."

He let this announcement sink in for a moment.

"Rose from the dead," he repeated softly. "From the grave."

The faces in the congregation were looking at him with a mixture of awe and bewilderment. Perhaps asking themselves, was this man mad, or was he the bearer of the most import tidings that had ever been spoken? Had the Corinthians looked upon Paul thus when he had preached to them, I wondered.

"Yes, this maker of wooden things," he went on, "a carpenter, Jesus Christ, the King of Kings, the Guamiquina of Guamiquinas, rose up from the dead and walked again among men. And He promised those who had remained faithful to Him that one day He would return and put an end to time; and that when time was over, the dust and bones of their bodies too would be made flesh again, more whole and more perfect than they had ever been, and their spirits would re-enter their bodies. And they would live forever."

Again he paused to allow Felicitas to tell her countrymen and women what he had said. She spoke with conviction, though at times with a certain distance, as if intent on reminding her audience that the words she was translating were not hers, and that all this was as new and as much a mystery to her as it was to them.

"And not only they, those who had known Him, but all men," he continued, "all, all who had ever walked this earth and would ever walk this earth, would be raised from the dead, and He would restore the world and it would become another Garden of Eden. And in that peace, in that time beyond time, the turtle will lie down with the crocodile. Yes, on that Last Day, when time no longer is and the world is timeless, all men and women who have ever lived, all our ancestors back to the time of Adam, and all those who are yet to be born, all our children and our children's children, will be made whole again. This is the teaching of the Resurrection of the Dead. Then God will judge men, and those who have followed His Word ..." – he held his breviary aloft for a moment – "... written here in this book and given to the priests of the religion Jesus Christ founded, those who have followed His commandments to love one another, to renounce their false zemis and cast aside their fetishes, and have been washed pure by the water of the sacrament of baptism, will be granted eternal life in the new Garden. But those who in this life have disobeyed His commandments will be cast into a darkness blacker than the darkest night, a fiery blackness called hell. The world and time and death are mysteries, mysteries that can only be explained by even more profounder mysteries. God's designs are this mystery of mysteries. And mysteries cannot be understood. They can only be believed."

At times you could have heard a pin drop for such was the power of his preaching. But how much of the import of his words his congregation could grasp I could not tell, for all this must still be essentially new to them, though I am sure that by now he has told it to them on many occasions.

"Faith, along with hope and charity, is the greatest of virtues," he told them, lowering his voice now, almost whispering. "Greater than knowledge or the illusion of knowledge, for it does not lead to pride and arrogance, things which are unpleasing to Our Father in heaven. For what father finds arrogance in his children pleasing? But God does not force faith upon us. He gives it to us as a gift, and to receive this gift, all we have to do is open our hearts to the words of Jesus Christ, who is the ultimate source of goodness in the world and the ultimate mystery, the Suffering Sacred Heart of the world. May God bless you all and now let us pray. Repeat after me: I believe ..."

Phrase by phrase and line by line, the Indians recited the Nicene Creed after him in Castilian, the idiosyncrasies of their painfully acquired and very imperfect mastery of that language lost in the unison of their childlike voices. There is a purity about the newly converted, an innocence that one rarely finds in old believers. How much of the doctrinal substance of the faith these simple souls are capable of grasping is open to question; but as Montenegro says, Christ did not give up His ghost on a Roman cross only for theologians, He died for all men, for the peasants of Germany and the savages of Hayti as much as for the Doctors of the Salamanca or the Sorbonne. Perhaps, he says, it is as difficult for those puffed-up in intellect as it is for those enslaved to the riches of the world to enter into the kingdom of heaven as it is for a camel to pass through the eye of a needle, though as Holy Scripture reminds us, with God all things are possible.

Ж

Theological idiosyncrasies? Unorthodox even, some might say. But in appearance, not in essence. The good news, if it is to touch souls, must be arrayed in the images and words that can enter the hearts of those who hear it. The Christian message is both simple and complex, and both simple and profound in its simplicity and mystery. It bids men to love God and their neighbours as themselves. What can be more sublimely simple than that? But it is also an account of all things, of the beginning, the purpose and the ending of the world, and of our living and dying in the world, and all things beyond the world, insomuch as it is possible for such creatures of limited understanding as ourselves to grasp such things. If men with the understanding of Augustine struggled to accept its mysteries, then how much more must the mind of a child struggle to grasp them? For the Haytian is child-like, a creature with all the virtues of a child, and the vices of a child. To confuse him with points of theology which he is not yet capable of apprehending would be exactly that, to confuse him rather than enlighten him. He needs to be led, gently by the hand but firmly, at a pace he can walk at with some ease, along the narrow path of correct thinking. Jesus Himself, for He too was dealing with child-like multitudes, spoke more often in parables than in the exalted language of theology. And is not theology itself, in its attempts to grasp the profound mysteries of the world and our living and dying in it, but little more than exalted abstract parable? Those who desire to save souls in far flung fields do better to concentrate on the substantia of the faith, not the accidentia; and in their natural religion, the Haytians certainly have some of the essentials of the substantia of the faith. The simple devotion of the Castilian peasant is as precious to God as the erudite faith of the Doctor of Divinity, and both lead to the same salvation. All men will be equal in the world to come. There will be neither Jew nor Greek, nor bond nor free, nor male nor female, for all are one in Christ.

How I yearn for dry land and an end to this rolling and swaying. And for the fresh meats and fruits of Hayti. I am lucky to have this 'cabin' to myself, which I share only with Savonarola's macaw, but I do not know which is more misery-inducing, the crampedness of this little space – I do not even have a plank one could call a table – or the dizzying expanse of sea and sky outside. The bird stares at me from the perch to which I have secured it with a string, its sulphur-yellow eyes, round and unblinking, full of some sort of malicious bewilderment, or so I imagine.

SEVEN

After mass, Montenegro led me through the kitchen garden behind the Dominican House, the modest dwelling beside the church where he and the other Dominicans live, a whitewashed, tile-roofed building in the style of the houses of the middling sort of colonist. The brothers, not without some ironic jest, refer to it as their 'abbey'. He told me a little of Franco Serrano on the way. An Indian with an intricate scar-design on his face and a particularly flattened skull was fastidiously watering the rows of calabashes, pea-nuts, cabbages, and herbs – most of the latter are from the Spains though some are of local provenance.

"One of the brothers," he told me, "found the misfortunate lying in his own vomit on the quayside and had the servants carry him here. He's been sober longer than a fortnight now, no doubt a temporary condition. If he had strength enough in his legs to walk any distance, I have no doubt he'd be down by the ships again, begging for sugar-wine and up to his old tricks. Not a very inspiring specimen of Christian humanity, I'm sorry to say."

The seaman was being lodged in what he called their 'charity caneys' – a half-dozen simple, yet decent, grass-roofed, round mud structures built in the Indian fashion and situated at the far end of the garden. The Preachers use them to house colonists and seafarers without means who have been stricken by various physical and spiritual disorders, with as much Christian charity that circumstances here allow. The Hospital built by Ovando, Montenegro told me, is overcrowded at the best of times.

Serrano, a rusty-haired, bearded, sun-crisped, red-faced man, well past his prime, and with several missing teeth, was lounging in a hamaca hung between two posts in the shade of one of the caneys. He was dressed in one of those homespun brownish-white-cotton robes the Indians wear.

"Sor Lucrezia would like to hear of the time you spent on tierra firme," Montenegro said bluntly, offering no excuse for my curiosity. "I've told her of the sinking of the *Trinity* and all that. Just tell her what happened after you had escaped from the Canibas."

Serrano's language was at times coarse, and I beg forgiveness for repeating some of it here, but to have prettified his manner of speaking would give a false impression of the man and his rough seafaring world.

"They had gold, plenty of it," he said, obviously thinking that that was my main interest, "ornaments and jewellery and the like. Any bugger who was anyone wore something. Armbands, badges, earrings the size of doughnuts, headbands, and little golden idols of half-animal half-demon creatures on strings around their necks. Never took them off. They're buried with them. If you can call it buryin'."

I asked him to explain.

"They put their corpses in the jungle until they rot, 'til all that's left is the skull and bones," he said. "Then they collect them up, scrape them clean, hang them up in baskets in their houses and have a fiesta, all dancin' and yappin' and drummin' all over the place."

"The Haytians also keep the bones of their dead in baskets, or in urns," Montenegro said. "But we preach against it and the practice is dying out."

"Then they'd bury them proper like, a few years later," Serrano continued, "the bones, that is, along with their half-animal half-demon gold little idols, and all the rest, for luck I suppose. An utter waste, of course, but then they didn't really have a clue about the true value of gold. The buggers were dog-ignorant in some ways. They said it came from a country to the north of them."

"So you learnt their tongue," I ventured.

"Oh, aye," he said. "'Tis simple enough. Though not very logical." Montenegro assures me that the Indian tongue, tongues rather, are anything but simple, though its logic is of its own. "They even have books of a sort, colourful things, written on a sort of paper made from tree bark. They can be clever buggers when it suits them."

"One thing at a time," Montenegro said. "Start with what happened after you escaped from Canibas."

"Five of us escaped," Serrano continued, "myself, Carlos Goya, the Don Padre Gerónimo, Gonzalo Morales and Young Pasqual, the ship's grommet. We spent days in the swamps, half-naked and without any means of protectin' ourselves save the prayers of Don Padre Gerónimo, livin' on raw lizards. We had no fire nor means of makin' it. And on the fruits we'd seen the monkeys eat. We lived like that for at least two weeks. Then one mornin' the Ucateks appeared, out of nowhere, a pack of the buggers, armed with bows and macanas ..." – a 'macana' is wooden club or cudgel – "... pokin' us as we slept on the ground as if we were dogs. Young Pasqual objected and got a clout for his troubles. Cracked his fuckin' skull. Those macanas are as hard as fuckin' iron."

At this outburst of vulgarity, Montenegro, who was in the process of lighting the end of one of his tabaco cigars – he carries a tinder-box with him at all times for this purpose – gave the seaman a reprimanding look.

"They gave us a hamaca to carry Young Pasqual in," he continued, "a kindness of sorts, though in our hearts we expected to meet the same fate as the others had. Morales said they'd at least have to fatten us up first, we were as thin as rakes at that stage. He had a sense of humour, Morales did. Their pueblo had houses like the ones here but they also had a mosque, a stone buildin', well, stone and mud, with a high grass roof, and decorated with all sorts of heathen gargoyles. As soon as he clapped eyes on us, their cacique started laughin' his head off and hootin' and howlin' and jumpin' around the place, and pullin' at Don Padre Gerónimo's beard. The buggers had never seen a man with a beard before and fancied it was some sort of wig or somethin'. But they soon gave up on that and brought us food: mahiz, which they make into a flour and bake a kind of bread with, and beans and fish, and red and green juicy apple-sized fruits they called tomatls."

The Indians here eat mahiz heads too, either fresh, or they barbacoa them, or simply place the kernels in a pot over a fire until they burst from the heat and the flour within forms them into sponge-like globules. Salted, they are quite palatable. But the Indians here do not make any kind of bread from them. Of tomatls I have never heard, nor of anything resembling Serrano's description of them.

"After a few days," Serrano continued, "when our strength was somewhat recovered – except for Young Pasqual, that is, he was still barely able to walk, and if the truth be told, he was never quite the same after that crack on his skull – they set us to work in their fields. They have no beasts of burden and figured we would do nicely instead. They grew mahiz and fresh calabash and beans, all mixed-up and higgledy-piggledy. We had to carry the mahiz heads in baskets on our backs. At night they'd herd us into one of their caneys, at first anyway, and lock us up for the night, like we was livestock. But then one evenin' they stopped lockin' us up, left the door on the latch, as it were, not that they had proper locks. I suppose the buggers figured we'd learnt by then that skedaddlin' off into the jungle didn't make much sense. Not that you could hide in it. And it wasn't as if it were empty. It was as populated as any fertile Catalonian valley. They expected us to work of course but it wasn't that hard once you got used to it – and I've had some ball-breakin' jobs in my time – and it wasn't that often. They did a lot of loungin' around, smokin' tabaco and yappin' and laughin'. There was always enough nosh. I'm no farmer, but I think it had somethin' to do with the way they used to plant everythin' higgledy-piggledy. There was always too much of somethin'. And once you'd got used to it, it wasn't that bad, not that bad at all in fact. There was buckets of fish near all the time and they kept a sort of guinea fowl, cutzes they called 'em, big bastards, the size of geese. They lived better than your average Castilian peasant really. Healthy buggers. Not like your sickly redskins here. None of them were pockmarked. They didn't drink much but there was always plenty to smoke and the two warlocks used to brew up a concoction of toadstools and weeds. It tasted like piss. But its effect wasn't like drink, not like proper booze that is, it ..." – for a moment he seemed to search for a word but then spat on the ground and continued – "... it made you see things differently, see things that aren't there, not normally there anyway, or maybe that are there but you don't see normally ..."

"See things differently?" Montenegro asked.

"Most of the time it was just things looked out of shape like, distorted," Serrano explained. "Or maybe it was just they felt different to look at. Sounds felt different too, and smell and the way things felt when you touched them. It was almost as if they were more real in some way. It depended on how much of the stuff you drank, mostly anyway. Different times it had different effects."

"And the things you saw that weren't there?" Montenegro said. "Or you thought were there but couldn't normally see?" He would have made a good inquisitor.

"You didn't actually see them, not like you usually see things ... or at least I didn't ... Goya said he saw things though, as clear as day. It had different effects on different people. Angels, devils, ghosts, it was if you were catchin' a glimpse of them out of the corner of your eye, but I'll be buggered if I could tell the difference. Whether they were angels or devils, that is. It was as if they were hoverin' about, just out of sight."

"Witches use similar potions," Montenegro informed me, "ointments that they smear all over their bodies at their filthy sabbats. Kramer and Sprenger describe it in some detail. A diabolical unguent. It makes the profane appear holy and the holy profane."

The *Malleus Maleficarum* was one of the dozen volumes given to me by Fray Francisco de Lillo, the order's secretary at Saint Stephen's in Salamanca, to deliver to the Preachers. The others included three bibles, several prayer books, a copy of Gerson's *Catechism: the A B C for Simple Folk*, and *A Guide to the Teachings of Thomas Aquinas on the Waging of Just Wars* from the University at Salamanca.

"Goya learnt the lingo real well. Took to it like a duck to water really. I suppose knowin' a bit of Jew-talk he found it easier to pick up. He was a reconcil-what's-it or whatever you call it. Nearly ended up bein' fried at the stake once in Granada, if the truth be told."

"The word is 'reconciliado'," Montenegro said.

I exchanged a quick glance with Montenegro. A 'reconciliado' is the Castilian word for one who has confessed to the sin of heresy and done penance. Such persons are forbidden to settle anywhere in the Indian countries.

"When in Rome, do as the Romans, he used to say," Serrano continued. "He had his earlobes bored and wore plugs in them, and with his skin engravin's he half-looked like one of them. He used to disappear into the jungle, for months sometimes. A real wanderer he was, and a proper seafarer. He could read maps and knew how to use a quadrant. Even made himself one out of the hard wood the Ucateks made their macanas from, cut it and notched it with one of their stone knives. He saw marvels in the jungle, he said, and gold, though he never managed to get his hands on any."

"Marvels?" Montenegro asked.

"Cities as old as the hills, with mosques the size of cathedrals, all overgrown with weeds and jungle plants, inhabited by tribes of monkeys and poisonous serpents. He said that to the north there was a great kingdom with countless cities, each with a mosque, and on the roofs of which a dozen men are sacrificed to the sun every day of the year. That the inhabitants believed the sun is a god and that it needs to eat human hearts every day or else it will not rise in the mornin's. On his last trip he said he'd seen a great bugger of an ocean to the west – and ships on it."

Montenegro and I exchanged glances. I thought he would interrogate Serrano further as to this but he did not.

"What happened to the others?" he asked instead.

"Morales went took a woman from another pueblo," Serrano

said. "It was sort of arranged for him. So he took off and lived with them. That's the custom. The men move in with the family of the wife, just like with the redskins here. Most of the time the only civilised company I had was Young Pasqual. And he went even more native than Morales. Had a special friend. Who used to have his way with him. If you get my meanin'. He was at an impressionable age, I suppose. The redskin may be a child of nature, Padre, as you say in your sermons, but he's got some pretty unnatural vices if you ask me. Thinks nothin' of a bit of sodomising on the side."

"Even Christians commit the most abominable sins," Montenegro said. He sees all Indians, even the most fallen among them, as his protégés, and invariably insists they should not be judged too harshly.

"Not sayin' they don't, Don Padre," Serrano continued. "I've spent half my life on ships. I wasn't born yesterday. But the redskin has no shame. If it's an arse and has a hole it, he'll fuck it. They were always touchin' each other, and they were as good as naked most of the time. The men have somethin' womanly about them, what with them not bein' able to grow beards and all, like young lads. And, as I said, none of them were pockmarked."

"And Pater Gerónimo?" Montenegro asked him.

"The cacique tried to tempt him with a woman but he wasn't havin' any of that. He tried to convert them but they weren't havin' any of that either. Hobbyhorses to water and all that. But what can you do if they're too stubborn to want to? He prayed a lot. And kept count of all the Feast and Holy Days. He'd managed to save his prayer book and they were all in that. He went off with Goya a few times and he found a pueblo where the cacique was interested in listenin' to him preach. He eventually baptised this cacique and his tribe. Goya used to refer to them as the Inocentes. Which I suppose they all were in a way, innocent, that is."

"Tell Sor Lucrezia the circumstances surrounding your rescue," Montenegro said.

I had been half-expecting him to ask Serrano to repeat the horrors of his companions being captured and slaughtered, and their corpses cooked and eaten, but he had not. Perhaps, like most men, he underestimated the stamina of my sex to listen to accounts of blood and gore with cool heads, thinking themselves better than we at facing painful truths. However, my impression was that, despite all his crudities and inexactitudes, Serrano was a credible enough witness, and though he had a certain cunning, I doubted he had the wit to invent such tales wholesale.

"The pox and the fever came," Serrano continued. "It got Young Pasqual and his 'friend' first. Don Padre Gerónimo said it was divine punishment. For rejectin' the faith. What seemed a bit harsh, like. But what else could it have been? Surely there can be nothin' natural about somethin' as evil as the pox. And, as I've said, they were healthy buggers, not like the redskins here. Three-quarters of the pueblo were dead within a fortnight. We buried them. Well, sort of buried them. We dug two long shallow trenches in the jungle and covered the bodies up with leaves and branches. I suppose the idea was to retrieve the corpses later like they usually did. I can tell you it didn't half stink after a couple of days. The Don Padre had a go at convertin' what was left of them again, but they still wouldn't listen. But then the ways of the Lord are mysterious, are they not, Don Padre?"

There had been more than a portion of bitterness, even a touch of thinly-veiled sarcasm, in his otherwise, strictly speaking, correct comment. I half-expected Fray Montenegro to reprimand him but he did not.

"Then one day," Serrano continued, "when it was over, some traders came to the pueblo. They were flogging stone knives, dyes, spices and the like. It was an often enough occurrence. They told us that the whole country had been afflicted and that what they called 'yanquis' had been spotted out to sea in floatin' castles. They meant ships of course. Christian ships. Their own ships are smaller than ours, more like rafts really, made of logs lashed together with hemp ropes. They don't have iron so they can't make nails. Nifty enough though, for what they were. We used to see them pass by now and again. Sometimes one would land to pick up fresh water and food. Anyway, these traders said that it was shortly after these so-called yanqui floatin' castles had been seen that the pox and the fevers had started. There was a lot of talk. I didn't understand most of it. Goya – he was better at the lingo, as I said – said that some of them believed it was the beginnin' of the end of the world. But the warlock, the one that had survived, the older one, an ancient bugger, said that could not be, that the time of the Last Day had not yet come, and it would not come for hundreds of years yet. The warlocks, Goya said, believed they knew exactly when the world would end, and had calculated it down to the very day, and that it had already ended and been recreated four times over already. They believed that after each Apocalypse things would just start over again. Load of bollocks of course. Though Goya said they knew how to count as good as any Salamanca scholar. Their weeks were longer than their months, you know. And they believed there was ten fuckin' heavens."

"The beliefs and rituals of primitives are often vague premonitions of the truth," Fray Montenegro said, turning to me – and again ignoring Serrano's crudities. "Man has an innate and God-given sense of the divine but without Revelation it inevitably becomes distorted, absurd and perverted, a travesty. The Haytians used to perform a ceremony here in which the warlocks had the women serve so-called 'sacred' casabe bread to their zemis, and then to the caciques and the common people. They believed it protected them against evil spirits."

"One of the blighters," Serrano went on, "one of the outsiders, a tiny effeminate-lookin' bastard with his two front teeth missin', started askin' who Goya and myself were, where we'd come from and so on. The Don Padre had left again by then. We'd taken to dressin' like them but we had beards, though we kept them short. And they'd never seen red hair before. So we stood out like sore thumbs. Anyway, when this arsefucker was told we came from the sea he started shoutin' and cursin' at us and spat in my face. I was about to clobber the faggot and smash out some more of his teeth for him but Goya stopped me. He was talkin' too fast for even Goya to understand everythin' he was rabbitin' on about ..."

"Mind your language," Montenegro said quietly.

"'Pologies Don Padre ... but the gist of it was that we'd brought the sickness out of the sea with us and would bring about the end of the world before the proper time. They talked long into the night, yappin' away with the warlock and the older men, and even some of the old women, in the mosque, the stone buildin' with the gargoyles on it. Goya managed to eavesdrop and catch some of it. He said they were tossin' coins – not that they had coins – as to whether to murder us, cut our throats. He didn't think waitin' around for them to make up their minds was a good idea."

"So what did you do?" I asked.

"We skedaddled, that's what we did. As fast as we could," Serrano went on. "Though in fact we didn't go very far. But we had the good sense to take what we needed. Some food, a net, some fish hooks, gourds, a couple of stone knives and traps. By then we'd learnt how to survive in the jungle, what you could eat, and how to catch parrots and iguanas and the like. There was a sort of cave about two miles down the coast. We'd intended to stay there for a few days before decidin' what to do but once we got there, there didn't seem any hurry to move. It was near a lake with fish in it, so we had plenty to eat. After about a week or so we got to thinkin' maybe they'd decided not to do us in after all. They weren't a bad crowd really. They'd treated us well enough over the years. So one day Goya decided to wander down to the pueblo and have a look-see. He was gone all day and for a while I thought the buggers had done him in. But when he came back he said he'd found the place empty, deserted, not a heathen in sight. They'd just up and gone, just like that."

"Where did they go?" Montenegro asked.

"We never found out. Not that there was anyone around to ask. The hills and the jungle were suddenly empty. If you didn't know what it'd been like before, you'd think there'd never ever been a soul livin' there at all, ever. Now and again we'd go down to the fields and help ourselves to what was still growin', mahiz and tomatls for the most part. The pueblo was goin' to rack and ruin slowly of course but the grass roofs were holdin' up well, on the mosque especially. Eerie really. Like a deserted graveyard or somethin'. At times you'd find yourself imaginin' you were half-hearin' the sounds of the little ones – the children – or the women poundin' the mahiz kernels to make flour. Goya even thought they might have all just gone into the jungle and topped themselves, hung themselves. He said he'd seen somethin' like that here once, back in the old days."

"Here?" I asked, finding myself looking at Fray Montenegro, strangely for moment taking on the demeanour of a man about to defend himself from some accusation he was innocent of.

"Oh, aye," Serrano said, giving Montenegro a look as if they were accomplices in something. Which I found equally strange.

"Not natural, is it," Serrano continued. "But I think they just moved away from the sea. After all, they did think the pox had come from the sea. Maybe they thought if they'd moved inland they would escape it. And if the traders were right – about it afflictin' the whole country – there must have been plenty of empty spots, some of them prime land. But then the buggers don't really think the way we do, so who knows?

"Then one day Goya spotted some smoke billowin' up from the pueblo and driftin' out to sea. It wasn't no cookin' fire, that was for sure. So we decided to go down there and have a look-see. Whatever it was, one thing was sure, somebody was there. We made our way down to the coast and sort of skirted along the edge of the jungle, keepin' ourselves out of sight. In most places the trees and the bushes came right down to the beach. We had no idea what was happenin' and didn't want to be caught with our breeches down, not that we were wearin' any. There was a small headland, sort of juttin' out into the sea, that we had to go round before we could see the pueblo proper like, and – would you believe it? – just as we came around the tip of it, there, just sittin' there on the water as if it was the most natural thing in the world, was a big fat Castilian caravel, flyin' the red and gold of Castille and the white and blue of Our Lady. Its boat was on the beach in front of the pueblo. I never ran faster in me life, and neither did Goya, screamin' and shoutin' to make ourselves heard. We must have been a right sight. Two half-naked long-haired madmen appearin' out of nowhere, ravin' and wavin' about like bloody savages. A moron of an Estremaduran near skewered me with a bolt from his arbalest. He was about to shoot before the fuckin' idiot realised we were shoutin' at him in Castilian. And some other fuckin' idiot was about to set the fuckin' dogs on us."

Arbalests, those steel-bowed crossbows, the one in which the bowstring is drawn by means of a windlass, is very common among the soldiers here. Much more so than the arquebus.

"It was a Tuesday," Serrano continued. "That was the first thing I asked them. What day it was. I'd thought it was a Monday. Only one day out I was, not bad considerin'. I'd kept count you see. Like the Don Padre. Kept civilised. Never eaten meat on a Friday, said a Pater Noster every Sunday, on what I thought were Fridays and Sundays anyways. When the boatswain told me I let out quite a hoot I can tell you. His lordship the captain gave permission for us to be taken to the ship, looked us over, asked us all sorts of questions for hours, and said we could work our way back to Santo Domingo and he'd throw in a pair of trousers for each of us into the bargain. A right hidalgo he was. Fancied himself."

"What was the fire?" Montenegro asked. I had completely forgotten about it.

"Ah, they were just torchin' what was left of the mosque and the caneys. A bit of devilment, that's all. They'd found nothin' worth anythin' to take so were a bit pissed off. Until I told his lordship the captain about the graves."

"The graves of the plague victims?" Montenegro asked.

"No," he laughed, revealing the few tabaco-stained teeth he had. "There was nothin' in them but bones and rot. They only put the gold ornaments in the graves when they bury the cleaned-up bones. We found a few dozen. We melted them down on the beach. I doubt if His Majesty ever saw his quinto. Then his lordship claimed the land officially for the King. He had us chop down some trees and build a big timber cross. We erected it on top of the headland. Visible for miles, it was. He read some arsey proclamation and then led us all in prayers of thanks for givin' us such a fertile and unpopulated land. Us! Pull the other one! Though, if you ask me, what good is land if you don't have anyone to work it? Then we sailed up the coast. Once we saw some of the ruins Goya had told me about. They were high up on a cliff. A few days later we found a pueblo and managed to catch a few of the Indians there, about thirty of them. About twenty survived. His lordship the captain sold them on the quiet here in Santo Domingo – for a hefty bag of dollars. Not that we saw any of that."

"Dollars?" I said, not understanding.

"Thalers," Montenegro explained. "Joachimthalers. Thalers. Talers. Dollars. The going rate for an adult slave is a hundred pesos."

He then questioned Serrano again.

"What became of Pater Gerónimo?" he asked.

"Missed the boat," Serrano said and shrugged his shoulders.

I asked him if the land he had described was an island and what was it called, but he only said: "In truth, Doña Sor, it is hard to tell, but if it was an island, it was a big'un. They call it Ucaton."

I also asked him if they had been able to see the Pole Star there.

"Aye, Doña Sor, some of the time anyways," he said.

On the way back to the church – it was time for Montenegro to celebrate the so-called Spanish mass – Montenegro told me more of how Serrano and Goya had been rescued.

"His story changes a bit every time he tells it, but the essentials remain the same. The caravel that picked them up was the *Roxana*. The captain was some Estremaduran with airs and pretentions whose name I can't recall, exploring without a licence, and raiding the Indians whenever the opportunity presented itself. All in secret, of course. Serrano says he made them swear an oath on the Virgin's Milk never to reveal who had rescued them. But there's precious few secrets on this gossip-prone island. Everyone just pretends there are. They were lucky, the two of them. If the *Roxana* had not already lost half its crew and was short of men, it might not even have taken them aboard."

"And this Goya's tales of cities?" I asked.

"The Pharaoh is reported to have said that some Indians – on his fourth voyage – told him that further inland there was a kingdom, called Ciguare or Ciamba or something like that, where gold is supposed to be as common as steel is among us. The Gold Land is always somewhere else, over the next hill, on the next island, somewhere further up the coast."

"What happened to Goya?" I asked him, remembering that Serrano had not said.

"He's here on Hayti. Somewhere near Concepción. But Serrano says he doesn't know where exactly. He said he thought he had an encomienda there."

"Surely they'll have a record at the Castle," I suggested. It seemed to be the obvious place to enquire. Castilian officials prefer nothing better than assembling archives.

"Perhaps," Fray Montenegro said, rather cryptically, I thought.

"The passage to the Cipango," I mused aloud. "a route to the Realm of the Great Khan? Perhaps ..."

"Maybe, maybe," he said, taking a last suck on his tabaco cigar, and dropping the still burning stub onto the gravelled path, extinguishing it with his sandaled foot. One of his favourite jokes is that, once, when asked by a penitent in the confessional if it was a sin to smoke while praying, he had replied: "Yes. But it is not a sin to pray when smoking." He does not believe it breaks a fast, but says by the time Rome makes a decision on that matter, he'll have already faced a higher and hopefully more merciful court.

Certainly, Serrano does not know if the passage that the Strassburg map depicts exists. In fact, I doubt if the fellow really believes the world is a sphere. But his companion Carlos Goya had, it seemed, spent months exploring. Perhaps ...

Before we parted, I asked Montenegro what he thought Ucaton meant.

"God knows," he said. "U-cat-on. Maybe it simply means me-no-understand. Wouldn't surprise me. There's a lot of places called 'me-no-understand' in this part of the world."

But, most probably, I thought later, surely it means something like 'Land of the Ucateks' or similar.

Ж

Franco Serrano's account to Sor Lucrezia of his
misadventures differed in no essentials to what he had
already told Fray Pedro and myself, but he had not told
us of Carlos Goya's travels. However, of course, the
thought foremost in my mind was that if Pater Gerónimo
Sanchez was still alive and making conversions, did
Carlos Goya knew of his whereabouts? I had the duty to
find out more. I wrote to Johannes Puccini that very
evening. I had no intention of going near the Castle. If
Carlos Goya was somewhere in the Vega Real, I had no
doubt that if anyone knew anything of his whereabouts
it would be Puccini. 'Our island alchemist', as I often
called him in jest, was a man whose principal vice was
idle curiosity, the vice which Augustine put second only
to lust.

Ж

I have decided to show Montenegro the Strassburger map. You
will no doubt think I am being foolhardy, but if you knew this
man, I am sure you would approve. And if I cannot trust this
man, whose all-consuming goal is to bring the message of Christ
to the untold multitudes of this island and the other Indian
countries, to jungles where men have never even so much as
heard the name of our Saviour whispered, then who, dear
Balthazar, can I trust? I am determined in this and will show it
him at the first opportunity that presents itself.

Ж

I have taken to saying my offices, at Prime, Terce, Sext,
None and Vespers, walking about the deck with
Savonarola's macaw perched on my shoulder. Lauds I say
in my 'cupboard' on rising, and Compline before retiring to
my hamaca for the night; and I have arranged for the
ship's bell to ring out Nocturns which I also say in my
'cupboard'. What a sight we must be! The praying monk
with his multicoloured bird! I must look like a tropical
Francis of Assisi preaching to the beasts. But the creature,
if it is to reach Christendom alive, needs fresh air, and I am
reluctant to let it out of my sight for any length of time lest
the seamen play some prank upon it.

The bird is a sort of parrot, a macaw being a sort of

bigger parrot with a rather distinctive type of beak. It is just over a foot and a half long from head to tail, which is not particularly large for a macaw. Most are considerably larger. The colour of the beast is truly wondrous, which is true of most of the birds of the islands. The feathers on its head are a bright red but these slowly change to orange and then yellow about its neck. The wing feathers are a multitude of hues: red, a purplish blue and brown. And its tail, which is near are long as its body proper, is red at the top and blue at the tip, on the upper side; however underneath, it is a sort of rusty red. The feathers on its back are brown but tipped with green. Its face, breast and thighs are a bright orange. In nature they are woodland beasts, flying about in pairs or in small flocks. They nest in cavities in trees. The cock is indistinguishable from the hen, unlike the birds of Christendom, where the cock is almost invariably the gaudier. The creatures need to be captured as chicks if they are to be trained as pets and to speak, though this one has never so much as uttered a syllable – despite what Savonarola said. I have a bag of palm seeds, their favourite food, to feed it with, though it will also eat nuts, fruits and vegetables of various kinds. Macaws, like parrots, are edible, and the Haytians prize their flesh as a delicacy, especially that of young birds, but it does not appeal to Christian palates.

EIGHT

Over the years there have been sundry schemes by the Casa de la Contratación to entice decent and upstanding Christian Castilians of all ranks and classes to settle here: the payment of salaries and stipends for remaining here for fixed periods of time, freedom from taxes for certain activities, generous grants of tracts of land, permissions to pan and mine for gold, and the granting of rights to the services of Indian labourers. At various times, even criminals, excepting of course heretics and sodomites, have been offered amnesties to settle here. Men have even been granted pardons for capital crimes on condition they undertake to stay here for at least two years – a seemingly generous exchange, but most probably based on the assumption that they would unlikely ever be able to afford the return passage. Those sentenced to banishment have also been allowed to settle here. In the early days only subjects of the late Queen were permitted to come, and then only those from certain of her countries, and subjects of the King not allowed at all. But these days men from all the Spains come here. A good half come from the Estremadura, which is in the south of the Iberian peninsula, though for a long time, immigration from that region was not allowed either.

All Jews are barred, as are Moors. Decrees forbidding conversos, or New Christians as they are more politely called, and of course moriscos, from settling anywhere in the Indies have been many and, as far as I can ascertain, various in their stipulations. At one time, so I have been told, all converted Jews and their offspring down to the fourth generation were barred unless they had obtained a royal permission, and all moriscos. Today the restrictions are more liberal. But in fact many New Christians and their descendants can be found here, the former in no small numbers. And even a few Moors, Ramírez, the Alcalde's morisco, being one of their number. But condemned heretics and reconciliados and their children are still barred.

Men can be granted legal title to tracts of land for fixed periods or in perpetuity by the authorities on behalf of the Crown: lands which have been declared forfeit because of some grave crime of rebellion on the part of their previous owners, or land which has been unoccupied, deserted by their original inhabitants or lain unused. In addition, settlers also acquire land through 'marriage' into Indian families of rank.

How all this functions in practice is a complex matter, as is bound to be the case when two systems of laws and customs coexist and have to do with each other, but I have gleaned some understanding of how it works from various conversations. Since the caciques have sworn fealty to the Catholic Crown and become free vassals of the Crown, and all have now done so, Castilian law and customs, naturaliter et de jure, take precedence over previous usages, bringing with them the unquestionable advantages of a written, civilised, Christian and superior regulation to a previously heathen and illiterate land. Native modes of title to property – title and inheritance among all the Haytian peoples is through the female line – have given way to Castilian. Thus the property of the wife becomes de facto the property of her husband and thereafter becomes de jure the property of their common offspring, if I properly understand the meanings of those judicial terms. However, what constitutes a legal marriage, in the eyes of the secular arm, is not clear-cut. When a ceremony of Christian marriage has taken place the issue is of course clear, but when the husband is a Christian and his wife not, they cannot be said to be joined in Christian matrimony. However, and Montenegro has been informative in this matter, the authorities generally consider such unions valid – if for no other reason, he says, than that it enables the ownership of land to pass into Christian hands. As regards canonical law, the situation seems to me less clear. Saint Paul says in his Epistle to the Corinthians: If any brother hath a wife that believeth not, and she be pleased to dwell with him, let him not put her away; the unbelieving wife is sanctified by the husband: otherwise your children would be unclean; but now they are holy. However, it seems to me most likely that Saint Paul was referring to unions made before one of the parties had become Christian, and not to unions what took place between Christians and pagans. Though I do not know this and it is not my place to judge. But I have no doubt that, men being what they are, there have been numerous cases of the unscrupulous taking unjust advantage of the misunderstandings and confusions of the situation; for which reason the Crown has since the beginning been meticulous in sending learned judges and notaries to adjudicate on these and similar matters.

After many failed attempts to impose an order of sorts on this state of chaos, the Crown has for several years now instituted what is called the encomienda system, often simply called 'the system'. The arrangement is similar to the arrangement of the same name implemented in the Spains after their liberation from Moorish tyranny. It enables a most modest Castilian, some of whom, it must be admitted, are men fit for little more than sweeping the streets of their native cities, to transform himself into an Indian lord.

Under 'the system' colonists are granted rights to the services of Indians to work on their lands for several months a year, the number of labourers being awarded depending on the rank of the recipient. A caballero, if he brings his wife, receives the services of eighty; a common soldier, if he brings his, receives sixty; and a labourer with spouse, thirty. In exchange for these rights, settlers are obliged to educate those who are obliged to work for them in the fundamental principles and practices of the Catholic religion, in so much as is practicable. In actual practice, this means that the Indians, who generally remain free vassals, have been for a large part gathered into pueblos adjacent to Castilian towns, settlements and encomiendas. "It is hoped that by obliging them to live in proximity to Christians," Fray Estaban, the Franciscan Prior, says, "they may gradually become more civilised, a task which would be infinitely more difficult if they were left to their own devices to run wild in the hills and the woods." Thus too, it is argued, the natural resources of the land can be most efficiently exploited, its rivers panned and its mines worked, producing prosperity for the benefit of all. Such, in principle, is the intention of Crown policy. But Fray Pedro – a very learned man, he is composing a catechism for the instruction of the Haytians – and Montenegro say that in practice the system causes much hardship and in fact hinders catechisation. But, since I have so far ventured no further afield than the outskirts of Santo Domingo, I have not been able to see the abuses they speak of with my own eyes.

Settlers are also allowed to purchase Indians who for some crime or rebellion or through capture in war have legally become slaves, as is the case in the Spains and all of Christendom, and even among the Turks and other literate nations. I am told that most of these slaves are Canibas – a race of men whose very mode of being renders all wars against them just – and that reducing them to this condition is the only way of taming them. It is difficult, from their appearance, to distinguish these ferocious men from the more indolent Haytian Indian, and accounts of the locations and extents of the countries and lands they inhabit are not exact.

Ж

Causes much hardship! The naivety of women! After every so-called Pacification, whichever domineering tyrant – styled Governor or Comendador or Excellentissimo or what have you! – happened to have been in charge at the time divided up vast numbers of the inhabitants as if they were mere cattle among his cronies, no small number of whom being the dregs of Iberian prisons. Thirty were given to this man, forty to that, and a hundred or two hundred to his special favourites. All on the pretext that they were to be instructed in the Catholic religion by their new masters, vicious idiots who like to call themselves 'conquistadors'. Crown policy! More the greatest act of piracy ever committed. And there is no end to it. The men they send to the gold mines where, fed with little more than soup, they wither away under a regime of labour that would break the back of the strongest Castilian peasant. And as for instructing these misfortunates in the Catholic faith: they are forced to work on Holy Days and on the Lord's Day itself, which means they work near twice as many days as a miner or a peasant in Christendom. The women are forced to labour in the fields, where they are so badly fed that their milk dries up and they cannot suckle their young. And with the men being separated from the women and allowed no congress with them, fewer and fewer children are being born. It would need quires of paper to describe the horror of it. Every royal decree stipulating the conditions under which they are to labour and what protections and rights they should have – and there have been many – are ignored with contempt and impunity.

A good Franciscan who came here on the Pharaoh's second voyage – not all of that order are insensitive to the bodily welfare of the native inhabitants of these islands – tells me that when he first beheld this land there were so many inhabitants that he was convinced that the Almighty had placed the greater part of humanity in the Antilles. Thus a nation sickens and dies, nay, is exterminated; a nation which when I arrived was perhaps sixty thousand, and in that short time of less than a dozen years, is now less than half that. When the Pharaoh discovered them, they were numbered in the hundreds of thousands.

Ж

"Who else knows of this?" was Montenegro's first question.

I had laid the twelve sheets of the map out on the large table in what we call our refectory in their correct order so one could see Waldseemüller's and Ringmann's bird's eye view of the world in one glance.

"No one here," I assured him, meaning none here on the Spanish Island.

"Prudent," he said, donning the reading lenses he keeps inside his habit. "The authorities take maps seriously. There are laws. And no shortage of spies and informers."

"Even if they have been printed and to be had in all the countries of Christendom?" I said.

"Yes," he said, bending over the sheets so that he could examine them in detail. "So this is how men now see the world?"

"This is how some men see it," I said.

"Jerusalem is not in the centre, not quite anyway," he said.

"It's kind of a portolano," I informed him, "more like a seafarer's chart rather than a true mappa mundi. It's based on Ptolemy's *Geographia* and on the discoveries of Americus Vespucci." I pointed out the inset portraits of the bearded cosmographers just atop the map's the frame: the Alexandrian Ptolemy with an astronomer's quadrant facing toward the east, and the Genoese Vespucci with his geometrician's dividers facing west. "The depiction of that part of the world mapped by Ptolemy – Asia, Africa, Christendom, all of the oikoumene – has been corrected in the light of the Portuguese voyages. This part ..." – I indicated the Indian countries – "... is based on Americus Vespucci's accounts of his explorations. "It shows the passage. A route through to the Great Southern Ocean, to Cipango and the Realm of the Great Khan."

"Which nobody has ever found," he said.

"Officially," I added.

"In this inset at the top," he pointed out, "there is no passage." He has sharp eyes.

"An oversight?" I suggested.

"Or a deliberate ambiguity?" he replied. "The mapmaker's way of saying that much of what he has drawn is merely speculation perhaps? And neither is it at all clear if this Southern Ocean can be reached by sailing around the Parrot Land, which I see he's christened 'America', after Vespucci one presumes."

It was a while before he spoke again.

"According to this, to reach Asia there is another ocean to cross, a distance greater than that between here and the Fortunate

Isles, between here and Africa even. Vespucci only sailed in
southern waters. How can the mapmaker know these things? Who
was he?"

"They. Two Alsatians," I told him. "A Martin Waldseemüller
and a Mathias Ringmann. I have been told they have printed a
thousand copies of this."

He asked me where I'd gotten it.

I must confess that I was miserly with the truth, and told him
only that it was a gift.

"An expensive one," he said but did not press me further.

"Serrano said they were able to see the Pole Star, so they must
have been north of the equator," I said, indicating the land just
north of the equator but below the passage.

"They might have been here." He pointed out the two large
islands off the coast of tierra firme near the passage. "Perhaps
they just thought they were on tierra firme."

"Riveria may not be a learned man but surely even he would
have known if they had been on an island," I said. "Would not the
inhabitants not have known and told him that this was the
case?"

"Most probably," he admitted.

Christian women, as I have said, are not numerous here.
Likewise, there are few Christian servants, but there is no
shortage of excellent native cooks, domestics and wet-nurses –
though many complain of their quality. Indians seem to require
little instruction to accustom themselves sufficiently to Christian
habits and ways, and their service can be had for little more than
rudimentary board, lodging and a suit of cotton clothes or a dress
per year. Unattached women are a rarity, though there are a
handful of propertied widows, some of whom are Indians. I have
also heard that there are, oddly enough, two gypsy women, from
Granada or thereabouts, who run a 'house' down on the docks –
I'm not sure where exactly – which is, I presume, officially a
tavern, but the nature of which requires no great imagination to
deduct. They are said to have a dozen or so Indian girls 'in
service'. I have seen two of them at the market, plastered in
make-up and dressed in locally made Castilian frocks, caricatures
of their sisters on the docks of Seville and Cadiz and all the other
ports of Christendom. That the oldest profession – as it is called
by lechers high and low who wish to trivialise the filthy
degradations of the whole business, as if its longevity justified it –
flourishes here surprised me initially, a failure of imagination on

my part. I have been told the gypsy 'house' is not the only one of its kind.

This evening Montenegro told me in some detail more of how, if left to their own devices, the Indians dispose of their dead. They have many different customs. Some corpses they preserve, some they bury and some they burn, all according to rank it seems. Some of these customs are still practiced in the hills, he told me. The corpse of a cacique was often preserved by drying it out beside a fire, and the heads of commoners were preserved in the same manner. Other times, they simply used to burn down the house in which a man had died in, or even just put a corpse in a hamaca in the woods and let it rot. Though they also buried some, in the ground or in caves. Another practice was to sew the bones of the dead into cotton zemis and pray to them as if they were the relics of saints.

"Which," he informed me, "makes it even more difficult to persuade them to part with the things. They will only do so if we give the remains Christian burials."

"And do you?" I asked him.

"We bury the bones in unconsecrated ground," he said, "and say a prayer – in Latin, which of course is beyond them – begging forgiveness for our deception. I console myself that no prayer is futile, not even those said at the gravesides of the damned. We have asked our motherhouse to send some genuine relics."

"Perhaps their ancestors are not entirely lost," I suggested. "Christ died for all men. Can it not be supposed that those who through no fault of their own were ignorant of the Gospel, and of His Church, but sought the truth and did God's will in accordance with their limited understanding of it would have desired baptism if they had but known of it? And the desire for baptism is enough, is it not?"

"Perhaps," he said, shrugging his shoulders.

I asked him what the Indians imagined happened to them in the next world.

"They believe the souls of dead are in a place called Coaybay," he told me, "an island somewhere in their so-called 'dream-world', but that at night they emerge and haunt the countryside, flying about in the form of bats, feeding on guayaba, or walking about in the bodily form they had in life." Guayaba is a fruit which tastes and looks like quince. "They say that these wandering corpses can be recognised by the fact that they do not have navels."

This 'dream-world', he told me later, is a realm of chaos where they believe all the spirits and demons who rule the world live, and who have to be constantly placated with absurd rituals and offerings. It is a rudimentary intuition of the divine order in the universe, he admits, but only barely so. He attributes the anarchy in their manners and customs to this, to their utter lack of any deeper appreciation that the divine by its very nature is ordered and harmonious.

The earth shook today. I was in the refectory with Hildegard and for a moment I thought that I had become suddenly dizzy from the heat – and then I saw the hanging lamp sway on its chain, was thrown into confusion, and felt Gloria the kitchen maid tugging me furiously and inexplicably by the arm of my habit and dragging me outside into the garden, shouting something incomprehensible to me in the native tongue, a look of utter alarm on her face. Once outside, Hildegard, who is proving adept at learning the Haytian tongue, explained that what had occurred was an earthquake. Then a few minutes later it happened again, with at least twice as much force. It was if the ground on which we stood had become the deck of a rolling ship. A few tiles fell from the roof and the dogs began to bark.

It appears that these shakings of the earth occur every few years and that what we had experienced was a minor shaking. One would expect that the experience would produce in one a sense of utter dread but it did not. How can I explain? For a moment I felt utterly in the Almighty's hands, utterly ... and felt a strange, deep and almost sensual peace, and was moved to tears.

Tonight we shall sleep on the patio, under an awning, for Hildegard says the servants say that there may be more shakings over the next few days.

In the dark early hours of this morning, about two hours past midnight, we were wrenched from our sleep by the sound of the most ferocious thunderstorm. Thunderclaps as loud as cannon reverberated through the sky and flashes of electric blue lightning in quick succession illuminated the hills. There was a moment when I thought the whole of creation, the heavens themselves and the hills and the very earth itself, was about to break asunder. Strangely, it did not rain.

Ж

I am sure the bird speaks. Today, returning to my
cupboard from performing my necessaries, as I was but
five or six feet from the door, I'm sure I heard its voice,
not loud and not so distinct that I could make out a
word of what it was saying, but distinct enough for me to
know that it was the voice of a macaw and not of a man.
Oddly enough, the words, or rather the sounds of the
words, or what I took for words, had a strangely familiar
rhythm or beat or cadence to them. But as I approached
the door to open the latch, the creature became silent, as
if preternaturally sensing my presence.

NINE

I am being spied upon. You said a woman has the ability to pass unnoticed in the world in a way that a man does not. It seems that is not the case here. After Vespers I was leafing through these pages – I make my entries mostly in the evenings, after the day's final prayers and before my spiritual exercises – and, perchance, I noticed that half a dozen pages were missing. Not the most recent pages, and not so many that their absence would be immediately noticed, so I do not know when they were taken. Nothing else that I know of is missing. Which leads me to the unavoidable conclusion that this theft is the work of a spy, not a common thief.

I keep this document in my drawered chest in the room I use for my administrative duties. Neither are locked. Locks, like everything mechanical or anything crafted from metal, are exorbitantly expensive here and our funds need to be preserved. I am furious. I should have kept it in our strong box. How could I have been so foolhardy? But what's happened has happened. Perhaps it was done when my sisters and I were at the Haytian mass, on the Sunday before last?

My mind is awhirl with rage and speculation as to who could have stolen my papers. I need calm to consider the implications of it all. So I have decided to put the whole matter out of my mind for the next few days – or attempt to – and apply my mind to other affairs. I will not let this pass but rashness could be folly. I shall sleep on it. What action best to take will come to me of its own volition.

As I wrote earlier, when I was commencing this account, the methods the navigator uses to find his way across the endless waters of the Oceanus Occidentalis, a full quarter of the extent of the globe, are of an astounding complexity. Perhaps now is a good time to relate what I have gleaned of them. The telling will distract my mind from my stolen pages.

On any voyage out of sight of land, the navigator needs to be able to determine both latitude and longitude if he is to sail with any degree of certitude, which is little enough at the best of times. To do this, he avails of numerous procedures of varying ingenuity.

Firstly, there is the matter of latitude. This can be determined –
at night only of course, and only if the sky is cloudless – using a
mariner's quadrant. This instrument consists of a brass quarter-
circle plate, the circular edge of which is marked out in degrees,
ninety degrees in all, with a small lead plum-shaped weight,
similar to the type used by builders to ensure that walls are built
straight, hanging on a string attached the right angle of the
quarter-circle plate – where the centre of the circle would have
been if the quarter-circle plate were a full circle. To take a
reading, the navigator aligns one of the straight edges of the
device with the position of the Pole Star – no easy task on a
swaying ship. Held in this position, the lead-weighted string
crosses the angle markings on the circular edge of the instrument
and thus gives the Pole Star's angular altitude in the arc of the sky
above the horizon of the sea. During the hours of starless daylight
and when on the other side of the equator – not that our voyage
brought us that far south – where the Pole Star is not visible, he
estimates latitude by using the quadrant to measure the angular
height of the sun. Then, with the help of his copy of
Regiomontanus' *Ephemerides*, which contains tables listing the
angular height of the sun in arcs and minutes for each day of the
year as seen from various latitudes, in a procedure that surpasses
my humble arithmetical abilities, he can estimate his actual
latitude. Needless to say, both these methods require relatively
cloudless skies and, as one can imagine, the opportunity for
considerable error on a wind and wave buffeted ship is not
negligible.

Estimating longitude is an even more haphazard affair. The
method invariably used, our captain told me, is called 'dead
reckoning', though some navigators have also attempted to use
the movements of the planets and the stars. Dead reckoning
involves estimating the speed of the ship by throwing a small rod
of wood attached to a long thin rope over the side at the bow.
There are two marks cut into the ship's rail, one fore and one aft.
When the floating rod passes the fore mark, the steersman starts
up an ancient seaman's chant, more syllables than words, the
meanings of which, if there be any, I was not able to make out.
When this rod passes the aft mark, he stops suddenly and the
officer on the deck notes the syllable he has stopped at. Each
syllable signifies a certain speed in Portuguese leagues or sea
miles per hour. A sea mile is about four Latin miles, as far as I
can discern; navigators make use of a great and confusing variety
of measurements of distance according to their nation and

inclinations. The method can hardly be that accurate, but it seems to work well enough. It is carried out on the hour every day, except when the vessel is moving very slowly, for in that case, the steersman would have finished his chant before the rod had passed the aft mark. And when the ship is barely moving, there is in any case little point in ascertaining its speed. Time is kept by a sand clock, which the grommet, the ship's boy, turns every half hour; and it, in its turn, is kept on time by the use of a portable and ingenious mechanical device, called a nocturnal, which indicates the time of the night by the rotation of stars around the Pole Star. The ship's speed is also sometimes estimated at night, when there is sufficient moonlight.

Thus, if the ship is travelling due west, or due east, and if the navigator knows his latitude and the length of the particular arc of longitude in sea miles at that latitude, he can estimate what proportion of that arc of longitude his vessel has transversed. By diligently recording all these daily measurements – assuming he knows the longitude to at least a few minutes of a degree at the journey's point of commencement – and by their careful addition, he can thus estimate his longitude at any given point on a voyage. However, should the vessel be travelling at an angle to the lines of latitude, say north-west or north-north-west, which is usually the case, then this deviation needs to be included in his calculations; and this is even further complicated by the fact that the sailing direction of the vessel and thus its relationship to the lines of latitude can vary several times throughout a normal day at sea.

The ship's compass is used to determine the angle at which the ship is travelling in relation to the lines of longitude and latitude. These angles, the ship's direction, in addition to the estimated speed of the ship, are recorded hourly by means of another ingenious device called a toleta. This is an engraved wooden board divided into two sections, an upper and a lower. The upper section consists of a compass rose with eight circles, one within the other, with thirty-two equally spaced peg holes on the circumferences of each, one for each of the thirty-two points of the compass, and to which pegs, one for each hour of the watch, are attached by strings lest they get mislaid. This part is used to record the direction in which the vessel has sailed, a peg being inserted into one of the inner-ring holes to record the direction during the first hour of the watch, into a hole on the next ring for the second and so on. The lower section of the board also has a number of rows of holes, each row marked with a number representing a speed – with more pegs attached to strings. On the hour the steersman simply inserts a peg into the relevant hole to record the estimated speed the vessel has been travelling at for the previous hour. Thus even the most unlettered seamen may record accurately both the speed and direction of the vessel, which the navigator then subsequently records onto his portolano chart. Straightforward enough when one understands the procedure, one may think, but this is all further complicated by the awkward fact that the compass needle does not point towards true north – that point on the top of the earth intersected by the invisible axis around which the heavenly spheres revolve – but rather towards what seamen believed to be an immense iron mountain in its vicinity. In the waters of the Mediterranean the compass needle deviates only slightly from true north – five or six degrees of the arc of a circle – but this becomes as much as thrice that as a vessel sails out into the Oceanus Occidentalis; perhaps because, as many cosmographers believe, and seamen too, the earth may be slightly pear-shaped. Don Cristóbal, our captain told me, is said to have speculated on the practicality of devising a method by which these compass variations – which in addition vary according to one's latitude – could be used to ascertain longitude with more accuracy than dead reckoning.

Was it one of my beatas? Hardly. And the servants are illiterate. Who would have the gall to commit such a violation? A person in the pay of the authorities? But who would have ordered such a thing done? That vain upstart: our Don Imperial Alcalde Mayor himself? Montenegro did say he had spies everywhere, or intimated as much. I can think of none other. I have no proof of course, but who else could possibly have had an interest in my affairs? It has to have been him. No one else would dare. Don Rudolfo Jesus de Paz needs a lesson in manners. But that needs to be handled with some tact.

Ж

I am not quite sure exactly when I began to harbour suspicions. Her curiosity in itself I did not find amiss. She was after all new to Hayti and a missionary needs to learn the customs of the people and the lay of the land in order to follow his vocation. So even when Alfredo Castro, the tile-maker, remarked that she was a 'nosey woman', and I asked him what he meant, and he'd said she's been 'asking a lot of questions', I was not surprised; nor indeed at her numerous questions to me. Perhaps it was when I learnt that she was spending our dark tropical evenings burning candles and filling pages of expensive Italian paper, several quires of which, along with a half-dozen years' supply of quills, she had purchased in Spain and brought across with her. Nuns, after all, even Hieronymite beatas, are not known for their love of scholarship. The island nurtures mistrust and suspicion. Hayti is a vipers' den of plots, counter-plots and rumours of plots. At times life there seems to consist of little else. This faction plots against that. That faction plots against this. The innocent comment does not exist and everyone knows it. Men are forever on the lookout for the slip of tongue that gives away another man's business, interests or his weaknesses. And Hayti is a small world. There are fewer colonists there than in a middling Castilian town.

Then there was who she was. The Marchionni are after all a family of usurers, and Genoa is as much of a bankers' republic as any of the other northern cities of Italy. And, it is well known, Genoese are known to serve whatever master furthers their private purposes. Bartolommeo di Marchionni, Fray Pedro had informed me, is the wealthiest slave merchant in Lisbon. He trades in Africans and Guanche from the Fortunate Isles, and he finances the greater part of the shipments from Africa to Hayti. He also, Fray Pedro says, had some hand in supplying the monies for the Pharaoh's first and second voyages. The Pharaoh, of course, was a Genoese too. And Bartolommeo di Marchionni provided the monies for Cabral's Portuguese voyage of 1500 to Calicut via the Africa coast and the Oceanus Indius Meridionalis – the one in the course of which Cabral claimed the Parrot Land for Portugal. That armada was as large as the Pharaoh's on his second voyage, and the journey was four times as long.

Was she mining my knowledge for some purpose? Or involved in some conspiracy of whose nature I was completely ignorant? Perhaps even spying on me and my brothers for one of our enemies in Castile, of which we have many? For the Portuguese? Or even for Rome itself? The Church's power is based as much on knowledge of the mundane world as it is on knowledge of the human soul. Such were the thoughts that went through my mind.

I knew nothing of her relationship with the Alcalde Mayor at the time, if her intercourse with him was anything beyond what was officially necessary, or something else.

There were also other possibilities. Numerous powerful and influential men have an interest in the affairs of the

island; interests they would be loath to see hindered or
compromised by meddlesome monks. Perhaps she was
serving one of those. Or perhaps it was simply that, being
by nature a curious man, I let that curiosity grow until it
transformed itself into suspicion. That is the nature of
venial vices. In any case, I became suspicious enough to
act. Above all, I wanted to be sure that nothing she was
about could compromise the private inquisitions I had
started carrying out when I was alone on the island; and to
the continuation of which Fray Pedro had given his
blessing. Much was at stake – at that time I had collected
four statements – and much still is at stake: the souls of
countless Indians who have yet to be given the good news
that mankind is not inevitably doomed to oblivion, that the
dead will rise again; and the souls of Spaniards who need to
be prevented from committing sin – if necessary by
compulsion.

TEN

Don Rudolfo Jesus de Paz, done up in another one of his costumes – a yellow cotton jacket, black ruffled pansied slops and dark blue hosen with an embroidered codpiece – was in the process of feeding his Irish wolfhound when we were ushered into his presence by Ramírez. The beast is massive and must stand seven feet tall when on its hind legs.

"Charlemagne's his name," he said. "A man should always feed his own dogs. They never bite the hand that feeds them. Unlike our fellow men."

He was no doubt surprised at my sudden appearance, though he made a good show at pretending not to be. I shall relate our conversation in some detail.

"Not quite like the rains of our beloved Christendom," he said when the seemingly ever-hovering Ramírez had left us alone. I had opened our conversation by commenting on the renewed rain, an endless downpour which had lasted near on three full days and had only ceased during the night. "But we'll begin paving the streets next year. Would have done it this year but labour's a bit of problem. Our fair city will be the Jewel of the Antilles some day. Mark my words."

I was still not sure how to allude to my missing papers without mentioning them, and without him quite realising that that was what I was doing; to somehow sow a suspicion in his mind that would cause him to tread more carefully in future.

"Now, that will be something to write home about," he added almost casually.

I looked him straight in the eye, but he just returned my gaze, smiling. The man didn't even blink.

"The day when our beloved Santo Domingo is known as the Jewel of the Antilles will be a day to write home about," he said by way of explanation, obviously wanting me to think that was what he meant. But I retained my composure.

"Ah, home," I said. "Your family is in Castile, I presume?"

"I was an only child," he said. "My parents, God bless them, have long since gone to the heavenly reward that hopefully awaits us all."

"Is there no Doña de Paz?" I asked.

"Oh yes," he said, "since last year, or as well as good as. We exchange correspondence – but she's not a great writer. She will be here in a couple of months. If God wills it. And our union will be sealed in His eyes."

Officials and colonists who can afford it, or are well-connected, enter into contracts of matrimony with Castilian ladies of good family whom they have never seen, either hoping one day to have them join them here, or to later join them in the Spains when they have made their fortunes and returned.

"The bulk of my correspondence with the fatherland is of an official nature," he continued. "Reports and the like. Our masters – la Contratación – are keen to be kept extensively informed on all manner of developments."

I still could not make out whether he was trying to provoke me again – if his 'something to write home about' remark had in fact been deliberate – or if he had been pretending stupidity.

"So you are alone in the world?" I said.

The expression on his face suddenly changed, either because of the unexpectedness of my presumed intimacy or because my words had scratched some raw nerve.

"We Marchionni," I continued, not giving him an opportunity to reply, "are a large family, a colourful melange. Bankers of course, but also soldiers, scholars, two bishops and a cardinal. We look out for each other. When one sheep gets into trouble all the other sheep – and some of them, I'm loath to say, are more wolves in sheep's clothing than sheep – flock about to help."

"Bah-bah black sheep," he said.

The absurd response just seemed to form itself in his mouth as if it had been the most natural thing in the world to say.

"It's one of the advantages of a large family," I said, flabbergasted.

"Jesus was an only child," he said. "But admirable, truly admirable. The way they flock about."

His pretence – that is if it was pretence – at taking everything I said at face value was impressive.

"Snap your fingers, my cousin – the cardinal – used to say," I said, "and I'll come running. Do you know Rome?"

"My father brought me there once," he said. "I must have been barely sixteen, if that. We saw the Pope. Fancy a tipple?"

For a moment I was at a loss.

"A snifter. A drink," he explained, extracting a pewter decanter from a drawer beneath his writing table. "I find it helps against this God-forsaken damp and greyness."

I declined.

"We were not a rich family," he told me as he poured himself what smelt like sugar wine.

"There is no shame in poverty," I said – with as much condescension as I could muster. He shot me a look of rage, or the perfect facsimile of it. "Nothing disreputable in it at all. Disrepute comes from breaking the rules, the laws of God, the laws of kings, and the customs of good behaviour."

He seemed unsure for a moment as to what I meant by the latter, which was what I intended.

"The customs of civility," I added, "of honour, of the unspoken rules – rules all the more binding for being unspoken. Overstepping one's station ..."

I let that sink in for a second. I am not quite sure how I expected him to react. To blather out some excuses? Offer some apology? Hardly. Needless to say, he did not. He simply laughed, so disturbedly and with such intensity that for a moment I thought he was going to succumb to a fit of apoplexy. But then I realised he was actually drunk.

"But a purse full of castellanos," he said, finding his composure again, "or better still a chest of 'em, or pearls, gleaming pearls as perfect as the heavenly spheres themselves ... or a virgin's arse, if you'll excuse the expression." He actually leered at me as he said that. "It does something to a man, raises him above the common herd ... and then there's the sweetmeats that come with it, all sorts of yummies. The pickings here – for a man of determination – can be significant. If one plays one's cards right. And if one steps carefully ..."

"And takes care not to offend those who do not take offence lightly," I suggested, "and have the power or the connections not to have to take it lightly,"

"Precisely," he said.

I've known men who exist in a constant state of drunkenness but still manage to fulfil their functions as well, or as badly, as if sober.

"The difficulty lies," I went on, "I should imagine, in that it's not always apparent who such persons might be, who's who, who knows who ..."

He looked at me for a moment, seemingly on the verge of saying something pertinent to that but then seemed to change his mind.

"How are the lady beatas?" he asked instead. "Settling in nicely, I trust."

"Very nicely," I replied. "They wish for no more than the

opportunity to instruct the poor Haytian children that Fray Pedro has placed in our care in right thinking and how to lead good lives,"

"Ah, yes, your charming bronze-skinned pickaninnies," he scoffed, staring at me. "The Indian is a wild flower. And in his natural habitat not without some tropical rustic charms. But he needs guidance – as you put it – in the right ways of thinking."

"As we all do," I added.

"On what is right for us," he said, practically barking at me, the emphasis loudly and clearly on the 'us'. "For ..." – he suddenly lowered his voice as if he was taking me into a great confidence, some lewd secret even – "... for what is right for Christians is right for all men, so for them too. If you follow my logic."

I did not of course. But after this puzzling statement, his mood, or perhaps it was merely his manner, changed abruptly again.

"I used to think," he said, "that one day I would return to Castile, rich and honoured. But now I realise I'll find my grave here. In a way, I suppose I'm sleeping in my coffin, like those monks do. But you, Sor di Marchionni, will you be buried here?"

"Such things are in the hands of the Almighty," I said pointedly, more than a little taken aback by the insolence of the question.

"Of course, of course," he said, pausing to pour himself another half mug of his sugar wine. "All things are in His hands, except of course those things He has given into our hands. This country, this our Castile in Asia, as it were, calls for strong wills, for determination. My duty is to see that the apple-cart is not upset. Nobody wants that you see, neither here, in Seville, nor in Rome either I should imagine. Have you seen my globe?"

I had, of course, noticed it on my first visit to him and had meant to examine it more closely at the time but the opportunity had not arisen.

"It was made by a man called Behaim, from Nuremberg, in the year before the Pharaoh landed here," he explained as we went over to it. "Or conceived rather. I had the sphere made by our carpenter but I gummed the gores to it myself and painted them personally. Of course, it does not show these islands. Not really."

He gave it a twirl and the globe, which was quite beautiful, rotated in its stand.

"The model rotates," he said, "but that of which it is a model stands still." For a moment I did not understand. "In reality the earth stands still and the world rotates." He touched it again and it stopped spinning. "Spain is a long way across the Oceanus

Occidentalis, and Rome too for that matter."

As he escorted me to the Castle gates, he said something along these lines: "There are those who say that Christ's commandment to be fishers of men only applied to the first apostles, not to their descendants. That there is no commandment, no obligation to missionise at all. Heresy I'm sure, not that I am qualified to pronounce on such things. But then we islanders lack the good offices of the Tribunal to guide us along the straight and narrow."

I remained, though with some effort of will, unprovoked by his thinly disguised sarcasm, if that is what it was.

"The same voices," he continued, "say that the Preacher friars should perhaps concern themselves more with the souls of Christian Spaniards than with the souls of those who perhaps were never meant to be saved. Who may not even have souls, some at court are saying."

ж

I knew nothing of this at the time. Perhaps if Sor Lucrezia had known the true character of Rudolfo Jesus de Paz, she would not have treated him so brazenly. That he became suspicious after this confrontation was inevitable. Suspicion is second nature to men of his ilk. His ability to sniff out those whose motives and interests were contrary to his own or did not serve his own, and how men were likely to act in pursuit of them, at times before they even knew themselves, had no doubt been indispensable in his rise from whatever miserable condition from whence he had originally sprung. And though he had not displayed it in the interview which Sor Lucrezia has described, I had also seen him display a not inconsiderable ability to charm, a skill he was capable of turning on and off like a tap. The ability to charm is, even in those, nay especially in those who are ruthless and cunning, a prerequisite to rising high in the services of princes, both royal and republican, and is sorely underestimated. Rare is the prince who is not susceptible to being seduced by flattery subtle and not so subtle.

ж

A ship from Dahomey on the West African coast has arrived in the harbour laden with Africans – the sons of Ham, Montenegro calls them – destined for the sugarcane fields in Maquana. A great number of these African slaves have been imported, he tells me. The first of them, a hundred men or so, were brought here to mine copper in 1505, when it was believed there were great quantities of that metal to be found. Now several hundred or thereabouts – getting figures of any kind is difficult here, he says, since everyone counts in a fashion to suit his own purposes – are imported every year. He says that Ovando was at first against the practice as the Dahomeyians were a bad influence on the Indians, but eventually saw the benefits of it, as the numbers of Indians were becoming less. The settlers also complained that the Indians were skilled in ruses to avoid work and knew the land so well that it was difficult to catch them again when they ran away.

My missing pages have reappeared. I found them in the top drawer of my chest, my mother's olivewood rosary beads laid casually atop them, presumably to give the impression that they had been there all the time. But the question remains: who did Rudolfo Jesus de Paz have do his thieving handiwork? And then replace the pages, attempting to make it look as if they had never been purloined in the first place? Presumably the same person? On reflection, I can only come to the conclusion that it must have been one of the servants. The thought that a disposition to treachery can inhabit the breasts of such a mild-mannered people is disconcerting – not that I have not been warned. I shall have to give the matter some thought. I will not have servants I cannot trust.

Ж

At about this time, I received a reply from Puccini:

To Fray Montenegro, Santo Domingo, from Johannes Puccini, Medicus Philosophicus, Concepción de la Vega.

Carlos Goya is well known to me. His encomienda is about a day's march from here, in what the Haytians call Caonabó's Valley, in what used to be the Maquanan cacicazgo. Anacaona was born thereabouts they say. Goya has built a small stone house there. The old buildings – the place used to belong to a local Maguán grandee – are still standing though and still used. He's growing sugar, or attempting to, like everyone else.

As regards the private concern you wrote of: I have cast your horoscope as best I could with the information you have given me and the indispensable assistance of my trusty copy of Regiomontanus. But it tells me not enough, though nothing that forebodes any immediate ill. I need to examine you in person. As above, so below, but: the microcosmos might be a mirror of the macrocosmos but the reflection we see is not easily deciphered. The key to intuiting diagnoses lies in the physical body; the stars inform, but less exactly.

Concepción is busier than ever. It just grows and grows. Men are making fortunes here and the price of everything reflects it. Bacon is selling at a comfortable price – those pigs were a good investment – and a thaler can be got for a fanega of casaba flour on a good day. There's more sugar being planted than anything else now. I believe that the time will come when the sweet crystal will prove more lucrative than the mines. Maybe it is already the case. The Castle is tight-lipped about these things, as we know.

As for my quest: it is bearing fruition. I believe I have found the herb. Well, it's a tree actually, the bark of one. But I will say no more in writing beyond that the bohiques swear by it for all sorts of fevers and tumours.

Ж

Montenegro has learnt of the whereabouts of the seafarer Carlos Goya. He – Montenegro that is – arrived at the nunnery this morning just after Terce, wearing one of those straw wide-brimmed sunhats the Indians wear, with a letter from an acquaintance of his in Concepción de la Vega in his hand, waving it about with some enthusiasm.

"I have located Carlos Goya," he said. "He has a place in the hills quite close to Concepción. I know a man there. His name is Puccini, a Florentine – though his mother was a Bavarian – a medical man, of eclectic abilities, a lay scholar of sorts. He says he knows him."

"Serrano's shipmate?" I said.

"Yes, yes," he said. "If what Serrano says is true and this Goya wandered about a bit ... well, he might know something about the passage."

It is a long journey to Concepción, several days' march through the Vega Real, which is a spacious empty landscape by all accounts. This may all be a wild goose chase of course and lead to nothing. However, it will be an opportunity to see something of the country. We leave on the Monday of next week.

Ж

The day before we left for Concepción Fray Pedro summoned me and suggested we take a walk in the vegetable garden. I knew immediately from his manner that it was so we could converse in private, out of the earshot of our brother monks and the servants.

He asked me how my inquisitions were progressing. I told him I had four sworn and signed statements and was in the process of composing my own which, I assured him, would be damning and include all that I had seen and heard in the years before he and my other brothers had arrived on Hayti. He nodded with silent approval, as is his way, while I related him the details.

"Good, good," he said when I had finished, "the more witnesses we have to the crimes that have been committed here, the greater the conviction will be with which we will be able to make our case."

"I am also in conversation with a Hieronymite who is witness to what is happening on the Lucayas," I told him. "He is willing to testify."

"You are being careful?" he said.

"Our correspondence has been sparse," I said, "and cloaked in euphemisms. I am expecting him to be here in a few weeks."

"Laudable," he said, nodding again.

Then he came to the real reason why he wished to speak to me.

"The time is approaching for us to act," he pronounced.

I nodded non-committally.

"I want them to hear the accusations with their own ears from the pulpit," he said, "during mass, when they are all gathered together, within sight of each other, each one knowing that the other has heard it and there can be no denying it. And I want you to deliver that sermon. You are our best preacher. You know these people and the circumstances better than any of us. Coming from your mouth the words will have the greater impact. I want them shamed collectively."

"And if His Excellentissimo orders us expelled?" I said. "He has the authority to do it."

It was a grey day, with only the odd sliver of sunshine on the waters of the bay. The oppressiveness of it seemed to mirror the hopelessness of the task we had set ourselves.

"It is a risk I am willing to take," he said.

"When?" I asked.

"Soon," he said. "We can discuss it further when you return from Concepción."

I had not told him the object of my journey. I had seen no need to.

"Of course," I agreed.

We were about to part when he said one other thing: "We must tread very carefully from now on. Under no circumstances must we give the Governor – or Rudolfo Jesus de Paz or anyone else – any pretext to throw mud at us. We must not only be above suspicion in all that we do; we must be seen to be. There must not be the slightest whiff of scandal of any kind."

Ж

It is better to marry than to burn, Saint Paul tells us. But for a bride of Christ, the burning never ceases. We smoulder endlessly, forever struggling to control the feelings that emerge out of our carnal bodies and the thoughts they give rise to. It is worst at night, in the privacy of the bare cell, the distractions of the day no more, the Antillean night bursting with the incessant chorus of the cicadas and of all the other creatures that inhabit the equatorial darkness, while attempting to sleep in the damp clammy heat of this place. And in that darkness memories of the day emerge: a pair of sparkling eyes, the shape of a comely limb or torso glanced at under flimsy fabric, or the sight of bare olive-hued flesh ... and with those feelings, deceptively pure at first, formless desires take on half-forms and transform themselves into images of lecherous concupiscence. Oh why, I ask myself, does He allow us to be tempted so, and so relentlessly? Why does He allow the flesh to drag down the spirit to its baser level? To that of the beast. Nay, even lower, for the beast's concupiscence, its lust to mount and be mounted, to dominate and submit, is something ignorant, and in that ignorance, there is a sort of crude innocence. We can only glimpse beatitude in a state of carnal and spiritual chastity. The body must be tamed, scourged into submission, compelled to submit to that higher spiritual self we call the soul. The more I pray and meditate upon these matters, the more certain I become of this profound truth. All desire and all disgust must be flushed out from our beings. Only in a state of bodily and spiritual chastity can the purified soul, liberated from its carnal fetters, experience the glories of creation in such a manner as to enable it to glimpse an inkling of the ultimate beauty of the Divine Creator from whom those glories emanate. Such moments of true purity are precious, for these glimpses of beatitude nourish the faith by which we try to live like nothing else, faith in the possibility of paradise, in the Resurrection of the Dead and in the ultimate perfection of all creation. But to achieve such moments, the body needs the whip, needs the scourge submitted to willingly, and the spirit needs to be cleansed of its attachment to the flesh. Only when it is free of the flesh and washed free of sin by the bliss of absolution does the soul gain the ability to attain such heights.

I still wonder if it was one of the servants who stole and then returned my papers. But they are all such meek and deferential creatures.

Sor Vitoria has taken to her bed with a fever.

Ж

It has happened again. This time as I was returning from washing my habit and hanging it up to dry. I do so with some reluctance as the seawater I'm sure will eventually rot it, but I do not want to look like an utter mendicant when we reach the Spains. Keeping up some semblance of a Christian appearance is important. The bird was making the same strange familiar sound that it made the last time, stopping, as it did the last time, just as I was to open the door of my 'cupboard'. Perhaps the creature actually hears me approach, but how? I was barefoot and made not a sound. Maybe its abilities really are preternatural.

ELEVEN

The Vega Real. Dawn. Since it is impossibly dark once the sun sets and we stop only in the evenings, a little after Vespers, this is the only time I can avail of to record some brief notes and impressions.

We have been walking for two days. We being Montenegro, Hildegard – a creature gluttonous by nature whom I thought the exertions of a short pilgrimage would do no harm – myself, and three of the Dominican servants to porter our effects and victuals. Mornings and from mid-afternoon on we make good progress; but when the sun is directly overhead in the sky – as it is at midday here, and unremittingly fierce – we have no choice but to seek shade and rest for a short while. We have all taken to wearing sunhats. The road or path – I am not sure what I should call it: it is narrower than roads in Christendom, the Indians never having had wheeled carts nor the beasts of burden to pull them, and so not requiring anything wider – consists for the most part of a long-trodden thoroughfare winding indolently through the lush landscape. It is pleasant to walk for the most part, but in places the surface had been rendered uneven by the passage of horses and mules.

The day before yesterday, as we ascended the hills outside Santo Domingo, we caught several glimpses of the ocean below us, an empty blue plain of water extending as far as the eye can see. It reminded me of the weeks at sea, of the killing of the shark that came from its depths, and how distant we are from familiar things, and, in our relentless sinfulness, from God Himself.

The hills and the valleys are bright green after the rains but for the most part empty, save for every few miles a cluster of three or four caneys, built on low mounds, half-hidden by fruit-bearing bushes and trees; and here and there, in the distance, the odd encomienda compound. Passing one of these Indian peasant hamlets, a pot-bellied girl child, as naked as the day she was born except for a bead necklace and whirls of arsenic-white paint on her cheeks, a concoction of some local herb or mineral, emerged from the herbage to silently stare at us as if we were some kind of apparition from another world. Once we saw a herd of feral pigs in some undergrowth. Descendants of the original eight that Don Cristóbal Colón brought him on his second voyage, Montenegro said.

Another time, we had to stand aside to let a caravan consisting of twenty or more Indians carrying large packs on their backs pass by. I exchanged some politenesses with their masters. Montenegro's disapproval was obvious – at least to me – but he refrained from commenting.

Due to the absence of privacy, I have been obliged to abstain from the discipline of my spiritual exercises. But in recompense, several times a day I remove my sandals, the ground permitting, and proceed barefoot.

We came across the ruins of an Indian settlement yesterday afternoon. It was perhaps a dozen manzanas in extent, in the flat dry country the Indians call 'zavana'. I am loath to call it a city for it possessed no walls or other buildings a Christian would consider proper to a city. Montenegro said it had only been abandoned a few years back. We lingered for a while among the ruins of the houses and the plazas called 'batey' courts where, Montenegro said, the Indians once played a ball game called batey and held heathen ceremonies called areítos.

I asked him to explain. I had heard mention of these areítos but I knew nothing substantial of them.

They were held, he told me, to celebrate the sowing and harvesting of the crops, to mark the solstices, and to celebrate the marriages of their caciques, the births of princes, or the first bloods of princesses, visits from other caciques and victories in war. As many as four hundred dancers would dance the dances and sing the songs.

"All their history and their legends were in their songs," he said. "But that is all in the past now."

"Sad," I said. "In a way."

"They were filthy heathen things," he said. "Devil festivals as bad as witches' sabbats. Their main aim was to invoke their idols and induce them to possess them. But first, they believed they had to 'purify' themselves, by bathing in so-called magic pools and engaging in disgusting bouts of communal vomiting. They used 'sacred' vomiting sticks carved from manati rib bones. And as for the music: they used to make flutes from human leg bones. And they danced naked. What is wrong is that the people are dying off, not that their ways are dying off."

The deserted ruins were being swiftly reclaimed by Mother Nature. Weeds and grasses overran the flat once-hard mud floors of the tree-trunk framed dwellings, all roofless now. It was a forlorn place, with the atmosphere of a long-neglected cemetery.

He said it was known as Pueblo Fantasma, and was a 'yucayeque', which is the Indians' word for 'town', and that there had been many of these yucayeques once. Then he shrugged his shoulders and said that the death of Isabela was the greatest calamity to befall this land and we needed to be getting on. A little later, when we had started walking again, he said: "Conversion to our ways is their only hope."

He has become uncharacteristically introspective over the last few days, but then each of us has their own intimate troubles and preoccupations.

Last night – I still have not quite recovered from the shock of it – Montenegro got drunk, drunker than I have seen most men. One minute we were sitting by the fire waiting for our evening fare, a mess of salty black beans and mashed casabe which our servants were preparing in one of their distinctive black-earth cooking bowls; the next I noticed he was drinking openly from a large earthenware bottle that obviously contained sugar wine, and I suddenly realised he was actually intoxicated.

"Isabela's death released the four horsemen on this God-forsaken land," he began, almost as if speaking to himself. "War, famine, plague and death – and the scum of Castile. What was done before, and I am sure much was done, was kept secret from her. They'd like to erase her name from memory. That's why it's called Santo Domingo, why they changed the name from New Isabela. And who could object to a town being named after a saint? But ever since Ferdinand has reigned alone, Ferdinand the bloody Catholic ... a drink?"

I shook my head, surprised that he had even offered.

"I once saw five men laid on grid-irons and roasted alive," he said, lowering his voice as if he was uttering some sacred truth. Those were his very words. "We were on way to the court of Hiquanamá, the Queen of Hiqüey. Some of her princes had rebelled. And with right." He took another swallow from the earthenware bottle. "Our so-called Christian compatriots treat the Haytians with more contempt than shit in the street. Or haven't you noticed? The drunken fucker – and I make no excuse for my language, Sor Lucrezia – who had ordered this atrocity, this blasphemy, then told the sergeant in charge – a man I know from Seville – to strangle his victims because their screams were disturbing his fucking repose. The sergeant merely had them gagged. Like roasted pig and singed hair, that's what a roasted man smells like, except you never get the stink of it out of your nostrils."

"What did you do?" I asked. The question, foolish now in retrospect, just formed itself on my lips.

His response was a devilish daemonic laughter, as if he were possessed by something from hell.

"What did I do?" he repeated, laughing again. "I'll tell you what I did, Sor di Marchionni." He moved closer to me and stared me in the face, looking at me as if I were some way an accomplice in what he had related, staring at me with such an intensity I could not believe that what his drink-crazed eyes were seeing could possibly be me. I was almost relieved when he took another mouthful of the poisonous alcohol. "I prayed, Sor Lucrezia di Marchionni, that's what I did, I prayed." He offered the bottle to me again. "You sure?" I shook my head and he helped himself again. "They called it a barbacoa," he laughed, "a barbacoa," and laughed again.

Then, with the typical unpredictability of the drunk, he suddenly got up and, bottle in hand, wandered to the edge of the circle of light created by our campfire and stared into the moonlit darkness of the valley below, where not so much as the light of a single lantern shone.

"A mission from heaven!" he said, almost to himself, speaking into the night, his back to me. "A just war!" He laughed again.

"The Hiqüeyans had taken to hiding in caves and holes in the ground," he continued, turning to me. "The soldiers were hunting them down with the dogs. I've seen the devils disembowel a man in a fraction of a minute. I once saw half a pueblo hung, strung up like fowl to ripen. The captain claimed it was the law: a hundred for a single Spaniard. They hung them thirteen at a time. Thirteen. In honour of Christ and His apostles, they said. I wrote to Salamanca but ... how can one write about such things ... and be believed?"

He staggered back to the fire, sat down opposite me again and drank some more, and was silent for a while. I became acutely aware of the sound of the nightly chorus of cicadas and other insect-creatures all around us in the dark.

Then he continued: "During the wars, the Pacifications as they call them ... The Haytians didn't have a snowball's chance in hell. Their weapons are as flimsy as the reeds boys play soldiers with. Things of wood and stone. Have you ever seen a troop of armoured men on horseback charging into battle calling on the Moor Killer?" I shook my head. "A man skewered on a lance like a wild pig or sliced open with a sword? The workings of our fine Toledo steel on a man's naked flesh? The Haytians would run into battle as naked as the day they were born except for their ornaments. It was murder and robbery, nothing less, organised by none other than our beloved Don Rudolfo Jesus de Paz, our illustrious Alcalde Mayor, from the comfort and safety of his Castle lair. I have seen with my own eyes the bodies of murdered Haytians being laid out on a butcher's bench, chopped up with meat cleavers like sides of mutton and fed to dogs. And they thought it was funny! A source of amusement! Redskin gobble up dog, they said, now dog gobble up redskin."

"What happened to Queen Hiquanamá?" I found myself asking, perhaps thinking that the question would make him somehow desist from continuing his recitation of this litany of horrors.

"They crucified her," he said, as if it were merely some incidental detail.

"Why?" I asked, horrified at the very thought that there might be some truth in what he had said, that he had meant that she had been literally nailed to a cross.

"Why?" he repeated. "For gold and the love of it. For gold and the love of it. Write that down!"

He was silent then for a while.

I briefly wondered what he had meant by 'write that down' – he's seen me making notes of course, but then the phrase is also just a manner of speech.

"Christopher bloody fucking Columbus he called himself," he went on. "Christopher the Christ-bearer. Columbus the dove of peace. The Apostle Thomas sailed east and brought the truth of our holy faith to the East Indies. The Apostle Christopher, the thirteenth apostle, sailed west to bring it to the West Indies. I believed that once, the fool that I was. Used to compare himself to Moses and Abraham, the fucker. Pleading poverty one minute, promising riches the next. The crews of the *Pinta*, the *Niña* and the *Santa María* were never paid a maravedí, you know. Dreaming of a yearly armada of caravels transporting cattle, pigs and horses one way, with slaves taking their places on the way back."

He then collapsed. I had the servants carry him – not an easy task, for he is a heavy man – to his sleeping mat.

It was the first time that I have ever felt any displeasure in his company. But for a while I meditated upon what he had said.

There was a crescent moon in the tropical sky, with the bright star of Jupiter above it and the less bright Saturn below it.

Mars, recognisable from its orange hue, was also visible. But I know little of astrology – or indeed of astronomy or cosmography.

We are due to reach Concepción late this afternoon.

Ж

I remember none of that. I remember getting drunk – I am no saint – and the next day, the day we reached Concepción, being as sick as I ever have been from excessive indulgence in the fruit of the vine, or in this case the stem of the sugar plant, and experiencing the dread of not remembering what I had said and done while in that shameful state. I thank God that it is a demon that possesses me only occasionally. But she said nothing, so I took it that I had neither said nor done anything too amiss, and found consolation in that. But there is no untruth in what she says I said. And did Christ not rage when, scourge in hand, He drove the usurers from the precincts of the Temple?

TWELVE

We arrived at the outskirts of Concepción de la Vega as dusk was descending and the mosquitoes were coming out. The silhouette of the fort, built by Don Cristóbal's brother, Don Bartolomé, was visible for a few moments against a grey-purple sky before we were enveloped in darkness. But Montenegro, who has been here many times, led us securely to our destination, the residence – some rooms at the far end of a walled courtyard – of Johannes Puccini. The medicus philosophicus welcomed me most enthusiastically, in quite elegant Italian-accented Latin, to what he called his 'humble abode', though it is no more humble than most dwellings here, and what he called 'dies bunt und giftig land' (multi-coloured and poisonous country). He wasted no time before offering us a jug of chicha, which, I noted, Montenegro, for once, took only the slightest sip of. He seems to remember nothing of his outburst; or, perhaps he does, but is so ashamed of it that he wishes me to believe he does not. I have no way of knowing if any of what he related is based on true events of any kind. And I know from experience that men are capable of saying anything – and doing anything – when in that state of extreme drunkenness.

The medicus is a well-built man, bald and clean-shaven, which is not the custom here, and obviously learned, though there is something of the jester about him. His right hand is deformed, with index and middle fingers missing, either from birth or accident; it is impossible to tell. He has two servants, a male and a female, with whom he converses in not very good Castilian, peppered with semi-crudities, and the local Indian language; and whom he seems to allow all sorts of liberties. The male, a gypsy-like Indian, his face tattooed with some sort of indelible black-brown ink, sports a bright-green parrot feather in his jet-black hair. He is in his third decade perhaps – I find it hard to tell, the Indians do not seem to age as visibly as we do – and has the unlikely name of Savonarola, and was even allowed to sit at table with us. Many of the Indians have Christian names and, I have been told, consider it a great honour when they are given one. There are a great many Juans and Marias among them. However 'Savonarola', the name of a Florentine heretic, can hardly be considered appropriate. A joke in questionable taste, to say the least. In truth, I cannot say I warmed to the medicus. There is something satyr-like about him and he has large frog-like eyes that give the impression of missing nothing.

Hildegard and I have been given a room and a bed which is more than adequate, and indeed a luxury after the hard fare of our various campsites in the Vega Real. I can hear music from below, a melancholic air played on a violetta, exquisitely played. Puccini, I presume. Fray Montenegro did say he was a man of eclectic abilities.

Puccini's residence backs onto a river called the Río Verde – though it's more mud-brown than green – and Don Cristóbal's fort, an ominous monument, around which the town grew up, is visible from the courtyard. Concepción is a noisy place, and indeed rougher than Santo Domingo, and its streets are in a far worse condition. There is little evidence of the Alcalde's latest Italian ideas. Montenegro says the fort was built not far from Guarionex's capital, Guaranico, which of course no longer exists. Guarionex was one of the most powerful of the caciques.

What Fray Montenegro finds to admire in the medicus philosophicus I fail to see. He has been here longer than Montenegro and in that time he has learnt much of how the peoples of the island lived before our coming. He quotes Plato – accurately or not, I cannot tell – saying that if Plato was right, and the first age of Man was the Golden Age, an age of happiness and natural virtue, then the Indians, who knew only how to smith gold, were still living in the Golden Age when Don Cristóbal discovered them. An interesting opinion, but a pagan one, not of course that all pagan ideas are false; but fanciful methinks. He is a Florentine, by birth at least, and Florentines love their Plato perhaps a bit too much; and his being a Florentine also perhaps explains somewhat why he gave his manservant the name Savonarola, who no doubt has no inkling of its significance. He is also prone to contradicting himself, for a little later he was suggesting that the people of the Antilles and tierra firme might be the descendants of the ten lost tribes of Israel. The ancient Israelites can hardly be said to have lived in Plato's Golden Age, or any golden age for that matter! Every now and again, showing a side of himself to which I have the impression Montenegro is oblivious, he utters an aside to me in Italian poking fun, indirectly, at something or someone – at himself too, often enough, I must say in fairness – as if we were both some intimate cabal of co-conspirators. But I do not like his humour: it is not generally base but it is invariably imbued with a rather unpleasant flippancy and cynicism. He impresses me as a man for whom there is little he will not ridicule. What exactly he doing here is not clear to me. Perhaps he paid for his crossing by acting as a ship's physician on one of the armadas and then just simply stayed here. He has a doctorate degree – if he is to be believed – which surely makes him the only medicus on the island with one; and it is, I presume, from the practice of that art that he principally makes his living.

This afternoon Montenegro broached the subject of Carlos Goya with Puccini over cups of 'chocol', a bitter but stimulating drink of the texture of Moorish kahwa. The drink itself is made from the nuts of the chocol plant and seasoned with axí pepper. The juice of the plant is used by the warlocks as a medicine, Puccini told us, and that he once met one who claimed dead men had been revived by it miraculous powers.

"He's a New Christian, a converso, you know," Montenegro said.

Puccini looked surprised and yet not surprised by this revelation.

"Like a good quarter of the Christians here," he said. "And in Spain. Even the Hammer of Heretics himself, the Blessed Tomás de Torquemada, is the grandchild of a Jewess. Set a thief to catch a thief. Poacher turned gamekeeper and all that, I suppose."

"As was my own grandmother," Montenegro said, which startled me somewhat. I saw immediately that he regretted saying it, though it was obvious that Puccini was obliviously familiar with the fact. The attitude of the converso towards the Jews proper is often more zealous than the attitude of the Old Christian towards them. It is common knowledge that many of the old converso families greatly influenced the Catholic Monarchs' decision to expel the Jews proper from the Spains. Some say that was because they believed that by doing so the Monarchs would remove both a temptation for them to backslide into their previous error and a shameful reminder that their forefathers had lived in darkness. "But Goya is also a reconciliado," Montenegro added, "a different thing entirely."

Puccini shrugged.

"He's a man of some learning," he said, "though it's more of the type one picks up in the better sort of tavern in places like Salamanca or Barcelona than at a university."

"You have no idea how he managed to get permission to come here?" Montenegro asked.

"Through the grace of Mammon all things are possible," Puccini said, rubbed the thumb and two fingers of his intact hand together in the universal and rather obscene gesture that signifies money. "As I wrote you, he lives in a place called Caonabó's Valley. With an Indian woman. He says she's a descendant of the infamous Anacaona or related to the family. It's a good day's walk from here. He's a sort of caretaker. The hidalgo who has the rights to it proper skedaddled back to Castile a couple of years back."

"Anacaona?" I asked.

"A queen," Puccini explained, glancing at Montenegro as if my question was somehow amiss, or inappropriate. "The sister of Behechio, the Xaraquan cacique. A wild woman by all accounts. She was hung during the Pacifications. By rights, of course, being a queen, she should have been shipped to Spain for trial, like Guarionex, for all the good that did him. He went down with the ships in the 1502 hurucan, along with two hundred thousand pesos of gold and the famous pepita de oro. The bohiques, the wise men, call gold 'el excremento de dios', the excrement of the gods. Not out of contempt, mind you, but with reverence. They consider it sacred. The pepita de oro was quite a turd. Thirty-six hundred crowns' worth of turd."

"Satan's shit," Montenegro half-murmured. Even when sober he is, at times anyway, not a man who minces his words.

"And why did this Guarionex rebel?" I asked Puccini.

"A so-called Christian raped his queen," Montenegro said. "A man I see every day walking the streets of Santo Domingo ..."

I looked at Montenegro and was about to ask him: Who? How?

"I will not soil my lips by uttering the blackguard's name," he said before I spoke. "It is a name that deserves oblivion. In his anger, Guarionex burnt down the church he'd had his people build."

"Our little island has a varied and complicated history," Puccini said, "the study of which is one of my amusements. The history of before we arrived – the world-before – and the history of what I suppose one could call the world-after."

"But surely," I said, "all accounts of before our coming are mere tales, legends, the truth of which can never be ascertained. We brought the written word, and without the written word ..."

But before I could finish, he had risen and was rummaging around in one of his chests.

"Not quite strictly speaking true," he said as he did so. "They use picture writing – or they used to – hieroglyphs, like the ancient Egyptians."

He handed me a sheet of the kind of paper the Indians make from tree bark and on which they paint symbols of birds and animals and with which they sometimes decorate their dwellings. There were no letters on it or anything that resembled writing, only pictures or rather what are called pictographs, painted in some black-brown ink.

"It tells of our coming," he said.

I could make out the cowls of the Franciscans – they had come over with Don Cristóbal on his second voyage – and what looked like depictions of Indians being baptised. But there were also symbols I did not understand at all.

"You may make a copy of it if you wish," he said.

I said I would be most pleased to do so.

"So you want to meet Carlos Goya?" he then said suddenly, looking at both Montenegro and myself in turn.

Montenegro began to busy himself with lighting a tabaco cigar, leaving me to attempt a diplomatic answer.

"We've heard that he has been to the unexplored islands to the west," I said tentatively. "Our order is interested in setting up further missions." A white lie of course, but for a good cause.

"Savonarola can take you there," he said. "He knows the way. Don't you?" The Indian nodded silently. He is not very talkative. "I can dispense with his fiddling for a couple of days. For the cause, you understand. I taught him to play when I still could myself. I'm left-handed. My violetta days are firmly in the past. But that's the way, isn't it? Bit by bit we fall apart." He held up his crippled right hand and flexed the stumps of his missing fingers by way of demonstration. So it must have been Savonarola whom I'd heard the other evening. I would never have thought. "The Haytians are a musical folk. Their speciality is the mayohuacan, a sort of large cylindrical drum made of wood. Three feet long and one and a half wide. Massive things. A good player can be heard a league and a half away. Music is how they communicate with their gods."

"Demons," Montenegro corrected him.

"The demons – they call them 'zemi' – they say teach them the melodies and words in dreams or when they are wandering alone on the zavana or in the woods," Puccini continued, addressing me rather than Montenegro, to whom little of this would have been new. "Their history is also recorded in songs taught them by the bohiques: the stories of their origins and the great deeds done by their fathers, grandfathers, great grandfathers, and ancestors in war – and in peace. If there is a key, it is in music, if it is anywhere. Don't you think?"

"A key?" I asked.

He made a gesture encompassing the yard, empty save for the pigs and the chickens and his Indian womanservant washing clothes at the water trough.

"To this temporary condition," he said. "This being, the flesh and its passing ... The Hibernians, not so long ago, are reputed to have marched into battle playing harps. But whether to inspire themselves to engage in the madness or to give the madness sense is hard to tell. Perhaps it was both."

Puccini and Fray Montenegro are still below, drinking.

I have made a copy of the Indian bark document Puccini gave me and have contemplated it many times but can make little sense of it.[1]

ж

"It's an ailment of the heart," Puccini said.

I remember his words and our subsequent conversation as if it were only last week.

"What do the stars say?" I asked him.

"They could be more auspicious," he said.

"So my days are numbered?" I found myself saying philosophically. My calmness surprised me. Perhaps I had expected his diagnosis, unknown to myself.

"All our days are numbered," he said.

"Except mine more exactly so," I found myself replying.

"You can put your habit back on again," he said. I had had to expose myself to enable him to put his ear to my chest to listen to what was going on inside me. "Not knowing the exact hour of your birth, I cannot be more precise than that, if it is indeed possible to be more precise. The casting of horoscopes is not an exact science. The natural unravelling of the preordained direction of our lives – call it what one will: Schicksal, kismet, fate – and to which all living things are subject, can be discerned and the outline of its course divined, but the particulars of it are unpredictable."

He then explained in detail the nature of what he called my ailment. I shall not repeat the specifics. Except for those

---

[1] See plates.

who finish at the hands of others or some other natural or unnatural calamity, all men sicken and die in shameful banality. Such things are between a man and his God and his physician. It is unseemly to speak of them. All I will say is that he said the end could come suddenly.

But I remember what I felt very clearly. It was suddenly as if I had left my body and was watching myself from the outside, as if a part of my soul had already fled its shell. For that is what I now know with even greater certainty what the body is: a shell, which we use and gets used up and is eventually discarded. Is that not why we mortify the flesh? To reduce our attachment to it, to remind ourselves that it is but a temporary abode, a fleshly tomb. To ease our ultimate discarding of it. The more I become aware of the numbering of my own days, the stronger has become my faith. And perhaps that is why I find myself writing so frankly here.

"The ways of the flesh are mysterious," he concluded, as if that physician's platitude were some sort of consolation.

"Is there a cause?" I asked him, almost out of idle curiosity.

He shrugged his physician's shoulders again.

"The climate perhaps. The damp. The heat. The strains. All things have causes. We can avoid them, stay at home, not leave port, take care. But ..." – his frog-like eyes (for that is an accurate description) looked at me – "... all things in this sublunary sphere, deep within them, have an inner impulse towards dissolution. Only the stars and the spheres of the world are eternal, unchanging. It's in the grass, in the trees, in the beasts and in ourselves. The Fates – I always imagine them as white-robed ghostly figures – idly spin the threads of our lives, and then cut them. Snip. The formal causes of things are but the servants of this impulse towards dissolution embedded within things. We are captains of our own destinies only in so much as we can steer with the tides and the winds, not against them. The stars merely reflect the process, and that imperfectly. In this world the passing of time cannot be avoided; only our perception of its passing perhaps."

His opinions on the spheres and his fondness for the Ancients and their philosophies and imaginings verged on the unorthodox, a disposition I put down to his being an Italian, and Italian ideas of orthodoxy are notoriously liberal these days. My own attitude to astrology is akin to Augustine's attitude to mathematics; it may be a noble science but its practitioners are for the most part charlatans.

"You said your quest had born fruition?" I said, no longer wanting to think about what I could not change.

His quest was for a cure for the Neapolitan pox – or 'the boils', as it is most often called on Hayti. Christians who succumb to this evil curse on Hayti exhibit the same symptoms as those who succumb to it in Christendom: initial millet-sized pustules on the private organ, fiery fevers, then pustules the size of acorns which when punctured or cauterised reveal themselves to be filled with a ghastly green puss, and all the other agonies associated with this plague. It does not seem to manifest itself among the Haytians to the same degree.

It is believed that it was brought to Christendom either by those Haytians carried back to Barcelona by the Pharaoh from his first voyage – by their infecting the air or by some other means – or by members of his crews who had been infected on Hayti through fornication with Haytian women. A number of the Pharaoh's crews died from it, including his pilot, Martín Alonso Pinzón. Puccini, who had studied the matter in some detail over the years, was of the latter opinion, which is now generally accepted. He had come to the conclusion that it had then spread from the brothels of Barcelona to Naples – and hence called the Neapolitan pox – via mercenaries in Charles VIII's army. He said he had read a report by a Venetian physician of the time who described the particulars of the disease in numerous captured French soldiers – hence called the French pox by some. A year later, he had told me, it had already spread to the German lands, causing the Emperor Maximilian to order all bathhouses and brothels shut up and a hospital for sufferers built outside the gates of Vienna. And it had since reached Goa where the inhabitants, not aware of its true origin, call it the Portuguese pox – just as the Russians call it the Polish pox, the Turks call it the Christian pox, and the Persians, in turn, call it the Turkish pox. He believed that the Haytians are immune to the effects of it but can infect others, as men are immune to the diseases of animals for the most part – even though they consume their flesh. But that is a not a thesis that I can accept.

"The cure is the bark of a tree that grows on Isola Beata," he said. "I am sure of it." Isola Beata is a small island off the southern coast.

Because the disease came from here, he believed, the cure would grow here too, there being a symmetry in things. Perhaps, I had told him when he had first spoken to me of this. But I had also pointed out that while he might find some medicine which would alleviate the agonies of the sufferers of this curse, was not the only sure cure for this plague the virtue of chastity. For if men obeyed the teachings of the Church and only gave reign to their concupiscence within the confines of holy matrimony, would not this largely self-inflicted malady – a punishment meted out to the unchaste, though also inflicted by the unchaste on their innocent spouses – simply not exist. Not, of course, that sufferers should not be treated with Christian understanding and mercy.

He showed me a small box containing what looked like very fine brown sawdust.

"Soak it in eight times its weight in water," he explained. "Boil until it has reduced to half. Remove the scum, dry it out and apply to the sores. The remaining liquid is made into a broth which causes sweating and drives out the fever. Worth a fortune."

They say the rich are more afflicted by it than other classes. A punishment for their sins, some say.

I asked him how he had found it.

"An old wise man whom Savonarola found gave it to me." That is what he calls the bohiques, the warlocks, the wizards. There is some truth in the appellation for they are not without some skill. They say those sicknesses they cannot cure are new and did not exist before our coming, and that before our coming they were a far healthier race. He had adopted Savonarola – if that's the word – several years back. The fellow wore a crude wooden cross around his neck but was a pagan through and through. "There are still quite a few around," he said, meaning warlocks. "Maybe there are truths concealed in the thinking of the Haytians that we cannot see."

I have often maintained, at times perhaps too zealously, that the beliefs of heathens are often indeed vague premonitions of divine truths, similar to that partial knowledge of the divine that can be achieved by natural reason, and there is no doubt a splinter of truth in that, but only a splinter. He was of the belief the Haytians' so-called dream-world, which they fancied their warlocks can visit in their poison-induced stupors and dreams, could be argued to resemble Plato's realm of perfect forms. He had once provoked me to anger by saying that perhaps it was even akin to Augustine's conception of eternity as a state of being outside all temporality. He suggested that because this dream-world is outside time, it could logically be the source of their warlocks' knowledge of the past and the future, which he ridiculously claimed they had, citing some dubious instances of this. For example, the Cubans are said to have a story of the flood and the building of a great canoa and that when the rains had stopped, a crow had been sent forth which returned with a green branch in its beak. He also cited the story that a particular warlock had predicted how one day men with clothes would come to their shores. Utter folly! And I told him so, but he was not to be budged from his stubborn opinions. Herbal cures and the like, however, do not touch upon greater truths, so I did not argue with him in this instance. After all, we should be in a bad way if our friendships depended on us seeing eye to eye on everything.

"It's called 'guayacán'," he explained. "The wise men have used it since time immemorial."

I smelled the sawdust. It had a pungent familiar odour, resembling something I have never been able to put my finger on. I wondered vaguely if it was used in the potions that Serrano had spoken of.

"Another cargo of Africans has arrived," I said.

"And from henceforth they shall be hewers of wood and carriers of water, servants of servants," he said, quoting the first of the books of Moses. "Remind me."

"Noah got drunk and fell asleep and Ham looked upon his father's nakedness. His line was punished. A verse of Holy Scripture often misread. Wilfully so at times. Balthazar was as black as the ace of spades. And he was a king."

"Aristotle teaches that some men are by nature slaves," he said.

"He was a heathen and is burning in hell," I countered without much thought. For of course, as Lucrezia di Marchionni had pointed out, it is presumption to suppose the damnation of any man, for who knows who would have desired baptism had they but known of it.

"Limbo surely," he said, "In Dante Alighieri's first circle, along with Averroes, Euclid, Homer and Julius Caesar, enjoying its green meadows ..."

"A work of poetic imagination," I pointed out.

He shook his head.

"You Castilians do wear your religion more heavily than us Italians," he said. "There is a darkness in it, a fanaticism. No Italian prince would dream of calling himself 'the Catholic', 'the Magnificent' perhaps, but not 'the Catholic'."

"Fanaticism?" I said, suppressing my outrage.

"Yes, a lusting after God," he said, "rather than loving Him in gentleness and humility."

"The teachings of Our Mother Church are clear," I said, refusing to be provoked into the sort of flippant theological cat and mouse game that so amused him. "No man is a natural slave."

"And the Canibas?" he countered.

"No man is the property of another per se," I told him, "and no prince, not even the most benign and munificent, may treat him as such, even if it is for his own good, but there are circumstances, very precisely prescribed circumstances, when men may be legally enslaved. The Canibas eat human flesh. What greater crime is there than that? They practice sodomy as a custom. They sin against the natural order, a sacred order. To sin against that is an abomination. Enslavement is a permissible punishment for a crime. Or for those captured in a just war. It has always been so, among all peoples."

"Some believe they are man-eaters and sodomites by nature," he said. "And that no punishment can cure them."

"A belief the only logical consequence of which would be to advocate their wholesale extermination," I said. "No human being is beyond redemption. All men are descended from Adam. All men have souls and thus free wills."

He offered me a cigar.

A reader of these words would be forgiven for assuming that there was much personal animosity in our arguments but that was not the case.

Ж

Savonarola showed me something today which, if I had not seen it with my own eyes, I would not believe that such a thing existed or was possible. It was a small ball. He was playing with it in the courtyard, bouncing it against a wall, with great dexterity, though I noticed he limps slightly. It was bouncing with a ferocity which I have never seen any ball bounce. Thinking it was some witchcraft, I asked him what it was and he said it was made of a substance made from the gum of a particular species of tree mixed with various herbs and grasses. I asked him to show it to me and he did so, graciously. His manners, most of the time, belie his savage appearance, an appearance which is little mitigated by the fact that the medicus dresses him in semi-civilised clothes. The ball was heavy, far heavier than the hollow balls played with in Christendom; yet when thrown and it hits the ground or a wall, it bounces into the air with more strength than was used to throw it in the first place. Even if dropped it rose into the air as high as the distance it has been dropped. It was heavier than an apple of the same size, and slightly spongy despite lacking the innumerable holes that give a sponge its quality of sponginess, yet it behaved as if it were light, not heavy at all.

Later Puccini told me that it is a batey-ball, the type of ball the Indians played batey with in the old days. He says these games were often played between clans in lieu of going to war with one another, in teams of ten to thirty of both men and women, or of men against women, or married women against maids, and with "both genders as naked as Greeks". He also said he's taught Savonarola to read and write and that he's "quite proficient" at it, and boasted to us he had succeeded in making "a bit of a scholar out of him". And that he had even taught him a smattering of Latin. The medicus' sense of humour is at times wry.

Fray Montenegro puts all the evils that have happened here – and if he is to be believed, there have been many – down to the lust for gold.

"But what does this lust consist of?" Puccini asked. The question was rhetorical. He likes to start his monologues thus. "Like all lust, is there not something mystical about it? In a perverse way. Gold is the perfect metal, the perfect substance. Unlike all other things that exist in the sublunary world, it does not decay, thus has something eternal, even heavenly, about it. It is a pure thing, devoid of impurities, clean. We call it precious, the same word we use when describing the blood of Christ ..."

"Rubbish," said Montenegro. "Utter rubbish."

I was tempted to say that Aristotle believed that gold is only precious because men think it is, but did not.

Puccini has investigated many of the herbs that the Indians use for medicinal and culinary purposes, or simply for the pleasurable effects they produce. The axí pepper, if taken in a sufficient dose, is a powerful purgative and expeller of malignant humours. The tabaco plant calms the nerves and induced sharpness of thought, a fact to which all who engage in this bizarre habit enthusiastically bear witness. It might be possible to cultivate many of edible plants the Indians grow in Christendom, where clime and soil allows, but none, as far as I can see, could be shipped across the ocean at a profit – with the exception of sugar, which is not native. Don Cristóbal believed that these islands would be a rich source of spices and herbs. He was convinced that he had found rhubarb growing wild, mastic for varnish, and aloe, all mistakenly; and some say that he believed it was so till his dying day. It seems, however, there was once a significant trade in what is called brazilwood or breselwood, the sawdust of which is the red dye powder used to colour velvet and other sumptuous fabrics. Don Cristóbal is reported to have said that he could "send all the slaves and brazilwood that could be sold", twenty-million-maravedís' worth of the latter, every year; and the Catholic Monarchs are reported to have instructed Ovando, in 1501, to see that no more brazilwood trees were to be cut down because such 'bad practices' had been followed and so many trees cut down that no more dye could be obtained. I do not quite comprehend this – for if no more trees were to be cut down, any further trade would have been impossible. However, it does indicate that there was once a substantial trade in this precious substance. At about the same time, Cabral, whose explorations I mentioned earlier, discovered a rich supply of these trees along the Portuguese coasts of tierra firme; and it is from whence that most brazilwood that reaches Christendom from these Indies has its origin now. But nothing I have been told or seen leads me to believe that these islands are comparable to the spice islands of the Portuguese, with their rich bounties of nutmeg, cloves, cinnamon and peppers.

Ж

My hand trembles as I write this. It has spoken in my presence. I have heard what it says. And I now know why the words seemed to me familiar even though I had never been able to make them out. I am ashamed to write what I am about to write. As on the previous occasions, I heard the voice on returning from the performance of my necessaries, but this time, being used to the sound, I simply lifted the latch of my cupboard, fully expecting of course that the bird would stop the moment it had sensed my presence but ... it didn't, it continued to speak as I opened the door and entered. I don't know exactly the moment I fully recognised what it was saying. Perhaps I already half-recognised it as I was opening the door. It all happened so quickly, and the moment I think I even vaguely recognised the words ... words I know so well, the holiest of words, words that shocked me to the core. I can still hear them. Or the mimicking of them. The holiest of words transformed into the filthiest blasphemy, by the lips, the beak, the tongue or whatever part of the beast that was speaking them. The words of God, the prayer Christ Himself taught us, Latin issuing from the throat of a creature that flies through the air. The first words I fully recognised were: Panem nostrum quotidianum da nobis hodie, et dimitte nobis debita nostra sicut et nos dimittimus debitoribus nostris. Give us this day our daily bread, and forgive us our debts, as we also have forgiven our debtors. It feels blasphemous to even write them down like this ... The creature had near-finished the prayer before I came to my senses and threw a blanket over its head and silenced it. Oh my God, what am I to do?

Plates 1

Figure 1 *Possible territories of the Haytian cacicazgos around the time of the Spanish Conquest in 1492, with Spanish settlements mentioned in the text. Names of caciques and cacica (in italics) give a tentative indication of their principal home areas. Jaragua is at times referred to as Xanaguá in the text.*

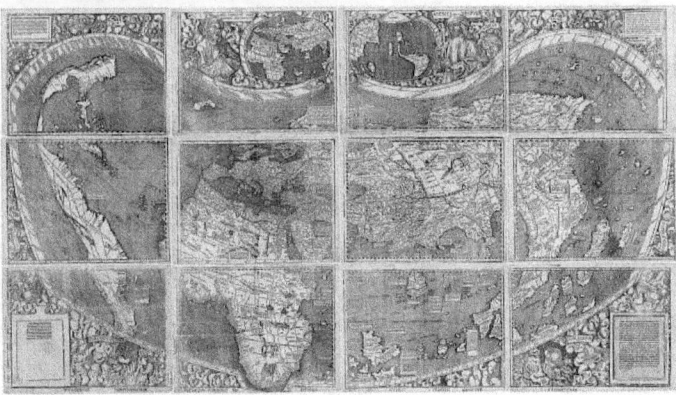

Figure 2 *Waldseemüller World Map of 1507, each section is 46 × 62 cm.*

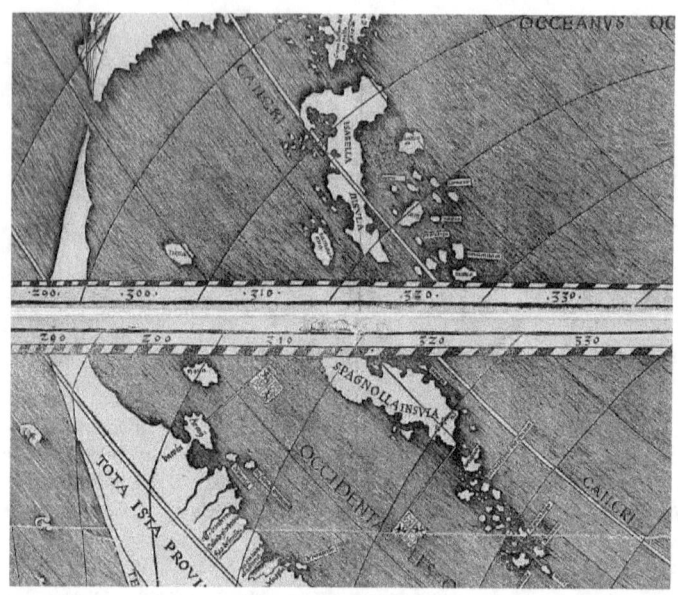

Figure 3 *The Caribbean islands as shown in the Waldseemüller World Map of 1507. Isabella Insula is Cuba and Spagnolla Insula is Hayti.*

Figure 4 *The Caribbean with names used in the text of principal locations.*

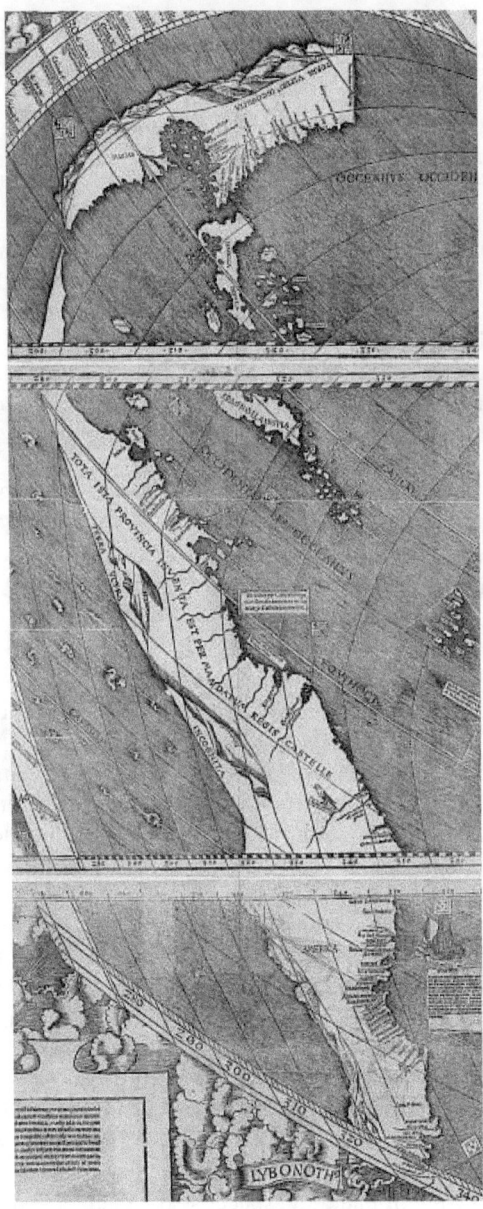

Figure 5 *The Americas as depicted on Waldseemüller 1507 World Map.*

THIRTEEN

Montenegro suggested I show Puccini the map. I had no intention of allowing Rudolfo Jesus de Paz to get his paws on it, so I had brought it with me for safekeeping.

When I had unrolled the sheets – I keep them in a tubular leather case I'd had made in Seville – and laid them out, the medicus took out his reading lenses and immersed himself silently in the detail of the Strassburgers' world picture for quite some while.

"Don Puccini collects maps," Montenegro informed me.

"Not something that I publicise," Puccini made pains to add.

He continued examining the map, reading the inscriptions silently.

"I have heard of this," he announced finally. "By Ringmann and Waldseemüller of Strassburg, if I'm not in error. You know what it's based on, the origin of it?"

"Very little," I said, "beyond what it tells us of itself. That the maps of Christendom, Africa, India and Cathay are all based on Ptolemy's *Geographia* but that these lands – where we are – are based on the accounts of Americus Vespucci."

He then looked at it again for a long time in silence before speaking.

"Ptolemy," he said, "was almost unique among the Ancients in believing that the Oceanus Indius Meridionalis was an inland sea like the Mediterranean and that you couldn't sail around Africa. But his genius lies in his geometry. And his thoroughness. Mariners find his *Geographia* map of little use, if any, but it still is the most common world map being printed – and most other world maps are still based on it. Most keep Ptolemy's overall scheme but have improved it, depicting Europe and the west coast of Africa the way we now know them to be. Which, ironically, lends the parts of those maps which are directly derived from the *Geographia* more credibility than they merit."

"And thus printing presses fill the world with half-knowledge," Montenegro murmured. He has a sceptical attitude to much that is new.

"I have a copy of one of Vespucci's so-called letters," he went on. "There are purportedly several of them. It was printed as a book called *The Four Voyages*. It describes his four voyages, but rather briefly. It's addressed to René II, Duke of Lorraine – and

King of Sicily and Jerusalem, if you please. Or perhaps the book is just dedicated to the good king. It's not clear. It's the letter that the western hemisphere of this map is said to be based on. I purchased a copy of it in Florence when I went back that time. It was selling like hot cakes. In places it's so utterly vague that it's impossible to make out where he's supposed to have been. But there are occasions when he's quite precise, and gives latitudes and longitudes, dates and the number of daylight hours on specific days at specific locations and so on. Most of the time he describes the peoples he came across. Near everywhere he describes as being exceedingly populous ..." – he lapsed into Italian here, as if quoting Vespucci's actual words; this he did often – "... inhabited generally by people who went naked and looked like Tartars, living in perfect liberty, not subject to any king or ruler, without laws, nor chastising their children. They observe no law or covenant with regard to marriage, he says, both men and women taking as many wives or husbands as they wish; for, he says, they are much given to lust, in which the women far exceed the men. He describes them as simple in their discourse but cunning and shrewd. Many of them are expert archers, he says, including the women – like the Amazons of old. He says most are man-eaters, and that some of whom 'will eat no other flesh than human' – though, if you ask me, the seaman who can differentiate between a cooked monkey leg and a cooked human leg is hard to find. He describes how once, during a landing, some of their men were abducted, and how later they saw from the ship how the body of one of them was chopped up and roasted over a fire on the beach. Some of the other letters, I'm told, are even more mouth-watering in their descriptions."

"How far south did Vespucci actually sail?" I asked. I had no intention of pandering to the perverse pleasure he was taking in the graphic details of Vespucci's descriptions of the anarchy and depredations of the Parrot Landers.

"Once, so far south that in April the days were fifteen hours long," he said. "Which would put him about here, somewhere between fifty and sixty degrees south of the equator." He gestured to where that was the map. "The coast there, he says, was utterly barren and desolate, and so cold that it was probably in fact uninhabitable. He says he was in the process of compiling a more detailed account – of all the four voyages – in which he would give all the navigational details. I don't know if he ever did though.

"Not the most reliable of characters, our Americus. In bed with

Castile, Portugal and God's own bankers themselves, the Medici, and the Lord knows who else. Even managed to wrangle himself a seat on the Casa at the end. And he does make sure – in an extraordinary feat of absent-mindedness – not to so much as mention the names of the captains he sailed under on any of his voyages."

He returned to the map: "The east coast of the Parrot Land is well mapped, but then the Portuguese are very much more meticulous, to say the least, in their explorations than the Castilians. See the detail on the coasts of Africa and compare that to the vagueness of our maps of the Castilian Indies – and we've been here for years now. Though they say the Casa has a master map, a map of maps, in Seville, in a room with a double lock that can only be opened with two keys, one held by the Cosmographo Mayor and the other by the Piloto Mayor." He outlined a section of the coast of tierra firme – that part of it marked out with Portuguese flags – with the little finger of his maimed hand. "All this area is Portuguese. By divine right as it were."

"As it 'is', not 'were'," Montenegro corrected him.

"Divine right?" Savonarola said. The Indian, I have neglected to mention, had appeared – a macaw perched on his shoulder – as I was laying out the map and Puccini had let him stay. Whether he had not understood the expression 'divine right' or was ignorant of how the Pope had divided the world into two equally sized spheres of influence was not clear. Like the medicus' cats, the Indian seems to have a free run of the place and even addresses Puccini by his Christian name.

"The Borgia Pope," Puccini explained, and bizarrely Savonarola seemed to know to whom the medicus was actually referring, "decreed that all the world, the unchristian world on the west side of this line, three hundred and fifty leagues west of the Fortunate Isles ..." – he traced an invisible line with his finger from pole to pole cutting through tierra firme – "... belongs to the King of Castile and everything to the east of it belongs to the King of Portugal."

"It has been given into their care," Montenegro added. "All that which men possess is theirs only by the grace of God. To care for."

Savonarola nodded. But it was impossible to tell whether he had actually understood the sense of what Montenegro had said or merely his words.

"In fact," Puccini continued, turning again to Montenegro and myself, "the Portuguese Crown has leased the Parrot Land to a company of New Christians on the condition that every year they send six ships and survey the coast southwards at the rate of three hundred leagues a year."

He then pointed to the western coast of tierra firme – on the Castilian side of the world – that part marked as Terra Ultra Incognita.

"But this coast here," he said, "as you can see, is only fleetingly mapped. Almost as if a ship has sailed that way but not methodically surveyed it. There is nothing in any of Vespucci's accounts that even hint at him sailing that far east."

"Do you think this passage leading to the Southern Ocean exists?" I asked him, pointing it out.

"Waldseemüller and Ringmann seem to think it does," he shrugged.

"And that it leads to a vast ocean which no man has ever seen?" Montenegro said.

"But if no man has ever seen it," Savonarola remarked, again interrupting, "how could these mapmakers know that it exists?"

"Deduction, finding out a fact, not perceptible in itself – not obvious – by deducing from facts which are known," Puccini said, in a lecturing tone. "It is the basis of all knowledge that cannot be perceived directly by the senses. But you have a point. Perhaps men have been there."

"Perhaps they have," Savonarola replied, in that odd insolent way of speaking that he sometimes uses when he is agreeing – or rather feigning to agree – with his betters, and which Puccini lets him get away with.

"The Pharaoh believed the passage existed," Puccini continued. "Vespucci thought it might but he never managed to convince the Casa to give him the ships and the money to look for it. Then there's the question of just how big the Southern Ocean might be. Which depends essentially on how big the globe is. And on which there are several learned opinions."

The medicus then provided us with a summary of his opinion on these matters which I am sure you will find of interest. Here is a précis of what he related, as well as I can remember it.

"The first man," he told us, "who made a mathematical estimate of the circumference of the sphere of the earth was Eratosthenes of Alexandria, about two hundred years before the birth of the Saviour. He did it by measuring the difference in the length of shadows cast at midday in Alexandria and at Aswan several hundred miles further south. The figure he arrived at was 45,000 Latin miles, give or take. No mean trick. Such geometrical calculations are not trivial. He is also supposed to have made a world map. His work is now lost of course, went up in flames with the library of Alexandria. But luckily Strabo, a contemporary of the Saviour, left us an account of Eratosthenes' works. Everything we know of the cosmographers of the ancient world prior to Ptolemy – which is precious little – we know only from Strabo, or from Ptolemy himself.

"Posidonius, who lived about a hundred years after Eratosthenes, came up with more or less the same figure. He based his calculations on the positions of Canopus, rather than the sun. At Rhodes, Canopus was only ever visible on the horizon, but at Alexandria, it was several degrees higher. But Strabo noted that Posidonius' estimate of the distance between Rhodes and Alexandria was less than Posidonius believed it was, so he revised Posidonius' calculations down to 30,000 Latin miles. Strabo made no measurements of his own. But he was probably one of the first to believe that India could be reached by sailing west.

"A hundred or so years later, Marinus of Tyre, whom some call the father of mathematical cosmography, estimated a global circumference of 27,000 or so Latin miles. But just as importantly, he also estimated that the oikoumene, from Hibernia to the furthest extremities of the Realm of the Great Khan, stretched over two hundred and twenty-five degrees of the globe; and that the Oceanus Occidentalis thus covered only a hundred and thirty-five degrees, 10,000 Latin miles in all. Ptolemy took the eight thousand places he included in his *Geographia* mainly from Marinus, and much of his mathematics, and gave each place a precise longitude and latitude. Then he positioned them on a sphere – at least I presume that is what he did, though there are no accounts of globes from the ancient world that I know of – and devised a mathematical method to represent that sphere as a flat surface. The problem of planes and curved surfaces. No easy operation to perform, I assure you. His meridian ran through the Fortunate Isles, as does the Strassburgers'."

"His meridian," said Montenegro. "I'm lost."

"An imaginary line from which longitude to the east and west is marked out," Puccini explained. "A sort of equator for longitude."

He indicated it with a sweep of his hand. Montenegro nodded but I am not sure he was quite following.

"Ptolemy's estimate of the earth's circumference was the same as Strabo's and Posidonius' – about 30,000 Latin miles," Puccini continued, "and he estimated that the landmass of Europe and

Asia only covered half the globe, a hundred and eighty degrees, considerably less than the two hundred and twenty-five degrees Marinus had estimated. Thus, according to his estimate, to sail from Spain to the Indies would mean crossing 15,000 Latin miles of open sea, an impossible feat for any ship ever built, or ever likely to be.

"The Pharaoh based his estimates mainly on Alfraganus, a Persian cosmographer, who lived several centuries after Ptolemy. He'd calculated the circumference of the earth at 14,000 miles, Moorish miles, not Latin ones. The Latin mile is shorter by about a third. Which gives us a figure of less than 20,000 Latin miles. And Alfraganus calculated a distance by sea from Spain to Asia of just over 4,000 Latin miles. But at Salamanca, the Pharaoh took care to mainly cite Christian sources: Toscanelli maps, Pierre d'Ailly's *Image mundi*, and even Aeneas Sylvius Piccolomini's – Pius the Poet, Pius II in a later incarnation – *Historia rerum ubique gestarum*. Toscanelli – with whom he was in correspondence – following Marinus, maintained that the landmass of Europe and Asia extended over two-thirds of the earth's circumference, leaving only one-third of it to cross to reach Asia by sea. When the Pharaoh did cite Alfraganus' theses, they say he neglected – deliberately or out of ignorance – to say that Alfraganus' miles were Moorish ones, not Latin ones, a detail the cosmographer-theologians of the university were certainly aware of, even if the Pharaoh himself was not. By all accounts, he didn't put on a very convincing display before the learned doctors. If Isabela had not got whiff that he was planning to bugger off to France to try his luck at the French court, that would probably have been the end of it. But she did get whiff of it. That anyway is the story."

"How do you remember these things?" I asked him.

"I was an Italian scholar once," he laughed, "in a previous incarnation. Like Pius the Poet."

Montenegro frowned at the irreverent flippancy.

"Once upon a time," Puccini continued, pretending contrition, "I was privileged to have access to the public library of my native city – founded and paid for by Lorenzo the Magnificent himself, in his latter, less magnificent days."

Again I wondered what had brought this strange man to Hayti. Greed and faith are what brings most men here. He seemed to possess little of either.

"And the practice of mnemonics," he went on, "the art and science of memory. The Taíno songs we spoke about earlier – the history ones, not the ones they learn from zemi – they are based on the same principles more or less. A different method though, or so my loyal and faithful Savonarola informs me."

Savonarola was bent over the map, examining it with what looked like intense curiosity. I wondered just how loyal and faithful he really was.

"So, to put it all in a nutshell," Puccini continued, "if Eratosthenes' estimate of the circumference of the earth is correct and if the extent of the oikoumene is less than what Ptolemy estimated – more like what Marinus estimated – then the Strassburger map is perhaps the truest world map we have and we are in a 'new world', and Asia is a long, long way away. The Ancients may have known things since forgotten, but they did not know everything. Nowadays every Nuremberger mapmaker knows that Ptolemy's *Geographia* errs grossly and contains much that is fantastical. And perhaps the same is even true of our celestial maps, if I may call them that, and of our understanding of the real positions of the planets and the stars, and their distances from us and from each other."

"As below, so above," Savonarola muttered, as if to himself; obviously a phrase he had picked up from his master, for it seems hardly likely that he is familiar with the works of Hermes Trismegistus.

"In any case," Puccini said, "this map seems to show the world the size that Eratosthenes thought it to be."

"Which, if true," Montenegro said, "means that Asia is near half a world away."

"That is quite possible," Puccini said. "Except for Cipango perhaps."

"And if there is no passage," Montenegro said, "then the only way to reach Asia is by sailing around these land masses."

"The northern route is blocked by ice," Puccini said, "and as cold as the third circle of Dante Alighieri's inferno."

I thought Savonarola would ask what ice was but he did not.

"Or around the southern tip of tierra firme?" I suggested. "The Strassburgers seem to think that might be possible.

"The world of mapmakers is a strange one," Puccini said. "They deal in secrets and they reveal secrets. But they also deal in dreams. Most things men buy and sell are much of a muchness. A man buying a horse can look it over, check its teeth, smell its breath and decide how much the animal is worth to him. But maps are different. Gems and precious stones are different too, of course. Both seller and buyer want the price to be high. But maps

... they are different again. The buyer never quite knows what he is getting. The man who purchases a map may be buying riches beyond imagination, the location of Eden or simply the waking fancies of a mapmaker."

He then showed us his own 'discreet' collection of maps. I am studying them now as I write. There are at least a dozen of them, most of them copied out by Puccini in his own hand in black ink on fine Italian paper during his stay in Florence two or so years ago, with each one clearly marked with the name of the cosmographer who drew it and the supposed date of its original composition.

Half of them predate Don Cristóbal's first voyage. One of these, by a Genoese, name unknown, dated circa 1450, shows the world in the shape of an almond nut. Another, by an N de Virga, dated 1415, gives a bird's eye perspective of the oikoumene as if one were looking down upon it from the Pole Star, and shows a clear route west to the east. A third, by Fray Mauro, dated 1460 – 'copied from a copy in the library of the Monastery of Saint Michael's, Murano Island, the Republic of Venice, of which the original has a diameter of six feet and is to be found in Lisbon' – shows the world as a perfect disk. Although all were composed decades before Bartolomé Diaz's voyage of 1487, during which he sailed around the tip of Africa, they all clearly show Africa as circumnavigable. But the more interesting – and surprising – of them are the ones showing these islands before Don Cristóbal Colón's first arriving here. One of these, by a Giovanni Pizzigano, a portolano, dated 1424, shows two Antillean islands, the Satanazes and the Seven Bishops. (The Portuguese tell how several hundred years ago seven bishops fleeing the Moor sailed into the west and founded seven cities in the Antilles. The Admiral searched for them.) Another, by Andrea Biancos, dated 1436, clearly shows the mar de baga, the seaweed sea. Another, composed by Grazioso Benincasa, dated 1436, shows the Antilles; as does the copy of Toscanelli's mappa mundi, dated 1474. And another, a portolano chart by the Albino de Canepa, dated 1489, shows the Islands of the Seven Bishops with their legendary seven cities, the Satanazes and a small island named Roillo.

"Have you ever thought about why our Haytians are dying off like flies?" I remember Puccini asking me that evening as Sor Lucrezia was diligently making her copies of his maps. Typically, it was of course a question to which he already had his own answer.

"Despair," I suggested, as he lit my cigar. "Backbreaking work. We passed a caravan of two dozen men and youths carrying a hundred pounds apiece on their backs on the way here. Their overseers – when they were not whipping, beating or cursing them – were being carried in litters like oriental satraps. We treat the poor creatures worse than we treat our beasts of burden. Like shit in the street. They have become so fragile and malnourished that even their own medicines no longer work."

"Perhaps," he said. "But perhaps not."

"A divine punishment?" I suggested sarcastically, though I knew he did not believe that.

He laughed. He had on occasion accused me of holding that belief.

"When the ships arrive here how many men are sick?" he asked.

"A quarter?" I ventured. "But I've seen ships arrive with over half the men unable to walk. It's almost unheard of for a ship to arrive without any sick. Why?"

"When the Tartars were besieging Kaffa to take it from the Genoese they catapulted the corpses of plague victims over the city walls," he said. "The Pharaoh brought the Haytian pox to Christendom. Is it not possible, in a manner of speaking, that we are doing the same? Catapulting, in a manner of speaking, the bodies of living plague carriers over the Oceanus Occidentalis? That that which is fatal to a Christian is a mere distemper to an Indian, and that which is a mere distemper to an Indian fatal to a Christian?"

"I do not believe it," I told him. "All men are of the same substance, in body and in soul, fashioned of the same flesh and the same blood, subject to the same ills. No, that cannot be true. The Haytians are men like us, not some other species."

"The wise men say they were a sturdy people before we arrived," he said.

"They were not mistreated then," I said.

Seeing he was not going to convince me to alter my opinion on that matter, he changed the subject and asked me if I'd had any news from Spain. I had discussed my correspondence with Spain with him on several occasions over the years; though nothing of our plan.

"Patience is counselled," I told him.

"How convenient," he said. There were times when he showed little respect for authority, ecclesiastical or temporal.

"These things take time," I said defensively.

"Still collecting testaments?" he asked.

I told him I was, but getting men to speak the truth and put their names to it was no easy task.

"Christendom is changing, Padre," he said. "The world is changing. There are new things in it. And the old ways of doing things are changing with it." He blew out some smoke, his big eyes viewing me more intensely than usual. He had been back to Spain – and Italy – two years previously; and I knew he was in regular, if erratic, correspondence with several Italian scholars. "Excuse me for saying so, but you have seen little of the world beyond monasteries and this island, a sheltered life ..."

I could have told him that listening to men's confessions week-in and week-out I had learnt things which would leave most men aghast, but I let it pass. I could also have pointed out that were it not for the Church – for all its failings – there would be little civilisation in the world. And that without the fear of hellfire, the history of last millennium would have been far bloodier than it had been. The barbarians, from whom it must be said we are all mostly descended, who had overrun the Roman Empire – a barbarous institution itself until Constantine had attempted to reform and save it – lacked all morality save for a perverse sense of honour. It was the influence of the Church that had made slavery a rarity in Europe. The Church has been the only moral instance, de facto and de jure, since the fall of Rome. And it still is.

"... you collect statements from wayward friars, copy them out meticulously," he went on, "you write to your superiors, you plead with them, and nothing happens. What I'm getting at is this: you do not understand politics. You are trying to arouse an elephant with a pinprick."

"I rely on the good will of good men," I told him.

"On men, no matter how good, who are enmeshed in the nets of power," he continued. "The Church is corrupt. There is not an altar boy is Christendom who doesn't know that. Offices put out to the highest bidder. Bishops who have not been to mass for years. Half the clergy can barely speak enough Latin to say a decent mass. The average Roman prelate has the morals of a whoremaster and exercises his office in the same spirit as a charlatan does his tricks. There are even mutterings that it has become so corrupt that it has become incapable of providing salvation, is a hindrance to it even."

"All institutions composed of men are fallible to some degree," I said. But in truth, he had uttered a heart-rending truth I found little argument to counter, beyond saying that churchmen were not immune to sinning and that the sacraments are no less valid because those administering them are not saints.

"And every abbey has the perfectly persevered foreskin of the Christ Child in its reliquary," he added, emboldened by the feebleness of my excuse.

"It's the devotion that a relic inspires which is important," I said, though not very enthusiastically. "Its provenance is secondary."

"Printing is changing things," he said. "Men are arguing like never before, and counter-arguing, and sometimes even coming to conclusions. And less and less in Latin, but in the tongues of the marketplace, of the tavern, of the bathhouse, in their own dialects. The Latin-speaking world is speaking less Latin."

"Babel," I suggested.

"It may well be," he admitted. "But it is not without consequences. Winds of change are blowing. Have you ever thought of circumventing the usual channels?"

I asked him what he meant.

"You could have your reports given to a printer. I am not without contacts ... in Florence, in Nuremberg, in Venice. A booklet, even a whole book, entitled ..." – he fished around in his mind for a title – "... something along the lines of, say, *A Report from the Antilles by an Anonymous Monk on the Habits and Customs of the Meek-tempered Inhabitants of those Islands and the Atrocities Committed Against Them by Men who call themselves Christians*, if that's not a trifle too longwinded, in the vernacular, with some sensational images, would, I should think, find a reading public, and perhaps stir up some moral disquiet. There are men of power who might find such moral disquiet useful to their ends. The quality of woodcuts and copper engravings is astounding these days."

"Nothing of value has ever been achieved by appealing to the mob," I said firmly.

At that, he let the matter drop.

FOURTEEN

We – Fray Montenegro, Hildegard, myself, Savonarola and two of our servants – reached Carlos Goya's encomienda shortly before the short tropical dusk. Caonabó's Valley is a long ten-hour walk from Concepción.

Of the journey itself, I have but one incident to relate, if it can be called that. About midway there we stopped to rest and restore ourselves on a wooded hill overlooking a vast extent of zavana stretched out below us under a seemingly limitless blue and grey sky. The view was of pools of sunlight and the shadows of clouds slowly drifting across the plain, clumps of evergreen trees – all trees are evergreen in these latitudes – and puffs of white mist on the hills opposite. All was silent except for every now and again the lone sharp cries of invisible birds echoing melancholically across the valley. I was reminded of how Don Cristóbal is reputed to have said how this land resembled Andalusia in springtime. Then, very gradually, I became aware of another sound, the sound of a flute drifting up from somewhere below us, a melody that seemed for a moment to simply issue all of itself from the landscape. I listened to this fey music for a moment, entranced by it, not thinking from whence it really came, and found my spirit swept up in it as the tune slowly changed from a melody to a dirge. All I could think of it being similar to, and that imperfectly, was to a requiem of sorts, perhaps sung by the finest castrati under the great acoustic vaults of some sumptuous Roman or Florentine church; and I had a vision of the Host being raised heavenwards in that sacred act of adoration and submission. But no sooner had my reason told me that it could not be so, I looked around me to see if I could ascertain where the music was coming from.

"Savonarola," Hildegard said, noticing my puzzlement.

Then I saw the Indian climbing up the hill towards us, putting the implement of his music-making into his shoulder bag. I remembered with a shudder what Fray Montenegro had said about how the Indians made flutes from human leg bones.

There was barely enough light to see by the time we arrived at the entrance to Goya's compound – it is surrounded by thick thorny bushes – and Savonarola explained our business to the watchmen. Both were armed with bows and arrows, and the wooden clubs called macanas, which looked anything but flimsy. I wondered if their arrows were poisoned. The dogs, two mastiffs, were on long iron chains, mercifully. One of the watchmen ran to fetch Goya, who subsequently appeared out of the near darkness.

He is a small and wiry, Roman-nosed man, with a mop of silver-grey hair, older than I had expected, terrier-like. He has holes in his earlobes, large gaping holes – and I do not mean like those which many seafarers have to sport a ring – and the lobes themselves are distended and flabby, like the ears of certain dogs, as if they had once held weights. He also has ugly black tattoos on his cheeks and forehead, like some of the Indians here have; but his markings are different in style, more angular. Montenegro introduced us through the wooden gate and Goya finally opened it for us.

"We don't get many visitors," he said. He has a strong Granada accent, even after all these years. "At least not of the type we welcome. And never female."

The main house is constructed of stone. Savonarola and the servants, after they had laid down our burdens in the portico, were dismissed. Following some further polite introductions, Goya invited us to be seated at a large hardwood table in the main ground-floor room, on stools made in the Haytian fashion with bamboo seats. He then shouted for a servant – or a woman I took to be a mere servant, who was heavy with child, who I did not immediately realise was more than that – and told her in a sort of pidgin Castilian mixed with some local words to bring us some food. Casabe bread, some iguana, and fresh calabash duly appeared, and we exchanged pleasantries while we ate. The iguana, heavily peppered with axí, had a taste very similar to that of wild fowl.

"So you are investigating how sincerely the Maquanans of these parts have taken to the faith," Goya said, quoting from the letter of introduction Puccini had furnished us with.

"Yes," said Montenegro. "That is the principal reason we are all here, to propagate the faith. Is it not?"

"But not the only reason," Goya said, perceptively and with more than a whiff of cynicism.

"Sor Lucrezia di Marchionni is only shortly arrived," Montenegro continued, ignoring the slight. "She is anxious to learn as much she can of the customs and usages of the peoples. So she is accompanying me with that intention. I have been told that the Maquanans here have destroyed their idols?"

"That is true," Goya said.

"But have they destroyed them in their hearts?" Montenegro asked.

"Have they?" Goya repeated. The question was directed at his pregnant servant. "Sit down!" he ordered. It was then I realised that she was his woman. "And tell the good friar what he wants to hear."

"Oh, yes," she said shyly. "The zemis are broken. All gone. No use anymore."

Later Montenegro decided to broach the subject that was on both our minds, our true reason for being there. He did so quite directly.

"There is a man in Santo Domingo," he said, "a seafarer like yourself – by the name of Franco Serrano – he says you and he were shipwrecked once ..."

"Serrano is a drunk," Goya said abruptly, obviously having no wish to engage in any conversation on the matter.

"True enough," Montenegro admitted, but did not pursue the subject any further, which surprised me somewhat. He is not a man easily deflected from what he has set his mind to.

I do not think that Carlos Goya is going to prove very informative.

The main house, in which we have been given rooms, is Spartan, like most of the buildings here; but being constructed of stone, though it has a grass roof, it is sturdy enough, and even has a second floor over part of it; and a largish wooden building adjoining it, currently empty, which I presume once housed horses or perhaps mules, a very common animal here. The other buildings in the compound are a ramshackle assortment of labourers' dwellings and the like, no small number of them utterly derelict, though several have been converted into pigsties. They are for the most part round, with walls of compounded grass and mud, and grass roofs supported by wooden posts, in the Haytian fashion. He has about fifty labourers, women and girls for the most part, a few with small children. He is rough and ready with them, but I have not seen him raise his hand against them, and neither does he carry a whip in his belt, which I have seen many doing. He has cleared land and planted sugar plants, and is in the process of building a mill. Several fields have been set aside where the women can grow their food: casabe, batata and beans for the main part, but also axí pepper bushes. They smile and curtsy when Hildegard and I pass them but do so without enthusiasm. It is not a joyful place, a humid oppressive air hangs over it.

There is no gold on the land.

"I had my people pan the local river for two months," Goya told me, "but they never came up with as much as a grain, even when I threatened them. Of course, they might have found some and kept it for themselves but I doubt it. They know better."

Ж

Unlike Serrano, it was apparent that Goya was not going to be naturally talkative; unless, of course, we were able to offer him something in exchange, that was. Which, as it turned out, we were, or rather, I was, in a manner of speaking. Or rather more, an opportunity presented itself by which I was able to gain his trust.

He came to me the morning after we had arrived and took me aside and said he wished to speak to me of a personal matter, a religious matter.

"You wish to confess," I said, thinking something in particular was burdening his soul.

"No, Padre," he said. "Later perhaps. It is something else."

I told him he could speak freely.

"I wish to take Juana as a wife," he said. "Properly."

I nodded, hiding my approval. It has always been Church policy in the Indies to encourage those Christians who had taken women as concubines to legitimise these illicit unions by the sacrament of matrimony. Near enough to half the settlers have taken well-born Haytians as wives, 'marrying' them in heathen ceremonies presided over by the warlocks. Such 'marriages' bring the advantage of enabling the settlers to inherit lands on the deaths of relatives, as Sor Lucrezia has already described, and to cast off these so-called wives with great facility, though they usually do not do so if there is any issue from these matches, which are generally fruitful. But, it must also be said, I have come across numerous incidents of great affection between the parties. The families of these concubines consider them legally married and those Christians, in name if not behaviour, who have taken them connive in this deception. Juana, I could tell by the tattoos on her face and arms, came of a nitaíno family.

His thinking was most probably that by getting properly married into the family, he would obtain some title to the lands, or at least to some of them, and to the encomienda he was caretaking, on the demise of the official encomiendero – though encomienda rights are not, strictly speaking, hereditary, not officially anyway. Goya was not the kind of man – a look at him sufficed – to be officially granted an encomienda by the Castle clique as a matter of course. But if he had some claim to the land via marriage and was willing to grease the appropriate palms ...

"She is not baptised," he said. "She says she is not ready yet. That she is unworthy."

"We are all unworthy," I told him. "Baptism is a gift, not deserved. But it wipes out all sins, all unworthiness. All she needs to do is to say the word and it will be done."

"The Franciscans say she must be baptised first," he said. "That I am damned every minute I live with her and that she is no more than my whore."

"You are already married," I told him, "in the eyes of custom. But it is not a Christian marriage. And in that the Franciscans are right, only two baptised persons can join themselves in Christian matrimony. Her baptism will be necessary ..."

I let him consider that for a moment.

Francis of Assisi was the most holy of men. But the zeal of many of those who attempt to follow in his footprints inclines them to interpret canon law a little over strictly at times. He was also a man who, to tell the truth, could have been as easily burned as canonised. There are many good men in the order he founded, though most of those sent out to the Antilles have as good as turned a blind eye – perhaps out of a misplaced reluctance to judge their fellow men – to the numberless horrors committed there.

"I will want to preach," I added, not being able to help myself from staring at his deformed earlobes.

"Of course," he said.

"But there is no chapel," I pointed out. "Is it not your duty as an encomiendero to construct one?"

"One shall be built," he replied.

"I will also need to hear your confession," I told him.

ж

Goya has suddenly become affable. Montenegro tells me that Juana has requested to be baptised, and that Goya and she are to be married. Today he showed us his near-completed sugar mill.

Don Cristóbal brought the first cane seedlings here on his second voyage. Many swear the fine spice, as they call it, is the future. The plant requires a hot wet climate; and though some is grown in Andalusia, it seems to thrive best on islands, such as

Madeira, the Fortunate Iles, the Cape Verdes and, I have been told, on Cyprus in earlier times. However, it is a bulky and heavy plant, and great quantities of it are required to produce the sugar cakes. So each encomienda that cultivates the plant endeavours to have its own mill.

As I wrote earlier, I have seen one in operation, just outside Santo Domingo, near Alfredo Castro's kiln. The machine has three upright rollers, each about the height of a small man and the width of a large wine barrel, situated over a wooded trough which receives the juice as it is pressed out of the cane. A mast or pole extends up from the central roller, and from both sides of this, a crossbeam extends by means of which the whole can be rotated. The cane is fed into the rollers by hand, a never-ending job. The sugar juice is collected and boiled – or sometimes even left in the sun to crystallise, though that, as you can imagine, is a slow process – to produce the valuable brown cakes. The harvesting of the cane plant itself – and vast quantities are needed – and its transportation to the mill, so that it arrives fresh, also requires many labourers; as does tending the fires under the boiling caldrons which produce the stuff of the cakes. The mill is rotated by two crews of labourers harnessed to the crossbeam like beasts of burden, circling round and round the central post endlessly, rotating the whole heavy mechanism as they go. Horses are too valuable to be used for such labour, mules too unmanageable, and oxen too rare. However, the final product is extremely valuable and great quantities can be transported even in a small ship, yielding substantial profit when sold in the markets of Christendom. I have been told that Africans, being better suited to the heavy work required, are increasingly replacing the Indians. Goya's mill, which is not yet in operation, is similar. He expresses great hopes for this enterprise. A couple of mills on the island are powered using Moorish water wheels but he has no suitable water course on the encomienda which could be used.

Returning from the mill, Goya also showed us his pigsties, of which he is also very proud. Montenegro said he hoped we would be given the opportunity of enjoying a roast suckling pig during the wedding fiesta.

"Don Padre Montenegro says you desire to speak to a prince of the people?" Goya said to me this morning.

"The missionary needs to understand the hearts and minds of those he wishes to conquer," I said.

"I think Anacasabe will suit your purposes admirably," he said. "She is a Christian. Of sorts."

"She!" I said surprised, though I should not have been. "Of sorts?"

"She refuses to give up her husbands," he said.

"Her husbands?" I asked.

"She has three," he explained. "Three brothers. The Franciscans told her that she could only keep one, but that he would also need to convert. She told them that they could baptise all three. Which they did. But then she kept all three anyway."

I refrained from telling him that in that case she could hardly be considered a Christian – of any sort. The custom of the caciques here and in the other Indian countries of taking several wives is widespread, though this is the first instance I have heard of a cacica taking several so-called husbands. While the former is an insult to the dignity of womanhood, the latter is an even greater insult to manhood. But, Montenegro tells me, they are not easily weaned from the uncivilised practice.

"I have business with her," he said. "You may accompany me if you wish."

This Anacasabe is obliged to provide him with labourers and some sort of negotiations are involved.

Ж

The macaw has not spoken since. But my mind is in turmoil, a whirlwind of possibilities and fears. I can barely garner the attention necessary to read this document, let alone comment informatively upon it.

My first thought was that the bird had learnt the words of the Pater Noster from my own lips, from my own whispered prayers. And the more I think about it, the more certain I become that it must be so. The bird must be clever though, for it is a prayer that I reserve for the most special of intentions and occasions, so it has had little opportunity to hear me recite it. The holiest words that there are, desecrated by the very act of them being uttered! I can still hear them. But are they words? Or the mimicked simulacra of words? I am overwhelmed with the blackest confusion. What if the bird should speak again and someone hear its blasphemy? They could surely come to no other conclusion than that I, the bird's owner, had taught it to say the Pater Noster out of some depraved and mad motive! Oh my God, what am I to do? I shall have to kill the thing.

FIFTEEN

It took us the best part of the day to reach the cacica Anacasabe's pueblo. I was obliged to leave Hildegard at Carlos Goya's encomienda; she said she felt a fever coming on and was not fit for travel. The pueblo consists of several large round houses, or caneys as they call them. Constructed of wood, palm leaves and woven straw, they are larger than the ones at the Preachers', each one capable of housing several families. Anacasabe's 'palace' is an exceedingly large long rectangular house, a so-called bohío, with a grass awning over the entrance supported by tree-trunk pillars.

Anacasabe, a big woman, fat, and no longer young, received us sitting on a caoba-wood throne decorated with the carvings of gargoyles, and surrounded by her attendants. She wore a white cotton dress embroidered in the most colourful manner and earrings made of 'guanín', a mixture of gold and copper, the proper name for which is orichalcum, I am told; and, on a leather thong around her neck, a silver medal with an image of the Virgin as Queen of Heaven on it.

Juana introduced me as a 'bohique' or perhaps it was 'bohica'. There is no word for 'nun' in the Indian tongues. Whereupon Anacasabe hugged me and shed tears – I have been told this teary greeting, as it is called, is a traditional means of welcome among them. It was a most moving gesture and more, I felt, than mere ceremony.

I did not follow much of the conversation that followed between her and Goya but Juana told us that it concerned one of Anacasabe's 'husbands', recently dead of a fever to which many others in the pueblo had also succumbed. When Anacasabe saw that I had understood that, she said something to me which of course I could not understand.

"She wants to know if that makes her a better Christian?" Juana translated.

I instructed Juana to ask her what she meant.

"Now that she has only two husbands and not three anymore," she translated.

It was a statement that reminded me of Felicitas's question about God not making the earth flat, another example of the sometimes absurd logic of these people. For a moment I wondered if, in fact, it could have been some attempt at humour of a sort. But I dismissed the thought and simply said that if he had repented of his sins before he had died, he would now be in purgatory – which Juana translated as Coaybay – and would in due time be in paradise.

"Anacasabe knew Colón," Goya said, turning to me. "He rescued her from the Canibas."

"Guamiquina Colón," she said, switching to more than passable Castilian, taking the silver medal from her neck and handing it to me to examine, "gave this as a gift to my father."

A noble gesture on the part of the Admiral, I thought. Though I have my doubts that Montenegro would be of the same opinion. But had the Admiral not discovered these lands, the people of these islands would still be living in superstition and ignorance. And surely the predations of some here upon them, while lamentable and wrong and not to be excused, are far less than those of the Canibas, who see them as nothing more than human meat. Also I ask myself: how plausible are these tales of Don Cristóbal Colón's brutality? He was not a young man when he came here; indeed, he was into his fifth decade. So if he was as brutal as Montenegro says, he must have come late to it. This I do not understand. For my experience is that men's characters are set in their early years and remain unchanged for the most part ever after unless touched by grace and improved.

Goya explained that I and my sisters were setting up a school for the education of girls of good birth, to which Anacasabe merely nodded several times, silently, approvingly or disapprovingly it was impossible to discern.

The introductions and politnesses completed, Goya said he had some 'delicate matters' to discuss with the cacica, and suggested that I might want to see a warlock. There are not many of them left, he said, but the few that are left still wield considerable influence. This warlock lived in a cave nearby, he said, Juana knew where it was. I heard the word 'simarons' mentioned several times as I left. Simarons are Indian bandits who roam the countryside not only robbing but also murdering and destroying property.

Ж

No doubt the 'delicate matters' Goya wished to discuss with Anacasabe concerned his planned marriage with Juana. I cannot be sure of course, but being from that part of the country adjacent to Concepción, she was most likely related

to Anacasabe's clan. Etiquette demanded that he inform
Anacasabe of course, but he might also have spoken to her
of the advantages of Juana deciding to accept the
sacrament of baptism – and them being properly married -
though I suspect it was the temporal advantages rather
than the spiritual advantages which he conveyed to her.

ж

The warlock, the bohique, who goes by the name of Guabancex,
lives in a cave about an hour's walk from the pueblo. Juana went
to the entrance first and called him out, announcing that I had
come to visit him and wished to speak to him. After several
minutes, and seemingly with some reluctance, an old man, his
tattooed beardless face smeared red with ochre, slowly emerged
and walked down the path to me.

"Who are you?" he said.

Juana translated.

I explained I was a nun – Juana again translated this as
'bohique' or 'bohica' again; my ear for the Indian tongue is still
untuned – who had come from across the sea.

"What do you want?" he asked.

"I have been sent ..." – I had to choose my words carefully, for
I knew I was facing a man, a sort of heathen priest in truth, who
from his savage appearance most likely knew nothing of our faith
and ways, and to enable Juana, with her limited knowledge of
Castilian, to translate correctly – "... by the great priest ..." –
which Juana also translated as 'bohique' – "... who speaks on
earth for the One True God ..." – which she translated as Yócahu
Vagua Maórocoti – "... to bring you His holy teachings." Fray
Pedro is of the opinion that the Indians will have to learn new
words and a new way of speaking if they are to be saved and
think correctly and be civilised.

To this he said nothing. He had the air of a man defeated but
there was no deference in his bearing. He obviously did not
consider himself my unequal.

"Your zemis are false," I found myself saying. I know it is not a
woman's place to preach, but do not the annals tell us of
numerous incidents of Christian women who by their piety and
example in ancient times converted the most obdurate of heathen
kings. And if I could convert this heathen, who I now felt sure
had never heard the Good News preached, would not perhaps
those over whom he held sway also convert? "They are devils and
demons. You are causing the One True God pain by continuing to

worship them. He is angry."

"So he sent the Castilla!" he said. I could tell by his tone and manner that it was not a question.

"But," I said, "if you turn away from the zemis and accept the teachings of the One True God and think and act in the good ways He enjoins us to act in, then His anger will melt away and you will prosper."

My words had formed themselves by themselves. I had neither thought about them nor prepared them. There was nothing in them that was not true but when I heard myself speaking them I could feel their hollowness; and was reminded of Saint Paul saying to the Corinthians that words spoken without charity were as hollow as the brass bells used in pagan temples. Was I, I wondered, without charity? And did not even know it?

The warlock listened quietly – while Juana translated my words – looking at me in bewildered curiosity with his squinting eyes, as if he was trying to make out the details of a ship on a distant horizon, or as if I was a being from another realm of things. When she had finished, he spoke slowly for a minute or so. I listened intently to what he was saying but could not make out a word of it. Then he simply turned his back to me and retreated back into the darkness of his dank cave.

I asked Juana what he had said.

"We are to our people what you are to yours," she said, "their mothers and their fathers in the things that cannot be seen. That is what he said."

But I was sure she was not telling me everything.

ж

While Sor Lucrezia and Goya were paying their call on Anacasabe I too – like Hildegard, but more about that anon – feigned illness and stayed behind at the encomienda. My purpose was to learn what more I could of Goya. The house and the compound were empty. All the labourers and their children were in the fields, Hildegard in her bed and Savonarola had also disappeared (or so I thought), giving me free reign of the rambling habitation.

Serrano's account of Goya's wanderings in the wilds of the lands they had been stranded in had planted the idea in my head that perhaps Goya had actually discovered some gold mines or some other source of riches, and that there might be some clue to this in his effects. Perhaps, I thought, he was biding his time for an opportunity to arise which might enable him to go back there, make his fortune, return to Spain a rich man, Indian princess in tow, and buy himself lands and titles. The ilusión indiana. The dream of rank and mammon. And no doubt pay off his debts.

All the settlers are debt-ridden. There are few men on Hayti who have not borrowed heavily to pay for their passages; or have not borrowed money from those who have set up as money lenders here, conversos for the most part, in order to bribe the likes of Rudolfo Jesus de Paz for favours and encomienda rights. The shortage of currency – coins other than small denominations of copper maravedís and silver reales are rarities – habituates them to constant borrowing and lending. The Pharaoh was commissioned to found a mint in Santo Domingo, and a treasurer was even appointed, but like much that he should have undertaken, it came to nothing. Nineteen-twentieths of all the coinage currently in circulation stems from the shipment from Casa de la Moneda in Seville – valuing a mere half a million maravedís, or was it half a million actual coins? – which arrived in 1506, as a result of years of complaint. And both debtors and unpaid creditors feel so hard done by all this, they take out their resentment on the poor Haytians. Men will not sell their children to get richer, but they will do so to pay off their debts; or even take their own lives for shame of it if they cannot. Creditors believe they have the right to take any measure if their victims cannot repay – with interest – the money they have borrowed from them, even to enslave them and their children, to rob them of their livings and the chattels they need to keep body and soul together, things decent men under normal circumstances would not dare to do. Usury is indeed a greater curse than greed.

The fact that Goya was a reconciliado – most likely he'd been charged with practicing Hebrew rites in secret, confessed, done penance and been reconciled – I admit, was also on my mind. A heathen who once worshipped false gods and idols is one thing; their falsity is obvious and once a man has been persuaded by reason and Holy Scripture that it is so, he is less prone to backsliding. But a man who once worshipped the One True God, albeit in a false and abominable manner, is another matter. Had Goya backslided? Were such thoughts worthy? I know not. For was not my very own grandmother, of whom I have but vague memories, also a New Christian? And are not those of us who have been granted the grace of faith and light, from whose eyes the wilful blindness of Judah has been removed, specially charged with rooting out the secretly practicing Jew? But perhaps the thought was also in my mind that, God forbid, during his sojourn among the heathens, Goya had even lapsed into demon worship of some kind. Serrano had hinted he used to take part in the rites they performed in the jungle.

Humiliating though I found it to do so, I examined Goya's papers. There were not many. The only document I found which I thought might be of consequence was a single sheet of paper, a curious table, the letters, names and numbers carefully scripted, the way one would a legal document or important statement of account. At first I thought it was a bill of accounts of some kind, perhaps done according to the Venetian method in which things are counted twice, but the numbers were not repeats of each other, not that I know how this system works. The thought also crossed my mind that it might be an astrological table or even something to do with the Hebrew art of numerology – seafarers are well known for their obsession with numbers.

I made a copy of it, which I still have, and it reads so:

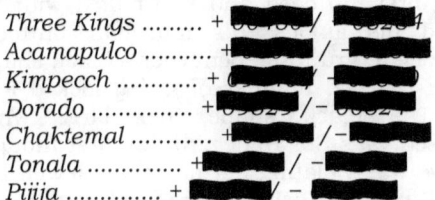

Three Kings	.... +
Acamapulco	.... +
Kimpecch	.... +
Dorado	.... +
Chaktemal	.... +
Tonala	.... +
Pijija	.... +

He also possessed some half-dozen tattered unbound books. Among them was the *Amadis de Gaula*, which must be the most popular book in the Indies, the charms of that chivalric tale being as much loved on Hayti as in Castile; and Sannazoro's paean to the pastoral charms of rustic life, the *Arcadia*, also popular enough; and an out-of-date Regiomontanus. Puccini had been right when he said the seafarer-turned-sugar-farmer was, in a modest way, not unlearned. But I digress.

Then I decided to explore Goya's rambling habitation further. A ladder-like wooden staircase led to the upper floor. Atop it there was a sort of recessed trapdoor, which I pushed open easily and climbed through, leading into one single large room, quite spacious, with sturdy floorboards, resembling more the upper floor of a barn than of a dwelling house; and perhaps it had originally served that purpose, to store dried crops or the like. It had small shuttered oblong windows of the kind found in fortified

---

[2] The numbers were crossed out in this manner in the Catalan edition of which this edition is a translation, as they were also undoubtedly in the original manuscript.

farmhouses in many parts of Christendom.

I was only there for a few moments and about to descend the ladder-like stairs again but then I heard a noise, similar to the grunting of a pig or some other beast, but which I intuitively knew was not. It was an animal sound, yet there was something perversely human about it; whether it was of pain or of pleasure it was impossible to make out. It was coming from outside, from beyond the shuttered windows. I made my way towards one of them, slowly, careful not to make a noise. I did not want my presence to be noticed for I knew not what the sound was. I thought perhaps it was the sound of danger or of a crime being committed.

I opened one of the shutters slightly, pushing it ajar slowly lest it creak on its hinges, so that I might get a view of where I thought the sound was coming from. What I beheld was something that in my wildest fantasy I could not have imagined. Below me, in the stable – I shall call it that – adjoining the back of the house, I saw them: the savage Savonarola first, tattooed and half-naked with his pantaloons around his ankles, his muscular buttocks visible in the dusty light, grunting, bent over a black shape, mounting it in the frenzied manner of a dog locked to a bitch in heat. The black shape, her large white hindquarters exposed, was Sor Hildegard. My first thought was that the savage was violating her against her will, but the way she moved in unison with his frenzied rutting and her squeals ... They were not of pain; they were of the shameless pleasure of the whore. It shames me to my depths to admit it, but the sight of them, engaged in the act of carnal congress, an act I had never myself engaged in – and God willing never will – struck me dumb. And, I confess, fascinated me as if I had become momentarily bewitched ... spellbound ... unable to control myself, as if possessed – nay, not 'as if' – possessed by a demon, the demon of lust ... I found my hand going to my tumescent member. I spilt my seed as they collapsed onto the straw-strew floor of the stable; and as I did so, I remembered the words of my fellow Preachers, Fray Kramer and Fray Spenger, from the *Malleus Maleficarum*: All witchcraft comes from carnal lust, which is in women insatiable ... they consort even with devils.

I have not been able to bring myself to do it. Every time I look at it, I see the creature's sulphur-yellow eyes staring at me, innocently unaware of the thoughts I have been nursing. I have decided to speak to the ship's surgeon. But what shall I say to him?

SIXTEEN

Back at Carlos Goya's compound.

Hildegard has recovered, as has Montenegro. She is her usual high-spirited self again. Montenegro has sent Savonarola to Concepción with a letter to Puccini, remarking to me after he had departed – for no particular reason it seemed – that he did not quite trust the man.

This evening the chicha came out and Goya talked. Perhaps now that he is about to be finally married in the eyes of God, a weight has been lifted from his soul and he feels he can trust us ...

Ж

And we domini canes, hounds of the Lord, have means of making men unburden themselves more subtle and more effective than the rack. Carlos Goya understood – I had no need to spell it out in so many words – that the price of an honest marriage to his woman was honest answers to our questions.[3]

Ж

... or perhaps it was the alcohol. He is a moody creature.

"So you have met Franco Serrano?" he said after Juana had cleared the table of the remains of our evening meal.

"He is in our care, in Santo Domingo," Montenegro said. "He has fallen on testing times."

Goya offered us tabaco cigars, Montenegro accepted, I declined, as I had declined the chicha. And surprisingly, Montenegro was also being unusually abstentious in that regard.

"What did he tell you?" Goya asked.

Montenegro told him, or rather gave him the gist of what the seaman had told both him alone and then both of us together on the Sunday after the Haytian mass.

"Well, what he told you was true enough," Goya said when Montenegro had finished.

"True enough?" Montenegro said.

"Serrano is a common sailor," Goya explained, "he notices

---

[3] Passage by Montenegro written in the margin of the original manuscript.

much but he misses much."

"He said you had made explorations?" I ventured.

"And that you fashioned a quadrant?" Montenegro added.

"I have a rudimentary knowledge of geometry," he said. "It seemed right to put it to use. I wanted to know where we were. It was something to keep me occupied. The devil and idle hands and all that."

"Serrano said the Pole Star was visible where you were," I said.

"Yes," he said. "We were north of the equator."

"On the mainland of Asia?" Montenegro suggested, no doubt thinking of the large northern landmass on the Strassburg map.

Goya shrugged.

"Maybe," he said. "I am no cosmographer. But I doubt it. We were only a few degrees above the equator. The mainland of Asia is supposed to be further north."

My first thought was that the southern continent, the so-called new world, what Waldseemüller and Ringmann call America, extends a full ten degrees above the equator – but I kept my own counsel.

"Serrano spoke of cities," I said.

"He spoke the truth," Goya said. "And there are more of them that I did not see than I saw. Some of them are bigger than Granada. Wondrous places. Ghoulish places. Rich places. Their hidalgos wear gold and precious stones. With mosques the shape of pyramids and the size of cathedrals. They sacrifice men on their roofs. Cut their hearts out and offer them to their idols. Their gods are whimsical beings and most of them can only be placated with human blood. Yet, at the same time, they believe that everything happens according to a great law of the universe, that everything repeats itself, that what happened in one age repeats itself again in the next, down to the very day, in great circles of time; and that if one can read the signs, anything can be foretold: storms, droughts and the like. I was told there is a city in the north, on an island in a lake with canals instead of streets, like Venice, where they sacrifice a dozen virgins every day so that the sun may rise on the next."

Montenegro glanced at me and I thought he was going to say something but he did not.

"I was told that to the south," Goya continued, "in the Parrot Land perhaps, there are more cities, in a kingdom called Birù."

"Your journeying about must have been full of dangers?" I suggested.

"I dressed myself like a heathen," he explained. "I wore

feathers in my hair and carried a rattle with me. And I'd had my ears done then. I looked like a wizard or a warlock of some kind. Who takes notice of the unwashed mendicant in sackcloth, begging bowl in hand, as he passes along the road or through the gates of a Christian city? Though it was a begging basket in my case. I usually kept my mouth shut, but I'd picked up enough of the lingo to be able to spot trouble. It wasn't the same the tongue the Ucateks spoke but similar enough. In fact, they speak many different tongues."

"Are any of them similar to Hebrew?" Montenegro asked.

For a moment I thought the question was a genuine query – and perhaps it was – but then I realised that Montenegro was letting him know that he knew Goya was a New Christian.

Goya looked at him intensely for a moment.

"No," he said.

"Serrano said you also saw the ruins of ancient cities?" I said.

"The cities of the seven bishops?" Montenegro suggested.

Goya shook his head.

"I think not," he said. "They were heathen places. All the mosques and palaces, what remained of them that is, were engraved with the images of zemis and gargoyles. Apparitions from the Inferno. No, they were not the seven cities. There was nothing Christian about them."

"What had befallen them?" Montenegro asked.

"What befell Rome?" Goya asked in return. "All things have their time, a time for living and a time for dying. A time to be born, and a time to die."

"For all is vanity," Montenegro continued, completing Goya's citation from the Book of Ecclesiasticus, "all are of the dust, and all turn to dust again. Serrano told us that the Franciscan who was with you, Pater Gerónimo, had made conversions? He talked of a people he called the Inocentes."

"There was a cacique who went by the name of Tabasco," Goya said. "His country was about two days march to the north of where we were. Don Padre Gerónimo got him to agree to be baptised. The Don Padre had learnt the local tongue too, the one spoken in those parts. There are many, as I've said. I was there when it happened, when the cacique finally agreed that he and his people be instructed in the Christian faith. He took the name of Inocente, and Don Padre Gerónimo said he could call himself Don Inocente, him being a prince and all; hence the name we gave them, the Inocentes."

"It is possible, you see," Montenegro said, turning to me. "By peaceful preaching and example, it is possible to bring men to the Divine. There is no need for Mohomedan methods."

Then, turning to Goya again, he said: "Tell us, tell us how this was done."

"It was done over many months," Goya went on. "But I think what really melted Don Innocente's stubbornness was Don Padre Gerónimo's telling him of Christ's Transfiguration."

Montenegro asked him what exactly Pater Gerónimo had said.

"He told them that Christ had cut open His own breast," Goya said, "and with His own hands extracted His heart and shown it to His disciples."

"The Sacred Heart," Montenegro whispered. I thought he was going to cross himself but he did not.

"He said," Goya continued, "that Our Saviour had done this in order to show that He was a god who did not demand the hearts of others as sacrificial offerings. Bands of soldiers from the cities used to come and demand tributes of boys and girls to sacrifice in their mosques."

"Soldiers?" Montenegro said.

"Yes, soldiers," Goya said. "They wore armour made from padded cotton. Their swords were of a hard wood but edged with shards of a black stone resembling glass. Sharp enough to cut a man's arm off. Sharp as Toledo steel in fact, but brittle as hell."

"What else did he preach?" Montenegro said, more interested in the arguments this Pater Gerónimo had used to reach Indians' hearts than in armaments.

"Christ, he said," Goya continued, "offered His own heart in place of all others. He said that it was Christ who made the sun rise, and not their idols. I cannot remember his exact words but that was the gist of it."

"The Miracle of the Transfiguration," Montenegro said, whispering again. "The First Glorious Mystery." This time he did cross himself. "Christ spoke in simple parables. And so too must we."

But I sometimes wonder if the parables are, in fact, that simple. At times, on reading them, I have noticed that Our Saviour often leaves His listeners to come to their own conclusions as to what is right and wrong, and what seems apparent on a first reading is often not so on a second.

"Then," Goya continued, "he told them how Christ was coming again, and that when He did, He would raise the dead and lead all those who had worshipped Him into an eternal paradise. He spoke with great eloquence. He was a very pious man, a man of great faith and charity, intolerant of all sin, and it pained him greatly that he had no bread and wine to celebrate mass. He said that Christ was coming soon from across the Eastern Sea and that He would put an end to all human sacrifice."

I looked at Montenegro and was about to say that surely that could not be right, but he had anticipated my disquiet.

"Simple people need to be spoken to simply," he said.

He turned to Goya again: "But you deserted him, you left him there."

"The captain of the *Roxana* said he could not wait," he explained. "He wasn't what you'd call a patient man. Everything about the voyage was illegal, not that that incongruous detail stopped him from erecting wooden crosses everywhere and claiming everything he clapped eyes on in the name of himself and the Catholic Majesties. Besides, it was possible that the Don Padre was no longer with the Inocentes. It could have taken me months to find him."

"And Morales?" Montenegro asked.

Goya shrugged.

"Never saw him again," he said. "He was happy enough where he was, I reckon. He'd had a few nippers by then. And, to tell the truth, all he had to come back to here was a pack of creditors after the skin on his back."

I decided to ask him about the passage.

"There is none," he said.

"How can you be so sure?" I asked.

"I asked," he said. "They know their own country. All I asked said the same, that there was none."

"Serrano said you saw a sea in the west," Montenegro persisted. "Big, 'a great bugger of an ocean' he called it."

"They call it the Sea of the Setting Sun," Goya told us. "The only way to get there is overland. I was told it could be reached in a two-week walk. That's twenty days. Their week is ten days long. They don't count time the way we do."

"The Great Southern Ocean," I suggested.

"It took me forty days from coast to coast," Goya said. "Give or take a few days for rests and diversions. I was wandering about a bit, keeping to the roads. I wasn't travelling in a straight line."

"You saw the Southern Ocean," Montenegro said, still not quite believing what he had heard.

"Yes," Goya said.

"Serrano said you saw ships," Montenegro continued. The Preachers are renowned for their persistence and their inquisitorial skills. "Indian ships?"

"One day from a cliff top," Goya explained, "I ... the waters stretched as far as the eye can see ... I saw a ship. A Christian ship slowly making its way up the coast, sailing north. It was nearing dusk. It was a ways out to sea but I'm sure that's what it was, a Christian ship."

"Castilian?" I asked.

"Could have been," he said. "Or Portuguese. It was too far out to make out its colours. The locals had told me about it. I'd gone to see it with my own eyes. It anchored overnight. Then the next morning it continued on its way, hugging the coast. It wasn't an Indian raft, I'm sure of that. Though they do build them big. And they do have sails. I saw a few near as long as galleys, twenty foot wide, packed with cottons and all sorts of goods. And it definitely wasn't a big canoa. They don't have sails."

Montenegro seemed satisfied and didn't question him any further.

Goya then said he had something to show us, got up, opened one of his chests and extracted a strange book-like object from it.

"Nobody here interests themselves in such things," he said, as he opened it up and showed us what it contained, "but you are learned people."

It was a sort of book, but not made in the manner to which we are accustomed. It was more a sort of scroll, the pages folded neatly between two intricately carved hardwood boards – caoba wood of some sort – the way parchments and other illuminated books are bound between wooden covers to protect them.

The 'paper', which was a very creamy colour, resembled the sort of pressed or hammered-out bark fabric the Haytians use as wall-hangings, with gargoyle-like images of zemis painted on them, usually in black, or red or white and various shades of brown and yellow-brown. But this was a lot finer, in truth more like a sort of papyrus; Goya said they manufacture it from the root of a certain tree which they grow for that purpose. There were coloured images on every page, drawings of strange creatures and men in what looked like feathered costumes, and of zemis and idols, as precisely painted as the images found in illuminated manuscripts. The writing in it was strange and indecipherable, obviously an Indian alphabet or some other device, certainly not Hebrew; nor did it resemble the flowery Mohomedan script used by the Turks, the Arabs and the Persians. Its provenance was obviously not the Spanish Island – the Haytian pictographs that Puccini had shown us were childlike in comparison – or any other of the islands of the Antilles, where by all accounts the people are even more simple in their ways. If it reminded me of anything, it was of those inscriptions you showed me on the Egyptian obelisk in front of the Church of Santa Maria in Aracoeli on the Capitoline that no one knew how to decipher anymore.

"How did this come into your possession?" Montenegro asked.

"It was left behind by the Ucateks," Goya said. "I found it in one of the deserted huts that time I went back to the pueblo after they – the handful that was left of them – had disappeared into the jungle. It was in one of the hanging baskets where they kept their books – which, I suppose, is what it is, really – to keep them out of the way of mice and the like."

"Their books?" I asked.

"Some of the warlocks could write," he said, "For quills they use the feathers of a bird called a cutz, which is ..."

"... a guinea fowl the size of a goose," Montenegro said, rather impatiently I thought.

"There were whole libraries in the cities," Goya said.

"Do you understand what it is about?" Montenegro asked, immersed in examining the curious artefact.

But Goya shook his head and said: "Lots of souls, Don Padre, multitudes of souls to save." I detected a note of derision in his voice, and I thought Montenegro, usually quick to notice such things, would reprimand him, but he seemed not to notice.

As the evening drew on, there was much more that Goya told us, more than I have the time to write of in any detail. He told us how people live long in the countries he had visited, once coming across a man who had lived, or claimed he had, a hundred and forty years. The inhabitants, he said, often call their countries after animals, such as the Cutz Land and the Deer Land; that for money they use beads, stone counters, fine feathers, red shells and chocol, which they also have, and give credit but know no usury; and that many of the ruins he saw had only been abandoned a mere fifty years ago and that many books had been saved from them. Of their houses he said that they are well built and excellently thatched and whitewashed, and that in the houses of the caciques, who take great pride in the ancientness of their lineages, there were many wondrous and colourful frescos; that their dwellings have no doors, nor locks and keys, and it is considered a great crime among them to burgle. But, he told us, in matters of agriculture and hunting and fishing, all is held in common.

They bathed a great deal, he said, in public, showing little shame, and had many perfumes. Of clothing, he told us, they wore mainly a large square mantle resembling a priest's chasuble and that many of these garments were finely embroidered and decorated with multi-coloured parrot feathers; and on their feet they wore sandals of either hemp or deerskin; and wore ornaments, and like the Indians here, they painted and scarred their faces, They also flatten their skulls for beauty's sake, and they consider being cross-eyed a very fine thing; mothers hang a swinging pendant between their infants eyes so that they may develop this deformity. And among some of them, the women file their teeth for beauty's sake.

They are much given to orgies and drunkenness, he said, making a wine from honey and water and the roots of a tree they cultivate for this purpose; and at their feasts there is much music-making and dancing and play-acting. They play many different types of flutes and trumpets made of wood, cane and bones; and similar to the Indians here, they also play cylindrical drums but their drumsticks are tipped with the gum substance, which they call 'kik', which the Indians here make their batey-balls from. Some of them smoke tabaco and other weeds in a sort of flute.

When Fray Montenegro enquired more closely about the deluded beliefs and the superstitions of these peoples, he told us that there was a greater variety of customs, dress and habits and superstitions among them than there is in Christendom; and some of them hold their own ways so dearly that they refuse to copy things from their neighbours even though their neighbours' things may be superior, such as their manner of building houses or making tools and the like. But many of them, he said, believed in the immortality of the soul, and that the beatitude they believed that could be attained in the life beyond was akin to that of the Moors, its chief pleasures consisting of eating and drinking and debauchery. They have no knowledge of the resurrection of the body, he said.

He said that in one country they sacrificed male and female slaves to a serpent-demon by throwing them into a deep well 'sacred' to that demon; and that in another they sacrificed dogs on the roofs of mosques, also by cutting their hearts out, as they do men, painting them blue first with the oil of some herb, but that this latter was done only and mostly when there was some great misfortune or tribulation. So great was their devotion to these demons, he said, that some men would even at times give their sons over to be sacrificed. They also sacrificed human beings, he said, by piercing them with arrows, but painting them blue first and putting mitres on their heads. The warlocks would flay the corpses of those they had sacrificed and wear their skins and dance among the people – for these sacrifices were also times of great festivity! Often, he said, the flesh of those whose hearts had been cut out was distributed among the caciques and the warlocks, and at times among the common people, to be eaten. Their own blood they would also sacrifice to the demons, he said, cutting themselves on the lips and piercing their tongues with thorns. Once, he said, he saw the idol of a demon in an oratorio being anointed with blood. The men stood in a line and pierced holes in their members and passed a cord through them, causing a great quantity of blood to flow, and, fastened together in this filthy and abominable manner, they anointed the demon.

Montenegro asked him if they believed their idols were demons or were only images of them. He said they knew they were only images but nevertheless worshipped them. They practised a sort of baptism, he said, their warlocks sprinkling what they called 'virgin' water – water gathered from the hollows in trees and in rocks – on the children with a bone. They fasted beforehand, and the ceremony itself is attended by great fanfare. He also related how they practised a form of confession in which they confessed their sins – murder, lying, adultery and other things that they believed to be their sins in their religion – to a warlock. This was to avoid calamities, which they believed were the result of their wrongdoings.

All these things, he said, were not practiced among all of them, though there was much that was common to them all. Of the great stone mosques in the ruined cities, he said, they still held them in great esteem, and when they passed them on the road they would enter them and offer prayers. However these days, in the country where he had travelled most, the people now only built mosques from clay and wood. He had seen serpents the length of two men and as thick as a man's thigh, he said, lions as black as ebony, and creatures like monkeys the size of men, who spent their lives sleeping in trees. All he had told us, he said, he had either seen or been told of, but I cannot recall which of them he said he had seen and which of them he said he had only heard about. And how much of this is all true to the letter, I have of course no way of knowing, for men do tell tales for the mere sake of it.

Later I said to Montenegro that if Goya had seen the Great Southern Ocean – assuming that was the sea which he had seen, and that he was telling the truth, which we had no reason to suspect he was not – then the Strassburger map was, at least in a great part, correct. And that if it was a Portuguese ship that Goya had seen, then perhaps the Strassburger map was not based on cosmographers' speculations but on some secret intelligence – and the consequences of all this could be most profound. I thought Montenegro would have much to say about this but he was curiously silent.

Ж

My first reaction to the Strassburg map was an intuitive desire that it be wrong. It was a desire from the bowels. I still want it to be wrong. And I pray to God that it is. I had not known why I felt so strongly at the time, but I know now, or at least I think I do. For if there is a Great Southern Ocean and Asia is half a world away across that ocean, an uncrossable expanse of empty water according to the map, then the question naturally poses itself: how did the inhabitants of Hayti and the other islands and tierra firme, or America as Vespucci has christened it, get to the countries they now inhabit?

If Hayti is an island off the coast of Asia, then the Haytians and all the other peoples of the Antilles came from Asia, and are thus unequivocally descended from Adam and definitely men like us. But if Asia is in fact further east, with a vast uncrossable ocean between the Antilles and there, then they could not have come from there, and the matter is not so unequivocally clear. Men like Rudolfo Jesus de Paz – and many others – would argue that they were incapable of even crossing the Oceanus Occidentalis. The logical consequence of which would be that these peoples are not descended from Adam. And the logical consequence of that does not bear consideration. I once saw the remains of a Haytian canoa capable of holding up to fifty men. Could such a canoa have crossed the Oceanus Occidentalis? A cacique once told me that in the time before our coming they used to cross to tierra firme in six days. Crossing the Oceanus Occidentalis is surely not impossible in such vessels? Goya and Serrano told how they had seen rafts with sails, as big as Christian ships. The so-called Ice Land is a country only reachable after weeks at sea, yet centuries ago Christians sailed there in smaller vessels than we have now. The Green Land, even further distant, and once a Christian diocese before the inhabitants there all died of a plague, was reached too. So is it arguable that, like us, the ancestors of the Haytians had in ancient times

made their way across to the Antilles from the Fortunate
Isles, the inhabitants of which resemble them in physique.

Ж

Today Juana received the Sacrament of Baptism and then
Montenegro joined her and Goya in Christian marriage. The
ceremony took place in front of the main house and was attended
by all the servants and labourers. Montenegro gave a brief
sermon.

"This earthly feast we have before us," he said, "is nothing
compared to the heavenly feast that awaits us." Then he told the
parable from Luke of the master of a house who held a fiesta but
to which none of those who had been invited came; and how the
master of the house, being angry, had bade his servant to go out
into the streets and lanes of the city, and bring hither the poor,
and the maimed, and the halt, and the blind, and go out into the
highways and byways, and compel those they found to come in,
so that his house might be filled. "Such is the love of the Lord,"
he said. In thanksgiving Goya gave a solemn oath to construct a
chapel, to be built on the site of the ruins of the small mosque that
once housed zemis in order to symbolise the victory of truth over
falsehood. And we were treated to a roast suckling pig at the
fiesta that followed.

On the morning of our departure, Carlos Goya gave Montenegro
the strange Indian book he had shown us earlier – "for
safekeeping".

"It proves that they are men," he said, "and not unlearned in
their way. You will know what to do with it."

"Yes, that is best," Montenegro said. "Such objects are safer in
the hands of the learned."

Our journey back to Concepción was without incident.

This morning Puccini brought us to what is called the Gold
Factory on the outskirts of Concepción. The appellation gives the
impression of something grand but, in fact, it is little more than a
collection of rough wooden sheds in a fenced-off stockade. There
are several guards, and a notary keeps constant watch and records
everything, noting the weight to the grain of all that is produced.
The law is that all 'gold' nuggets collected everywhere in this
part of the Vega Real – and other gravels which look like them,
for it is not always so easy to tell the difference – are brought
there to be purified. But Puccini also told us that although it is the

law that the purification and collection of all precious metals take place at these factories, of which there are several on the island, there is no shortage of private enterprises being carried out in the hills and remoter places. The Alcalde Mayor's eyes cannot be everywhere, he said, and for a share of the proceedings of these outlaw enterprises, most of his men will turn a blind eye.

The 'gold' brought in is not pure gold but an alloy of gold containing various other metals, in the manner in which brass is a mixture of copper and zinc, and pewter a mixture of lead and tin. Its alchemical name is electrum. It is extracted from the sandbanks and gravel beds of rivers in the form of nuggets of varying sizes, some so exceedingly small that they are called 'gold dust'; and much electrum is also mined by digging tunnels into hills.

The purifying sheds are not a pleasant place. We were not inclined to subject ourselves to the stink of it for any length of time. But we did stay long enough to see how the alchemists – they were the rudest and scabbiest of men, tropical Vulcans, but I could not help thinking of them thus – crushed the electrum gravel in a crude mill into fine pieces to prepare it for the purification process proper. They then mix these pieces with much water and a quantity of quicksilver, perhaps equal in quantity to the crushed electrum, in a small barrel, and agitate the whole solution as one churns butter. During this process of rapid agitation, Puccini informed us, the quicksilver attaches itself to the gold; and when the agitation is ceased, the gold-quicksilver amalgam sinks to the bottom of the barrel, where it is left to rest for a while. Then the water, which has absorbed all sorts of impurities liberated from the electrum by the alchemical action of the quicksilver, is poured away. The remaining amalgam is then carefully spooned from the bottom of the barrel and transferred to leather bags which are left to hang; and in the next few hours the quicksilver drips out and is collected in pots for use again, for quicksilver is not cheap and has to be brought from Spain, there being no local source of it. The Fuggers, he said, have a monopoly on the buying and the selling of it, in Spain and in the lands of the Empire. What thereafter remains in the bags is a gold dust of a very high quality. The stinking sulphurous water, which is returned to the stream from whence it originally came, causes great damage to fisheries, of which the Indians sorely complain, he said.

After the notary, with whom Puccini is acquainted, has carefully weighed the gold dust and given a stamped receipt to the miner or encomiendero who brought the electrum in, it is then placed in another bag, secured with a lead seal and placed in a sort of strong room, the only building constructed of brick in the place. Every evening, an hour before sunset, these bags are removed to the Concepción fort under guard. The receipts are honoured at the annual ingot casting at the arsenal in Santo Domingo, a great ceremony attended by all the men of authority on the island, meticulously overseen by the royal notaries. Those who have brought gold in are given their portions, as is the Governor his, and the King's quinto is shipped with great fanfare to Seville. Debts are also settled at this time, but many is the miner who goes away empty handed, for they do not live frugally.

Attempts have also been made to extract gold from galena – which is the alchemical name for the ores and gravels from which lead is extracted – by the use of furnaces but this has not proved fruitful. The demand for lead itself is high here, and much is produced for ammunition and to make cladding for the hulls of ships to protect them from the sea worms that abound in the warm waters. Iron too is mined and worked. The Indians themselves knew nothing of these arts before our arrival; though they have skill in the working of gold or rather orichalcum, which they call guanín. This they did not produce themselves but got by trade from some distant islands and tierra firme. They also have skill in fashioning ornaments and beads from bones, shells and stones and the like, and of which I have seen some very fine examples.

Ж

I once asked Puccini what in truth had brought him to Hayti.

"The Fountain of Youth," he laughed, "Dreams of bathing in its perfumed waters, dreams of eternal beauty, of eternal youth and eternal significance. And unpayable debts." He always had the gift, if one may call it that, of seeming to be jesting and yet not.

The Fountain of Youth is a pagan fable, I told him; to which he replied: "As opposed to a Christian one?"

Carnal beauty and youth, I remember saying to him, are fleeting things, and it is part of the divine plan that they are so; at most they are but faint glimpses of beatitude.

"Prester John is said to drink from its waters," he said.

He was, of course, attempting to provoke me and I knew better than to fall for his bait or argue with him when he started quoting ancient books at me.

Another time he said to me: "Perhaps the beliefs we need to live well by, to live to the full, in the world, are not necessarily beliefs which are correct about the totality of things. I am not denying there is eternal life, but could it not make some sense, from the point of view of living well, in a way, as many of the Ancients held, to actually believe there is only this one mortal life?"

"To live by a lie?" I retorted. "To believe in something that one knows not to be true? That is the philosophy of a madman!"

"Then I am mad, Padre," he said and laughed that ambivalent laugh of his.

Puccini's mind sprouted ideas with the fecundity of weeds in a vegetable patch but he lacked the judgement, despite his erudition, to discern which of them are worth believing in and which deserve discarding. Perhaps he enjoyed his doubt, and made a sort of philosophical game of it. I believed then, that beyond confiding them in private to me, a priest, he had kept those doubts and heretical speculations to himself.

Ж

Returning to Santo Domingo now.

Yesterday afternoon a troop of soldiers passed us on the road, appearing almost preternaturally out of the dust cloud created by their horses, their Indians, armoured mastiffs and pigs jogging along beside them: a barking, squealing, neighing, metal-clad clattering mass. Their grey-haired commander, a man who looked as if his years had rendered him more handsome than he had perhaps been in his youth, sporting silver earrings and the badge of the Order of Saint James the Moor Killer on his breast – a red cross in the form of a sword – greeted us chivalrously and asked us if we had seen anything amiss on the road.

"There is much amiss in this country," Montenegro said. "Anything in particular?"

His tone surprised me; he is usually more polite, in any case when not in his cups.

The commander's adjutant, a helmeted Berber in chainmail, his Moor-coloured face dust-bleached, seemed to find the remark amusing; but being behind his commander and thus out of his sight, the latter did not notice.

"We're searching for a gang of simarons, Red Francisquito's gang," the commander said. "Half a dozen redskins and a pair of renegade Black Ladinos, with stolen horses. Probably holed up in some cave somewhere. They set fire to a sugar mill two nights ago. That's what's amiss, Padre. In particular."

"Is it now?" Montenegro said scathingly.

I exchanged a concerned glance with Hildegard.

"And vengeance is thine," Montenegro added, paraphrasing scripture.

"Well, we'll catch them," the commander said, obviously not recognising Montenegro's sarcastic misquoting of Deuteronomy, "if it takes all month. We've plenty of meat for ourselves, and the dogs." He indicated the pigs. The soldiers invariably travel with a herd of them in tow.

As they rode off, again disappearing into a cloud of dust of their own making, Montenegro told me who the handsome commander was: "The noble and gallant caballero Captain-General Gonzales de Esquival. The Haytians simply call him Carnage."

His animosity seems particularly personal.

I asked him if he knew de Esquival well.

"I would not say we know each other," he said. "But I know what kind of a man he is well enough."

"And this Red Francisquito?" I asked.

"A cacique – once – by the name of Guaro," he explained. "A Christian, baptised in any case, and no fool either. He was educated by the Franciscans in Santo Domingo for a while as a boy. They call him Francisquito because of his size. He's a small man, a near dwarf of a man. He and his simarons have been running wild for years. Paints himself red, never uses any other colour, hence Red Francisquito."

Later we came across a heathen shrine at a crossroads; we are taking a somewhat different return route to the one we travelled to Concepción on. Fresh offerings of casabe, fruits and parrot feathers had been made at it.

Later, after our evening meal, I asked Montenegro what had happened to Puccini's hand.

"A shipboard mishap of some sort," was all he knew. "On his last voyage back."

Ж

I finally mustered up the courage to speak to the ship's surgeon. He is a Basque by the name of Bikendi, a big fellow, and quick with the saw by all accounts. He's reputed to be able to cut through a man's thigh in three minutes, cauterising the stump included, and losing but half his patients to fevers. He certainly proved himself with Goya. The reputation of his race for being knowledgeable, secretive and sharp merchants is not undeserved. Their fishers must provide half the cod eaten in Christendom; and with over a hundred fasting days a year, that is not a small quantity of fish. For years nobody knew where their fishing grounds were. There is a story that Cabot, when he was exploring the northern waters between the Green Land and Asia, to his great surprise, came across armadas of their boats there. They had been fishing thereabouts for years and had breathed not a word of it.

I told Bikendi the bird uses bad language, that it curses and swears.

"Like a sailor," he said, rather predictably, and laughed.

"Yes," I said. "Something like that."

"Can't you just punish it every time it does it?" he suggested. "Pull a few feathers out. That should hurt it enough. It'll soon learn. I once had a dog ..."

If only, I thought. But the bird did not speak often enough for that.

"I've tried," I lied, "but it's stubborn. Won't learn. I know they are supposed to be clever creatures but I think this one is particularly dense."

"I see," he said, looking at the bird. "So how can I help you? We don't have a lot of medicines on board ship but we have some. If it's the runs you have, I have something that never fails. It's my own concoction ..."

"It's not about me," I said. "It's about the macaw."

"Oh," he said, looking at the bird again. "What's wrong with it? It looks healthy enough to me."

"I want you to cut its tongue out," I said.

He seemed not to understand.

"I want you to cut its tongue out," I repeated.

But he had understood. The expression on his bearded face had been bewilderment, not incomprehension.

"I am a man of God," I explained. "It comes out with filthy language while I'm saying my prayers. I cannot have that."

"You could give it away," he suggested. "Even sell it. It might fetch ..."

"No, no," I said, trying to think quickly. "I have grown attached to it. I'll pay you of course."

"'Twould be a tricky thing to do ...," he started to say.

Then I showed him the coin, a silver ducat.

The expression on his face changed to that of greed. I hid my disgust.

"As I said," he said, "it will not be easy, I will have to manufacture a device of some kind, and the operation itself will not be without risk."

"I understand that," I said.

He must have been thinking what a sanctimonious prig I was, a perverse sanctimonious prig.

"I will need a few days," he said. "As I said, I will have to manufacture a device. It takes the devil's patience to learn the creatures anything. Seamen have the time for it. And well, the language of the common sailor ... but if you can't unlearn it from swearing and cursing, I suppose snip-snip is the only thing for it."

SEVENTEEN

Santo Domingo.

Sor Vitoria passed away in our absence. She died three days or so following our departure to Concepción. Such is the rapidity with which the so-called seasoning fever carries away its unfortunate victims. Her grave, a fresh mound of the red-brown earth of this place, out of which the first bright green shoots of grass have already begun to sprout, lies headstone-less and solitary at the end of our garden, overlooking the bay. Death and fecundity can be nowhere more intimately entwined than in these tropics with their unremitting warmth. She was no more than twenty-two in years. Her father is still living; or, at least, still was when we left Seville. I shall have to write to him. We are all severely grief-stricken.

ж

The news that met me on our return to Santo Domingo was that Serrano had been arrested. That in itself, to tell the truth, did not surprise me overly; for Serrano, I had no doubt, was as much a petty crook as a drunk. But then Fray Pedro informed me that the Alcalde Mayor had sent Ramírez, his morisco dogsbody, with a troop of Castle soldiers to take him. When asked why the man was being taken into custody, Ramírez had replied: "We'll find that out when we get him to the Castle, Padre." Such are the puffed-up! So it was as plain as day that Serrano's arrest had little to do with petty crookery. So the next day, I was obliged to make my way to the Castle.

Rudolfo de Paz received me in his lair. Dressed like the fop that he is, he was counting money as I was ushered in by Ramírez, stacks of silver coins on the table in front of him. Counting money is one of his favourite activities.

"A tipple?" he said.

He was drinking a glass of Jerez wine.

I declined.

"The Pharaoh's pigs," he said, referring to the money, "from the licences to hunt them. Last year we took in over three thousand pesos. The creatures are a bloody plague. But a lucrative one."

I refrained from pointing out that because of the depredations of him and his like, it wouldn't surprise me if there were more pigs than people on the island now. But I got straight to the point. I was afraid of the man, but I was determined that it not prevent me from speaking plainly to him. I said Serrano had been in our care, our spiritual care, and that I wanted to see to him.

"Non possumus, I'm afraid, Padre." But before I could object, he took pleasure in explaining why. "The poor man is no longer with us. In a better place now, I suppose. But you would know more about that than I do, I dare say. He was not in very good health. Too much liquid sugar. Did what we could. I took a great interest in his case. Saw to his arrest and detention personally. But sadly he just went and died on us. Sad, but there we are. Ashes to ashes."

Hiding my rage, I asked if he had been given the last sacraments, and by whom, thinking that if he had been granted that final grace, then it must have been by one of the Franciscans, whom perhaps I might be able to question later.

"It was terribly sudden, very unexpected," he said, wincing. It's a habit of his when he is about to say something disagreeable that will give him pleasure. "There was no time. But he did make a last confession – in a manner of speaking. A rather comprehensive last confession. Does that count?"

The serpent-like creature likes to talk, so I said nothing. He was sure to tell me more.

"Serrano had a long and interesting yarn to tell," he continued. "He was a seaman on the *Trinity*. That was that ship that was lost a few years back on the way from Santa María la Antigua del Darién. I'm sure you remember."

I remained stony-faced.

"They ran aground on some God-forsaken sandbank and had to take to a boat," he went on. "They were hoping to reach here or Xaymaca but the currents and the winds carried them to some terra incognita. Numerous adventures followed. A right seaman's tale. Man-eating Canibas. Riches beyond imagination. Eventual rescue. The usual sort of thing. And smuggling and illegal voyages. Two activities which, as I'm sure you are aware, the Crown takes a very dim view of, a very dim view indeed. The King does not take too kindly to being cheated of his quinto. It was a very exhaustive account. Perhaps Serrano saw his days might be drawing to an end. His health ... Men sense these things. Their memories seem to improve considerably when the prospect of meeting their Maker becomes tangible, when the possibility of final unpleasant consummation looms. They fancy they can somehow put off the inevitable by spilling it all out, making a clean breast of it, as it were. In my humble experience."

He gave some more details of what Serrano had confessed – which the serpent had no doubt tortured out of him – but there was not much in his account that differed in any essential from that which has been described earlier in these pages. But then he came to Goya.

"The deceased had an accomplice in all this," he said. "A Carlos Goya."

He paused for a moment but I held my tongue.

"A Jewman," he added.

Again I said nothing.

"A reconciliado to be precise," he continued, "from Granada. A man who had denied the faith but to whom the Tribunal of the Holy Office of the Inquisition, in its unfathomable mercy, had given a second chance. But you know more about these things than I do, I'm sure."

"Such mercy is extended only to those who have repented, made a solemn undertaking to mend their ways and accepted the penances laid upon them," I felt obliged to point out.

"But the law, the King's law, is very clear about such persons," he said. "It is a serious crime for Jewmen to set foot upon the soil of these dominions. As is aiding and abetting ... aiding and abetting a man who is, without doubt, a reconciliado and quite possibly a secretly practicing Jew to boot. Once a Jew, always a Jew. Perhaps he has accomplices. Blood is thicker than water and all that. Even than the water of baptism."

He stared at me for a long moment and I wondered if he was referring to my own ancestry, but then how would he have known? Puccini knew of course, and now Sor Lucrezia too – a foolish indiscretion on my part perhaps? – though I was sure my secret was safe with her.

"And," he continued. "I think one can safely assume that a man who has broken one law has little compunction in breaking others. I am presuming of course that Serrano told you none of this."

I chose to consider that as a statement rather than a question and again said nothing.

"And to top it all," he continued, "apparently this Jewman fellow is still amongst us, living in Concepción or thereabouts. Needless to say, when I learnt of all of this, I got my people in Concepción to initiate inquiries. Posthaste in fact ..." He paused, wondering how I would react but I continued to play the silent priest. "You have just returned from there yourself, I believe?"

"You are well informed," I said.

"It is my business to be," he said. "I keep tabs on things, as you know."

As indeed I did know.

"Sailors' tales," I suggested unthinkingly, perhaps wisely or unwisely, I do not know.

"This Goya character did a lot of wandering, sniffing about," he said. "Serrano seemed to think he might have found the Gold Land."

"There is not a beggar," I pointed out, "a would-be hidalgo or caballero in the Indies who does not believe that over the next mountain range or on the next island some country lies in wait, its roads paved with gold, its roofs tiled with the stuff. Serrano's brain was addled from too much liquid sugar, as you say. I'm surprised he didn't tell you this Goya had found the Fountain of Youth or some other cock and bull story."

He seemed to find that funny.

"Perhaps," he laughed, "but I can assure you he was very sober when he made his ... last confession. Very sober indeed." Again he paused. He is a cruel man. "He said this Goya made a map."

"A map!" I repeated, genuinely surprised. Serrano had not mentioned any map to me, nor had Goya.

"Yes," he said, looking at me for many moments more than was decent or polite. The foppish fox was trying to ascertain if my surprise had been genuine. "Serrano said that this Jewman made a quadrant of some sort and drew himself a map."

I remembered what Goya had said about his making a quadrant, how he had dismissed it as something to keep him occupied, about the devil finding work for idle hands. But I had found nothing even resembling a map in Goya's meagre papers. Rudolfo Jesus de Paz spoke again before I could speculate any further.

"Now, if that is the case ..." – he paused for a moment and winced that perverse wince of his – "... secret mapmaking, spying, perhaps for some foreign power, for the enemies of the King. That makes this whole sorry tale very grave indeed."

The thought did cross my mind to tell him that I had met Carlos Goya. He would in any case, my reasoning went, eventually find out, so might it not be better to spit it out there and then, to have done with it – but had I not already denied, or as good as, that Serrano had revealed anything to me or that I knew anything of Carlos Goya? So I decided to remain mute.

I was about to go when he spoke again.

"There's an execution tomorrow," he said. "A poisoning case. The crime of women, servants and primitives. Of a creature who attempted to poison his master."

"Attempted?" I said.

"Yes," he said. "No doubt about it. He made a full confession."

"Like Serrano?" I suggested. He did not detect my sarcasm, or pretended not to.

"Yes, just like Serrano," he said. "Abominable crime. And particularly abominable because his master trusted him. He used to let him feed his dogs." Because they will never attack the hand that feeds them, a Haytian needs to be greatly trusted before his master will let him feed his dogs. "The judges were quite severe. But justice often is severe. The dogs first – an appropriate embellishment I thought – and then he's to be roasted alive – on a spit, rather slowly."

I told him what I thought in no uncertain terms. There is not a Castilian in the Indies who does not live in terror of being poisoned by his Haytian servants – with casabe juice or frog-slime arrow-tip poison – and who does not imagine he has been poisoned every time he has the vomits or the shits, which is often enough. As for confessions: rigorous examination may be indispensable to root out evil; and no man should be capitally punished if he has not subsequently freely confessed or unless there is some other overwhelming proof of his evil-doing, but the safeguards need to be followed meticulously. Which is rarely the case when a Haytian is accused by a Castilian.

"The redskin is not like us," he said calmly when I had finished. "You know that as much as I do, except you won't openly admit it. His vice is sloth. His society is based on sloth."

"As ours is based on greed," I suggested, but he ignored that insight.

"He's a near-feminine creature," he went on, "not even capable of growing whiskers or a beard – with the vices of a woman. He's a child of the woods, a recalcitrant child."

"And perhaps with the virtues of women too?" I retorted.

"If every man just did as he pleased, no civilisation would be possible," he said, "no greatness. We should all be running around naked, adoring idols and living in grass hovels, singing and dancing our lives away. Civilising the savage calls for severity at times. For the bridle and the bit!"

"Even if it exterminates him?" I replied. It never ceases to surprise me that a man who has taken the trouble to learn the tongue of a people – a tongue whose grammar bears no resemblance to civilised tongues – can hold that people in such contempt. "That would be the greatest crime ever committed."

He shrugged his shoulders.

"Or an act of God," he countered. "But I think you exaggerate. In time, as the savage accepts the ways of Christian civilisation, we will become milder, and this will be a happier land, happier than it ever was, and its inhabitants will learn to work and live in stone houses. If some wild and dirty tribes must fall by the wayside, then so be it. Unfortunate, but the progress of Christianity has never been without its casualties. Nations come and go. As a priest, you should know that better than anyone else. The land of Israel was not empty when Joshua and Caleb led the Hebrews out of the desert and sacked its cities. There are quite a few examples in our Holy Book of whole peoples whom the Lord commanded to be wiped from the face of the earth, I believe, but I'm not a great reader."

"With Christ came a new dispensation," I retorted. "The parable of the Good Samaritan enjoins us to love the stranger as we would ourselves."

"Perhaps, Padre, perhaps," he said. "Theology is beyond my remit. But it is not us who are exterminating – your word, not mine – the nations of these islands. They die of sickness for the overwhelming part. And no man sickens and dies unless the Almighty allows it. Or have I misunderstood some essential tenet of our holy faith?"

I controlled my rage.

"But theology aside," he continued, "do you really think that it is our aim to so deplete the workforce of these islands to the extent that we have to – at great expense – import black men all the way from Africa, dangerous prisoners-of-war and criminals who'd cut our throats as soon as look at us?" He had a point. In 1503, Isabela forbade the import of Berber and African slaves on the grounds that many of them had rebelled and gone over to the Haytians and infected them with the spirit of disobedience. But a good proportion of the African slaves landed in recent shipments were mere youths, some of them barely out of childhood. But I held my tongue. "We may be accused of many things but to accuse us of a lack of self-interest is preposterous, I would suggest, respectfully. We shall make this land better, more fruitful than it has ever been. Future generations of Christian gentlemen will sit at table and, while enjoying the fruits of our labours, will consider all that we are doing today. At times, no doubt, they may well lament how it was all done, utter some pangs of regret for an imaginary lost Eden, and perhaps condemn our occasional excesses, and laugh at our follies; but they will find, on balance, that it was all well done, and inevitably done, that there was a kind of destiny in it. And who but a fool stands in the way of destiny?"

"And smug and ignorant men they shall be," I told him.

"This Goya," he said, ignoring my comment, "told Serrano that the people of the countries he had visited practiced human sacrifice. Are you suggesting that we, as civilised Christians, stand by and allow that? But enough of morality. This poisoner is a convert, officially at any rate. We need somebody to take his last confession. Perhaps you or one of your brothers could oblige?"

"To save him from further torment?" I suggested, with as much sarcasm I could muster.

"More of a legal nicety," he said.

But I agreed of course.

Before I left he asked me if I wanted Serrano's body. "It's still quite fresh", he said.

The last thing he said – he had no doubt saved it for the moment of my departure – was: "There was something which Serrano didn't tell me. Something that didn't occur to me at the time of my ... er ... conversation with him."

"What was that?" I asked him.

"The *Trinity* was lost," he said, "but it didn't quite sink, not immediately anyway. Which meant that they would have had time ..."

"Time?" I said, barely keeping my patience. "Time for what?"

"Time to unload the gold they were carrying," he said. "There was a not inconsiderable amount on board, I'm told."

"Perhaps they had other concerns," I countered. "Like water and food."

And I was thinking that if they had managed to salvage the gold, Serrano would surely have blabbered it out in the numerous conversations I'd had with him.

"Perhaps," he said. "At first I thought they might have buried it on the sandbank ... or even left it on the ship thinking to come back for it later. They would have known where they were ... more or less ... but then sandbanks come and go. The more logical thing would have been to load it onto their boat and take it with them. After all, they thought they were not that far from Xaymaca. But things went wrong and they ended up where they did. I try to imagine it. Let us suppose that Serrano's tale of them being captured is true. It would probably not have happened immediately after they landed – I somehow think that there was not a Caniba welcoming party on the beach waiting for them. No, they were probably captured later, even days later. But even if it had been a matter of hours, they would have had time to bury it. The logical thing to do, all things considered. They would hardly have intended to stay on the beach. They would have wanted to find water, food ... and gold is heavy. It would explain this Goya making a quadrant later. With a quadrant, he could have made a map, a map with the location of where they'd buried it. A bit of an oversight on my part ... not to have asked our dear departed before he departed, of course. But when it did occur to me ..." – he held out the palm of his hand and blew upon it, as if blowing away some dust or a feather – "... he was gone. Gone to the winds. Just like that."

The man is a serpent, truly a serpent.

"In any case," he added, "I'm expecting news from Concepción before the week is out. I am confident that this Goya will be able to throw some light on the matter."

Gold. Gold. Gold. Jesus de Paz and all his like are obsessed with it, by the very thought of it, and will follow any old wives' tale and fancy they think will enable them to get their paws on it. But his suspicion that the gold from the *Trinity* had been saved and subsequently buried, and that Goya had made a map of where they had buried it, was not illogical. If that were the case, then Rudolfo Jesus de Paz would torture the truth out of Carlos Goya and, no doubt, try and find the gold – and he would also learn of our visit to him. The scenario that presented itself to my mind was thus: buried treasure or not, once in de Paz's hands, Goya would confess all, and anything else the Alcalde Mayor wished him to confess; and that confession would be signed, witnessed and dispatched to Seville on the next available ship. Our order, it would 'reveal', was conspiring with Jews to do all manner of things – preposterous of course, but devious words and manipulative phrases can lead men to believe in the most outlandish things. I could almost see the document before my eyes as if it had already been penned. It would claim how out of a misguided concern for the welfare of His Catholic Majesty's Indian vassals – the serpent would phrase it oh so politely and humanely – certain monks of the Dominican Order of the Preachers had conspired with secretly practicing Jews who were intent on a malicious revenge for the expulsion of their tribe from His Majesty's dominions; and how these secret Jews had smuggled themselves to the Indies and were making clandestine explorations and maps of those, as yet, undiscovered heathen lands which had been granted into His Majesty's care as a sacred trust by the late Supreme Pontiff Alexander VI in his bull *Inter Caetera Divinae*. It would paint flowery fantasies of riches undreamt, hint at involvement with the machinations of His Majesty's foreign enemies, and God only knew what else. Such were my thoughts as I left the Castle. I heard the poisoner's confession that very afternoon. He had, in fact, attempted to murder his master, but to reveal more would be to breach the sacred seal of the confessional. We said a mass for the departed soul of Franco Serrano the next day and laid him to rest in our churchyard.

Ж

Executions take place in a field outside the northern gate. One took place this morning, of an Indian who attempted to poison his master. The criminal was accompanied by Fray Montenegro, a grievous duty I do not envy him. We could hear the man's screams here in our nunnery, faintly but clearly. I instructed my beatas to offer up a decade of the rosary for the repose of the man's soul. If good men require to be prayed for, then how much more do evil men require our prayers?

Ж

It was a ghastly event, as the administration of justice invariably is, in every country of the world that I have seen or have read of or been told of. The whole sanguinary affair was presided over by de Esquival, Carnage himself, who remained mounted on his mare throughout, gaping at the proceedings as heartlessly as a stone. There were very few Christians among the public audience, barring de Esquival's troopers. The Haytians, who made up the bulk of the crowd, were mute and showed no enthusiasm for it, as is invariably the case at these events. The poisoner's corpse – what remained of it – was left hanging on a tree as an example. It was only when I had recomposed myself sufficiently – it always requires a day or two for me to regain some balance of mind after these events – did I feel confident enough to speak to Fray Pedro regarding the implementation of our plan, without of course revealing anything of my conversation with Rudolfo Jesus de Paz or anything regarding Carlos Goya. I suggested that it might be politic to postpone its implementation until the Governor had returned from his tour of the other possessions, that its impact would be greater if he learnt of it with his own ears and in the presence of his retinue. His expected return was at least several weeks away and those weeks would give me time to pray for the wit to think up some ruse by which I could manoeuvre myself out of the predicament de Paz had placed me in – or failing that, for some divine intervention.

Ж

Montenegro brought a Hieronymite priest over to our nunnery this morning. At first I thought it was out of politeness, we being of the same order. He was a wizened grey-haired bearded man, his cheeks and stubby nose burned a dark brown by the sun and elements. After introductions – his name is Pater Alonso – Montenegro told me he had recently returned from the Lucayas. These are the islands that dot the northern coast of Cuba. Don Cristóbal first made landfall on one of them.

"Tell her what you told me," Montenegro said then, quite abruptly.

"It started with trickery," this Pater Alonso said, "but now they are raiding all the islands and bringing in every living soul they can lay their hands on."

"Trickery?" I said. "I do not understand."

"The Indians on the Lucayas," he explained, "believe that after death their souls are transported to mountains in the north where they are purified of their sins, but then, once purified, they will be brought to a warm land to the south, a sort of paradise. The slavers pretended that they were supernatural beings and that they would transport them on their ships to this paradise where they would meet their departed relatives and friends. Only a few fell for it of course. So then they started to use violence. They've taken three thousand in the last six months alone. God only knows how many they've slaughtered in the raiding they've done. And they've thrown a thousand overboard who've died on the voyage, like so much jetsam. Tribute to the sea they call it."

"Throwing valuable merchandise overboard?" I said, deciding to play the advocatus diaboli.

"Victuals cost money," he said, no doubt thinking me callous. "They reckon by packing as many of the poor souls aboard as a ship can hold, even if the third of them die of thirst and hunger on the voyage, they can make a greater profit than if they took less and fed them. One seaman told me that it's possible to find one's way to and from the islands without a compass or a chart ..." – the Lucayas are twenty leagues or more from the northern coast of the Spanish Island – "... simply by following the trail of bloated carcases bobbing around in the sea. A market has been set up on an island off the coast. Wives are separated from husbands, children wrenched from the arms of their mothers. They are shared out by the drawing of lots. Then they brand them in the face. Half of the Lucayas have been laid waste already. Empty except for wild animals and birds. The Useless Isles they are calling them now. Because they are neither a source of gold nor of the labour to mine it."

"Puccini told me they are also raiding the Giants and the Barbudos," Montenegro said, "and God only knows where else."

"But ...," I began, not quite sure what I was going to say, but Montenegro was not listening.

"... the inhabitants of which," he said, "the Pharaoh himself described – and I quote his very words – as being 'artless and generous with what they have to such a degree that of anything they have, if they be asked for it, they never say no, but do rather invite the person to accept it, and show as much lovingness as though they would give their hearts'. He promised to protect them from the predations of the Canibas. Vespucci raided them once too, kidnapped a few hundred of them and sold them in Seville."

But can all this be true? All these tales of atrocities? Can it be the case that a whole class of men, Christian born and bred, can have been so uninfluenced by the command to do unto one's neighbour as one would do unto oneself? Have the teachings of the Church and the sacraments been in vain? Can it be that Christians behave no better than infidels and pagans, or worse? That those who believe in the right things do the wrong? To be sure, many of the Christians here are puffed-up and greedy and arrogant, but that there are so very few who are virtuous is a proposition that our faith, it seems to me, prohibits me.

Later, as the good Pater Alonso and Montenegro were about to leave, Pater Alonso asked permission to use our facilities, leaving Montenegro and me alone together for a few moments.

"There is a problem," he said, looking about him rather

ridiculously, as if somebody might be eavesdropping on us. "Carlos Goya. The authorities have developed an unhealthy interest in him. Unhealthy for Goya, that is. And possibly unhealthy for us, both of us, should it be known that ... If anyone asks – and I mean *anyone* – I think it would be wise if nothing about our meeting him was said. Say simply that I was in Concepción to visit Puccini – for health reasons – and on other business of which you do not know the details. And that I asked you along with me simply in order that you become more acquainted with the country. If pressed, if it is unavoidable, say you met many people, but cannot remember all their names."

But then Pater Alonso reappeared and our conversation was cut short.

EIGHTEEN

I had a long conversation with Alfredo Castro last week. Castro is the master tile maker I mentioned earlier and who came here with Don Cristóbal Colón and his seventeen ships on the second voyage in 1493. He is a tall skinny man, well into his fourth decade, bald as an egg, sports a blue Basque beret to hide it, though he is not a Basque, and has a surprisingly good set of teeth for his years. He has some sort of facial twitch or tick, which gives one the impression that he is winking at one much of the time, and obliges one to make an effort to concentrate on what he is actually saying and not be distracted by the constantly changing expression on his face.

"The truth is," he said, beginning his tale, "to this day I still don't know what was in our heads when we signed up. That is was a dream-armada sailing to the Gold Land? Streets paved with gold? Mountains of gold? Rivers of the stuff?"

I take liberties with regard to his precise words: an artisan, his language is coarse and not given to great discrimination, but this is how I believe he would have spoken, had he been graced with more refinement; though I will attempt to keep the flavour of his speaking, for truth's sake.

"The journey across was smooth enough," he told me, "twenty sunny days from the Fortunate Isles to the first sight of land on this side. Then we spent weeks hopping from island to island, seeing the sights. We even landed on the Baptist's for a bit. It was near to two months after our first sight of land when we finally got to La Navidad, or rather what was left of it."

La Navidad was the first settlement the Admiral founded. It was out of necessity, his flagship the *Santa Maria* having been wrecked, making it impossible for him to return to Christendom with all his crews. He had left thirty or more men there.

"The place was cinders and ashes, burnt to the ground. Not a Christian alive. We found no more than a half a dozen bodies to give a Christian burial to. The local cacique, a crafty devil who went by the name of Guacanagarí, gave us a cock and bull story about it being Canibas that had done it. And he also gave the Pharaoh some gold by way of compensation – though how much nobody ever really found out – and supplied us with food. So it suited the Pharaoh to believe him, you might say. We searched the pueblos all round. I was with the party that found the Moorish cloak, a fine piece of work, in a bohío. Some of the men who'd been on the first voyage recognised it as belonging to one of the men who'd been at La Navidad. It was still in its chest, as new as the day it was bought, all folded neatly. Worth a couple of maravedís, a fact even the most wooden-headed thieving Caniba would surely have been aware of, you'd imagine. We found the anchor of the *Santa Maria* in another bohío in another pueblo. But the Pharaoh wanted it not to be Guacanagarí's lot that had done it. So that was that. Maybe it was Canibas. Who knows? But Bernaldo Boyle, the Apostolic Nuncio, and the hidalgos didn't believe a word of it. They wanted to garrotte Guacanagarí on the spot, burn the pueblos and enslave the lot of them. But the Pharaoh stood his ground. Some were for building the settlement there but the Pharaoh was against it. So we all got in the ships again and sailed further up the coast, beating against the wind all the way – for twenty-five days, longer than it took us to cross the Oceanus Occidentalis, to cover just over thirty sea miles, a hundred and thirty land miles. We stopped where we stopped because we hadn't the strength to go any further, and that's the truth of it. By then it had been half a year since we'd left Cadiz. Half the provisions had spoiled, and we'd near enough run out of vino. The casks had leaked. And half of us had the fevers and the shits.

"Anyway, we unloaded the ships and set about building the so-called City of Isabela. The Pharaoh decided to christen it that in honour of the Queen. To formally mark its founding – on the Feast of the Three Kings – Bernaldo Boyle officiated over a high mass on the headland, assisted by his twelve apostles – that's what we used to call his twelve Franciscans. We put the stockade up first and then started on the stables, the barracks, the arsenal, the storehouse and the church. And on the Pharaoh's mansion. Two storeys high it was eventually, bigger than the church itself. He even ordered pewter cutlery, silver cups and jugs, brass candlesticks and tablecloths from Spain, not that they ever arrived. It was never really properly finished. Don't know how we managed to build what we did really, considering, but we did. You wouldn't believe the amount of trees we had to cut down – we needed wood to bake bricks and tiles, for the forges, and to cook of course. We even built a few ships later on.

"We probably would have starved if the redskins hadn't been willing to trade for food. We still had loads of beads and mirrors and those little Flemish hawk's bells at that stage. The Ciguayos, as they called themselves, were in and out of the place all the time. They used to kneel and cross themselves in front of the statue of the Virgin that Bernaldo Boyle had put up in front of the church. They loved copying us and were totally mystified with the most common things. They were as bewildered by locks and keys as a monkey would be. They traded as if they were giving one a gift, or something like that, and food they often just gave us, if they were not short of it. Could never put my finger on what was going on in their heads. The Pharaoh used to trade with them for gold, which in those days was like stealing toys from a child. But – officially – the Pharaoh was the only one allowed to play that game.

"His plan was that half of us would farm the land. The Pharaoh and his cronies would do the trading, Boyle and his apostles would do the converting, and the hidalgos the protecting – which meant sitting on their arses most of the time. Not a very popular plan, to tell the truth. After all, what's the point of sailing halfway across the world to break your back behind a plough when you can do the same just as well back in Castile?

"The business with the horses was the first big trouble, a sign of things to come really. The Pharaoh wanted to work them but the Granada hidalgos were not having it and there was a ferocious row about that – and other things. Bernaldo Boyle and the Pharaoh didn't see eye to eye on much. Some men were garrotted. For fomenting rebellion, the Pharaoh said. My kiln was a mile or so away, and sometimes I used to sleep there, so I wasn't able to follow all that was going on that well.

"Then the sicknesses came, just out of the blue, a few weeks after we'd landed. We were knackered from the journey of course, and the lack of proper food and vino. A few men had already died. But then suddenly we were dropping like flies. It hit the redskins too, worse, far worse than it hit us. Vomiting, rashes, fevers, you name it. We were burying men from dawn to dusk. Boyle's twelve apostles – no disrespect – were earning their crust, and that's a fact. And the Ciguayos were doing whatever they did with their dead, and they had some strange customs in those days. Still have, many of them, not that there are as many of them. And with them dropping like flies too, they stopped coming to the settlement with food – or bringing gold in. So we had to more or less fall back on the supplies we had brought with us on the ships.

"The Pharaoh started to send de Hojede out to look for gold, sometimes with fifteen men, sometimes with fifty, always on foot, and always accompanied by the royal accountant. He could have sent the hidalgos – it's not as if they were doing anything, and they'd have been willing enough, despite the trouble about the horses – but he didn't trust them as far as he could throw them. De Hojeda would come back saying there was loads of it, that it was all over the place. Don't know if he actually brought much back. If he was, nobody was telling us about it. And besides, the redskins were learning its true value then, or beginning to anyway. They're not as stupid as we like to think they are. I suppose we were also copping on to the fact that our baubles were worth a trifle more a million miles from Spain than they were in your Seville bazaar. We'd already traded away a lot of them for food – and for gold, not that we commoners ever saw bugger all of that. And in the middle of all this, most of the ships sailed back to Seville, leaving us with five.

"By April or so, when most of the buildings were sort of habitable, and the first floor of the Pharaoh's mansion was done, his lordship decided to launch an expedition into the interior, announce our presence in style. So one fine morning, five hundred men marched out in rank and file. Half of those that were left were bed-ridden, not that they had beds. I remember it well: the Pope's and the Queen's colours flying high, drums rolling, trumpets sounding, the Pharaoh at the van, Bernaldo Boyle beside him, the hidalgos in their polished corslets and crested helmets and on their horses, a hundred arquebusiers, their weapons on their shoulders, and as many arbalesters, quivers full, with two dozen builders trailing behind. The plan was also to build a fort somewhere. The redskins – and God only knows how many of them had died of the sicknesses by then – had never seen the like of it: the horses, the pigs and the dogs especially, armoured men, steel, arquebuses ... Though, as we learnt later, trying to hit one of the buggers with an arquebus was near impossible, unless they were in a crowd, but the noise terrified them. Give me a decent arbalest any day – or even a hand-drawn crossbow."

The arquebus, while it can strike terror into the heart of an enemy, is considered inaccurate and prone to misfiring due to damp powder; and many an arquebusier has blown himself up either because of a fault in the construction of the weapon or through carelessness with the smouldering wick and bags of powder he is required to carry with him when in combat.

"And while the Pharaoh was out playing Alexander the Great, there was a fire," he continued. At times I really did think he was winking at me. "Half of the buildings were destroyed. One disaster after another really, when you look back on it. You should've seen the look on the Pharaoh's face when they returned. But the main thing was they'd brought casabe back with them, carried by press-ganged Ciguayos.

"They'd left Margarit with fifty men in the Vega Real to build a fort at Santo Tomás. The Vega was teeming with Indians in those days. But they weren't back a week when Margarit sent word saying that the redskins were deserting their pueblos around the fort and he believed that Caonabó – he was the cacique of the Ciguayos – was planning to attack and slaughter the lot of them. There was a rumour going around at the time too that it was Caonabó, not Guacanagarí – or the Canibas – who was responsible for what had happened at La Navidad. Anyway, the Pharaoh then sent de Hojeda with four hundred men, nearly as much as on the original expedition, to reinforce Margarit at Santo Tomás, but it was really more of – what do the military men call it? – a preventive strike. Before they left, there was the usual mass and prayers to the good old Moor Killer. The Pharaoh himself spoke from the pulpit. The church was packed, the doors open, more than half the men outside; but they heard him, he could shout when he wanted to. I can remember his words as if it were only yesterday. 'Your mission, men,' he said, 'is to pacify the Vega Real. To demonstrate Christian power and skill at arms, and bring them to respect us. But show them that no harm will come to them as long they do not oppose us. Pacify them – and by terror if needs be.' The men were to live off the land.

"Then, to top it all – de Hojeda and his army weren't gone two weeks – when the Pharaoh decided to sail off in search of the Gold Land and the Garden of Eden, taking two of the remaining caravels and a nao with him. He left his brother Don Diego in charge – he used to dress as a priest you know, could barely speak a word of Castilian – along with Boyle. It was another six months before we saw him again.

"In the Vega ... well, four hundred half-starved and women-hungry Castilians, armed to the teeth, wandering from pueblo to pueblo living off the land ... not a pretty sight at the best of times. If Caonabó hadn't been planning anything, he soon was. And most of the other caciques with lands in the Vega – Guarionex, Behechio, Higuamaná and Mayobanex – were joining him. But, funnily enough, Guacanagarí didn't. He stayed out of it. Sniffed which way the wind was blowing, I suppose. That was the first war. The redskins started to destroy their own crops so our men couldn't live off them, even stopped their own people from planting, a sort of scorched earth campaign, you could say. It went on for months. And in the middle of it, Margarit – half of his men had died of the boils – and Boyle skedaddled back to Spain on the ships that Don Bartolomé, the Pharaoh's other brother, had arrived on."

Montenegro speaks well of Margarit. He says that he subsequently pleaded for a just treatment of the Haytians before the Monarchs in the Alhambra. Of Bernaldo Boyle he has never spoken.

"Then the Pharaoh returned," Castro continued, "and announced he'd discovered a place called Cuba and that it was part of the mainland of India. He'd made the crews take an oath on the Holy Trinity that it was so, on pain of having their tongues cut out if they later said otherwise. Though word soon got around that the redskins there had told him Cuba was an island. Not to be believed really, but that's the truth of it. He was in a terrible state. He appointed Don Bartolomé Governor and spent the next few months bed-ridden, no doubt plagued by nightmares about what Margarit and Boyle were saying about him back in Spain.

"Don Bartolomé had more forts built, the one at Concepción and the one at Magdalena. But a few months after the latter was built, a cacique calling himself Guatiguará, if I remember correctly, a vassal of Guarionex, attacked the place and slaughtered every Christian he could lay his hands on. Forty men it must have been. The Pharaoh, who'd recovered by then, led the campaign against Guatiguará personally. He didn't manage to catch the bugger but they took a lot of prisoners. Fifteen hundred men, women and children. A sorry sight. The Pharaoh took the best of them, maybe five hundred, and loaded them onto the few ships that were there at the time and shipped them off to Spain. But such is the fate of the vanquished, is it not? He reckoned they'd fetch five thousand maravedís a head at the cathedral in Seville, not that we sees a coin of that." Slaves in Seville are auctioned off at the bottom of the steps of the cathedral. "Them that was left was shared out among the rest of us, each according to his rank, as the saying goes. I took two of them for the kiln. And, would you believe it, one actually turned out to be a potter. I caught him at it one day, making a cooking pot. The bugger had slipped it in the kiln behind my back. It wasn't half bad, as good as a lot of the stuff that's churned out in Castile. From the point of view of technique that is. But the decorations he'd made on the sides of it were ugly as hell. So I set him to making plain plates and jugs and cups and the like – though it wasn't until I'd set up shop in Santo Domingo that I'd started making pots in any quantity. The Pharaoh used to order crockery from Spain in the first years, even chamber pots, not that any arrived that I knew of. Anyway, the bugger knew his clay, that's for sure. Clay is not just clay, you know. It needs to be worked differently, fired different, depending on where it's from, not that differently, but enough to make a difference ..."

"What happened then?" I asked him. Like many craftsmen, he imagines the details of his trade are of interest to all, and no doubt he would have continued expounding endlessly upon it if left to his own devices.

"Oh, he never really took to it with any enthusiasm," he said. "I treated both of them well enough. I like to treat a man fair, give him his due, no matter what his condition. But I suppose they just couldn't let bygones be bygones. They just disappeared into the woods one night. There one day, gone the next. They're like that. Here one day, gone the next, if you give them half a chance."

"I mean at Isabela?" I said.

"Oh, the Pharaoh told the rest of them they could go," he continued, "that they were free, the old ones, the kids too young to work, nursing mothers and the like. At first they didn't understand but ... My God, did they run when they did. Never saw anything like it. They were terrified of us. Thought we were going to set the dogs on them, for sport or something, run after them and capture them again and eat them. And the truth is we were hungry enough." He laughed at that, but I felt unable to join him in his mirth, harmless though it was in its way. "Some of the nursing mothers left their children on the ground. Terrible thing to see really, mothers abandoning their infants like that. But then, they are not quite like us; so maybe, when all is said and done, we shouldn't judge them by Christian standards. They say the Queen was none too happy about the ones the Pharaoh sent back on the caravels. Half of them found watery graves. It was brought up at his trial, they say, when Bobadilla arrested him that time. Some even say that was what the trial was mainly about. 'How dare you enslave my subjects,' she said to him. Or so they say. Though there were other shipments as well. Some of them were sent back, you know.

"Anyway, as I've said, the Pharaoh didn't capture Guatiguará, but de Hojeda did capture Caonabó. It was during a siege at Santo Tomás, I think. He was brought into Isabela in chains. A small man – in a bad way really, they'd beat him about a bit, as you can imagine – but you could tell by looking at him he was a tough little bugger. When he was presented to the Pharaoh, he just shouted at him and spat on the ground. The hidalgos – most of the men in fact – wanted to garrotte him on the spot but the Pharaoh had qualms. Caonabó might be a savage, he said, but he was still a king, or at least a prince, and only kings had the right to try kings, so he decided to ship him back to Spain. He never made it of course. Died of a broken heart on the way across, they say.

"All this was too much for Guarionex and the other caciques, so they decided to march on Isabela. There were about five or six thousand of them. If they'd done it earlier, just after we'd landed, they could have raised five times that, but what with the sicknesses and the famine caused by their own stupidity, destroying their own crops and that, they were probably hard pushed to raise even that many. But the Pharaoh got wind of it – from Guacanagarí – and sent Don Bartolomé out to attack them first. Maybe two hundred men on foot, most of them armed with arquebuses and arbalests, twenty hidalgos and thirty to forty mastiffs or Irish hounds, and maybe a thousand of Guacanagarí's warriors. Don Bartolomé attacked their camp at night – which they were not expecting, it being against their sense of right and wrong to fight in the dark – and captured most of the caciques, including Guarionex himself.

"The Pharaoh could have shipped them all off to Castile but that would have meant they would simply have been replaced by their brothers or sons, or even their sisters or wives. Behechio was replaced by his sister, that Anacaona woman. They had their own ways of settling these things, and to tell the truth, to this day I still don't quite understand exactly how it works. But not the matter. If that happened, then he'd have to start all over again, as it were. A bird in the hand is worth a dozen in the bush, as they say. So he got them all to swear an oath of allegiance to the Crown in a big ceremony, with mass, flags, the lot. The royal accountant drew up articles of submission for them to sign, not that they could read a word of it, but they could make their marks, and that was good enough, and all legal like. They also agreed to pay the tributo and provide food and lodging for the Franciscan missionaries. I don't think it was quite clear to them that the tributo was not a once-off thing, or a thrice-off. But they all made their marks."

"But how," I asked him, "did so few win against so many? And do so again and again?"

"The sicknesses was the main thing," he said. "A Hieronymite once said to me that God had not so much sent the sickness to punish them ... For weren't we afflicted too? Plagues and diseases are punishments, he said, for the original sin of our first parents –

'the condition of our birth', he called it – and for the sins we commit willingly. And do not Christians sin as much as other men? No, he said, the sicknesses were not sent to punish the redskins, who were for the most part innocent of the faith – and even then, those that had been preached to had only been preached to for a short time, and then not well. It takes time for men to accept the truth. Even those that had converted, as had a lot of Guacanagarí's people, were still but infants in the faith, not to be judged with the full rigour of the law. No, he said, God was not cruel. He had merely allowed the sicknesses to come at a time that would bring us victory, for our victory was essential to the spread of Christianity. Angels on pinheads if you ask me. Of course, we had good Toledo steel, cannon, falconets, and the horses and the dogs. A pack of mastiffs or Irish hounds let loose on a bunch of naked savages is not a pretty sight. No, not pretty at all.

"In the beginning they didn't quite know what to make of us, whether we were even flesh and blood. They thought we'd come from the sky. Though they soon learnt that we were flesh and blood. And the Pharaoh, for all his faults, was canny. He was forever asking them about their way of waging war, how they would fight each other and all that. He used to have long palavers with Guacanagarí about it. He had even brought that Fray Pané fellow over with him especially to learn their lingo and their customs, so he could find out what they believed and who was vassal to whom and all that. They were used to fighting each other by their own rules; and if you knew those rules, it was easier to outwit them. The truth be told, they were not a warlike people, not really. Sometimes you had the impression that they'd as soon settle a war with a game with one of those funny bouncy balls as with a proper battle. But, at the end of the day, it was the sicknesses that did it. Not that you'd get any hidalgo to admit that. There's little glory in shit, boils, fevers and vomit."

"How did the tributo work?" I asked him. Fray Montenegro has told me much of the current system but little of what had preceded it; he has little interest in the mechanisms of politics or commerce, and neither was he here at that time. I wanted to have a clear image in my mind how it had come to an end and come to be replaced. To achieve any comprehension, beyond a superficial one, of the present state of affairs of any country, I feel it is always necessary to understand the circumstances which preceded that state of affairs.

"Every redskin over fourteen belonging to the caciques who

had accepted the Catholic Monarchs as their lords was obliged to deliver a hawk's bell of gold dust," he told me, "or, in places where there was no gold, twenty-five pounds of cotton, four times a year. Though later they were allowed to provide labour instead. There was a lot of building to be done, at Isabela and the forts. The gold dust and the cotton were to be delivered to the royal accountant at Isabela or to one of the forts every three months; though sometimes soldiers went to the pueblos to collect it. The Pharaoh had copper tokens minted and each time a redskin came in with the goods he – or she – was given one. They had to wear them around their necks. When they came in the next time, they handed in the old tokens and got new ones with new dates stamped on them. If they were found without the right one, there was hell to pay. The caciques were to see that all this was done. It worked much of the time. For the most part. In a muddled sort of way."

At this point he became distantly pensive, as he did at several points during our conversation, and was silent for a few minutes, winking and twitching more frequently. It was as if his spirit was being transported by some mechanism of his mind back to the times he was telling me of, and he was again seeing in his mind's eye all the sights he had experienced.

"There reigned a great bewilderment among them," he said when he spoke again, "what with the sicknesses and the lack of food. They had to move from one place to another to pan the rivers for gold, so that at any one time half of them were not tending to their gardens. Neither was the authority of the caciques what it had been before. There was less fighting, but it never really stopped; and the hidalgos and the soldiers marauding all over the place, exploring for gold mines, just added to the general chaos. Couldn't last really. Three years later, when the Pharaoh was off in Spain, Guarionex rebelled again."

"Again," I said, somewhat surprised. My impression from what he just told me was that victory over the Indians had been complete.

"Aye," he said. "The buggers kept coming back for more. Guarionex's territory was less affected by the famine. I was in Concepción at the time, setting up a kiln, when it happened, or rather when we heard the rumours. And they gave cause for concern, as the saying goes. It had been known for a while that the redskins had gotten their hands on arquebuses – when they'd taken Magdalena that time, and other times too – and arbalests, but they hadn't really learnt to use them, the arquebuses that is ...

but now it appeared they had. Though we didn't know then, or weren't sure, whether they'd managed to get their hands on any powder. Put a different colouring on things, as you can imagine. But Don Bartolomé was quick enough to act. Again he attacked at night, several camps at the same time, and captured Guarionex and the caciques who were in cahoots with him. It wasn't clear what he was planning to do with them. Ship Guarionex off to Spain? Try the others on the spot and garrotte them? They were caciques but hardly kings, more like impoverished caballeros really. Guarionex, of course, was different. He was what they call a guamiquina, a cacique of caciques.

"Anyway, before Don Bartolomé had decided anything, a procession was making its way to Concepción. There must have been a good few thousand of them, three or four maybe. They'd come from Guaranico. Men, women, children, old ones. Unarmed. As naked as the day they were born, or as near as. It's not true that they didn't wear any clothes ever, you know. The older women wore short cotton skirts a lot of the time, and the caciques and the warlocks were wont to wear embroidered shifts on occasion. Quite a few of them had taken to wearing Christian castoffs whenever they could get their hands on them. Anyway, this was the last thing anyone had expected. But old Guarionex was well-loved, that's for sure. We'd heard they were coming just before they arrived. Don Bartolomé and the hidalgos were waiting for them, mounted on their horses, along with the rest of the garrison, just outside the gates. There was also a priest, an old man, beard down to his tits, a Franciscan. I knew him from Isabela.

"The sun was blasting out of the sky, I remember that. The rest of the settlement was there too, maybe two hundred Christians in all, along with a sprinkling of women and kids. We didn't know what to expect really. Then we saw them. They just appeared in the distance – out of the heat haze – silent, slowly walking towards us like some ghost-army. There was a woman at the head of them, carrying a baby, wearing feathers. Guarionex's wife, or one of them, or maybe his sister. I'm not sure. The silence was unnerving. They are a noisy lot usually; at least they were in those days. But that day that crowd was as quiet as a funeral procession. Don Bartolomé ordered the falconets primed – there were two pieces – and the arquebusiers to load their weapons and mount them. He had Guarionex brought out, in chains, an iron collar around his neck, led by one of the hidalgos, like a dog on a leash.

"By then the crowd had stopped, maybe a hundred varas in front of us, but the feathered woman with the child kept walking towards us. She walked right up to Don Bartolomé. She was a small thing, and looked even smaller standing there in front of Don Bartolomé in his armour and crested helmet on his big brown mare. I was standing nearby. To be honest, I thought he was going to order the arquebusiers to fire – when he'd ordered them to load and aim – but this little woman with her child walking up to him like that ... it sort of took him aback.

"It looked like she was going to say something to him. But she didn't. Instead, she turned to Guarionex and started to talk to him, in Haytian. Don Bartolomé looked at the Franciscan, expecting him to translate, but the priest just shrugged and said she was talking too fast for him to follow. 'Tell them to disperse,' Don Bartolomé said, ignoring the woman and Guarionex. 'Do it now! Tell them to disperse!' The man's Castilian was atrocious. He could barely speak a sentence proper. The Franciscan cupped his hands and shouted at the Indians, translating what Don Bartolomé had said, repeating it several times. I didn't understand a word of it of course, but it sounded like he was more pleading at them than ordering them. Then the woman turned towards the crowd – turning her back on Don Bartolomé on his mare, which just infuriated him further. Then she shouted at the crowd – what I don't know of course – completely ignoring Don Bartolomé, which threw him into even more of a rage. 'Dogs to the front!' he was screaming. 'Dogs to the front! Show them the fuckin' dogs!'

"We had nearly fifty dogs that day. They'd bred well over the years. The mere sight of them was enough to put the terror of hell into anyone, Christian or heathen. I saw the Franciscan look at Don Bartolomé, an expression of horror in his eyes – yes, that's what you'd call it, I suppose, horror. He made to say something but before he could get a word out, Don Bartolomé was screaming at the top of his voice again, trying to make himself heard above the dogs – they'd smelled blood. 'What's the bitch saying?' he was screaming. 'What's she fuckin' saying? Tell her I'll do it. I swear by the Holy Trinity and the bones of the Moor Killer I'll set the fucking dogs on them if they don't disperse.' Then suddenly there was silence. Guarionex's woman stopped talking. Even the dogs seemed to have stopped howling and barking and straining at their leashes. The redskins began to get down on their knees, kneel down, first a few at the front and then, like a flock of birds all of one mind, they were all on their knees.

"Guarionex's woman knelt down too, this time facing Don

Bartolomé. She said nothing. She just knelt in front of him. The dogs started barking and howling again.

"'Tell them to get up!' Don Bartolomé was screaming at the Franciscan again. 'Tell them to get up! Tell them if they don't get up they're meat, tell them ... I'm going to count to ten.' And he started counting. 'One, two, three ...' I think he'd just reached five when the Franciscan too knelt down, facing Don Bartolomé on his mare, closed his eyes and started to pray, out loud, almost calmly. 'Blessed are the meek! Blessed are the peacemakers!' he was saying. I don't know the rest of it. Guarionex's woman was weeping, tears running down her tattooed cheeks, rocking the baby in her arms to shush it. Then, slowly at first, all the redskins began to chant, in unison: 'Guarionex, Guarionex ...' and something else which of course I didn't understand, but not insolent, more like a plea, a desperate plea ... a cry of utter despair. Yes, I think you could call it that. A cry of utter despair.

"'Six!' Don Bartolomé shouted. 'Seven!' But then he stopped. It's not often you see shame on a man's face. Not here. This is hard country. But I saw it that day. Don Bartolomé Colón was suddenly ashamed of himself, more ashamed than I've ever seen a man. And it wasn't that kind of inconsequential shame you see on a man's face when he realises what an idiot he's made of himself after a few jugs of sugar wine. No, it wasn't that, nothing like it at all. But it was unmistakable and everyone saw it and for a few moments, if I didn't know better, I'd swear the clouds had stopped moving and the sun had stopped in the sky and even the dogs had fallen silent again. You could feel that shame in the very air, spreading from one man to another.

"'Eight,' I heard him say, but it was not much more than a whisper, and then suddenly he was pulling on the reins of his mare, turning her around and riding back into the stockade, the eye of every Christian upon him. I could say with his tail between his legs but that would be like making a joke ... like farting in a church. So I won't say it.

"I forget who Don Bartolomé's captain was that day. I forget his name, that is. But I remember what he looked like. As blond as a Northman. But he had the good sense to see that there was no danger from Guarionex's people, that they had simply come to beg for their cacique's release. Don Bartolomé had no doubt realised the same – in the very moment, I think, as he was about to set the dogs on them ..."

A womanservant brought us some chocol and he was silent while she served us. He lit a tabaco cigar before speaking again.

"It's impossible to know what goes on in another man's mind," he continued. "Don Bartolomé should have known from the beginning that there was no danger but there was more to it than that ... Much wrong has been done here, by all of us, done more by some than by others ... Sins have been done ..."

As he told me this it seemed as if he had become unaware that I was there – as if he was actually again reliving the events he had described in his mind's eye, as vividly as he had on the day. For a moment I thought he was going to confess some of his own sins but then, suddenly, he emerged into the present again and decided to continue his tale.

"There were quite a few religious in Concepción that day, Franciscans mainly," he went on. "Fray Pané was there, he was living and missionising in Guaranico at the time, along with his right-hand man, Diego Colón II ..."

"Diego Colón II?" I asked, mystified.

"Pané's interpreter," he explained. "He was one of the Haytians the Pharaoh brought back to Spain with him from the first voyage. He returned with him on the second as an interpreter. He was baptised Diego Colón, so everyone calls him Diego Colón II. He's still alive. Lives in Santo Domingo. Has some sort of pension."

I wondered briefly, for a moment, how the Christian cities of Spain must have appeared to one of the first Indians to have crossed the Oceanus Occidentalis in the opposite direction. I was about to ask him what he imagined an Indian seeing civilisation for the first time might have thought, but he was already speaking again.

"If there had been a massacre, there would have been no covering it up," he said. "The captain, I'm sure, did not want his name mentioned in dispatches to the Alhambra. Funny, isn't it. What has to be covered up and what not. I suppose one needs a very sensitive nose for that sort of thing. In any case, he had the good sense to order all the soldiers and everyone else back inside Concepción, and when that was done, the gates were simply shut and barred.

"Guarionex's people stayed there all night. We could hear them singing. They are musical people. They'd dance their lives away like gypsies if given half the chance. But it was more like a lament they were singing that night, a sort of keening, like at a funeral. It was like listening to a choir of phantoms at times.

"The next morning, Guarionex and his caciques were released, with the usual promises and declarations of friendship and oaths of loyalty and all that. Don Bartolomé, you might say, had realised, as the Pharaoh had a few years earlier, that the devil you knew was better than the one you didn't. And Guarionex's lands were the richest. I moved to New Isabela shortly after that."

"And it was around then that the tributo system ended?" I said.

"Yes," he said. "Roldán's rebellion, if you can call it that, put an end to all that, more or less."

Francisco Roldán's name, on the few rare occasions when it crops up in conversation, invariably provokes evasiveness, as if the black sheep of a family had been mentioned at a gathering at which strangers were present; the conversation is hastily moved on to another theme. As to what sparked Roldán's revolt against Don Bartolomé: I had heard that it was because Roldán had been furious because Don Bartolomé had dared to punish one of Roldán's men for raping, in one version, seducing in another, one of Guarionex's wives. Perhaps it was the same incident Montenegro had referred to, the incident as a result of which Guarionex had burnt down the church that time.

"Roldán and Don Bartolomé didn't see eye-to-eye on a lot of things," Castro continued. "One of them being the tributo. Another was the Pharaoh's shipping slaves back to Spain, one of his favourite schemes. The Spanish Island, Roldán said, was useless without the labour to exploit it, and what with the redskins dying off from the sickness and hunger, shipping off men and women in their prime was lunacy, only cutting our own throats, killing the goose that lays the golden egg – with, of course, the lion's share of the profits going to the Colóns. He was not disloyal to the Crown – though they tried to say he was. When he raided the arsenal in Isabela, he made a point of saying he was doing so in the name of the King. And Don Bobadilla, when he arrived, recognised this. It was the Pharaoh that was sent back in chains, not Roldán. The common man, he used to say, and the redskin would make this country rich. We came here for gold and land, he said, not to spend our time collecting the tributo for the Pharaoh. We needed labour to mine the gold and work that land, labour that the Pharaoh was shipping off to Spain. And the tributo meant that most of the redskins could hardly feed themselves, not-a-mind produce extra. Learning the redskins decent Christian agriculture, he said, would make more sense than shipping them off to Seville.

"After the raid on the Isabela arsenal, men joined him in droves. They tried to capture Concepción but failed, so they ended up roaming the countryside, living of the land, skirmishing, making alliances. But everywhere he went he told the caciques that the tributo was abolished. Eventually, he and his men settled in Jaragua, along with their wives and servants and hanger-ons. Don Bartolomé and Don Diego could never muster enough men to defeat them, and especially not with all the redskin allies Roldán was gaining.

"The Pharaoh returned from Spain the following year to find not only did he not control the island but that Isabela had also been abandoned – and Guarionex had rebelled again, taken to the hills. The Pharaoh and Don Bartolomé wandered about and still tried to collect the tributo but there was less and less of it, which caused even more trouble. All the redskins they captured – the ones they thought were worth anything, that is – were marched to New Isabela to be shipped off to Seville on the next available caravel. Guarionex was also captured, along with Mayobanex, but this time they were not released, which of course made it near impossible to collect the tributo in Magua and Samaná. Roldán demanded that they all be released, and he made sure every cacique in the island knew he was demanding it, not that they were released. There was a lot of to and fro but eventually there were negotiations and the Pharaoh and Roldán actually met and hammered out an agreement. The Pharaoh agreed to declare a general amnesty – he had it nailed to the church doors in Concepción – and to grant a safe conduct pass to all those who wished to return to Spain. Three hundred men took the offer up. Roldán and the remaining roldanistas were granted encomiendas – the first granted. Most of them moved to the Vega Real and thereabouts, though Roldán was made Alcalde for Jaragua and he stayed there. Of course, then the colombistas also wanted encomiendas. The cat was out of the sack, you could say. And the Pharaoh had little choice but to grant them lands and the vassalage of the minor caciques.

"That's the origin of the system, I suppose. Though, even then, the Higüey and the Guacajarima caciques were still lords of their own lands, more or less; and the Anacaona woman was still queen in Xaraguá. Not that that lasted long. But most of the land that was worth anything had been shared out. Sounds neat and tidy, the way I'm telling it, but it was anything but really.

"Then Don Bobadilla arrived in New Isabela with his armada – and with the slaves the Queen had sent back – to be greeted by the sight of the decomposing bodies of seven Christians hanging on the gallows in the Plaza de Armas. That was in '99. The Pharaoh and Don Bartolomé were up country at the time, chasing redskins – and surveying the new gold seams, the richest found so far – but when they returned, Don Bobadilla arrested them. The Pharaoh tried to put the whole mess down to the machinations of conversos and Jews but Don Bobadilla said that was for the King and Queen to decide – and that they had ordered the Pharaoh be brought back to Spain. So the Pharaoh and Don Bartolomé were shipped off to the court at Granada."

After the Pharaoh's trial and acquittal of all the charges against him, one of which was in fact the illegal enslavement of some of the inhabitants of this island, Their Majesties Ferdinand and Isabela issued a solemn proclamation so that all settlers should know that all the inhabitants of the Spanish Island were free vassals of the Crown and not slaves. So how then, you may well ask, my dear Balthazar, is it that some have been enslaved or are labouring under such conditions which can only be described as so akin to slavery as to be indistinguishable from it? Though Indians are no longer shipped to Seville. But it is the fact of things. On the other hand – though I am no legal scholar or expert in natural rights and I know little of the details of such things – it seems to me indisputable that wars waged against those who sin against nature herself, man-eaters and sodomites, are by their very nature just, and that captives in such wars may be rightfully enslaved. Peace with such creatures is impossible. Saint Tomás of Aquino, if he had had to do with such peoples, would surely also have argued so. No Christian can stand idly by and say, like Cain, 'I am not my brother's keeper', and merely watch such crimes being committed. Peoples such as the Canibas need to be brought to their senses, to ways of truthful thinking and productive lives. Leaving them to their own devices, to roam at will, free of all hierarchy and restraint, recognising no laws but only their own crude and irrational customs, would be a failure with regard to one's duty to treat all men as one's brothers, even if that means, on occasion, the judicious use of rod. And this may require their enslavement. That this duty is abused, and large numbers of Indians who are not Canibas have been enslaved wrongly, or as good as, is of course a grievous wrong and to be unreservedly condemned.

As to how much of all of what Castro related to me is true, I do not know. Montenegro intimated that Castro himself was a so-called roldanista but, if he was, he gave no indication that he been anything but a bystander to the events he described.

"The redskin is not like us," he added when he had finished this account, in the tone of a storyteller who was about to finally reveal the moral of his tale. "I wouldn't say they have no souls for they can suffer well enough. It's more that ... it's sort of as if his feelings mimic ours. He's sad when his child dies but it is not quite our kind of sadness. In form he is like us – just like the Jew or the Moor – or would be if he didn't mutilate and paint himself, though he does that less now – but in essence he is different. His pain is pain, his joy is joy, but it's not quite the pain or the joy we Christians feel, even among the baptised among them. At first I used to think they were just pretending, play-acting, but now I know their feelings are real enough. It's not deliberate, it's the way the Good Lord made him. He can't help it, but once he knows who's master, you can get along quite well with him. The problem is that when he gives his word, it's not the sacred thing it is among us. A part of him thinks it's all a game, in a way. This makes him treacherous by nature. You know they believe they came from caves, the caverns of creation they call them, out of darkness, not from a garden. They have very little sense of sin, no sense of being cast out, of any need of salvation. Little sense of shame. They think nothing of walking around as naked as the day they were born. At least in the beginning, they did. Though the monks have learnt them some shame. That at least has been achieved. Your average redskin can be as stubborn as an ass and lazy. A dog has more get-up-and-go. Half the time it's as if he's going around in a daze. The work of one African is worth that of four of them. You have to be hard with him. It's the only way he learns. Fair, mind you, but hard."

This opinion – though usually expressed less philosophically – and variations of it, is common enough among the colonists; and though it is harsh and uncharitable in many respects, and blind to the many childlike virtues of the Indians, I cannot help thinking that it is not without more than some truth.

"What happened to the Anacaona woman," I asked him finally.

"When her brother, Behechio," he told me, "the cacique of Xaraqua, died, she became queen – or cacica rather – in his place. Though Roldán had been commended lands in Xaraqua after his peace with the Pharaoh, he had come to some accommodation with her and it lasted quite a while. All in all, there was not much trouble during the two years when Bobadilla was running the shop. But when Ovando arrived things changed. That was in '02. He had instructions from the Casa to move the Indians – the ones who belonged to the caciques who had submitted – from the countryside into special Indian pueblos which were to be built near our towns."

Montenegro says that it was in fact Isabela who instructed this – in the conviction that obliging Indians to live in close proximity to Spaniards would more easily facilitate their catechisation – but that Ovando made sure all these so-called Indian pueblos were built near gold mines; and that the Queen's stipulation that the Indians be paid a wage and given rations for any labour they performed was simply ignored, and there was great suffering among those who consented or were compelled to move. I do not doubt the Queen's piety but at times I am forced to conclude that she was a particularly naive woman in very many regards, or in this at least. Of course, Montenegro will not hear a word whispered against her and says she was dishonestly advised.

"Needless to say," Castro continued, "the redskins were not exactly over the moon about that prospect and most of them took to the woods and the hills. That's the Haytians' true element really, I suppose, the hills and the woods. He's not by nature a townsman. Ovando's twenty-seven ships had also brought two-and-a-half-thousand gold-hungry men, hard-headed Estremadurans for the most part, most of them without as much a pot to piss in. Near-half of them succumbed to the seasoning fever and the boils but that still left a lot of them wanting land, mines and no end of redskins to do the donkey work. So Ovando decided to conquer the remaining free caciques. One of whom was Anacaona – and Xaraqua was quite a prize. He set off with about four hundred men, banners flying and all the rest, the usual scenario. They say she received him well, along with all her vassal-caciques, held a big areíto and feasted Ovando and his little army for two or three days. But, they say, at the end of the areíto, Ovando got wind of a plot, that it was all a trick, and Anacaona was scheming to have them all murdered in their sleep. Maybe there was a plot, maybe there wasn't. God only knows. You can never tell with them. Anyway, they say, he asked all the vassal-caciques to gather in her bohío so that he could speak to them in a body and then had his men fall upon them and tie them up – about eighty of them, they say – and then ordered the bohío set alight – with the buggers in it. He had Anacaona brought back here. Strung her up on the Plaza de Armas. 'Out of respect for her rank,' he said. But I wasn't there so I can't swear that was the way it was. Must have done something, she must, pissed him off in some way, must have. That's my way of thinking. Either way it was wrong, I suppose, to go to such extremities. It's not much talked about."

It seems Anacaona too was also in some respects a naive queen, fatally so. I forgot – the heat of this country slows the workings of one's mind at times – to ask him about Hiquanamá, the Queen of Hiqüey, who Montenegro claimed was 'crucified'.

ж

I have just paid the surgeon a call. I would have done so earlier but the storm has only just now abated. While it raged I was confined to my hammock, sick as a dog, too weak even to empty the pot in which I do my necessaries, and with the ferocious swaying and bouncing of the ship ... I have only just cleaned up the mess.

His cupboard, larger than mine by several square feet but still a cupboard, is situated at the bow. He bid me enter with some enthusiasm. It was packed with jars of medicines tied, or 'lashed' as seamen say in their idiosyncratic parlance, to the shelves on which they were stacked, and various forbidding-looking instruments of his trade.

"I think I have solved the problem," he said, extracting a wooden box from a chest of drawers and opening it.

The device he showed me was a sort of scissors-forceps sort of thing, assembled out of various metal and wooden parts, the operation of which was not immediately apparent.

"This part here," he explained, opening and closing it, and indicating that part of it which resembled a forceps, "is a device I use to extract shot from flesh, though I have had to adjust it somewhat by the addition of these ..." – he indicated two miniscule cup-like structures – "... they should enable me to wedge the macaw's beak open, like this ..." – he opened the forceps. "While this part here ..." – he indicated the inner scissors-like device – "... these blades, will, hopefully, slip over the beast's tongue ..." – he closed the inner contraption as one would a scissors – "... and cut it cleanly at the root. Should only take a moment if all goes well. The main problem will be convincing the creature to open its beak in the first place. It's not yet quite working with the precision I desire. I shall have to spend some more time on it."

The thing, I must admit, was quite elegantly fashioned. He had even smoothed and polished the wooden parts and on his writing table, I could see the rather detailed drawings he had made of the apparatus, each part indicated by a letter, in a very clean hand. Christ too was a craftsman, I remembered. Perhaps we should all have a craft.

"My pleasure," he said as I left, "I love a technical challenge."

Plates 2

Figure 6 *Taíno Indian thatched dwellings, caney (left), bohío (right), Oviedo y Valdés 1851.*

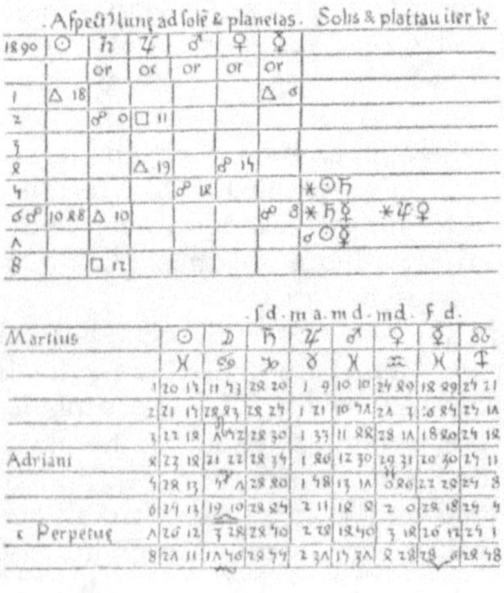

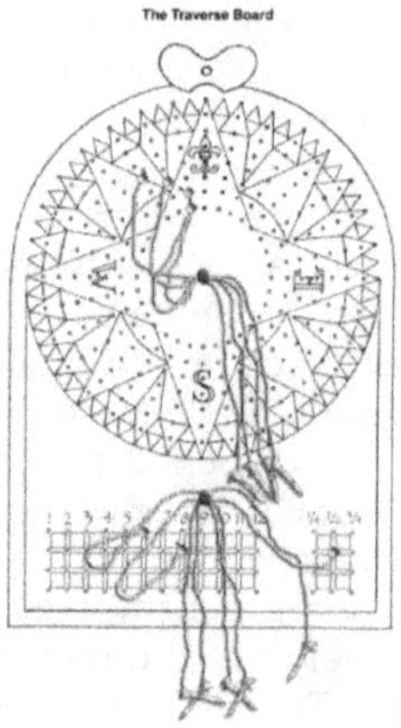

Figure 7 (left) *Table from Regiomontanus' Ephemerides.*
Figure 8 (right) *Toleta or traverse board, used to record a ship's course, both distance and angular direction.*

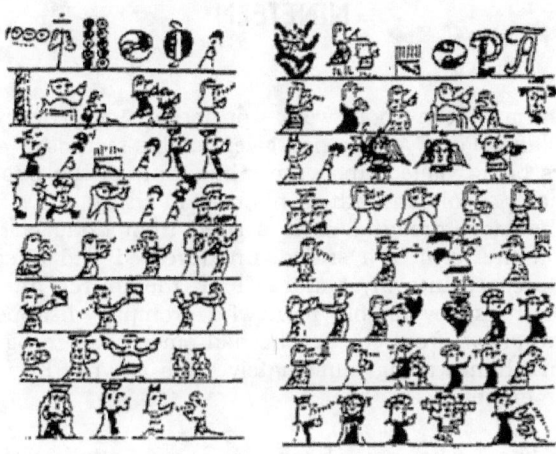

Figure 9 *Facsimile of the Taíno Indian document on wood bark paper given to Lucrezia di Marchionni by Johannes Puccini, as printed in the 1924 Catalan edition of* Hayti.

Figure 10 *The Cuban red macaw, also called the Hispaniolan macaw, now extinct, by John Gerrard Keulemans, 1907.*

NINETEEN

It must have been about week – or perhaps near two weeks – or so after Pater Alonso had given me his testimony of the horrors being visited upon the inhabitants of the Lucayas, and made a solemn oath in his own hand as to its truth, that the most dreadful news arrived from Concepción. It came in the form of a sealed, unaddressed and unsigned letter, pressed into my hand as I left the church after the Haytian mass by an old man who promptly disappeared into the crowd from whence he had emerged. I recognised Puccini's handwriting immediately. This is what he wrote, as I remember it:

I don't know what you already know, so I shall start from the beginning and give you a full account.

Four days following your departure from Concepción I had the dubious pleasure of an unannounced visit from some officers of the law. There were three of them – one of them your friend Gonzales de Esquival, Carnage himself, obviously in command but curiously mostly silent throughout, letting his minions question me. They said they were seeking the whereabouts of "a one Carlos Goya who may or may not be known by that name". But a visit to the royal notary at the fort would surely have told them where Goya's encomienda was located, so there was obviously more to it.

"I know him," I admitted. There was no point in denying it. "And he goes by that name, his Christian and family name, as an honest man does."

"We have reason to believe he is not an honest man," the bigger one said. There was a bigger one and a smaller one, not counting Carnage, like in some farcical double act in a bad Bavarian morality play.

"Do you know his whereabouts?" the smaller one asked again.

Carnage said nothing during all this. He just sat there, stretched out in full armour, helmet in one hand, the other one resting on the hilt of his Toledo sword. But he didn't need to. His simple presence was intimidating enough.

"He has an encomienda," I said and gave some vague and pretty useless description of its whereabouts. I knew they would eventually find out at the fort – if they did not already know – but I didn't want them thinking that I was that familiar with Goya and possibly involved in whatever they

suspected he was involved in. "Half a day by horse, I believe."

"You've never been there?" the big one asked.

I told him I had not been, which was a lie of course.

"But you have business with him?" the smaller one asked.

A right Castor-and-Pollux pair, they were.

"I buy pigs from him, on and off," I explained, which the truth. "He has them delivered or brings them himself."

"This is a serious matter," the small one said.

"A judicial matter?" I ventured.

"A matter of state," the big one said. "What do you know of this man?"

"He trades fair," I said.

Then the Captain-General asked about you by name. He said they believed you might be able to be of "assistance", but in what they did not specify. I told them I was not privy to your movements and affairs, diplomatically. In fact, my distinct impression was that de Esquival was as much interested in your movements as in Goya. Needless to say, I let not a whiff pass my lips that you and Sor di Marchionni had been to visit Goya. I told them only that you had spent time in the countryside catechising.

Savonarola set off early that afternoon for Caonabó's Valley. And I learnt later that Carnage had dispatched Castor and Pollux, accompanied by some Maquanan porters, to the same destination about midday the next day. They were mounted; but even so, I was sure that Savonarola would get there well before them. It also rained heavily that night, which would also be to Savonarola's advantage. The following is what he told me, more or less in his own words, when he returned several days later.

"There was smoke rising from his encomienda," he said, "large thick clouds of it. I saw it immediately when I reached the path down into the valley. I got to the compound a little later, but by then the fire had burnt itself out. There was nothing left but smouldering timbers and ashes. Everything had been consumed by the flames, the buildings and the huts around them. There wasn't a soul in sight. I could make out the remains of bodies in the ruins of the stone house. Two of them. The building had already half-collapsed and the burnt-out beams holding up what was still left standing looked as if they might give at any moment so I couldn't get a proper look at the bodies to recognise them, even if that was possible given the state they were in. In any case, I thought it more urgent to return here and tell you what had happened."

"All the buildings were destroyed?" I asked him. For if it was so, then that meant it was hardly likely to have been

an accidental fire.

"Yes," he said. "Every last one of them. It was done deliberately. I am sure of that."

"Simarons?" I suggested. "Red Francisquito? Guaro?"

But he only shrugged his shoulders and said it was possible.

Francisquito Guaro and his gang have been raiding the country around here recently, but mainly small stuff, a bit of burning and pilfering. No murders until now have been laid at their doorstep that I know of. He will come to a bad end but not, I suspect, without causing much more destruction – and God knows, he has his reasons.

But that is but the half of it.

Castor and Pollux have not been heard of since. There's not a trace of them. The general opinion is that Francisquito and his gang waylaid them on the road. It does seem a likely explanation. Francisquito Guaro has audacity enough. A troop of horse was sent to retrace their tracks but nothing – except Goya's burn-out encomienda – no bodies, no sign of their horses, nothing's been found. But, as you know, it's a wild country out there and there's no shortage of places to dump bodies. Just the kind of tactic Red Francisquito would adopt. Armed men disappearing in the hills and naught is heard of them again. Nothing like the unknown to strike terror into men's hearts. The Concepción watch has been doubled and some of the better-off encomienderos have been scurrying about hiring mercenaries and Taíno guards. So that's that. Carlos Goya is simply no more. And his woman too by the looks of it.

But – and I hesitate to write this – something feels amiss. I trust Savonarola with my life as I would trust no other man, as you know. But I have this inexplicable feeling, a vague intuition that he is holding something of this whole affair back from me, some detail, not that I have the faintest idea what it could even be. It's probably just my imagination. Savonarola knows Guaro. As you know, it was Guaro who brought him to me, in the days before he took to outlawry. Perhaps it is simply that. God, all that seems an age ago and only yesterday at the same time! Even then I think, without rightly knowing it, I sensed in Guaro something of what he was to become. Or maybe it is simply that no matter how educated in and accustomed to our ways the Haytian becomes there is always something about him profoundly unknowable.

If I hear more, I will write again. But somehow I doubt I will. Goya is dead and that is that. And the bodies of Carnage's men will simply rot to nothingness in the hills.

*I'm entrusting this letter to Savonarola. He will know how
to get it safely into your hands. I could trust no Christian
with it. It would be wise to destroy it once you have read it,
needless to say.*

And that was that, as Puccini said, or so I supposed at
the time. And thus too, in a way, were my prayers
answered. Or had they been? Rudolfo Jesus de Paz would
now never learn of our visit to Carlos Goya nor its purpose.
But to beg a divine intervention in the manner in which I
had done so ... Had it not been but little better than what
the Haytian is about when he abases himself before his
zemi ragdolls to beg for health or success in hunting
parrots? No matter how genuinely heartfelt, keenly desired,
pure, noble and good-willed – as if we can ever really be
sure that our wills are pure and good. No, true Christian
prayer is a feminine act, an act of submission, an opening
up, of the heart and the soul, inviting Our Saviour, in His
divine and transcendent wisdom and according to His
mysterious designs, to impregnate us with the grace of faith
and perhaps some guidance, and with the hope that our
sins, mortal and venial, may be forgiven.

There was now no hindrance to my preparing the sermon
in which I was to announce our interdict. I spoke to Fray
Pedro, telling him I had revised my previous opinion,
suggesting that perhaps we should not wait for the
Governor to return – it could be quite a while yet, best
strike while the iron was hot, present him with a done deed
on his return ... but Fray Pedro seemed not as confident as
the last time we spoke of it.

"The deed being done," I argued, "he will not have had the
opportunity to nip it in the bud."

"But have we the right?" he said. "The right to deny men
access to God? To deny them salvation? And there's talk of
trouble on John the Baptist's ..."

"They will have no salvation unless they see their sins for
what they are," I pointed out. "Besides the Franciscans will
still hear confessions and say masses. It will be a symbolic
act. But one that cannot be ignored, in Spain or in Rome.
We need to make an uncompromising stand and speak
clearly and loudly. They need to be accused of their crimes
to their faces. We need to create a scandal. A scandal that
cannot be ignored." Which of course was what he himself
had been arguing.

Ж

In a good year, the royal quinto from pearls can amount to fifteen thousand ducats. They are principally found along that part of the coast of tierra firme known as the Pearl Coast, the richest fisheries being in the waters around the island which Don Cristóbal discovered on his third voyage and which he christened Margarita. I have been told that the first substantial quantity of these jewels was actually acquired by Pedro Alonso Niño, who had been Don Cristóbal Colón's captain on the *Santa Maria* and had also served the Admiral in some capacity on the third voyage. Niño acquired them by trade, in exchange for the usual hawk's bells, glass diamonds, beads and tin baubles, and reported that there were many well-ordered markets on that coast and gold could also be had in quantities. The Indians he dealt with, he said, haggled as vigorously as any Castilian wife would with a peddler. Parts of this Pearl Coast are reputedly inhabited by Canibas.

Ж

Pearl fishing is the most cruel and detestable drudgery, worse than the mining or digging of gold, to which our fellow so-called Christians put the peoples of the islands. As part of my general inquisition, I had occasion to interview a Franciscan who had seen it with his own eyes, once, when catechising in those parts.

This is the account he said to me as I remember writing it out: "The fishers are taken from the Lucayas – for the Lucayans are excellent swimmers. They are then sold secretly to the hangmen – I can think of no better word – who run the trade. They are forced to dive down four or five ells deep underwater where, swimming without breathing, they collect the oysters and put them into nets. When they rise, they swim to a small boat or canoa where their owners wait for them, and having given over their catch, they are forced to dive again and again, being beaten with sticks if they are slow to do it. The poor creatures, even after a short time of this, are barely recognisable as human anymore. Their hair turns from black to the combusted, burnt or sun-colour of sea wolves. Their skin becomes caked with salt and is rendered so deformed by it that they look like monsters in human shape more than men. They are forced to hold their breath for so long and so often that the pressure of it bursts and tears the tissues of their lungs so that after a few weeks they are spitting blood. Their owners – for it is slavery and nothing else – feed them on the oyster flesh from the discarded shells and casabe roots and mahiz, none of which has nutrient enough to sustain such labours. If they don't die of exhaustion, they drown or are eaten alive by marine monsters called tuberoms and maroxi which can swallow a man whole. They are locked in stocks at night and sleep on the ground. The pearlmen complain that they pay an exorbitant price for them – as much as a hundred and fifty ducats. Before they've used them up, they can turn a profit of fifty crowns on a bad one, and even as much as hundred crowns on what they term a 'good one'. It is forbidden of course, and not done publicly, but it is done all the same and there are witnesses to it."

Thus, by such methods, are riches torn with matricidal hands from the bowels of our common mother.

TWENTY

The whole of Santo Domingo is in an uproar. "Are we to be deprived of all our hard-earned wealth?" I heard one man say. "Are we to be deprived of our beasts of burden?" I heard another man cry. But I get ahead of myself.

The day started like any other Sunday morning at the so-called Spanish mass. The modest church, as usual, was packed and the congregation decked out in its Sunday best, the ladies in Castilian dresses, either imported or home sewn, and the most notable gentlemen in the uniforms and regalia of the knightly lay orders to which most of them belong – Saint Raymond's Calatrava, Saint Julien's Alcántara and Saint James's Moor-slayers – sitting together in the front pews. Not a hint of anything amiss as Fray Montenegro mounted the pulpit, as he has done on countless uneventful Sundays. The theme of his sermon, he announced, was to be the third verse of the third chapter of the Gospel of Matthew: 'Ego vox clamantis in deserto. I am a voice crying out in the wilderness.' Then he began to preach. I shall write down what he said as best and in so much as my memory allows.

"I am going to speak to you today with the voice of Christ," he pronounced. "With the voice of Christ crying out in the desert of this island. A desert that you have created, an Eden destroyed by aristocratic avarice. It will not be a voice you want to hear, but I beg you, for the sake of your immortal souls, to take heed of the words I will speak to you before it is too late, for death and judgment come like a thief in the night."

He paused for a moment. Already one could feel this was obviously going to be more than a preacher's customary admonishment of his flock.

"You are all in sin," he continued. "In deadly mortal sin. You are living in it! And you are dying in it! You have sinned against the people of these lands. The system under which you live and profit has blinded you with greed and made you into tyrants. You have used the inhabitants of this island with the most horrific cruelty and wreaked unheard-of havoc upon them. Your hands are stained with the blood of the mildest creatures that God has ever created."

There was rage in his voice, but sadness too.

"Who gave you this authority to wage such wars upon them and to enslave them," he went on. "God? Christ Himself? You make them mine gold day in and day out and starve them and then you complain they die on you. Die on you! No, you murder them! Do you think they are not human beings? That they have no rational souls? That they are not descended from Adam? Do you not know that you are obliged to love them, to love them as you love yourselves? Do you not understand this? Are you unable to grasp this, the greatest commandment? Do you not understand that all mankind is one?"

He then quoted some verses from the Epistle of Saint James. "Faith by itself, if it does not have works, is dead. Even the demons believe and tremble." Adding: "Without good works you can no more be saved than the Moors and the Turks who have no, nor wish to have, faith in Jesus Christ. And your works here on these islands are not good."

The congregation was listening in stunned silence.

"We have laws, you say," he continued. "But your laws and the system which you live and profit by ... The loaded dice thrown by cheats and ruffians in the lowest tavern of the world are honest devices in comparison to the way you interpret and administer those laws.

"You do this and continue to do this to a people more capable of goodness and morality than perhaps any other – perhaps because their needs are simple – and as capable of morality and goodness and civility and good manners as the rest of mankind, a people who have waited patiently down the centuries for the Word of Christ to come to them.

"You come here every Sunday and offer up your prayers, but the Almighty does not accept the offerings of oppressors. In the words of Ecclesiasticus, also called the Book of Wisdom: 'He who sacrifices a thing wrongfully gotten, his offering is ridiculous. The gifts of unjust men are spurned. The Most High is angered by the offerings of the wicked. No multitudes of such sacrifices can wipe away sin. He who brings an offering of the goods of the poor does as one who has murdered a son before his father's eyes. The bread of the needy is their life. He who takes away his neighbour's living murders him.' "

He paused for a moment and looked down at the pew where Rudolfo Jesus de Paz was sitting among the brethren of his order. De Paz's face was stony and expressionless.

"You know what you have done and are continuing to do," Montenegro went on. "You know what your neighbours have done. Yes, your neighbours, the man sitting to the left of you and the man sitting to the right of you. These crimes are not a secret among you. Some of you openly boast of them. To list them would be pointless, for you know the shameful details of your deeds far better than I do.

"When the Pope divided the world so that the newly discovered heathens could be converted in an orderly manner and there would be peace between the two greatest Christian nations, he gave leave for this enterprise to be financed by trade – a legitimate enterprise between nations. He did not by the stroke of a pen divide up all the ignorant peoples of the earth – their lands, their estates, their chattels, their properties and persons – between you and the Portuguese. It was not a licence to commit theft."

Then he spoke of Cuba.

"And newly, not being satisfied – for the basest appetites, those for illicit flesh and gold, are never fully satisfied – many among you have set your eyes obscenely upon the feast of Cuba and have set about reducing those poor people there, a people who have never done you any wrong, indeed have shown you hospitality and kindness, to the same vassalage and misery as you have reduced the inhabitants of this island. They have been forced to flee to the hills – as the people here once did – where now as I speak they are hunted like pigs. Some, in despair, have hung themselves, their wives and their children, to escape – may God have mercy on us! – the clutches of men who call themselves Christians; one of whom – I shall not soil my lips with his name – exercised such ferocity that two hundred hanged themselves to escape his cruelty and his dogs. That man has since paid his debt to nature and the devil. As you in time will pay yours. You may scoff – as men once scoffed at Christ – but you know it is the truth. And this I know to be the truth because it was told to me by a priest, whom for his protection I shall not name, who also related to me that in three or four months, more than six thousand children have perished, as good as murdered, because their parents have been led in halters – like dogs on leashes – to work in the mines. Once, he told me, he saw with his own eyes three thousand men, women and children put to the sword, on a whim, without the least pretence or occasion, by Spaniards whose minds had been possessed by wicked devils, who slaughtered them in cold blood, and with such inhumanity and barbarism he says no age can parallel. Thus too is Cuba laid waste, its people exterminated, as they have been here. You are turning that island too into a desert."

Rarely have I heard such silence in a crowded church.

"The other day," he continued, "a certain holy monk of the

Franciscan Order who had just returned from the island of Cuba came to me. Among his duties was to attend the execution by fire of a certain cacique, a man by the name of Hathney, a man originally of this island who fled your cruelty and avarice to seek refuge on that island. Every man among you has heard of him. Some of you know him. After the executioner had bound Hathney to the stake, he gave leave to this Franciscan to speak to the condemned of God and of the eternal glory and bliss that would be his if he – in the small time remaining to him on earth – would repent, make an act of faith in the essential articles of the Holy Catholic Church and accept Jesus as his Saviour, pointing out that if he did not, and he died in sin, his fate would be an everlasting torment infinitely more excruciating than the fire he was in a few moments to face. Do you know what this Hathney said, my brothers and sisters? Do you know what this heathen who was to shortly meet his Maker said?"

He paused and cast a glance in the direction of the Alcalde, who, all the time as motionless and as expressionless as a statue, was staring ahead of himself as if into a void of nothingness.

"This Franciscan told me that this Hathney was pensive for a while and seemed to think deeply on the matter," he went on. "But he then asked a question. The question was this: he asked the monk whether the Castilla were also admitted into heaven. The Brother Franciscan of course answered that the gates of heaven were open to all who were Christians. And what did this cacique, this Hathney reply?"

Again he paused. He is not lacking in stagecraft.

"He replied, and I use the very words this good Franciscan used to me: 'I should rather roast in hell than go to heaven and spend eternity in the company of a nation as cruel, as blood-thirsty and as rapacious as the Castilla.' Thus, my brothers and sisters," he added a little more quickly, for I think he now sensed the congregation would take no more, "have you honoured God and the holy Catholic faith in these Indies. That is the greatest sin you have committed. You have driven men to deny Christ and His teachings, the hope of the world, the only hope of the world."

One of the Alcalde Mayor's caballeros made to rise and turn his back on the altar and leave the church, and a few others seemed about to do the same, but the Alcalde bade them by a sign to reseat themselves and be silent.

"And why have you done all this?" Montenegro continued. "Out of the lust for gold, a material thing, for nothing else. The proper place of gold is the adornment of God's churches, where its preciousness can remind us of the precious blood that He shed ..." – he held his wooden crucifix aloft – "... so that your sins may be forgiven.

"Your way is not the way of Christ, nor of His preaching, nor His way of converting souls. It is the way of Mohomed, even worse. Those the Mohomedan subjects by force of arms to profess faith in his religion, he leaves them their lives. Yes, you are worse than the Moor.

"So thus, and with a heavy heart, we, the Preachers of Saint Domingo in the Indies, from this day on, will not give out the Eucharist nor dispense the sacraments until such time as you, who are living in a state of mortal sin, as all do who live and profit under the system you have imposed on these people, have repented before God, begged forgiveness of those you have wronged, and made restitution to those you have wronged – if, God knows, that is possible.

"And now, I beseech you," he then concluded, "to join me in a prayer for the souls of the dead – especially for those dead, whom when they were living, you so grievously wronged – in the hope that you too may be forgiven your sins."

He then joined his hands in prayer and began to recite the Pater Noster. I can still almost hear the words ring out through the deafeningly silent church. When the prayer was concluded, he continued with the sacrament of the mass, and when the time came for him to distribute the Host, he simply did not do so. Thus the mass ended, without communion. I sincerely believe that most of the congregation had not yet quite fully realised what he had said to them.

Afterwards he spoke to me.

"It is done," he said. "And what is done cannot be undone."

The Alcalde was within earshot – I'm sure he heard the remark – but he said nothing, merely bowed slightly as he caught my eye, his face as expressionless as it had remained during the entirety of the sermon.

As we were leaving, the Captain-General de Esquival was in conversation with a group of settlers, complaining loudly, but I did not catch what he was saying, except for the phrase "fucking interfering monks".

Some had already hardened their hearts so much that I doubt if they even heard my words in any real sense; though Rudolfo Jesus de Paz had, despite the ossification of his heart. Some were confused, and knew not what to say; and in the consciousnesses of a small few, I had given germ to sentiments of guilt. But none, not a single one among them, repented.

Ж

A delegation of the chief men of the island, including the Grimaldi's agent, led by the Alcalde Mayor himself in person, went to the Dominican House this morning. And chance would have it that I was privy to much, though not all, of what was said. They were in the refectory when I arrived, some unrelated and trivial business having occasioned me to make my way there. There was a dozen of them in all, and they were sitting at the long table in conversation with Fray Pedro and Fray Montenegro. As I waited in the entrance I could hear and see much of what was going on.

The Alcalde did most of the talking, addressing himself to Fray Pedro, studiously ignoring Montenegro, who remained silent throughout.

"The logic of what you are preaching," he was saying as I began to eavesdrop, "is that His Catholic Majesty, the lord of all these lands, a lordship given to him by the Pope of Rome himself, has claimed rights that are not his to claim. In short, that he is a usurper."

"No," said Fray Pedro firmly. "We say no such thing. We act as he, no doubt, as a Christian, would command us to act if he was privy to the truth."

"So you know the King's mind?" the Alcalde retorted. "Better than he himself? Some would say that smacks of arrogance, at the very least, delusions of grandeur even."

"We know he is a good Christian," Fray Pedro replied. "That is enough."

"And it was as a good Christian that he gave us our lands and rights over the Indians," the Alcalde replied. His tone was determined and serious, with not a whiff of his usual unpredictability or frivolity. A man with a face for all occasions indeed. "In return for conquering these lands and fighting heathens. Or do you say that he had no right to do so?"

"No, we say only that you are abusing the rights he gave you,"

Fray Pedro replied. "The Indians are free vassals, not slaves."

"We want a retraction," the Alcalde said. "Nothing else will satisfy."

"And an end to this mad nonsense about restitution," one of the Alcalde's companions added. The remark was followed by a bout of laughter.

Fray Pedro looked at Montenegro.

But the Alcalde spoke again before Fray Pedro could reply.

"Would you agree that what you are saying is new?" he said.

"In its particulars," Fray Pedro agreed.

"And that it has not been heard on this island before, or indeed anywhere else? In its particulars at least?"

"Yes, in its particulars," Fray Pedro agreed again.

It was impossible to tell if the Alcalde was attempting some reconciliation or preparing some final stab.

"Then," he said quite coolly, "we could describe it as a new and unheard of doctrine?"

Fray Pedro made to reply but the Alcalde raised his hand to bid him be silent and he complied.

"Therefore it is possible that it is wrong, in error? That is possible, is it not?"

This time he waited for Fray Pedro to respond.

"It is always possible to be in error," he admitted, "but ..."

"So," the Alcalde went on, cutting him short again, "further meditation and prayer upon the matter might lead you to recognise your errors ... Should you be in error, that is?"

Fray Pedro could hardly disagree.

From the look on most of the faces of the rest of the delegation, I could see that they were thinking the Alcalde Mayor was being ridiculously and incomprehensibly mild and conciliatory. Which was obviously not to their liking.

"So for this reason," the Alcalde continued, "I will refrain from taking action if – and only if – you and your friars pray and meditate upon what you are preaching, on all the consequences of your ill-advised decision for the Christians of this island, and on the consequences of that decision for your mission itself."

Then he stood up and the rest of the delegation did likewise, as did Fray Pedro and Montenegro, belatedly.

"You have a week," the Alcalde said, "a week to meditate upon this matter and the consequences of what you are preaching." He then looked at Montenegro. "Next Sunday I shall expect Fray Montenegro to mount the pulpit of our humble church again and relate to us the result of your meditations."

He then turned and without any ceremony strode out of the room, the Captain-General de Esquival at his side and the rest of the delegation trailing behind him. I don't think he even noticed my presence at the doorway as I stood aside to let them pass.

Ж

De Paz – and this I learnt later – had already drafted a letter the Casa de la Contratación demanding that I and Fray Pedro, and the rest of our brothers, all be expelled back to Spain, and in the following days went about to all the men of standing in Hayti and asked them to sign it. And all those he approached did so willingly.

Ж

As I learn of all the numerous and grave abuses that are committed here, I have felt forced to ask myself: Should not Christians, being men whose knowledge of the truth is greater and who possess a higher moral sense, not be better men than Moors and Jews and those who follow all the other multitudes of false religions and superstitions? Should they not behave with greater charity than these? But I have had to remind myself that spreading the tenets of Christianity to all corners of the globe and to all people is a good and proper thing, a fact surely obvious to all right-thinking men; and that the failings and the sins and cruelty of individuals and companies who are making the Indian countries safe for missionaries, ploughing the heathen fields so to speak, do not invalidate this. The actions of many Christians here, besides being sinful in themselves, make the task of catechising more difficult and at times even impossible, but they do not detract from the correctness of our mission. Christ never claimed His Word would banish sinfulness from the world. Sinfulness is part of our nature and will be part of it till the end of time.

The Governor has returned. His ship arrived from Xaymaca this morning, sailing up the Río Ozama all banners flying. He is reported to be out of himself with rage.

TWENTY-ONE

His Excellentissimo made a point of coming to the Sunday mass this morning, accompanied by a retinue of some of the most important hidalgos on the island. Needless to say, the Alcalde Mayor was also present, accompanied by his caballeros in their regalia. I have rarely seen a church so chock-a-block, nor a congregation so expectant.

Montenegro seemed to begin in a conciliatory tone.

"Last Sunday, from this pulpit," he commenced, almost timidly in fact, "I said things which were harsh on your ears and afterwards some of you, embittered against me and my brothers for what I had said, came to us and said that I had spoken wrongly and that I should consider again what I had I preached. I promised I would do so. I said I would meditate and pray upon the matter. I have done so."

The Alcalde and His Excellentissimo exchanged satisfied glances, seemingly sure that what they had wished had come to pass and this whole matter would be put to rest, and Fray Montenegro's outburst of last Sunday put down to overzealousness on the part of monks who had spent too much time in the tropical sun – but obviously not enough time to have learnt to appreciate what the Alcalde referred to as the 'peculiarities of the tropics'.

"Holy Scripture is our guide," Montenegro continued, "so I went there, to the Book of Job. And I read: 'I will go back over my knowledge from the beginning and I will prove that my words are without falsehood.'"

I swear I thought I saw His Excellentissimo about to rise and the Alcalde about to make a move to lightly touch him on the arm to gently restrain him from doing so, but surely I must have imagined it.

"In other words," Montenegro continued, "I have gone back over what I said and in all humility examined my conscience and have come to the conclusion that what I said to you last week was the truth. But also that much of what I said dishonours the truth." He paused for a moment. "I have dishonoured it not in my overstating it but in my understating it." He paused again, as if expecting some uproar but there was none, only silence. "So I say to you again, loud and clear: If you persist in the state in which you find yourself, the state of mortal sin, you are all lost. Mortal sin. Consider those two words: Mortal. Sin. And what they mean. A man who dies in mortal sin is beyond salvation. He will spend eternity in hell. Another word to consider: Hell. There is nothing worse than the sufferings of hell. Its agonies are beyond your imaginations. And it will be just ..." – and here his voice rose again to its usual powerful pitch – "... for you men who profess to follow Christ have unleashed a hell fashioned within your own hearts upon the harmless people of this part of the world."

Then the strangest thing happened. Or rather it was Montenegro's reaction to it which was surprising. A small multi-coloured bird had flown into the church and was hopping between the beams and rafters above us. The smaller beasts and birds having less fear of men here, it is a thing that occurs frequently. Its twittering and the flapping about were impossible to ignore. Montenegro paused and looked up.

"Once, several hundred years ago," he recommenced, inspired by the unexpected intrusion to digress from his theme, "a mere blinking of the Almighty's eye, in England, there was a missionary, a holy man by the name of Bede, called the Venerable because of his piety and wisdom, who one day was preaching to a pagan king, and the king asked him what is eternal life. Now as this Bede was preaching – they were in a palace of some kind – a bird flew in, circled above their heads for a while and then flew out a window again." His Excellentissimo, the Alcalde and Fernández de Oviedo – I am not sure what his official position is, but he is a man of some influence and a scholarly reputation – exchanged puzzled glances, thinking perhaps that their troublesome monk had totally taken leave of his senses. "Our earthly lives, Bede said to this king, are as the few moments this bird has spent in this palace. It enters by one window and departs via another, and while trapped within this palace, glorious and beautiful as it is, that is all the bird knows. Such are earthly lives, he said, but short sojourns in a glorious palace; and we live in that palace in a state of ignorance of the eternal vastness that lies beyond it, outside the windows through which we enter and exit it – namely, our births and deaths. But while trapped in this earthly palace we have the opportunity not only to determine life within the palace but also the opportunity to determine what fate shall befall us when we exit into the eternal vastness beyond. We can create for ourselves the most beautiful of heavens or ..." – he paused again, but only for the slightest moment – "... or the cruellest of hells. You, in creating the cruellest hell for the innocent people of these islands, are making your own souls fit for nothing but eternal damnation"

The bird flew out a window just then, as if the timing of its appearance and disappearance had been some sign or a conjuror's trick.

"What I preach is not, as some of you have maintained, a new and unorthodox doctrine," he continued, his voice thunderously loud and clear, and full of certainty. "It is the teaching of Tomás of Aquino, the greatest theologian of the Church. The fact that a man is a heathen and has not heard the Word of God, or having heard it, wavers in believing in the good news, annuls neither his natural rights nor his human rights. The people of these islands are the true owners of their own countries, their estates and their persons, as Christians are in their own lands. They do not lose these rights because of their backwardness or their savage condition. We do not have the right to dispossess them. It is a sin to do so, a mortal deadly sin, and that sin will not be wiped clean until you have gone down on your knees – yes, down on your knees! – and begged forgiveness of those you have sinned against, made a true act of contrition before the Almighty – and made restitution! Yes. Res-tit-ution!" He emphasised each syllable of the word with venomous distinction. "The thief is not forgiven his sin and then allowed to keep the goods he has robbed and pilfered from his victims. Discovering these people gave you no rights over them beyond the duty to bring them the Gospel of Love by preaching and example. Nothing more. You have no more rights over them as they would have over you if they had crossed the ocean and landed on the shores of Christendom. That is the teaching of Tomás of Aquino. Or is there perhaps a more erudite man here among you who wishes to stand and contradict the greatest theologian and philosopher of the Church?"

Needless to say, none dared stand.

"There is a story that is commonly believed among you," he continued. "It is of the cacique who ordered gold poured down the throats of his Castilian captives. What cruelty, you say. Perhaps the Haytians tell the same story. Except that they most likely say why it was done. Perhaps they say that when the cacique was asked why he had ordered its doing, why he had chosen to put them to death in this way, he said: 'Would you not kill cruelly those who have raped your mother? Do not these Christians thirst for nothing but gold, which is their god?' Do we ourselves not put to death those among us who have committed dreadful deeds in a manner appropriate to their crimes? Do we not burn the heretic and the witch? Do we not chop off the hands of the forger at the wrists? Do we not cut out the tongues of blasphemers and bearers of false witness at the root?"

I was sure that at this stage some would stand up and leave the church, but nobody did. Such was the depth of their shock.

"Thus, I repeat what I preached one week ago from this very pulpit," he continued. "You are all living in sin, in deadly mortal sin. You are dying in it! And we will not confess a man of you until you mend your ways, any more than we would confess a vicious highway robber who had not the intention of mending his criminal ways. And in this we have not a shred of doubt that we are serving both Almighty God and fulfilling the Christian will of His Catholic Majesty. You owe these people, who are God's children as much as you yourselves are, your brothers and sisters from Adam, restitution for the wrongs you have done them. And I say: the only just wars being waged in these islands are those against you. For, as the Prophet Hosea wrote: 'They that sow the wind shall reap the whirlwind!'"

Perhaps he meant to say more, perhaps not, but at that moment, as the words of Hosea rang out under the rafters above us, His Excellentissimo rose, turned his back on the altar and, followed rapidly by the Alcalde Mayor and his entire retinue of hidalgos and caballeros, marched furiously down the aisle and out through the open doors of the church.

Only God Himself knows what consequences will follow from all this.

Not a peep from the Castle yet, even though it's been three or four days since Montenegro and the Preachers threw down the gauntlet – for the second time. The silence is deafening. Is it all simply going to be ignored, dismissed as a moment of madness, as if Montenegro's words are nothing more than a country sermoniser's Sunday ranting to his parishioners? Or is the Governor's intention simply to send a damning report to the Spains and let the Casa or the King decide what is to be done? Wash his hands of it? Or is this merely the quiet before the storm?

Still nothing. Not a word. Or if there has been, neither Fray Montenegro nor Fray Pedro has said anything. Life seems to have returned to normal. But surely it cannot have.

*

Felicitas was here again today on an errand and took the opportunity to question me again in that curious manner of hers. I think you will find an account of it amusing.

"Doña Sor Lucrezia," she asked, "what does the King of Spain do with the gold from the rivers and holes the Castilla dig in the hills?"

"His Majesty makes it into coins," I told her.

"The ones with an image of his head and symbols of his office on them?" she said.

"Yes," I said, bemused.

"For what purpose?" she asked.

"He uses it to pay his mercenaries, his soldiers. He keeps many armies," I told her.

"Why?" she asked. I think it is her favourite word. "Does he have many enemies?"

"Yes, he does," I told her.

"And what do the soldiers do with these coins?"

"They use them to buy the things they need, food mainly."

"From whom?"

"From merchants."

"And what do these merchants do with the coins?"

Not to be believed, is it?

"They use them to buy the food from the peasants?" I told her.

"But why do the peasants need these coins?"

"They use them to pay their taxes."

"Taxes?" she said, obviously not understanding.

"Tributo," I explained.

"To the King of Spain?"

"Yes. All the lands of the Spains belong to the King. The peasants pay him tributo for the use of it."

"So that he can pay his armies?"

"Yes."

"And if the peasants do not pay this tributo?" she went on.

"The King punishes them," I told her.

"By cutting off their ears?"

"No, he confiscates their crops or locks them up."

"In cages? Like captured parrots?"

"In prisons," I said. "It's not the same thing. Or he takes the land from them."

"Is that why he has many enemies?"

I shook my head in bemusement and laughed. The simple ignorance of these people can be exasperating at times, and can try one's patience.

We enrolled two more mestizo girls today. Both about twelve years of age.

Ж

Our captain is more learned than most members of his guild but he is generally a quiet man and not given much to conversation. Bikendi tells me he drinks and at times, I must admit, I have seen him pacing the quarterdeck the worse for it; but he is as miserly with his store of sugar wine as he is with his words, generally allowing the crew only the minimum of rations. However, he has engaged me in conversation on occasion and attempted to describe to me some secrets of his trade.

He is employing a method to measure our speed and the distances we are travelling which is quite different to the method used on my voyage out. Several times a day one of the seamen casts a log over the stern – literally a log of wood, though it has been shaped into the form of a block of about two feet in length and has a lead weight attached to it so that it anchors itself into the water and does not skim over it when we are sailing fast. This so-called log is attached to a light knotted rope – two hundred varas or so in length, marked with the knots at equal lengths from each other – which is allowed to unravel for a fixed period of time, measured by a sand clock. Then the knots are counted off, so many knots meaning so many sea miles per hour, and the distance we have travelled can be deduced. It is a Portuguese invention.

He is also experimenting with the use of what he calls a mariner's astrolabium, a well-crafted brass instrument invented, he said, by Martin Behaim. This circular device is a foot in diameter – it needs to be large because, as he explained to me, its accuracy is directly proportional to the length of its circumference – and hangs freely on a hook so that it may be used on a rolling deck. The device resembles the planispheric astrolabium – I think that is the word, my knowledge in these matters is meagre – which astronomers use to chart the movements of the spheres; but in order that it is not buffeted by the wind when the navigator holds it up to take his readings, it is heavier, and instead of being crafted from a single sheet of brass as is the astronomer's instrument, it is manufactured in the form of a four-spoke wheel, for the same reason. The Pharaoh is reputed to have used one on occasion, and twice calculated his longitude by timing lunar eclipses with it; and once, when shipwrecked on a Xaymaca beach, he deceived the Xaymacans into believing he had magical powers by predicting a lunar eclipse. Our captain tells me that it enables him to determine the relative positions of the planets, usually during specific alignments of the moon and Mars, compare them with the times of the same alignments predicted in the tables of his Regiomontanus, and by an arithmetical sleight of hand – I call it thus for it is thus to me – to determine his longitude with a greater precision than he could by any method of dead reckoning. However, to use it effectively, it is necessary to know the time with great accuracy, a matter which is not easily achieved in foreign seas and lands. He had seen a small clock, he told me, small enough to put in one's purse, the last time he had been in Seville, that might suit this purpose; it had been made in Nuremberg, Behaim's native city. This mariner's astrolabium can, of course, also be employed to calculate latitude, with the further advantage that it enables the position of the sun to be read without the mariner having to stare directly into it.

The book – or perhaps I should call it a codex, for it is not a proper book – that Goya thrust into my hands on the morning we left his encomienda has been on my mind. In a perverse way it is a beautifully manufactured thing, a work of intricate craft, but can anything but wickedness come of keeping it in the world? In the eyes of greedy men – self-styled Christian conquistadors who, if they could sail as far, would plunder the very moon itself of its silver – it would be an inducement to further seeking out the Gold Land. Obsessed, they would plunder and pilfer all they stumbled upon, bringing mayhem and devastation upon the Indians, murdering their princes or reducing them to buffoonish lackeys as they have done on Hayti – and condemn themselves to eternal damnation in the process. Yet, in the eyes of more virtuous and more open-minded men, would it not be evidence that, as Carlos Goya himself put it, these undiscovered people are 'not unlearned in their way' and thus capable of receiving the good message of Christianity? Perhaps it should be studied, in the manner a physician studies ailments – for is not the catechist a spiritual healer, and without precise knowledge of the nature of the spiritual diseases his flock suffers from, how can he hope to cure them? And if these peoples are not discovered, will they not forever remain outside the civilised community of the world? Yet, once they have been catechised, can such perverse objects be allowed to remain in their hands, forever a reminder to them of the dark unenlightened ways of their ancestors and a permanent allurement to backsliding and taking up those ways again? To us, at most, the thing – and, as Goya said, they have whole libraries of them – possesses a perverse beauty; but, in their barbaric and childlike eyes, it must be simply beautiful without any qualification, perhaps even sublime to them. Lusts and greed are in sorts triggered by beauty, or at least by the appearance or perception of it. Gold shines and glitters. As do women and boys in their fleshly way. And with what easeful facility does not the mere perception of beauty become lust, the desire to possess, to hold, rent and ravish?

I have wondered also about the ship Goya said he saw, or thought he saw, on what he believed could be the Great Southern Ocean. If the central passage does not exist, and Goya was sure it does not – and more than ten years of searching for it have not delivered a shred of evidence that it does – then the only way a Christian ship, either Castilian or Portuguese, could have reached those waters was by sailing around the southern extremity of the Parrot Land or the northern extremity of what the Strassburgers depicted as a great island but which – if there is no central passage – must be part of tierra firme. But is such a thing possible? It is a conundrum, to be sure. But many things pass unrecorded and even unnoted except by those directly involved, part of a shadow history of the world, which the powers and principalities of the world, for their own reasons and by various methods, obvious and devious, for laudable reasons and vicious, conspire from bringing to the light of day – like the innumerable crimes and negligences that have been committed against the peoples of the Indian countries.

TWENTY-TWO

The quiet before the storm has broken.

A brusque note arrived from the Alcalde Mayor this morning commanding me – 'a distressing duty' he called it – to attend him at the Castle 'between noon and one hour past, concerning a grave matter' and 'to bring the nun Hildegard of the Ordo Sancti Hieronymi' with me. It was in the hand of a secretary, that of Ramírez most probably. I suspected immediately that it portended no good. So I steeled myself for whatever was to come and told Hildegard to dress in a clean and unpatched habit and make herself ready.

Ushered into Rudolfo Jesus de Paz's bureau by Ramírez, we were met by the sight of Montenegro and his interpreter Felicitas, her hands and feet manacled in heavy rusty chains and a fat filthy-bearded guard in chainmail standing at her side. The Alcalde, in yet another multi-coloured costume from his seemingly endless wardrobe, was fanning himself with a bunch of ferns.

"Welcome, Sor di Marchionni," he said. "I see you have brought your plump little beata along, or should I say your plump little harlot."

Shocked to the roots, enraged at the behaviour of the man, I was about to protest but he just pointed his bunch of ferns at me and shouted: "Hold your tongue!"

I was about to shout back at him but Montenegro caught my eye and indicated by an almost imperceptible nod that I should, as it were, hold my fire.

"Do you know what this is?" the Alcalde asked me, meaning the ferns he was fanning himself with.

"A weed," I said, managing to restrain myself. "A common weed."

"Well, it's common enough, I suppose, I'll give you that," he said, and turned to Hildegard. "But you know what it is, don't you, Sor Hildegard?" He turned to me again. "It's a poison, Sor di Marchionni, a special kind of poison. A particularly devilish and Haytian sort of poison. One that only works on the innocent." He looked at Hildegard again. "On the unborn."

"I have no idea what you are talking about," I said.

"I will explain," he said scathingly.

"Please do," I said. I was going to say more but he cut me short.

"It's an abortivum," he said.

He paused before continuing. He is an abominable man.

"This fat little whore here ..." – he indicated Hildegard with a contemptuous jutting movement of his goatee – "has been fornicating behind your back – probably with some pox-ridden sailors – and one fine day found herself with child."

"How dare you," I said.

"Shut up," he snapped. "I'm not finished."

"Then kindly do so," I said with as much righteous venom I could muster.

"And finding herself with a sizzling bun in her oven," he continued, sneering, "decided that she would get rid of it, murder her own unborn child, an innocent gestating blissfully in her womb. Drop it down the latrine. But to do that, she needed an accomplice. Now, it so happens that the natives of these islands are well-versed in such diabolical arts. There is nothing in their religion – if one can call it that – which forbids it. Is that not so, Don Padre?" But Montenegro remained silent, refusing to be provoked. "As there is nothing in their religion which forbids them strangling their sick to help them to their demise. Or taking their own lives with impunity when it all gets too much for the sensitive souls. In fact, I have been told that they fancy that a death by hanging ensures them immediate entry to their heathen paradise – the only good reason for not stringing them all up. They have murdered half the Christians on John the Baptist's. Taíno and Canibas together, the bastards have joined forces. As part of your just war, no doubt." But Montenegro continued to keep a cool head and said nothing. "So this little pregnant whore had not far to look in find an accomplice. And where was this accomplice to be found?" He looked at Felicitas. "In the priests' house, no less, concealed like a viper in the very bosom of Mother Church herself." He turned to Montenegro. "A witch's art, poisoning, is it not, Padre?" Again, Montenegro refused to be provoked.

"Have you any evidence of this?" I asked him, realising by now, and with horror, that what he had told us, in as an unpleasant as manner as he was capable of, was simply too outrageous for it not to be essentially the truth.

"A little bird told me," he sneered. "Of course, I have bloody evidence. What do you take me for? A fool?"

"Not that," I said.

"I have ears and eyes all over this island. They keep me informed. Gardeners, cooks and servants are particularly observant, and always short of a few maravedí or two. A quiet chat in a back-alley or in some lonely spot in the zavana with some of my men usually persuades them to cooperate. Do I need to spell it out for you?"

"A paid informer? Not a very reliable source of intelligence, I would have thought," I said.

Inwardly I was raging at Hildegard but a mother's instinct is always to protect her young. And am I not a mother to my spiritual charges?

"Of course," he turned to Montenegro again, "a confession could always be obtained."

But Montenegro persisted in his silence.

"It would be necessary for a conviction of course," the Alcalde continued. "If this matter were to come to trial?"

Now I was confused. What did he mean by 'if'?

Then I realised that the whole theatrical production – deadly real though it was – was not for my benefit, but for Montenegro's. Rudolfo Jesus de Paz was taking his revenge. To undo what that been done? To somehow force Montenegro to retract what he had said in his sermons? To silence him somehow? Or at least muddy the waters of the whole affair to such a degree as would damage the Preachers' case and call the integrity of their cause into question? Such were the thoughts that rushed through my mind. I sensed that Montenegro had already realised this. The Alcalde had spun a web, hence Montenegro's silence. He was waiting to see what the contours of that web would be.

"But perhaps it need not come to that," he added, and was silent for a moment, leaving the possibility hanging in the air. There was no need for him to say that there would be a price.

"You thought you had made fools of us with that sanctimonious sermon of yours," he said, addressed himself to Montenegro. "We are no saints. I know that as much as any man. No, we are men, and men of action at that. We are what we are and stand by it. We desire gold and seek it out and take it. Even if the half of us perish doing so. We are not meek. But you, Padre, you and your mealy-mouthed brother monks follow in our wake with your holier-than-thou words. You allow us to do your dirty work so that you can save your precious Indian souls, pick up our leavings."

"What do you want?" Montenegro said finally.

"To give you a choice," the Alcalde replied. "A choice between saving one you know or saving many you do not. A moral dilemma I believe is what the theologians call it."

Montenegro, demonstrating great restraint, simply waited for Rudolfo de Paz to come to the details of what exactly he wanted of him.

"Item one," the Alcalde said, it was obvious that he had planned this down to the last detail, "you leave the Indies on the first available ship. I cannot banish your order from this island but I can get rid of you. "Item two: you hand over to me all your papers, all those so-called statements you have been collecting. I know exactly who you have been yapping to. And you shall swear a solemn oath on the Holy Trinity itself that all the copies of these so-called witness statements you have amassed and will hand over to me are the only extant copies, and there are no others. And that includes the libellous account you have been busy composing yourself."

The Alcalde then turned to me.

"Our good priest here," he said, "has been busy collecting statements from disgruntled fellow men of the cloth and embittered no-goods on alleged abuses allegedly committed against his beloved redskins. Getting men to spin him tales and sign their names to them. Collecting slanders and libels against the men who have the responsibility of ruling these lands, the King's men." Then he addressed Montenegro again. "Needless to say, both whore and witch will enjoy the Castle's hospitality until you have made up your mind."

"There will be no need for that," Montenegro said calmly. "I will do as you wish."

"Very prudent, Padre," the Alcalde said, "very prudent."

He indicated to the guard to untie Felicitas's bonds and turned again to me.

"You also may take your not-so-little harlot back with you to your nunnery," he said, "though perhaps the gypsies' whorehouse might be more to her liking."

I held my tongue.

Then he turned to Montenegro and said: "Did you really think I would allow you to drag the glories of our splendid conquest – this holy crusade – into the dirt and create a black legend? Politics is a dangerous game, Padre. The heads of losers can end up on spikes. You should thank God that yours hasn't. I think you'll both find it in your interests that all this is 'kept in the family', as they say. That's the way I want it. Not a word to another living soul. If I hear anything – and I mean anything, anything about this matter, even a whiff – well, I will be forced to reconsider the leniency I have exercised here today."

TWENTY-THREE

In the midst of all this, I received a letter that struck me an unexpected blow. From the savage Savonarola, no less. It seems Puccini, to a certain extent, had succeeded to some degree in making 'a bit of a scholar out of him'. His style displays a surprising, if odd, elegance. The letter also explains much and relates events which I know to have happened and which he describes truthfully, and for that reason, despite its blasphemy and the parroting of confused concepts and ways of thinking he could only have picked up from Puccini, I have decided to include it here. Like Puccini's earlier letter describing the fate of Carlos Goya, it was delivered by an anonymous Haytian – this time a lanky youth, missing an ear, no doubt removed by some good Christian – while I was taking my customary late-afternoon walk in our garden. This courier also mumblingly informed me that he had left some 'things' for me with the cook, before promptly disappearing.

The letter appears to have been written over several days.

To the Honourable Don Padre Montenegro, with respectful regards, from Agüeybaná, also known by the Christian name of Savonarola.

Your friend Don Johannes Puccini's last wish was that these papers and medicines and other things be sent to you in Santo Domingo. His goeíza, that which you call the soul of a living person, has left his body for the last time. His parting was sudden and has caused me profound grief, for I miss him the way I would a younger brother.

He was bitten by a serpent, the one that lives in flowers and mimics their colours so truly that even to the sharpest eyes the beast is barely detectable. I do not know the name of this creature in your tongue, perhaps it has none, but it is well known to us. I knew that once he was bitten he would die that day or the next. For the venom of this serpent is deadly to men, beast and bird. It bit him on the hand. It took half a day for the poison to reach his heart and stop it. Before he ceased breathing forever he asked me to play some Italian airs on the violetta. "For significance's sake," he said. I could never make out whether he believed that music entices a deeper significance out of things, evoking an awareness of the deeper order within, or whether he believed it imbued things with significance.

Sometimes I thought he believed it did both, not first this and then that, but both simultaneously, like fruit and seed, both necessarily occurring at the same time, both being the cause of the other. Or whether he believed something else entirely. I held his hand as his goeíza metamorphosed into his opía – into that which you call the soul of a dead person – and evaporated into the world. I buried his empty husk in a secret place in the hills, in a cave, as is our custom, though as you know, we have many customs in this regard. But I have always felt that, since it is from caves whence men and women came originally, caves are the most fitting place to lay to rest what physically remains after death.

But who knows anymore what death really is? Before your coming with your pigs and your cats, your locks and your keys, and all your other marvels and monstrosities, and your suffering god and you monks, we thought it was one thing. But now we are told it is another, and that you Christians, in your hearts, despite outward shows of sorrow, believe that it is a cause of rejoicing. Don Puccini once said to me death was no thing and that to fret about it was to fret about no thing. 'A load of fuss about no thing,' was the expression he used. Though he said other things as well. He was a man of contradictions, but who is not?

A 'no thing'? But does not the tree in the woods still exist when it is out of sight? Does not everything that has ever existed have once existed? And forever continue to have once existed? So, does it not, in a fashion, thus continue to exist forever? In a time outside time. In the dream-world. If that has meaning in your tongue. The bohiques say that it is the dream-world that is revealed to us when we sniff the dust of the stars into ourselves, and that all that has come to pass in this world continues somehow forever to pass in the dream-world. Johannes, who often partook of the dust, used to say of it: it arouses us from slumberous waking perception and gives us a glimpse of things the way they are seen by what he called the angeli, which he said were a kind of zemi that sometimes took human shape. Music and the song of the birds at dawn, he said, can have a similar effect on our spirit-senses. He also used to say that though the passing of time may not be avoided – the demiurge's relentless reckoning, as he called it – our perception of things passing, which was time, may perhaps be perceived differently. The world, he used to say – this world, for he believed there were many – was created by this demiurge, an evil being of great mischievousness and cleverness. It is as plain as day that it is so, he used to say. But he also said that in the ultimate finality of things time must be a mirage of sorts because only in the eyes of Atabey and Yócahu, the gods hidden behind the demiurge and from whom all things ultimately emanate, do things really exist; and that Atabey and Yócahu are outside time, and that time is a trick played on us by the demiurge. And that Guamiquina Jesus Christ – the Destroyer of Time, he used to call him – had been sent into this world by Atabey and Yócahu to destroy time. As I said, he was a man of contradictions.

Death makes me think of such things.

When I returned to Concepción, sickness was raging again. When the pestilences first ravaged us, we implored our gods and our zemis and offered them all manner of sacrifices, but they replied only with dumbness. Many smashed their zemis or burned them in the hope that they would at least hear our anger and distress and return to us, but the zemis, like the victims of the pestilences, too had become silent husks. Some of the Franciscans say the pestilences are a punishment for not thinking the right things – or 'believing' as you monks always say – and not honouring your fetishes; and that if we thought the right things, we would not draw down Guamiquina Jesus Christ's wrath. They say it is Guamiquina Jesus' way of showing us that Atabey and Yócahu and all the rest of our own gods have deserted us. Or that they were never there in the first place. Or that they are nothing but evil zemi who had deceived all the generations before us, my mother's generation, her mother's, her mother's mother's, all the way back to the time of the birth of the fifth sun, back even to the time we emerged from the caves – the Franciscan monks too are contradictory men. And they say that we have lived in wrongness all this time and that all we thought we knew of the world and the dream-world was but no more than like the silly imaginings of a naughty child. That your world is superior to our world, yours the right and ours the wrong. That all these wrongnesses which we are is the cause of us dying off like the sickly pups of a litter. Oh, how you all endlessly babble on about right and wrong, about good and evil!

The old people tell us that when you first came out of the Sea of the Rising Sun on your ships, more suddenly than any hurucan, you said you came in peace and friendship and the caciques lavished you with gifts, as was our custom; and in those days we had much to give. They gave Colón things of gold because you said it was the thing you desired above all other things beyond our welfare. For how can one who wishes friendship reject the heartfelt desires of those who wish to befriend him? And does not he who gives gifts receive gifts in return? For is not the giving and receiving of gifts the only way for different men to live in peace on all the various islands of the world? But Colón said because the caciques had sworn friendship to his king and queen on the island of Castile and had once given him gifts, which he called tributo, that they were henceforth to give him gold and cotton every three moons until the end of the fifth sun. He said it was only by the perpetual giving of gifts from each cacique to the one above him that there could be harmony on the islands of the world, and that this was the way on all the other islands of the world; and that the highest caciques were the Christian King and Queen of Castile. At times, it is true, he gave us gifts of little brass bells and images of your zemi, but he said that these were a regalo, not tributo, which means they were things only given once and at pleasure. Higher men, he said, received tributo and lower men received regalos. But has it not always been otherwise, that those who possess much are required to be generous, even if they don't always follow that custom? When we buried the holy pictures and the statues of your zemi you had given us in the fields so that the casabe and batata would grow more fruitfully, his men burnt several of our people while their flesh was still living because they said they had insulted Guamiquina Jesus. But what good are zemi who do not increase the fruitfulness of the earth, we said; and that it was no insult, for did we not also bury our own zemi in the fields when we planted.

All these things – the pestilences, the endless talk of right and wrong, and of gold, and of superior and inferior ways – were a strange and new way of thinking for us, and we were without understanding of it and were thrown into confusion.

But do not all things come to an end? And now is the time of the ending of our world, our 'apocalypse' as Guaro, the one whom you call Red Francisquito, calls it – a word from your magic book. Johannes was extinguished by a serpent, a creature you say whose nature is to bring time and death and wrongness into worlds. Was the serpent thus superior to Johannes because it poisoned him? Is Guamiquina Jesus Christ a nobler god than Atabey and Yócahu because he has driven them out of our hearts and our world? Is your world better than ours because it is extinguishing ours?

Such are my thoughts.

*

Perhaps you wonder how I met Johannes. I shall tell you.

Perhaps you wonder why I tell you. Johannes said that you were a man who did not wish that what was happening should be happening and that you were collecting testimonies from other Christians on what he said you called the abuses committed against us, and that you were writing these down because Christians consider that things that are written down are truer than those that are not; and that you intended to give all these written testimonies to the Guamiquina of all Christ-bohiques on the island of Rome because you think that he would put a stop to these abuses if he was convinced of the truth of them. That may be so, or it may not be so. But I am writing you these things not because I think or hope it may be so or not. I do not seek to right a wrongness. The wrongness cannot be righted. No, I make these marks because my inner spirit tells me that in a few years from now all that will remain of the people of the cacicazgos of Maguana, of Xaragua, of Marién, of Maguana and of Higüey will be a few shards of our pots in the earth and that – though it is the way of all things and all gods and demiurges – it does not seem right. I know that all I do is make a few marks on one of those shards, no more. This makes no sense in the larger schemes of the heavens, the worlds and this earth. But I do it nonetheless.

I spent my boyhood at Anona – named after the fruit you call 'pine-apple', it grows well there – the place you call 'Pueblo Fantasma'. I think you know it, or rather what remains of it, for it has been desolate for many years. It is that overgrown place on the zavana just off the road from Concepción to Santo Domingo. You must have passed it many a time. It was a big pueblo then, what we called a yucayeque, as big as what you call a town or even a city, with perhaps two thousand souls; it is hard to count these things, but there were many. I remember well the areítos that once took place there, and the batey games and the ceremonies that were part of the rhythm of the world-before. My uncle, Cayacoa, was cacique there.

One day, I think I had been fifteen years in the world, many years ago now, four Christians on horses, alone, without any of their allies, came from New Isabela to collect the gold and the cotton tributo – this was before Santo Domingo had been built. I had of course seen Christians before but only from a distance. I had seen horses before too, and often come across the sweet-smelling droppings of these wondrous creatures, and your dogs too, armoured like their masters, but also only from afar. In my child's world, Christians and their animal familiars were ghost-like entities that moved through the woods and the zavana, appearing and disappearing, following some mysterious and arbitrary design of their own, feared and awed by all of us. But seeing them at arm's length, in my uncle's bohío, to not only hear their words but to see the expressions on their bearded faces, was another thing entirely; and not to only see the horses but to smell them and sense the heat and power of their monstrous bodies, for they were monstrous creatures to me in those days; and to see the terrible dogs on their leashes, beasts the like of which were unknown on our islands before your coming and whose droppings are disgusting. I can still see the details of those men's armour and the medals of your goddess Maria that they all wore, and the way they stood, hands on their weapons; and their gestures and manner of moving, their way of listening to and hearing only those things which served their own designs, and the hardness in their voices. I felt their crude presumptions of natural mastery over us, the arrogance of men who are blind to the substance of the other, except to the extent that the other can serve his needs. Yet, I also remember recalling how the Franciscans had told us that Christians believed that all men were siblings, descended from the same first parents, and that is why Christians are enjoined to treat all men as brothers and sisters!

I struggle to find words either in your tongue or in mine.

But I was also fascinated by them, by their foreign strangeness, by their otherness I suppose one could call it. Johannes once told me that there were certain bohiques among you, women for the most part, who exercise a power called glamour, a spirit thing, a magical thing, by which they cause a delusion of the senses, and especially of the eyes, in their victims so as to seduce them into submitting to their will, and whom you burn, as you do us when you deem we have offended you. Perhaps it was this glamour that I felt. And I thought, perhaps not at the time but certainly later, how much more potent this magic must have been for those of my mother's generation when they had beheld Christians for the first time; for surely it is a power which weakens with familiarity. I have also since wondered if we too had exercised a glamour on you, once.

So, spellbound in my innocence, I watched these Christians while they talked with my uncle and he slowly began to argue with them in Castilian, though about what I could not at that time understand. But then suddenly they were shouting at him and one of them had slapped him across the face with an armoured glove and another had unsheathed his sword and the dogs were barking and straining on their leashes. A handful of our men ran forward – they were not armed – and tried to defend my uncle; which made the Christians even more angry and suddenly they had all drawn their swords and were poking our men with them, drawing blood and causing them to cry out in pain. Then, in the flash of an eyelid, suddenly one of the war dogs was loose, and then another. Have you ever seen one of these evil creatures go about its devilish work, Don Padre? Seen one of these beasts slice open a man's living flesh with its claws, tear out his living entrails with its teeth in as little time as it takes you monks to say a few words of your Pater Noster? If you have not, I urge you to take some time to imagine it. Suddenly overcome with righteous rage at the horror unfolding before my very eyes, I grabbed a macana from where it was hanging on a post, ran towards one of the Christians and, with every ounce of strength I possessed, clubbed him on the head, twice, perhaps thrice, perhaps more, his iron hat ringing out with every blow, until he fell to the ground as lifeless as a sack of mahiz kernels.

Then I ran, the three other Christians chasing me, their swords drawn. In an instant I was outside, fleeing for my life. For no reason I could think of – perhaps I thought to reach the pathway to the woods on the other side of it – I headed for the batey court, zigzagging across it, expecting at any moment to be hit in the back by a bolt from an arbalest. But when I reached the pathway – not hearing my pursuers behind me – I briefly turned to look. The Christians were following me but, weighed down by their armour, they were far behind me, and they had stopped; and they were no longer together, but spread out, each man alone, and without their horses and their dogs. Neither were they carrying their arbalests, which I then remembered had been in holsters on the horses.

Between them and my uncle's bohío, a large crowd had assembled, of men, women and children, armed with macanas, sticks and stones, making their way towards the Christians, shouting: "Death, death to the Christ Men!" Stones and rocks began to fly through the air, bouncing like batey-balls all around the Christians, hitting the one farthest from me on his breastplate – none of them had shields – and then, a moment later, another bounced off his iron hat and he began to stagger and stumble. By then, I had stopped running. The people were upon him as he fell to the ground. I saw the macanas and the sticks rise and fall over the group that had gathered around him as they began to beat him to death. For a few moments the two other Christians made in the direction of their fallen brother but then they too found themselves immersed in a hail of rocks and stones, thought better of trying to rescue him, and began to run away.

The crowd caught up with one outside the caney where we kept the zemi and the images of Guamiquina Jesus and the goddess Maria that the Franciscans had given us. He flayed about wildly with his sword but there were so many with long macanas and sticks that it availed him none and he was eventually tripped over and fell to the ground. My uncle's youngest sister crushed his skull with a rock the size of a large calabash. But I was there when we caught up with the last one. Guaro hit him on the head with his macana and he fell. It took him the longest to have the life beaten out of him, but it was done. In the silence that followed, I felt his goeíza become his opía, and evaporate into the world.

While all this was going on, the entrance of my uncle's bohío had been barricaded and the roof set on fire, trapping the dogs – who were too busy about the bloody business to which their Christian masters had reared them to think of trying to escape – and when they did, it was too late; they were then too blinded and choked by the smoke to succeed. They suffocated and their bodies burned, as did the bodies of my uncle and Mabiatué, his counsellor, and the Christian whose head I had battered in. All that was left of them, both men and beasts, were their charred husks and blacked bones.

The gravity of what we had done was apparent to all and we knew that the Christians would take a terrible revenge upon us. Some said we should send an embassy of men of rank to New Isabela and offer gifts and ask forgiveness and say that those who had killed the Christians had run away into the hills – for surely, they argued, the Christians would want to keep receiving their tributo of gold and cotton, so what possible use could it be to them if there was war between us? Others said we should fight the Christians when they came, for what was this word 'tributo' but the Christian word for 'robbery'. Who had ever heard of such a thing in the world-before? Who had ever heard of a man being required to give gifts again and again forever to men who possessed much – as you Christians surely do? Of men telling other men what they were to do? Others said that we should scatter over the zavana, hide ourselves in the woods and the caves in the hills, as others had done in the past. For there was nothing the Christians hated more, they said, than insurrección, they hated it even more than they loved gold and would punish us terribly.

Then Guaro spoke. He said that if all the peoples – the Maguanas, the Xaraguas, the Mariéns, the Maguanas and the Higüeys – fought together against the Christians, we would surely drive them from our island. The Christians were still few, he said, and we still outnumbered them and their allies and their horses and their dogs many times. He said that it was better to be a dead man than to be the property of another. For was that not what we were, the best part of the year, except when we were eating, shitting or sleeping?

Guaro then took the Castilian standard the three Christians had brought with them and held it aloft for all to see.

"The yellow of this rag," he said, his voice booming over the batey court, "stands for the shiny gold the Castilla hunger for. The red stands for the lakes of blood they shed to still that insatiable hunger."

And he then set it alight.

"They have grown used to our bowed heads and bended knees," he said, "and grown ever more proud in their ways. But pride makes men vulnerable. They forget to expect the unexpected. But we will do the unexpected. We will not bow our heads and show them ours backs for the whip. No, we will attack them before they get here, fall upon them in a mass. You have seen them run and die. We shall make them run and die again."

As I write these words I can still see him standing in the middle of the batey court addressing us, and still almost hear his powerful voice. He had a fine voice then, as he does now.

Then – he had planned it all of course, he understood the magic of gesture – four of his men emerged from the crowd, each one carrying an arquebus and the rods these weapons have to be erected on so that they can be properly aimed and fired, and joined him in the centre of the batey court.

He made a sign – they already had their firing wicks alight and had loaded gunpowder into the muzzles of the weapons – and they pointed their arquebuses above the heads of the people, and discharged them in unison into the air. The thunder sound echoed across the zavana and the birds in the wood beside the batey court rose up into the sky, screeching and scattering in all directions.

The arquebuses had been captured during the first wars against the Castilla and their allies, he said, and hidden by his father in one of the caves on the Breast, which is the hill behind Anona, and smeared with turtle fat to preserve them from rotting. His father, he said, had foreseen the day when we would need to fight again. He did not say that these wars had been lost and we had been forced to agree that every man and woman of us would pay you tributo, pan the rivers for you and every three moons fill the bells you had given us with gold dust, or if we could not find any gold, to give you bales of spun cotton.

"When the other peoples of our island," he said, "see that the Castilla can be punished for the innumerable inequities they have inflicted upon us, they too – many of whom the Castilla have even more grievously wronged than they have us – will rise up against these intruders."

The power of the human voice and words spoken with passion and eloquence, or even simply having the appearance of being so, can be a terrible thing. And though some were unmoved by his preaching and went to hide in the hills, most stayed.

The next day Guaro became cacique and selected his council of advisors. Then – he waited till the day after those who had decided to go on an embassy to New Isabela to beseech forgiveness had departed, for he knew that the Christians knew how to make men talk – he revealed to us how we would surprise the Christian soldiers when they came. Of those who went to New Isabela with gifts: we never heard of them again.

"We shall lie in wait in the woods on the path from New Isabela and attack them there," he said. "It will be many days before they get here and we shall use that time to lay traps for them." He talked of digging pits with sharpened stakes in them and carrying rocks into the trees to drop on the Castilla as they passed below us.

His argument was that through surprise and numbers – for you were less in those days and we were more – we would win; and that word of your defeat would spread from one end of Hayti to the other, like a fire across the zavana in the dry months. That we would be armed with arquebuses was the last thing the Christians would expect, he said. We had little powder of course, and only a handful of lead balls, either of the larger ones or the smaller ones which are fired a dozen or so at a time; the making of powder and of lead was a secret you Christians had guarded well. But, Guaro told his advisors – and this I learnt later, for I was not privy to their councils – the main purpose of these weapons was to strike terror into the heart of the enemy rather than wound him, for arquebuses are notoriously inaccurate weapons and do not work well on rainy days; though the wounds they make are terrific, as I'm sure you know. Arbalests are much more accurate and easier to use, but we had only the four we had taken from the horses of the dead Christians.

The Christian army appeared thirteen days later, thirteen long foreboding-filled days and nights during which the bohiques spun their disks and looked into the dream-world. I was out trapping hutias that morning. I saw the cloud of dust created by the men, their horses and their dogs as they approached over the zavana, a cloud of death bearing towards us. Our warriors had been waiting for days in the woods on both sides of the way between Concepción and New Isabela, the women bringing them casabe bread, while youths like myself and some maidens went about trapping hutias and parrots for them.

The battle had already begun when, running as fast as I could across the zavana, armed with my macana, bow and a quiver of arrows tipped with frog poison, I reached the edge of the woods. I could hear the thunder of arquebuses, the cries of men and the barking of dogs, and was met by men running towards me, terror on their faces, running from the flames. For the wood was on fire. The battle was already ending in defeat. I ran too, back across the zavana to Anona, towards home, thinking, I suppose – though the thoughts that were rushing through my heart as I ran were so chaotic that they were not really thinking – that home is the place to run to when one's world is falling apart. That was what nearly all those who escaped death in the battle did. They ran home, the way a hunted hutia makes for its burrow. But I never reached Anona. One moment I was running, the sounds of dogs and arquebuses somewhere in the distance behind me, and then the next moment: nothing.

I came to consciousness two days later, in pain, my mind wiped clean of any memory of what had happened or where I was, as if I'd drunken a pot of sugar wine. Though later the memories came back. A hand offered me a gourd of cool water, Guaro's hand.

"You were hit by a ball from an arquebus," he told me. "It ripped your thigh. The shock of it must have knocked you over and caused you to hit your head on a rock. That was what put you to sleep."

He had dressed my wounds with turtle fat.

"And the others?" I asked.

He wasted neither time nor words in answering me, as was his manner when he was not trying to inspire men to do impossible things.

"The Castilla defeated us," he said. "Anona does not exist anymore. Most of those we know are husks. The shit-eaters burnt everything."

I pressed him to tell me more, but he said what was done was done, knowing the details was not what was important then. That there would be time enough to remember and lament.

In the days that followed he was silent for the most part so I did not learn much, not then anyway, of what had happened, nor what he felt in his heart about being, in some measure, responsible for our destruction. He had emboldened us to fight the Christians, and had led us to believe that it was possible to win a victory over them and that one glorious victory would cause many of the peoples of our island to rise up. Perhaps it was possible, but only that, possible, in so much as anything is possible. The glamour of his own passion and eloquence had seduced him, as well as us, into believing that it was more than that. His arguments had been wishful thinking. Both he and we had forgotten our past defeats. But he had also believed that it has been the intention of the Christian commander to massacre our people in any case, as a lesson and an example to any others who dreamt of insurrección. But then, had I too not had a hand in causing what had happened by raising my hand against the Christians on that fateful day?

He said: "Our gods are husks. The world-before will never be again. We have to leave our customary ways behind us."

Later I learnt that we had fought well but that the Christians had set the woods on fire.

"Even the wind was against us," they say of that day.

I asked him how he had survived, escaped.

"I didn't try and run home," he said.

The Christians had followed our warriors back to Anona and Gonzales de Esquival, or Carnage as we called him from that day on, who was the commander that day, had ordered his men to give no quarter. Over six hundred were cut down, bludgeoned to death or ripped apart by the dogs. Six hundred men, women and children. That is why we call him Carnage.

Several days later, when I could walk again, or at least move around, Guaro said it was time for us to part.

"There is a Castilla I know in Concepción," he said. "I have had dealings with him. I am going to pretend to give you to him."

"Give me to him?" I asked astounded. "By what right? No man is yours to give."

"I said 'pretend to'," he said.

"The Christians pretend that we owe them tributo," I said, "and their pretending makes it so."

"I will make an agreement with him that after five years you will no longer have to do his bidding," he explained. "You will be safe with this man. He is not like the others. I am going into the hills. There will be a price on my head. I will need to be able to move quickly, like the flight of an arrow. You can barely walk. I cannot take you with me. If the Castilla find you out here, they will kill you or sell you. As this man's slave you will be safe from the other Castilla. You will be his property. The Castilla respect little, but one of the things they do respect is each other's property. I know him. He will not mistreat you. You have no choice. We have to leave our customary ways behind us. There is no more home to run to."

He then gave me some Christian rags and told me to put them on, and a crude wooden cross that he had fashioned to wear on a string around my neck.

"It will help keep you safe," he said. "Crosses sometimes have a strange power over them."

He also put on some Christian rags himself.

"Don't want to turn up looking like savages from the woods, do we now?" he laughed. But I don't think the joke translates.

Then the both of us, dressed up as Christians, set off for Concepción.

Thus it was that I came to be with Johannes and learnt your tongue – for he was a good teacher – and how I came to be called Savonarola. Not as you may imagine because Johannes was not able to pronounce Agüeybaná. He was adept in that regard and like you, Don Padre, spoke our tongue; though also like you, with a funny stilted awkwardness. He said the name came to him when he saw the wooden cross hanging around my neck and the Christian rags Guaro had given me. He laughed when he gave the name to me and said it was the name of a bohique from his native city in Italia, who by his preaching had convinced the rich to throw all their luxuries into a huge fire erected in the plaza mayor there – 'a bonfire of the vain things', he called it. I have always suspected that there was more to the joke. But if there was, he never told me.

You have your pictures of the world you call maps. We too had pictures of our world. They told us where our gods dwelt, where Atabey slept by day and the Lord of the Dawn slept at night; from whence the seawaters came; where the island Coaybay lay, on which the opías of our dead dwelt, watched over by the dog-god Opiyelguabirán; of what the earth was to the heavens and the heavens to the earth; of how to live and how to die; and when to sacrifice, when to rejoice and when to celebrate our areítos, what songs to sing, what tales to tell; and when to be full of sorrow; when to play batey on the now desolate and weed-filled batey courts. We had our maps of that which you call the soul. We knew the contours of the dream-world.

I search in my own tongue for words to better and with greater accuracy explain all this and to translate it into Castilian so that you may better understand, but I cannot find them. There are some things I cannot say in your tongue, and there are some things which you say that I cannot put into my mother's tongue, and which I think I understand but perhaps not. We both call the grass green in our different manners; but is that which you call green and we call green the same thing in your eyes as it is in ours? Is our sense of holiness the same as yours?

You monks forever preach to us about that which you consider to be good and holy, forever saying that all humanity sprang forth from the womb of a woman called Eve and that we are all siblings, brothers and sisters, and that once all humanity spoke with a common tongue and there was great understanding between the one and the other. 'Humanity' is a word I learnt from Johannes. He said that it is a word denoting all men, all women, those who are neither or both, children, you, us, the black men you have brought with you, the Canibas, high men and low men, whole and unwhole, all of us. He said that all this is written in your books. Of course those books could be a load of shit, just like your maps could be. The fact that something is written down does not make it true.

Right and wrong. Right and wrong. You monks are forever going on about it. Your right and our wrong! As if darkness could exist without light, wetness without dryness, inside without outside, black without white, satiety without hunger, life without death; as if the night does not know another truth than the day. You do not see that all things exist only in conjunction with their opposites, and the world is whole only when these opposites are in living balance. Your obsession with your rightness brings forth only its opposite.

And you count and you count. Your notaries and accountants accompany you everywhere, writing things down as if the writing down of what they write down makes true what they write down. They put numbers and prices on everything and note them endlessly in their books as if the relation of one man to another can be measured in maravedís, pesos and ducats. You would count the blades of grass on the zavana and the feathers on the birds and the clouds in the sky and put a number on them if it was possible.

Your right and our wrong!

Our picture of the world is evaporating as completely as a dawn mist over the zavana; perhaps it was never more substantial than that. Soon it will be no more. I see a tree and I see a gibbet. The very air itself has become pestilent. We are suffered to exist on whims. The sun is dying and the stars are going out. We were forced to pay you tributo for the privilege of inhabiting the earth, and when we could not pay it, you made our bodies your property. Our thoughts fly about like straw in a hurucan; they are chaos. Our maps of the world have been erased. Our maps of our souls have been erased. It is as they had only ever been writ on the water of the Lake of the Iguanas. Without them, we are becoming invisible even to ourselves.

The news will no doubt have now reached you that the caciques Urayoán, Orocobix and my namesake Agüeybaná have made common cause with our ancient enemies the Canibas and have risen up in insurrección against you on the island you call John the Baptist's and have put to death great numbers of Christians there. This no doubt strikes terror into the hearts of the Christians here on Hayti. But for us it is a cause of joy. Perhaps we have become like you. For did not one of your greatest bohiques, a Christian called Tomás of some tribe or country called Aquino, not say that one of the greatest blisses of Guamiquina Jesus' world beyond death is watching the eternal torments of those who shall suffer eternal pain in the inferno Guamiquina Jesus has created for all those who offend him.

Because of all this, secret meetings were taking place in the hills. I decided to go to one of them. We came together in the ruins of a roofless bohío in the remnants of a pueblo known to me as a child, now visited only by the spirits of our dead at night in the form of bats searching in vain for their descendants. We were not many, for we are not as many as we once were, but we were of all sorts: men and women, nitaíno and naboria, those who work in your fields, and the ones you call simarons – because they move from place to place at the speed of a flying arrow, burning down your sugar mills – and even three black Castilla, a people most of whom you also misuse dreadfully.

The bohique Guabancex, being the eldest among us and the most familiar with the spirits and the dream-world, spoke first.

"Siblings," he said, "I have vomited and fasted and purified myself. I have inhaled the dust of the stars and gazed long into the spinning disk. I have looked into the heart of the world and seen nothing but the husks of dreams. The gods and the zemis are husks. The Christians are devouring the world. The tides bring only grief and childbirth has become a cause for lamentation. The time of our passing has come. The duty of those who are compelled to bear arms is to bear arms. The duty of those us who cannot, who have seen all they were ever destined to see, is to end their time in dignity."

Then Guaro spoke. He had aged little from the time we had last met. Perhaps men who are possessed of such wills as his age less gradually than common men, or perhaps their fiery spirits make such an impression upon us that we notice less their changing appearance.

He said: "Either we become as the Castilla and, like them, learn to worship gold – for no man is born worshipping gold, it is a religion which must be learnt – and make it the measure of all things. And learn the use of locks and keys, for that is also a thing which must be learnt. Or we choose not to, but to be what we are, for good and for ill. If you choose to become like the Castilla, you shall perhaps live long enough to have children, and perhaps some of those children will not be snuffed out by the pestilences. But your children will forget you. If you choose not to become like the Castilla, you will be hunted to the death by monstrous dogs and have no children, but the children you will not have will not forget you. The gods, who are now husks, and fate have already decided that. But what you want in your hearts was not laid down by the gods. I do not have it in my heart to become a Castilla, to make a shiny rock the measure of all things and to learn the way of locks and keys. Perhaps I am too old in spirit, too set in my ways, too stubborn to accept the new world. But so it is. And when they kill us, for they surely will, and they have taken final possession of all the islands, as they will also surely do, our spirits shall haunt this land by night and give them no rest. Our dead shall still live in the night air and the Castilla will live in fear of them."

We talked long into the night, drinking chicha around the fire, the embers of the dying stars in the darkness of the night above, visible through the rafters of what was once a roof. When the now dead moon had risen, revealing in its silver light the contours of the dark hills of our forlorn land, Guaro spoke again.

"At Anona," he said, "we were foolhardy. Perhaps, as some suggested then, we should have run to the hills and hidden ourselves in the woods. But when I look back on that time, I remember it as a time when the sun still shone, even if more faintly than in the world-before. There was still light or at least the possibility of it in our world. I believed that some things were still possible. And I wanted others to believe that. But now there is only the fading of the light, and soon there will be darkness, an invisible darkness, a darkness darker than that of the darkest moonless night. The days of great battles are bygone. All we can do now is go from place to place, and by moonlight, swiftly and silently like the flight of an arrow, wreak terror and havoc among the Castilla, and remind them that we still exist. Join me if you will. But, unlike life, which offers many things, I offer you nothing but struggle and death."

At dawn Guabancex went into the woods and hung himself honourably from the branch of a caoba tree. He had asked that his husk be left there, unburied, his bones uncleaned, so that his opía might haunt the land.

Johannes, as you know, used to absent himself for long periods, walking around the island in search of medicines and precious plants. So his absence is not considered unusual. I will no longer be here when he is missed. The chest I send you contains the things he said he wanted you to have. His gold, not that there was much, I have taken. I will find a use for it.

"The imperfection of the world," he used to say, "is its second mystery, the first being that such a thing as the world exists at all." He often told me how he believed the world was the imperfect reflection of a reflection of a reflection of some perfection, a base thing, the lowest and most forlorn of all the spheres of being of which he said there were ten. And that this lowest sphere, our world, where nothing holds its form, was an eternal battlefield between the forces of darkness and of light, each vying to mould the form of this world in its own image. And that our salvation lay in only in greater knowledge of our own souls and the universe-soul, which is the soul of all that exists in the heavens, on the islands of the earth and beyond, and that one lifetime was hardly enough to acquire such knowledge. But I no longer concern myself overmuch with such questions. It is simpler to live as if one were already dead, as if all that is to happen were already done.

I leave Concepción tomorrow.

The macaw can be quite talkative.

The macaw can be quite talkative!

Damn him! Reading those words now for the second time – I have not looked at the letter since it was delivered to me two months ago – it all becomes suddenly and excruciatingly clear. Among the 'things' the one-eared Haytian youth had left for me with the cook was the macaw.

The macaw can be quite talkative! Damn him!

How had she put it? A smattering of Latin?

The damnable bird has not learnt to mimic the Pater Noster from me. At most I have but whispered the prayer but a few times in its presence. The macaw might be cleverer than the average of its kind but not so clever as to be able to learn to say the Pater Noster off by heart, in a tongue it had probably never heard before in its life, from hearing it a few times, and whispered at that.

No, to learn a macaw to talk takes time, patience, perseverance, and only one person had spent enough time with the bird: the savage Savonarola. It seemed Puccini had thought Savonarola a bit more than a smattering of Latin. The Haytian was clever, and more than adept with tongues other than his own. His letter was ample evidence of that. And in turn, Savonarola, in his perversity, had learnt the bird the prayer.

The knowledge both relieves and horrifies me.

That he was lecherous and incapable of controlling his animal urges – nay, wallowed in them – I could somehow understand. For is not the Haytian in a manner of speaking a child of nature, innocent and sinful at the same time?

The perversity of it!

The guileful savage had known the prayer was holy.

Is our sense of holiness the same as yours?

Damn him again!

Or else he would not have learnt the bird to say it, or written those final taunting, calculating words: The macaw can be quite talkative!

Oh Lord, how much they must hate and loathe us and all to do with us!

Not that that changes anything of course. For who would believe that a savage was capable of such perverse dexterity?

But I must remain calm ...

Among the rest of Puccini's effects Savonarola had sent me were several samples of the bark of the guayacán tree Puccini believed can cure the Haytian pox, along with detailed drawings of the plant from which it came, the method of its grinding and preparation, its medicinal qualities, recommended doses and methods of application. There was also as a map indicating where on the Isola Beata the trees can be found. And a letter, uncompleted, to an Albrecht Schweinsteiger care of the House of Fugger in Augsburg, a connection he had never mentioned to me, which he had seemingly been in the process of writing before his untimely demise and which outlines his theories as to why the herb is effective. And Puccini's collection of maps.

"Let the dead bury the dead," Sor Lucrezia said when I told her of the fate of my friend and she saw my grief. I said an early morning mass for him and begged forgiveness for his sins, which were grave and of which there were no small number.

I remember at the time recalling a conversation we once had. We had been discussing reason and he had asked me to give an example of how through reason alone we could approach the divine. A simple enough intellectual task, so much so that in fact I suspected he was setting some philosophical trap for me. But I accepted the challenge.

"You agree that it is beyond question that God is a being the greater of which cannot be conceived," I said.

"Hardly a proposition that any sane man could deny," he admitted.

"And that it is greater to exist in the mind and in reality than in the mind alone," I added.

He could not but agree to that too.

"Therefore God must exist in reality," I continued with some satisfaction, "because if he did not, we could conceive of a greater being. Thus spoke Anselm of Canterbury to the fool who had said in his heart that there is no God. An example of pure reason approaching knowledge of the divine. Indeed, proving the existence of the divine. I know no better."

"The greatest proof there is," he admitted. "Except to those who don't believe it's greater to exist in reality than in the mind alone."

He did not like being bested in metaphysical argument.

"So death then, and sickness, and pain," I said, "the deaths of seemingly innocent babes and the suffering of apparent innocents? How can we explain such things? If there is a loving all-powerful God. Which we have just proved there is."

When catechising – for that, in hindsight, I suppose, is what I was doing – it is always a useful strategy to address the objections that might be raised by those one is preaching to before they themselves have had the chance to raise them.

"Because we are being punished?" he said.

"Yes," I remember saying, feeling no trivial measure of satisfaction in seeing him on the defensive for once. "No other reason is conceivable. Because none are innocent. We are all sinful by nature. We are all fallen creatures. We are punished because we offend God, the essence of goodness, and continue to offend Him. The terribleness of the punishment can only be explained by the terribleness of our sinfulness. The evil in the world is our own doing. By its fruit shall you know the tree."

"There have been other explanations," he said rather lamely.

"Such as?" I asked, succumbing to curiosity, wondering which one he would choose.

"That the evidence of our senses," he said, "or reason based on experience as I like to call it, suggests that much that is in this world of earth and flesh and pain was not created by the Loving God, but by a sort of demon, a demiurge. *My maker was divine authority, the highest wisdom and primal love.*"

I was at a loss for a moment but he explained.

"Those were the words Dante Alighieri inscribed above the gateway to his inferno," he said. "Some would argue that it is impossible that the highest wisdom and primal love would create a world such as this one, let alone create hell itself. Reason – based on experience – would seem to teach us that good does not always triumph over evil. Perhaps the struggle between good and evil is never-ending."

"Ideas taken seriously by none except fanatical idolaters in Persia," I told him, "and fashionable intellectuals in Italy. Pure reason, like Anselm's, can lead us to the divine, but your so-called 'reason based on experience' tells us but trivial things – and can deceive. It does not tell us that men have souls or what is right or wrong. Christ used the world to illustrate eternal truths. He did not find eternal truths in it. Sin comes from Man. The hell we have created here on these islands is of our making, created by our greed and cruelty, not by highest wisdom and the primal love."

Another time he said – and it is something that I often remember: "Two thousand years of philosophy. One and a half thousand years of Christianity. But what essential thing have we not learnt?"

But I wander from the point.

I see now how he was guilty of a sort of heresy, a purveyor of a garbled Kabbalistic theology, the poisonous Gnostic idea that salvation is only for some elite of adepts, and Manichean falsities. Yes, I can see that now. Hate the sin and love the sinner! So we are enjoined. But what if the sin is inextricable from the sinner? I console myself by thinking that in this case that was not so. The ideas that Puccini played with were no doubt heretical in nature. But I use the words 'played with' advisedly, for though he was no doubt unduly attached to and enamoured of his cunning ability to perform all manner of philosophical conjuring tricks – in truth, he could run rings around the devil at times – I have no proof, sadly, that he did not hold those ideas deeply in his heart.

The presence of a false idea in a man's mind is not in itself 'formal' heresy, it is 'objective' or 'material' heresy, graver than simple irreverence, but still not, strictly speaking, heresy proper, the worst of sins. A man, for example, may hold an idea in innocent error, be momentarily overcome or seduced by a fleeting opinion, or be plagued by doubts. Even Christ in the depths of His Passion cried out in despair. Or a man may hold ideas unwillingly, being led astray by others, indeed be the victim himself of heretical rhetoric. And such confusions can be remedied by simple preaching and example. No, pertinacity, the obstinate adhesion to a dangerous and erroneous doctrine, is required to make heresy formal, that is, into what is generally understood as the crime of heresy. The heretical idea must be willingly held, deviously held, stubbornly held, unrepentantly held, and, in addition, preached. Puccini's sin was in conveying his heretical thoughts, arguing them – even if it was only for rhetorical amusement – to a soul in his care and over whom he exercised influence and hence had a responsibility to. No man has the right – by deed, word or thought – to endanger the immortal soul of another.

That was my friend's sin, and nothing can convince me that it was not grave. For the savage Savonarola, despite his blindness and obvious inability to rein in his depraved animal lusts, did have a rudimentary sense of right and wrong, an interest in spiritual matters and, as evidenced in his letter, in the nature of his soul and the divine order. He could have been led to Christ; instead, he was led into an unholy marriage of faulty reason and black magic.

I am running out of ink but our captain tells me we should reach the Azores within a week or less. No doubt the price of it will be exorbitant. As we approach Christendom I find myself yearning for things I have not tasted in years: olives, cheese and good wine. And oranges. To mark our progress thus far the captain has announced to the whole crew he is going to tap a barrel of sugar wine tonight. The prospect of a proper drink is heartening.

The shame of it! The whole crew got mad-raving drunk and I along with them. Two dozen sailors pissed out of their minds in the midst of these heaving God-forsaken waters along with the captain ... I remember only how it started ... I woke up on the floor of my cupboard, bruised, my habit filthy, stained with God-only-knows what dirt, my head about to crack, my bowels poisoned ... The shame of it! I lay half-awake for I don't know how long, the only sound the bird fidgeting on its perch, the ship as silent as a graveyard, my soul beseeching the Almighty to punish me, to fasten me into the stinking depths of a deep latrine and have the whole ship's filthy crew shit on me until I suffocated in my own foulness ... Oh, what demons do at times possess us!

Plates 3

Figure 11 *Depiction of cannibalism in the New World by the engraver Johann Froschauer, from an edition of Amerigo Vespucci's* Mundus Novus *from Augsburg, Germany, 1505. Possibly the earliest surviving printed image of American Indians.*

Figure 12 *Girolamo Benzoni* La historia del mondo nuovo, *Venice, 1565. Depicts collective suicides of Taíno Indians on Hispaniola in the years after the discovery. Benzoni arrived in the Americas in 1541 and spent 15 years there.*

Figure 13 *Illustration from Theodore de Bry's edition of* Narratio regionum indicarum per Hispanos quosdam devastatarum verissima *(a translation into Latin of Bartolomé de las Casas'* A Brief Description of the Destruction of the Indies*), Frankfurt-am-Main, late 16th century. De Bry's images were possibly the most common images of the conquest of the Americas in circulation in Europe at the time. His books on the Americas were published in several editions, and after his death, his son and other family members continued publishing new editions with new illustrations.*

Figure 14 *Illustration from Theodore de Bry's edition of* Narratio regionum indicarum per Hispanos quosdam devastatarum verissima, *late 16th century.*

Figure 15 *Illustration from Theodore de Bry's* Narratio regionum indicarum per Hispanos quosdamdevastatarum verissima, *late 16th century.*

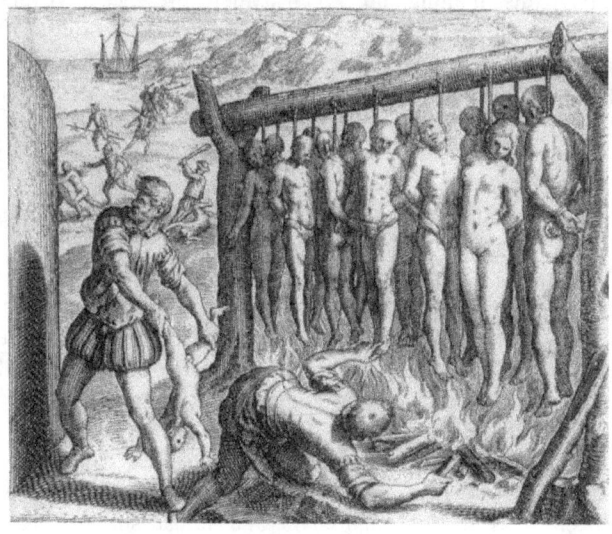

Figure 16 *Illustration from Theodore de Bry's* Narratio regionum indicarum per Hispanos, *late 16th century.*

TWENTY-FOUR

The Alcalde Mayor's bride-to-be, a flaxen-haired woman of very handsome looks indeed, arrived this morning on the *Incarnation*. He met her at the quayside and, with great fanfare, escorted her as she was carried in her litter to the Castle by her two Guanche servants. Also on board the *Incarnation* was the Captain-General de Esquival's bride-to-be, whom I have not yet seen. Both couples are to be married the day after tomorrow in a private ceremony in the Castle chapel, a Franciscan officiating, with His Excellentissimo and his lady wife, the Donna Marias de Toledo, also in attendance. A more public festivity is planned for the evening of the same day. It will be a fortnight or so before the *Incarnation* sails again as repairs need to be carried out, and when it does, Fray Montenegro will sail with it.

I have often wondered how the dead appear to us when they are granted leave to do so. Some say they manifest themselves no more substantially than a wisp of smoke. Others say that it is even less than this, nothing more than a mere presence invisible to earthly eyes, detected by the mind rather than the senses. Yet others maintain that the deceased appear as if they were solid flesh and blood, no more ghostly, strange or unsubstantial than they were in life; and appear so much so that the beholder of an apparition may not even be immediately aware that he is in the presence of one. If what I saw was a ghost – Carlos Goya's ghost – then the form that apparitions of the dead take is most definitely the latter.

The details: It happened in broad daylight, late morning, at the twice-weekly market on the Plaza de Armas, amidst the whole multitude that packs the square on these occasions: hawkers, servants, maids, seamen, soldiers, wild Indians and every other type of person who inhabits this island. I saw him from a distance across the square behind the pigs' and goats' pens. I didn't recognise him immediately. His face was painted white and red and his hair was black – he must have dyed it – and longer than it had been, more in the Indian style, and he had small clumps of green feathers hanging from his mutilated earlobes. He was also more or less dressed in the Indian fashion – I say more or less because many of the poorer Christians and those of mixed race, the so-called mestizos, have also taken to wearing plain homespun cotton. I don't know what feature of him I recognised first. Perhaps it was his eyes, or his nose, which is quite pronounced, or something about his general demeanour. When I was sure it was him – or his ghost? – or thought I was, I made to go towards him through the crowd; but the market was so packed I could barely move and, in the hustle and bustle of the throng, lost sight of him for an instant. When I looked again, he was gone and there was another man, an aged Indian peasant, standing in the spot where he had been, a man so different in appearance that I could not have possibly mistaken him for Goya, even momentarily. But it has been insufferably hot and humid these last few days and nights. Perhaps I just imagined it all.

I have finished transcribing Fray Pedro's copy of Ramón Pané's brief account – and it is brief, and unclear in many parts – of the customs, medicines and superstitions of the Indians as they were at the time of our first coming here, and of the first conversions among them. He also tells of a strange prophecy among them, related to him by an old cacique whose name is not clear; the friar's Castilian is faulty, he is a Catalan, and he had knowledge of only one of the Indian dialects; and, he freely admits, he had to rely much on interpreters, though he makes no mention of the Diego Colón II of whom Alfredo Castro spoke or any other interpreters by name. This cacique, Pané relates, claimed he had been told by their most powerful zemi, one called Yucahuguamá – which means the lord of casabe, for 'yuca' is another word they use for casabe – that 'one day a clothed people' would come to their land who would conquer them and they would all die of starvation. At first, he says he was told, the Indians had thought that this prophecy had referred to the Canibas, but since these only steal from them and then run away they concluded that in fact the zemi Yucahuguamá was foretelling the coming of 'the Admiral and his people'. All in all, it is a rough account and, Pané says, he would have written more and with greater accuracy if not for the shortage of paper at the time.

I have decided to entrust the care of this manuscript into the trustworthy hands of Fray Montenegro. You did say I was to find a person 'above suspicion' – your very words – to convey it to you; and that that might not be an easy task. I think he will see that it will be in his interest to deliver these pages to you personally, and that making your acquaintance will be an opportunity for him to argue the Preachers' case to a man of influence in Rome. So I am hoping he will agree to this. I intend to speak to him at the first opportunity.

Rudolfo Jesus de Paz is now a married man, as is the Captain-General de Esquival. A messenger from the Castle arrived yesterday morning inviting me and my sisters to attend the festivities which are to take place at the still uncompleted Palace. It was signed by the Alcalde himself. As you can imagine, after all that has occurred, it surprised me somewhat to have received an invitation. A sincere attempt to mend damaged bridges? Even if I draw on all my reserves of Christian charity and its injunction to think well of our Christian fellows, I cannot with a pure heart believe that.

I have spoken to Montenegro about conveying this manuscript to you. He has agreed in principle. I told him only, not mentioning your name for now, that you were a man of some influence, pious and humane, and devoted to the welfare of mankind, and that you had requested me to provide you with a firsthand account of conditions in the Indies, an unbiased account. For, I said, you suspected that many of the official reports that reach Rome are biased accounts of the truth of these matters, coloured by the various interests of their composers. I emphasised most strongly that this document was only for your eyes and those of none other, and that I would seal it accordingly. I would, I told him, deliver it into his hands when he was safely aboard the *Incarnation*, for I would not put it beyond the wiles of Rudolfo Jesus de Paz to have his effects searched before he boarded, a possibility to which he concurred.

Ж

And that, in short, is how this document came into my hands.

TWENTY-FIVE

A horrifying event has occurred, and like many tragedies, or the beginnings of them, with the suddenness of a thunder flash from a blue summer sky. I must describe it in detail, starting at the beginning.

The evening was perfect for the double nuptial fiesta. The gardens of the Palace could not have been more splendidly decked out. The uncompleted building, its arched colonnades decked out in the yellow and red bunting of Castile, provided a splendid backdrop to the event. An equatorial crescent moon and a sprinkling of the brightest stars hung over the bay, gently illuminating the whitewashed buildings of Santo Domingo and the mirror-black sea, where a few ghostly ships lay at anchor in the calm. The air had cooled after the heat of the day, and there was but the whiff of a sea breeze. Rarely is Santo Domingo so pleasant and so picture-like.

My beatas and I arrived two hours after sundown, minus Hildegard of course, who is confined to her cell. I do not yet know what to do with the girl. Dispatching her back across the Oceanus Occidentalis would be an expense beyond the means of our purse, and she has no close family on which I could impose to pay her passage. To subject her to a long sea journey in her current condition would be a cruelty, if not to her then to the innocent child she is illicitly bearing. She still refuses to say who the father is. I suspect finding her a position of some kind in a respectable household here would be near impossible. So I suppose that in the end there will be nothing for it but for her to remain with us as a servant of some sorts. Her skills in many areas are, it must be said, superior to those of my other cares.

But to return to this evening's events: Long tables and benches had been laid out in the form of a large square. Torches had been erected on perhaps two dozen or so poles to provide us with illumination. The servants, done up neatly in grey cotton livery, were already roasting three large pigs on spits and preparing other meats, fowls and fishes in the Indian barbacoa fashion over slow-burning fires. The smell was mouth-watering. A large tapped barrel of Jerez had been placed beside the wooden platform on which the high table stood. On the table too was an object the shape and size of a birdcage, draped over with a brown cloth – or

rather that is what I first took it for, a birdcage containing perhaps
a parrot, draped over to keep the beast in darkness to prevent it
from getting excited in all the commotion.

Most all of the guests were already in place as our arrival was
announced, including Fray Pedro, Montenegro and the other
Preachers. We had barely been seated a few minutes when a
herald blew a horn and Ramírez, our master of ceremonies,
announced – with perfect elocution and in a booming voice I
never suspected he possessed; he is a paragon of humble
demeanour and discretion normally – the entry of His
Excellentissimo the Governor and his wife, citing all the former's
titles: Viceroy of the Indies, Marquis of Jamaica (the island the
Indians call Xaymaca) and Duke of Veragua. His
Excellentissimo's dwarf-buffoon, who was not announced – his
name is Cervantes – removed his feathered cap and bowed to us
all with a flourish. Neither was a tall beak-nosed man, dressed
entirely in bright green; Fray Estaban, the Franciscan Prior,
whom I have met several times but whom I think I have only
mentioned once in this account, informed me that this was His
Excellentissimo's astrologer, whose name is Millan. Both these
two, I am told, accompany the Governor everywhere.

Ramírez then announced the two married couples, who arrived
next, and the other leading personages of the administration,
citing their titles, who followed. The Captain-General de
Esquival, attired splendidly in ruffled pansied slops and hosen,
cut a far dapper figure than when we had met him on the
Concepción road. Then, when the notables were seated, Ramírez
rang his bell and the servants began to go around the tables with a
jug of water and a bowl so that we could wash our hands. Fray
Estaban then led the whole of the company in grace and the
serving of the food and drink commenced. While we ate, a trio of
musicians entertained us, the sounds of their guitars, the clicking
of castanets, and their songs evoking memories of the hills and
olive groves of Castile and Andalusia.

The Preachers, the Franciscans and ourselves had been seated at
the same table, and Fray Pedro, Fray Estaban and myself, as the
respective heads of the religious orders on the island, had been
placed at the head.

"Perhaps His Excellentissimo has seated all of us sinners
together to give us an opportunity to reconcile with one another,"
Fray Pedro said, remarking on this fact. A silly remark really,
since the arrangement was surely natural.

"A most laudable Christian desire," Fray Estaban said. "And

not impossible to achieve if those of us who are enjoined to serve God serve Him and leave those enjoined to serve Caesar to do Caesar's work."

"All men are enjoined to serve God," Fray Pedro said.

"And to give unto Caesar what is Caesar's," Fray Estaban replied. "And His Excellentissimo is Caesar here, appointed by a God-anointed prince."

"We will not be moved," Fray Pedro cut him short. "We are set in our determination and sure of the righteousness of it."

But then, mercifully, for I did not relish the idea of an argument between these two men, Ramírez rang his bell again and announced that we were to be treated to a performance from a troupe of dancers from one of His Excellentissimo's many estates.

There were perhaps two dozen of them, young men and young women, equal in numbers; all chastely dressed I must add, in white cotton, the men in shifts and pants and the women in dresses. The men had painted their faces red, white and black, their traditional colours, for the occasion, not something that is encouraged in normal life, and they had feathers in their hair; the women wore garlands of multi-coloured flowers in theirs. Both sexes wore bands of small snail shells on their arms, legs and ankles. Four drummers, playing intricately engraved mayohuacan drums as big and as loud as Puccini had described them, pounded out the beat and the rhythm. Round and round they wove, weaving in and out of each other in rows, leaping and singing, some of them holding hands or with their arms around each other's shoulders, all the time stamping their feet and shaking themselves to the beat of the mayohuacan drums so that the bands of shells they wore tinkled to the rhythm; while others played timbrels rimmed with their beloved hawk's bells. The sound and the sight of them was most pleasant and showed the elegance and chaste joy that these people are capable of if properly tutored. In the end, they all faced the high table and bowed gracefully to His Excellentissimo – their cacique, their guamiquina – and to the other notables before disappearing again into the night. A marvellous – there is no other word for it – display of grace and innocent dexterity which put all the company in jolly spirits. I was reminded of how, as Montenegro had previously told to me, such areítos were once performed with upwards of four hundred dancers. What a wondrous spectacle those ancient events must have been, I thought, but then remembered what Montenegro had told me about them.

Mercifully, in the hour that followed, during which we were treated to more Andalusian airs by the three guitarists, the conversation at our table consisted exclusively of trivialities and snippets of harmless gossip. And for that I was thankful to Fray Pedro. He seemed determined to speak only of innocuous subjects, as a way, I suspect, of demonstrating, though silence on the matter, the strength of the Preachers' resolve with regard to their refusal to dispense the sacraments to the Christians as long as they remained in a condition of ... I suppose one could say ... collective sin. It was as if he were saying: Look, we are so resolved and certain in this matter that I feel absolutely no need to even discuss it, or justify it in any manner at all, and I have no intention of being drawn upon the subject, so let us simply discuss the weather and how our respective gardens are doing and the like. And Fray Estaban, a man who, despite his earlier comments, generally gives the impression of preferring a quiet life, played along, not wanting to wave the red cape at the bull. Montenegro, who was seated beside Fray Pedro, was noticeably silent, and abstemious in his drinking, which was probably no bad thing.

When we were sated – not a condition we are habituated to, for our daily fare here is at times frugal, despite it being a land of eternal spring and harvests most of the year – Ramírez stood and rang his bell again to gain our attention.

His Excellentissimo spoke first, beginning by congratulating the happy newly-wedded couples, wishing them numerous and sturdy offspring and singing the praises of the Alcalde and the Captain-General, mentioning the many services which they both have rendered him over the years, and through him, the Crown. Montenegro caught my eye several times. The look of quiet fury and derision on his face made me again thankful for his abstemiousness. His drunken outburst that night on the way to Concepción was still fresh in my mind.

I shall quote, or rather attempt to quote – for, despite His Excellentissimo's rather strained Castilian, he spoke with great feeling and eloquence – some few words of his rather lengthy speech.

"My father, God rest his soul," he told us, "was a man of vision. And I, in my own modest way, also like to think of myself as a man of vision. When he first landed on these shores, he found a people living in utter ignorance of Christian civilisation, a people to be sure with many laudable qualities but with only the vaguest ideas of right and wrong, and of property, a people prone to the most barbaric practices, a people living a life bereft of all the spiritual and material advantages of being part of Christendom. But those dark days are fast receding and the native inhabitants of these Indies are now slowly being integrated into the only true family of mankind, the community of Christianity. On Jamaica, on John the Baptist's and in the more recently founded colonies of Golden Castile and New Andalusia on tierra firme, everywhere I have seen good work being done and the wealth of our nation being increased. Gold is being extracted from the earth. Pearls are being extracted from the seas. Our knowledge of the world is increasing. Our sea captains are making new maps and providing us with information on lands and realms which a mere generation ago existed only in our dreams. And so that all this wealth can be even further increased, our notaries are busy counting and numbering it. But most importantly, the souls of men are being brought out of darkness and into the light."

He then raised his cup and bade us offer a hearty toast to all those who risk their lives in Christendom's cause.

"A rose-tinted picture, some of you may say," he continued. "And not without some justification. I myself would be the first to admit that all is not sweetness and light in these lands which have come under our tutelage. There are abuses – adventurous men are by their nature prone to strong passions – and at times there are tasks to perform which require severity and severe men. No, all is not perfect, and will never be. Not even a world organised according to the highest principles of the Christian religion, the highest moral code that there is, can be free of imperfections. Such is the unhappy human condition."

These words, obviously, were meant for Fray Pedro and his Preachers, but also I suspect addressed to some of the Franciscans and myself, and any colonists whose consciences may have been unsettled by Montenegro's sermons.

"But the invisible hand of God," he continued, "moves in the most mysterious ways, and works so wonderfully that even out of the sinful selfishness of men can come an increase in wealth and of goodness and righteousness in the world. I ask you, but most especially those of you who suffer sincere qualms of conscience, to consider that. We have our differences, but are not all of us, in our different ways, creating a Christian global empire, a new order in the world one might even say? I do not consider those differences not to be grievous, not at all. But, in the depths of our spirits and our hearts, do we not all serve the same cause? I am sure that if you consider, deeply and calmly, all the various circumstances that have brought us here – to the ends of the earth, one could say – banishing from your thoughts your own particular causes and passions, you will recognise this to be so."

Then he made a sign to Ramírez who came forward and whisked the cloth from the birdcage-shaped object. Except it was not a birdcage, it was a clock. The polished brass and varnished wooden casing of the exquisitely crafted mechanism glinted in the torchlight.

"A new timekeeper," His Excellentissimo pronounced. "For a new time."

The dwarf-buffoon Cervantes was the first to clap, with an enthusiasm that bordered on pure sycophantic mockery. I could have sworn he almost winked. They say the Governor at times puts a collar on him and walks him about on a leash, as one would a dog. I can well believe it. But His Excellentissimo took it in his stride and bowed to our enthusiastic applause.

The Alcalde and Captain-General de Esquival, mercifully as briefly as politic allowed, then thanked His Excellentissimo for the honour of the fiesta. The formalities concluded, the guests then began to mingle and some even to dance in the square surrounded by the tables. Santo Domingo, as I think I wrote earlier, is a man's world, but there were quite a few ladies present this evening, far more so than at other gatherings I have attended.

I'm not sure what or which of the two of them I saw first. I think it was Savonarola – which astonished me in itself – he was wearing the grey cotton livery of the servants, both were, and for a fraction of a moment I absurdly thought he was actually working as a servant. But when I saw Goya, I was thrown into complete turmoil. I was standing in brief conversation with Fernández de Oviedo and another official from the Castle. Both Goya and Savonarola were moving towards us when I saw them, or rather in the direction of where we were standing, but I'm sure neither of them saw or even noticed us. They were moving in unison, their eyes not on us but on something or someone behind us. But this time, I knew, instantly, it was Goya I was seeing, not his ghost, and that he was inexplicably alive. Never have I seen such iron determination on men's faces, such single-mindedness, and, as they passed us by, I knew we were invisible to them and that the object of their iron determination was behind us.

As I turned to see where they were heading I noticed that

both of them had a hand behind their backs and were clasping the handles of long knives half-hidden under the folds of their servants' clothing – and that they were making a beeline for the Alcalde and the Captain-General, both of whom were engaged in conversation with their wives and Ramírez in a group to the side of the still-playing guitarists.

Then – in my memory it happened slowly, as though in a Florentine ballet, but in reality it happened in as little time as it takes lightning to flash – I saw their knives come out, and the vicious blades glitter momentarily in the torch and moonlight. And I saw Rudolfo Jesus de Paz's wife turn and her mouth open – I could have sworn it was actually an instant later that I actually heard the scream that issued from her – and step protectively, perhaps thinkingly or perhaps instinctively, between her husband and Savonarola, who had cast himself forward at the Alcalde, his knife-bearing arm stretched out straight and rigid as if it were a lance.

The long blade of the knife pierced her breast with a terrible and almost inaudible thumping sound. As she bent forward, as if embracing the blow, and fell to the ground, she dragged Savonarola down with her, his hand still glued fast to the knife, frantically trying to extract the blade from her ribs.

Then three things happened simultaneously. As the Alcalde's Irish wolfhound jumped growling on Savonarola, Goya, startled, stood still in his tracks, giving the Captain-General time to swiftly draw his sword from its scabbard and bring it down on Goya's outstretched arm with such force that it cut clean through it, through both flesh and bone, just above the wrist. Goya screamed as his hand, still clasping his knife, tumbled to the ground; and then he turned and ran as the Alcalde, letting out a cry of what I can only describe of utter despair, knelt down and embraced his bleeding wife; while Ramírez, his sword drawn now too, began stabbing Savonarola, repeatedly, and with a ferocity I would not have believed him capable of if I had not seen it with my own eyes.

Goya, screaming, tore through the crowd, which parted to let him pass as the sea parts to let a ship through it, with Captain-General de Esquival, sword in hand, pursuing him, roaring: "Assassin! Assassin!" But Goya had not gotten very far when he suddenly fell to the ground, out of shock or loss of blood or because he had tripped over something – I couldn't see – and the Captain-General was upon him and the crowd closed in upon them both.

When I reached the throng, finding myself standing beside Montenegro, the Captain-General was shouting for a surgeon. A ship's officer said he would fetch one and rushed off into the night; and, as he did so, I saw the Captain-General kneel over Goya, who lay on the ground, seemingly still conscious, his eyes wide open but seeming as if they were seeing nothing. The Captain-General took off his neck scarf and used it as a tourniquet to stem the flow of blood from Goya's bleeding stump. Then, just when the bleeding had reduced itself to a trickle, His Excellentissimo and his retinue appeared, and the crowd made way for him.

"The bastard's still alive," the Captain-General told the Governor. "But he's lost a lot of blood. I've sent for a surgeon."

His Excellentissimo nodded.

"Who is he?" he asked.

Montenegro looked at me but I don't think I would have spoken anyway.

"Looks like a redskin," the Captain-General said, "but I don't think he is one. That's a Castilian snout if I ever saw one."

His Excellentissimo looked at Goya more closely, bending slightly over him.

"But those ears," he said, "they don't look like Castilian ears to me."

"Let me through, let me through," a voice called out, and a small man, a Basque by the sound of him, pushed his way through the crowd.

When he reached His Excellentissimo and the Captain-General, bowing profusely to the former, he introduced himself: "Bikendi Bolibar, surgeon of the *Incarnation*, at your disposal, Excellentissimo."

"This creature," His Excellentissimo said, indicating Goya with a disdainful gesture, "has lost a hand."

"'Tis a clean cut," the Captain-General added.

"Yes," His Excellentissimo said. "A clean cut. Can you cauterise it or whatever it is you do in cases like this?"

The Basque knelt down beside Goya, looked at the stump, waved his hands in front of Goya's eyes, presumably trying to ascertain something or other.

"I'll need a knife," he pronounced finally. "With a nice big flat blade."

The Captain-General sent one of his men to fetch one from the cooks.

"I want this man to live, Señor Bolibar," His Excellentissimo said. "It's of the utmost importance that he lives. Understood!"

The surgeon bowed.

"I shall do all in my power, Sire," he said.

"We need to get to the bottom of this bloody business," His Excellentissimo added, almost to himself, but then addressed the crowd: "And we shall, fellow citizens, we shall."

The man who had been sent to fetch the knife returned with a cleaver, and the surgeon ordered it to be heated up at one of the cooking fires.

"I need it hot, just about to redden," he said.

I was busy assembling my beatas then, so I did not see what he did when the knife was brought back. But I heard Goya scream and then saw him being carried on a makeshift stretcher in the direction of the Castle.

As we were leaving Montenegro tugged on my sleeve and requested a few private words with me. I bade my sisters wait while we stepped aside and found a quiet spot.

"I presumed you recognised him," he said.

"Yes," I said, "I recognised him. The other day ..." I was about to tell him that I had seen Goya at the market but he interrupted me.

"We shall have to come forward," he said. "Both of us. Separately. Say we did not recognise him at the time, or were not sure. The shock of it all and all that! But that now we are sure. Something like that."

"I do not understand," I said.

"They will make him talk," he said. "That's why they wanted him alive. There cannot even be the faintest whiff – not the whiff of a whiff – that we are even remotely connected with what has happened here this evening. You must go to the Castle first thing in the morning, I will go shortly afterwards."

"But the Alcalde will ..."

"He does not know we visited Goya," he said, "though he may suspect it. He never actually asked me if we did, and I did not tell him that we did. Go to de Esquival. The Alcalde will be in mourning. Say you did not want to disturb his grieving. His wife is dead. De Esquival will suspect nothing, most probably. God willing. Go there immediately after Terce. I will get there an hour or so later. Say you were with me when you visited Goya's encomienda. Say I brought you there. I was showing you how our catechising efforts in the countryside were progressing. Tell the truth. Say that I went there to baptise Goya's Indian woman and marry them. If I turn up just after you have left, he'll have no time to wonder too much why I did not come forward just now. But be sure to tell the truth. That way our stories will be the same – and I will say nothing that contradicts anything you tell him, hopefully."

"And what about Savonarola?" I asked.

"Just another dead redskin," he said. "I doubt if there'll be any interest in him. But if you are asked, simply say you weren't close enough to get a good look at him. If he presses you, shows you the body – which is possible – then say you recognise him as Puccini's servant."

I nodded agreement and we parted.

The moon had set as we made our way home through the pitch-dark streets of Santo Domingo by lantern light, the only sound that of the dogs howling. I have left instructions to be woken at first light.

TWENTY-SIX

The Captain-General de Esquival received me immediately as soon as I was announced and listened intently and politely to what I told him, which was in its essentials what Montenegro had suggested I say, though I did emphasise that I 'believed' rather than 'knew' that the assassin was Carlos Goya. When I was finished he was silent for a few moments before speaking.

"Carlos Goya," he said eventually. "Are you sure, Sister?"

"As sure as I can be," I said. "It was dark. And, as I said, I believed he was dead. Killed in a simaron raid, I was told."

"That is what we all believed," de Esquival said.

He speaks Castilian with a trace of some accent I cannot put my finger on.

"And then the shock of it all," I continued. "And, of course, it only occurred to me after yesterday evening's dreadful events that his identity was probably a mystery to you."

I could not help but remember what Montenegro had told me what the Indians called this man, a man of, at times, seemingly considerable charm and, unlike the Alcalde, with an impressive gravitas of manner – despite occasional outbursts of crudity. And that Montenegro, on the few occasions he had mentioned him, had himself as often as not referred to him as Carnage as by his proper name. Perhaps the good priest does exaggerate at times, but if he does, I sincerely believe, he does so out of a deep sense of right and wrong. And is it not so that the man who tells untruth sincerely is more virtuous than the man who tells a truth for devious purposes?

We were on the shaded terrace overlooking the river. He bade me take a seat on a bench and he then sat down beside me, an intimacy I cannot say I was comfortable with.

"I'm afraid, Sister," he said, "I am going to have to ask you to identify this Goya." Adding, as if reading my mind and was intent on reassuring me, for I had suddenly had a vision of having to descend into the bowels of the Castle and enter some filthy dungeon: "He's in the infirmary. Where he's well-guarded. Very well-guarded. And restrained. He will be of no danger to you. You can be sure of that."

Then, just as suddenly as he had sat down, he stood up.

"Shall we?" he said and indicated with an outstretched arm and a slight bow that he was expecting me to follow him.

The surgeon Bikendi Bolibar was examining Goya when we got to our destination. The prisoner was in a room of his own. There were two guards outside and the windows were grilled.

"Our patient is still unconscious," Bikendi said, in his thick Basque accent. "Quite normal under the circumstances. Just as sleep enables our bodies to recuperate from the strains and troubles of our days, the wounded often drop into this sort of unconsciousness. Sometimes they never awake from it again. But he has a strong pulse and little fever, so the prognosis, as we physicians say, is favourable. In layman's terms: he will in all probability recover. My considered opinion is that he will regain consciousness sometime today. Perhaps in the next hour. Perhaps this evening. If God wills it. But it's impossible to predict these things with great accuracy. Medicine is not an exact art."

While he spoke I noticed that one of Goya's ankles was manacled to the bedpost with a heavy chain.

"I'll come back this afternoon," Bikendi added and made to excuse himself.

The Captain-General nodded his approval.

"Well?" he said when Bikendi had left us.

"Yes, it's him," I said.

"No doubts?"

"None," I insisted. "It's definitely him."

We left the room and the Captain-General instructed one of the guards to go sit in the room with Goya and not to leave him alone under any circumstances.

As he escorted me to the Castle gates – the guards have been doubled – I asked after the Alcalde.

"The poor man is distraught," he said, "as I'm sure you can imagine. She died in his arms, you know. He hasn't spoken a word since."

He was thanking me profusely for my assistance and was bidding me farewell when, with perfect timing, Montenegro appeared, slightly short of breath, or perhaps pretending to be.

The Captain-General greeted him coldly but not impolitely.

"I presume you are here about Carlos Goya," he said.

Feigning surprise, perhaps a bit too exaggeratedly, Montenegro looked at me and then at the Captain-General again.

"Yes," he said. "But how ...?" He let his words trail into silence.

As I left, the Captain and Montenegro were heading away in the general direction of the main Castle building.

Ж

"She told me everything," de Esquival said to me when Sor Lucrezia was out of earshot.

"Everything?" I said, momentarily afraid that she might have.

"The holy sister explained ..." he began and summarised what she had told him, which was more or less what I had instructed her to say – the truth but as little of it as possible. I stifled a sigh of relief when he had finished.

"So Sor Lucrezia thinks she's recognised him too?" I ventured.

"She's certain of it," he said.

"I would need to see him again," I said, "to be sure. Yesterday evening, in the confusion of the whole dreadful business ... I'm fairly sure it was him, but I cannot be absolutely certain ..."

"What do you know of him?" he asked.

He was being polite – he is known for his ability to turn the charm on and off – but I could feel the animosity behind the words. From all I knew of him, and from what had been related to me by many persons whom I trust, he is a man skilled in the arts of manipulation, knowing exactly when to charm, or act the bosom comrade, the flatterer or the threatening brute.

I told him I had married Goya – to a woman of good birth, I emphasised, who had genuinely accepted the faith – and that Goya had made a solemn undertaking to build a chapel on his encomienda. I picked my words carefully. He is not a man to be underestimated and I had no intention of doing so.

"But," he said, pretending as if the thought had just that moment formed itself in his mind, "you must have found him strange. The man is a freak. To put it bluntly, he looks like a bloody heathen or a Moor."

"He said he had been shipwrecked once," I said. "On one of the other islands or tierra firme. He wasn't quite sure where. And had feared he would never see a living Christian again. But he kept the faith. It would not be the first time a Christian adopted the apparel and customs of a heathen people in order to live unmolested among them. Si fueris Romae, Romano vivitomore. As the Great Ambrosia said."

"My Latin fails me," he said.

As if he had any!

"When in Rome do as the Romans," I explained.

"No matter. But I would hardly call it apparel," he almost

jeered at me. "Mutilation is more like it. The man's face looks like a page from the Moorish bible."

"Extreme, yes," I agreed, "but even Christians pierce their ears and wear silver rings in them. There is nothing in Holy Scripture that forbids some mild modification of the body for purposes of decoration, not for laymen in any case. Though you are right of course, in Goya's case it is rather de extremus. Though some might argue that it is more a matter of degree ..." I let it at that. He sports a silver earring, a vain man, and I was sure my point was taken. "I presume he is still alive?"

"Oh yes," he said. "You know he was a wanted man? Before this."

"I do not understand," I said vaguely, so that at the most the statement was a lie by omission rather than commission.

"Alcalde Mayor de Paz issued a warrant for his arrest a few months back. When my men got to his encomienda, it was nothing but cinders."

"So I'd heard," I said. "Simarons. Red Francisquito. But it seems he survived. If it is him. As I said, I'm fairly sure but not absolutely. I would need to see him again to be certain. What was he wanted for?"

"For questioning," he repeated, rather sharpishly. But then he became surprisingly conciliatory. "I was not informed as to the precise details at the time. And I never got to see him in the flesh, of course. I would ask the Alcalde but he is distraught and ..."

I wondered if he was telling the truth.

"Of course," I said.

"There isn't anything – in hindsight – something you perhaps only barely noticed at the time, thought insignificant," he said, "which in the light, or rather the dark shadow of yesterday evening's events, might tell us something about him, perhaps even why the Alcalde was anxious to question him?"

I pretended to search my memory for a while before slowly shaking my head.

"We have our differences, Padre," he said, his tone suddenly both confidential and distant at the same time, avoiding my eyes, instead looking out over the bay towards the ships at anchor in the shimmering morning heat. "Let us not beat about the bush on that. The situation on John the Baptist's is grave. And now this. I believe the original intention was to murder His Excellentissimo himself. If they had succeeded, we might right now be facing a general insurrection on all the islands, and even in the Veragua colony. These heathens communicate with each other a lot more than we sometimes think they do. Our hold here is not unassailable. Our crusade here ... and that is what it is when it comes down to it. We are fulfilling God's plan for these lands, you in your way, I in mine. For how can we but not? How can any man but not? For is not everything part of God's plan?"

Had he really expected me to discuss theology with him? Provide him with some justification? Perhaps he had. He's a strange fish. Or, was he merely being disguisedly facetious?

"They wander in and out of our houses at will," he continued. "They make our beds and wash our linens. They serve us at table. They cook our food. But they are strangers to us. Perhaps one day, many generations hence, we shall come to understand them and they us. But that day is a long way off. None of us really has a clue what really goes on in their heathen heads, baptised or not. One fine day they might simply decide to rise as a mass and murder all of us in our beds. No Christian here feels much guilt when he dispatches one of them, so I doubt that they lose much sleep when they get the chance of doing the same to us. But they must not get the chance. They must never unite against us. We rule with an iron fist out of necessity."

He paused in his monologue. Out of necessity! The nerve of the man! How men justify power, I thought, and the dreadful abuse if it.

He continued looking at the bay. For a moment it struck me how beautiful the sight was, how blue and peaceful the sky and how magnificent the ships. A nao, a ship whose hold is as roomy and as spacious as a whale's belly, had raised her sails and was slowly sailing out, no doubt packed to bursting with ill-begotten plunder.

"We have our differences, Padre, as I've said," he continued. "But we also have a common interest, one of blood and of faith. If we were driven from these islands, the Church would be driven from them too. And, I think, when all this unpleasantness is finally resolved, you and your fellow Preachers will find that Rome knows which side its bread is buttered on."

He turned to me.

What he had said – I am loath to confess – was not wholly devoid of truth.

"So is there anything?" he asked, looking deliberately and intensely into my eyes. "In hindsight?"

I tried to think of something, some detail that could easily be dismissed as inconsequential, but I could not. But I knew I needed to say something that would lead him to believe that I had understood the import of his observations and admit, albeit begrudgingly, that I recognised the 'common interest' he had spoken of.

"Perhaps the Alcalde somehow suspected that some conspiracy was afoot," I ventured, "and had reason to believe that perhaps Carlos Goya had some connection to it, was involved in some way? The Alcalde, as we both know, has always made his business to be informed. He has eyes and ears everywhere, as they say."

Every Governor of Hayti has nightmares of some disgruntled colonist with grandiose fantasies setting himself up as some sort of king-cacique and successfully recruiting Haytians to his cause by promising them freedom and all sorts of things. As Roldán had tried to do, and not without some success.

"But," I continued, "even in hindsight, I cannot say I noticed anything about this Goya that could be in any way construed to be relevant to what happened yesterday evening. But perhaps I am unobservant, naive even, in these matters. Except of course his appearance, which you have already pointed out, perhaps should have warned me as to his character."

He thought about that for a moment, pretending, and I have no doubt he was pretending, that he believed that I had been utterly sincere in what I had said.

"Very well," he said finally, seemingly – no, most probably pretending to seem – convinced. "So, in that case, let's go and take a look at our assassin. So that we can be absolutely sure about his identity."

I made a grave nod of agreement.

The guard stood up abruptly as we entered the room.

"He's come to, Sire," he told de Esquival. "He's asked for water. I've sent for some."

Goya looked in a terrible state, as pale and as withered as a spectre – he must have lost a lot of blood – and was groaning horribly to himself, twisting and turning under the soiled cotton covering they had laid over him.

"Has he said anything?" de Esquival asked.

"No, Sire, only asked for water," the guard said.

De Esquival turned to me.

"Well, Padre, is this your Goya?" he asked.

I nodded.

He shook the groaning man gently by the shoulder as if he was trying to rouse him from sleep. Goya opened his eyes.

"Do you recognise me?" de Esquival asked, almost and

perversely so, as a parent would address his child. But Goya merely turned his head away.

A Haytian manservant arrived with a jug of water and a mug. De Esquival insisted on serving it to Goya himself. He took several long slow sips from the mug. To anyone who did not know de Esquival or of his reputation, the touching scene was the image of charity itself, as might be painted by some Florentine master commissioned to depict the parable of the good Samaritan for some altarpiece. Oh, how our eyes can deceive us as to the true nature of things? For I had not the sliver of a doubt in my mind that de Esquival's display of false charity was to confuse the dying man and that, when it suited his purposes, he would suddenly withdraw it and replace it with the viciousness he was capable of in order to throw his victim into a state of even greater terror and confusion.

Eventually, he put the water aside, laid his hand momentarily on Goya's shoulder – another false gesture of comfort – and indicated with a jutting motion of his head that he wished to speak to me outside.

I hesitated for a moment, fearing that this was all I would see of Goya. My plan had been to somehow convince de Esquival, on the pretext of hearing Goya's confession, to grant me some moments alone with Goya so that I could question him as to what had happened at his encomienda and subsequent events; and indeed if he had actually saved and hidden the gold from the *Trinity*. But seeing the condition Goya was in, and knowing he had the fresh blood of an innocent woman on his assassin's hands, it was also clear to me that I was duty-bound to attempt to confess him and offer him what might very likely be his final chance to reconcile himself with the Almighty.

But the Lord works in mysterious ways.

"He's at death's door," I said the moment we were outside.

De Esquival looked at me, seemingly genuinely deep in thought, perhaps not pretending.

"I have seen it many times," I added. "We priests ..."

But he did not let me finish.

"I have a proposition to make to you," he said.

"A proposition," I repeated, taken somewhat off guard.

"Yes, an arrangement," he said, "a rendering unto God the things that are God's and unto Caesar the things that are Caesar's."

Just as Estaban had argued. The Franciscans have a lot to answer for. When Christ said we should render unto Caesar it was a command to render unto Caesar only that which is rightfully Caesar's. It was not a command to connive in the wilful enslavement of men, women and children, or in the laying waste to entire countries. But I held my tongue.

"His Excellentissimo is determined to get to the bottom of this," he said. "Absolutely determined. And so am I. We need to know if this half-redskin has accomplices."

"Of course," I said, waiting for him to come to his 'proposition'.

"I could have my men question him," he went on, "but ... you've seen the pitiful state he's in. He's at death's door, as you said yourself. I doubt he'd survive their ministrations. But there is another way."

"Another way?" I repeated. I had no idea what he was thinking.

"The proposition I have to make to you is as follows and quite simple," he said. "I will allow you to hear his confession ..." – he paused, but only for less than the blinking of an eye – "... under certain conditions."

The priest in me was suddenly outraged, furious. Words fail me. How dared this murderer, this greedy slimy puffed-up caballero, this serpent in human form, dare to tell me, a servant of God, that it was up to him to determine when and to whom God's holy sacraments could be dispensed, to decide the fate of the eternal soul of a fellow creature, a creature who, no matter what his sins, was created by God in His own image! But I held my tongue.

"However," he added, "if your private interdict forbids ..."

"Continue," I said.

"I will allow you to hear his confession," he continued, "on the condition that the penance you impose on him is that he make a full, legal and official confession regarding the events of yesterday evening to the lawfully constituted authorities on this island. Namely myself."

Again I was about to explode with rage and he knew it.

"His soul is in your hands," he continued, cool as a breeze. "If you cannot do this, I will have no choice but to have him questioned ... rigorously. We'll get something out of him but ... men are not always as truthful as one would wish under rigorous questioning and ... but, as I said, I doubt if he'd survive the ordeal. On the other hand, the fear of impending eternal damnation and the eternal fires of hell can concentrate a man's mind marvellously, as I'm sure you know."

I knew I had no choice. My plan, if one can call it that, had been to ask him if I could hear Goya's confession in any case.

"The forgiveness of sins requires remorse, true contrition,"

I began, "but also a commitment to sin no more ..."

"I think his opportunities in that regard," he smirked, "have become rather limited ..."

"And," I overspoke him, "a commitment, in so much as it is possible, to make amends, to make recompense."

"As you so elegantly pointed out in your sermons," he said. For a moment the satanic venom in the man's heart was visible in his eyes. But I found the fortitude to ignore it.

"Such amends could of course," I added, "consist of confessing one's crime to, as you put it, the lawfully constituted authorities."

I had not known I had such deviousness in me.

"Not of course," I was careful to add, "that I could agree in advance that any absolution I may grant him would necessarily be dependent upon me giving him such a penance, to make his absolution dependent on anything other than my good judgement as a priest, the laws of the Church and my conscience. But such a penance would not be unusual under the circumstances."

It was the truth, but spoken insincerely, though not for a wicked purpose. I had no choice if I wanted to fulfil my duty and hear what might very well be Goya's last confession.

"My thoughts precisely, Padre," he said, smiling deviously. The look of triumph on his face was sickening. "I think we understand each other." He had dragged me down to his level and he knew I knew it.

He held the door of the sickroom open for me and we entered it again. He bade the guard leave with a precursory wave of his hand – contempt for all those below him comes naturally to him – and then he left, leaving me alone with Carlos Goya.

TWENTY-SEVEN

What I am now about to relate, I must state and emphasise unequivocally, are events and facts which Carlos Goya confided to me outside the seal of the confessional. That seal is sacrosanct and the breaking of it is never permissible, no matter how grave the circumstances, for whatever reason whatsoever, be they of state or of church or of the common welfare. The spiritual takes precedence over the merely carnal, the salvation of men's souls over all other things in the universe; for the soul is the essence, the body merely the form, though they be intricately entwined with one another. Even the Captain-General de Carnage, low and particularly sinful creature that he is, understood this fundamental truth and did not even consider, I am sure, to suggest that I abuse my role as priest and confessor to Goya by breaking that sacred seal. So the following is what Carlos Goya told me, outside the seal of the sacrament, in his own words as they exist in my memory, omitting the many interruptions that his condition caused, and the repetitions and such, for he was a badly wounded man, suffering a fever, his life very possibly near its final completion and judgement.

"Francisquito Guaro and his simarons," he began, "arrived about noon. They were mounted – they had five horses between them – and were drenched to the bone. It had been raining for days. There were eight of them, not counting Savonarola – they'd picked him up somewhere between Concepción and Caonabó's Valley – and they were all armed, four of them with arbalests.

"They said they needed food, and shelter for themselves and their horses. They were polite enough. But once the horses had been stabled – and Francisquito was quite fussy about that, making sure they were out of sight – and they were inside the house and my watchmen no longer around and I was about to tell Juana to prepare them some food, his tune changed entirely. 'Your cosy little setup here is finished,' he said, and then turned to Savonarola and told him to 'tell Señor Goya who's coming to visit'. 'Two of Carnage's men will be here shortly,' Savonarola told me. 'With a piece of paper with your name on it and Rudolfo Jesus de Paz's official seal,' Francisquito added with some relish. 'It appears your presence is required at the Castle. Why is that?' I said nothing. But my guess, at the time, was that my life on the other side of the world – my youthful follies – had caught up with me."

"The Holy Office does not concern itself with mere youthful follies," I told him, though of course I knew nothing of the details of what false thinking and practices he had been required to abjure.

"Perhaps not," he said. "But in any case I reckoned I was in serious shit – if you'll excuse the expression – if that was the reason. I could think of no other. But then Savonarola said, 'They were also interested in that priest, the one I brought here a while back, with that crazy woman who dresses like a priest.' 'I don't know what you have been up to,' Francisquito added, 'and I don't much care. Maybe you haven't been up to anything but the Castle thinks you have. Which, as far as you're concerned, amounts to the same thing.' "

"Alcalde de Paz believed that you had saved the gold from the *Trinity*," I told him, "and buried it ... and were planning to go back. That is why he had ordered your arrest."

But he said nothing to that. He just looked at me.

"They had arrested Franco Serrano," I explained. "And questioned him."

"And what did he tell them?" he asked me.

"Much," I told him. "But nothing about any gold on the *Trinity*."

"There was no gold," he said, dismissively, as if I were a fool who had asked a fool's question, "not on the ship in any case."

"But ...," I began to remonstrate, intending to say that everyone said there had been ... We have become so obsessed by this metal, which both delights and disgusts us, like the charms of some sophisticated whore, that we are willing to believe any rumour regarding it. But maybe there never had been any gold on board. "Serrano said you'd made a map?" I said instead. "That you'd discovered the Gold Land."

But he neither confirmed nor denied that. He simply made a grimace that was halfway between a self-loathing sneer and a smile, and asked for more water. I did not press him.

"So what happened then?" I asked.

"Francisquito said: 'When Carnage's bastards arrive we're going to kill them. And when we've killed the bastards, we're going to burn this place down. Maybe I should kill you too – but you're kin now.' He speaks good Castilian. The monks taught him well."

I told him I did not understand.

"They're all related," he explained. "Juana, Savonarola, Anacasabe and her lot, and Francisquito, by blood, marriage and in the dream-world."

It is a tradition among the Haytians – now, like much else, nearly but not completely died out – to exchange areíto-songs with one another and thus forge bonds of kinship between each other in their spirit world, their so-called dream-world. During the early wars, when the Pharaoh defeated Guarionex, the latter took refuge with the cacique Mayobanex, but Mayobanex refused to surrender him because he said Guarionex had thought him and his cacica areíto-songs. Such was the high regard these exchanges were held in, and kinship in general.

"'And when that is done,' Francisquito added," he went on, "'you can either come with us or take your chances with the Castle. The choice is yours.' Then, just at that very moment, there was a shrill whistle from outside. One of the Black Ladinos was keeping watch from a tree. It was the signal that Carnage's two men had arrived. The rest happened quickly. 'Sit', Francisquito barked at me, 'and don't move! And not a bloody word out of you!' I nodded and sat on the bench facing the door. He signed to his men and, with the efficiency of a well-practiced crew raising a sail, they took up position in various corners of the room, out of the line of sight of the windows.

"We waited a while and then we heard horses outside and the sound of men dismounting, and then the sound of their boots on the portico steps. They didn't knock. The door simply swung open and both of them appeared in the doorway, their brown cloaks dripping from the rain, hands on the hilts of their swords, and me sitting there like the lord of the manner, which I suppose I was in a way – or like a village idiot more likely. There was a moment of confusion. One of them opened his mouth to speak but what came out was a scream as the arbalests twanged and shot their bolts into the both of them. Then Francisquito laid into them with his sword and two of the others, the second Black Ladino and a Haytian, laid into them with their macanas and began finishing them off. Savonarola just watched emotionlessly, as if it were pigs they were slaughtering not men, as if it were all just some job about the farm that needed to be done. It took a few minutes to kill them. They screamed a lot until they didn't anymore. There was a lot of blood. But that's the way it is, Don Padre, is it not?"

He asked for more water.

"Then they dragged the corpses outside, stripped them

naked, shared out their weapons, and pulled the arbalest bolts out of them and washed them. Waste not, want not. It was all very matter-of-fact, as if they had borne the dead men no ill will at all. Even when they were killing them, there was no more wrath in them than it necessarily takes to stab or beat a man to death – it's not something a fellow can do in cold blood, normally – no other pleasure taken than that taken in a job well done."

That was how he described it.

"And your lady wife?" I asked. "Señora Juana?"

"Silent as a mouse during the whole thing," he said. "Just stood there, out of the way, with not a word out of her. Women and Indians are mysterious creatures. But if it were not for her ... While Francisquito's lads were dealing with the bodies, she simply went and made us food."

"De Esquival's men had some Maquanan porters with them?" I said, remembering what Puccini had told me in his letter. "What happened to them?"

"They skedaddled," he said. "Took to the hills."

I was keen for every detail and I knew this was the only chance I would get.

"The next day Francisquito spoke to me again," he continued. "'What's it to be?' he said. 'Us or the Castle?' He's a dab hand at the flowery speech but when he wants an answer, he doesn't mince words."

"I see," I said, thinking that was that was the end of that – except for the burning of the encomienda – intending then to ask him about the time he had obviously spent with the simarons and the events leading up to the attempted murder of Rudolfo Jesus de Paz and de Esquival. But there was more.

"Then Francisquito had his men hang the naked corpses, upside down, by their feet, from the roof beams in front of the house, and ordered all the servants and the labourers to assemble. Then he made a speech from the portico steps. He looked like the devil himself in his red war paint. He knows how to rouse men, to get them to see things the way he wants them to see things and ..." – he hesitated, searching for the right words – "... to see things maybe the way they should be seen and yet, at the same time, the way they are in some way. He spoke in the local dialect. I understood most of it.

"'Fellows,' he said, 'these two Castilla ...' – he never called us Christians for some reason, funny that – '... are dead by our own hands. See!' He hit one of the bodies with a macana, beat it so fiercely and with such energy that it swayed to and fro on the rope it hung from, like a pig hung for gutting. 'See', he said, his voice booming as if he was addressing the very hills themselves. 'See, as dead and lifeless as the stones on the ground, as lifeless as any lump of dead flesh.' He left the swaying corpse come to rest before speaking again. 'See how they hang there, like dead parrots. All their vudu is gone.' Then, matter-of-fact like, he took a rusty knife from his belt and began to cut off the privates of one of the corpses. When he'd done it, he held the bloody lifeless things up in the air for all to see. 'See,' he repeated, 'all their magic is gone.' Then – he has a sense for theatre, for the spectacle, I've seen him perform many times since – one of his simarons appeared with two pigs on leashes, two large sows from my piggery, and Francisquito simply threw the cock and balls on the ground for the sows to eat. Which they did. He did the same with the other corpse, saying, no chanting more like, 'Vudu gone! Vudu gone!', repeating it over and over again."

"Vudu?" I asked, for I did not know the word.

"It's Dahomey talk for magic or something," he explained. "He liked the sound of it."

"Madness," I muttered and crossed myself.

"Ach, Don Padre," Goya retorted, "I've seen fucking worse – here and in Christendom. And there was purpose in it."

"Purpose in it!" I exclaimed.

"He then made every man, woman and child come forward one at a time and, handing each one the macana, had each one of them take a turn at beating the corpses," he said. "To show that we were not invincible, to make them all feel that they had a part in what had been done. To ensure their silence. The bodies were pulp at the end of it, pulped meat. 'Go,' he said then, 'go to your dwellings and remove everything you value, for now we are going to burn every stick of this place to the ground.'

"Then he placed the bodies in the house and set it alight," I said, the sequence of events forming in my mind.

"Yes," Goya said, "And no. As I said, he wanted everyone present – man, woman and child – to feel they had a part in what was being done. He's a clever devil. Wise in his way, at times. He didn't do it. He got my labourers and servants to set the fires."

"He forced them to it?" I said.

"No. He convinced them that they wanted to do it," he said. "They did it willingly, more than willingly, with enthusiasm. As I said, he has a way with words."

I remembered what Savonarola had written about Francisquito's mastery of rhetoric. What enemies of the faith have we created?

"They torched everything, every bloody thing," he said. "I had dreams for that place." I remember his laugh as he said that, that strange bitter laugh of his.

Then he was silent for a few long moments.

"It all happens so quickly," he said. "What's it all about, Padre?"

"Our lives are a mere passing through," I told him, "a pilgrimage, a testing of our worthiness."

I should have heard his confession then. But I wanted information I could use, for the faith's sake. So I let him continue.

"And from that day to this one," he said, "I've been wandering the land by moonlight and striking terror into the hearts of Christians."

"But you are a Christian yourself," I found myself saying.

But he just looked at me, a half-smile on his face, almost as if he was pitying me, but contemptuously.

"You will hear my confession?' he said.

"Of course, my son," I said. But he had told me nothing of what had happened the previous evening. News would eventually reach Spain of it. There would be questions. The more I knew, the better I would be able to answer those questions. And that would serve my cause. Such in any case was my reasoning, I think, at that moment. So I continued to question him.

"But why did you attempt the lives of Alcalde de Paz and Captain-General de Esquival?" I asked.

"It wasn't them we were after," he said. "It was His fucking Excellentissimo we intended to kill. But ..."

"Savonarola's motives I can understand," I said, "but yours ..."

"I need to confess," he insisted.

"How did you hope to get away with it?" I asked him, persevering.

"We didn't," he said.

But I could see he was growing weak so I did not persist.

Of what he confessed I can say nothing.

When he was finished I gave him absolution and told him what his penance was to be – to confess his crime to the lawful authorities. He and Savonarola had viciously taken the life of an innocent woman. And while the authority exercised over the Haytians by the Castle is a usurpation, he was not a Haytian, he was a Spaniard and a Christian and lawfully subject to it. Such was my reasoning. Perhaps it was reasoning to suit my own ends. But it would also save him from unnecessary torment at the hands of Carnage, so it was not without charity.

But as I was about to leave him he said: "There is one condition."

"A condition?" I said, totally taken aback.

"I want to see my wife," he said, "I will not sign anything willingly if I can't see her once more."

"Where can she be found?" I asked him, thinking that the chances of finding her were probably meagre. Indeed, I was about to say to him that he would see her again in the world beyond this world – for had she too not become a Christian – but not in the way we see things in this physical world. But he had an answer to my question before I could say anything else.

"She will find me," he said.

I told him I would speak to the Captain-General.

Of the motives which tempted Carlos Goya to such a suicidal and desperate act and which he revealed to me under the seal of the sacrament, I cannot speak plainly. So I will quote scripture, or rather allude to it. Did not Samson, betrayed by the harlot Delilah, shaven and eyeless, and chained to the pillars of the temple of Dagon, not bring about his own destruction and those of his enemies when he brought that temple crashing down upon both his own head and the heads the Philistines? And did not the harlot Rahab betray her own kind for her own sake and that of her family when she betrayed Jericho to Joshua and the army of the Israelites?

Ж

Affairs of all sorts have kept me from recounting anything here over the last week, so I shall summarise what has taken place since my last entry. Our ploy worked. Captain-General de Esquival suspected nothing – not that we were guilty of any misdemeanour – and Fray Montenegro convinced Carlos Goya to make a full confession of his crimes, which was made and duly notarised. With the details of it I am not familiar. And the Captain-General, in an act of mercy that can only commend him – whatever his other sins may be – allowed Goya's wife, the Haytian Juana, the grace of a visit to her husband on his deathbed. Goya passed away in her company. So there will be no trial.

Ж

In an act of mercy that can only commend him!

Sor Lucrezia di Marchionni's charity is commendable but misplaced. I have no doubt in my mind that the Captain-General would have had no hesitation in handing Goya over to his brutes if he was not satisfied that Goya's confession was the truth, or what he wanted to hear, or whichever suited his designs. He is a calculating man as well as a cruel one. And I have little doubt he had anticipated with some glee the sight, never to be, of Goya on the scaffold in the hands of his bloody executioners.

And, I sometimes wonder if in fact Goya was helped on his way. Poisoned. By his wife. In order to spare him the agonies of the scaffold. Rudolfo Jesus de Paz is not incorrect, loath though I am to admit that he is right about anything, when he says that the poisoner's art is one the natives of the islands are particularly adept at, though surely no more adept than many an Italian princeling. I have no proof but a feeling in my bowels tells me that it is not unlikely. In truth, the more I ruminate upon it – and I have much time to ruminate as the *Incarnation* slowly ploughs its way through the watery wastes of the Oceanus Occidentalis – the more I consider it to be a real possibility; Bikendi had been moderately confident that Goya would live. I saw her shortly afterwards, in the street, a few days later.

"He's at peace now," I said, in an honest if somewhat conventional attempt to comfort her. "He repented. I heard his confession. But you know that. The grace of the sacrament washes all sin away. God will embrace his soul." Words to that effect, in any case.

She looked at me with her dark brown eyes. She is in fact a fine-looking woman though, for whatever reason, I had not noticed this when I had first met her at Caonabó's Valley. I had seen only womanly meekness, a creature with the humble demeanour of one had been born to be a servant and would never enjoy any other condition but that of a servant, or a servant-wife. And there in the street, in the full light of the early afternoon sunlight, with her olive complexion, and her jet-black hair under her ill-fitting straw sunhat, and her simple clean cotton dress, I perceived a dignity and nobility in her bearing that I had not noticed before. Or so I thought.

I had expected her to reply with some sincere politeness appropriate to the situation but she did not. She just looked at me for a few brief moments and then suddenly cleared her throat, and spat in my face.

How deceptive our perceptions can be!

By the time I had regained my composure and recovered from the insult, she had disappeared into the crowd, and I could not find the will to attempt to follow her.

If it is true that she did poison him, did she do it without his knowledge? Or did he himself wish it? Knowing it meant eternal damnation? Surely he knew that such a fate pales to nothing in comparison to any agonies of the flesh? Was his confession just a ploy? The thought fills me with despair. But I cannot forget that strange look he gave me when I asked him if he was a Christian the last time I saw him in the Castle, that look of half-pity and half-contempt that at the time I thought was ... I don't know.

Perhaps the forlorn and endless vastness of this grey sea is weighing too heavily on my spirits ... Hayti already feels so, so far away now, as I write these lines.

TWENTY-EIGHT

"Hoping I had forgotten, eh," the Alcalde Mayor said as Montenegro laid the various testaments and statements he had been collecting on the Alcalde's caoba-wood writing table.

The Alcalde, dressed in black widowers' weeds as was befitting his bereavement, looked as gaunt and as broken-spirited as he had at the funeral of his wife. Fray Estaban had officiated and His Excellentissimo himself had spoken a eulogy, a quite elegant one, and moving. One would never have guessed that he'd had perhaps but a single conversation with the poor woman. He'd praised her as 'one of the cream of Castilian womanhood and an example to her sex'.

The Alcalde began to go through the documents, leaving Montenegro and myself to stand as he did so. His grief had obviously done nothing to soften his manners; if anything, quite the opposite.

"*A sworn account of the wilful depopulation of His Majesty's West Indian possessions,*" he said as disdainfully as he could manage, reading the title first, "*as witnessed by Fray Juan of the Order of Saint Francis on the Feast of Saint Clare in the Year of the Our Lord fifteen hundred and* ... blah blah blah ... *inhabited by so many persons that I was convinced on first seeing it all that the Almighty had placed the greater part of humanity on these islands* ... indeed ... *the cruel and unjust execution by fire of* ... blah blah blah ..."

Casting that statement aside, he turned to the next.

"*A sworn account of the established tradesman by the name of A* dot *C* dot *of the early years on the Spanish Island, who has resided on said island since 1493, having arrived with the Admiral Don Cristóbal Colón on his second voyage, who being unable to read and write has signed this with his mark in the presence of a witness on Ash Wednesday in the year* ... blah blah blah ... *even to the cutting off of their hands and leaving those so abused to bleed to death* ... blah blah blah ..."

A.C. Alfredo Castro? The description certainly fitted. And Montenegro is more than casually acquainted with him, or such is my impression.

The Alcalde moved on to the next statement.

"*A sworn account of the horrors of pearl fishing on the islands of tierra firme,"* he read on, in the same disdainful tone, *"as witnessed by Fray Sebastián de Toledo of the Franciscan Order of the Friars Minor on the feast of the Conversion of Saint Paul ...* my, we are pedantic, you should have been a notary ... *tuberoms and maroxi which can swallow a man whole ...* sea monsters, a ripping yarn no doubt. How imaginative! *A sworn account of the enslavement and wilful extermination of His Majesty's subjects on the islands known as the Lucayas as witnessed by Pater Alonso of the Order of the Hieronymites ...* blah blah blah ... *bloated carcases floating around in the sea like dead fish ...* gory but a nice poetic turn of phrase all the same ..."

Finally, he came to Montenegro's own account, the most substantial of them, more than fifty sheets of paper written on both sides in Montenegro's economical hand.

"And last but not least, your own little masterpiece," he pronounced and began to skim through it as contemptuously as he had the previous testaments, again reading out the title and the odd phrase that caught his eye. *"A sworn account of the atrocities committed against His Majesty's subjects on the Spanish Island and Cuba as witnessed and related to him by honest religious and other persons over several years by Fray Montenegro of the Order of the Preachers of Saint Domingo ... sparing no age, nor sex, nay not so much as women with child ... they divided among themselves the young men, women, and children, one obtaining thirty, another forty, another one or two hundred, the more one was in favour with the domineering tyrant which they styled Governor ...* naughty, naughty ... *thus a population of hundreds of thousands of persons was reduced to ...* blah blah blah ... *more than the number of grains of wheat in a wheat field ...* arithmetic is obviously not your strong point, Padre, is it? ... *Turkish savagery ...* blah blah blah ... *a crueller oppression than that inflicted by the Egyptians on the Hebrews ...* my, my ..."

"I retract none of it," Montenegro said quietly. "Let us complete this shameful business."

"As you wish," the Alcalde said.

He handed Montenegro a sheet of paper.

"Read this out loud," he told him, "date it and sign it with your full name and ..." – he turned to me – "... if you, Sister, would then be so liberal as to sign it too, as a witness."

But he also, and I have no doubt of it, wanted me to witness Montenegro's humiliation and his own display of power, and perhaps exercise a belated revenge for my daring to try and put him in his place. That is if he had actually noticed that was what I had intended that day I went to see him at the Castle after my papers had gone missing.

Montenegro extracted his reading lenses from inside his habit and began to silently read the statement he was being compelled to sign.

"Get about it, man," the Alcalde suddenly barked, and then cast a quick glance, full of nastiness, at me.

Montenegro cleared his throat, braced himself, and read: "I, Fray Hugo de Montenegro of the Order of the Preachers of Saint Domingo on the Spanish Island of the Antilles, do hereby swear in the presence of Señor Rudolfo Jesus de Paz, Alcalde Mayor of said island, and Sor Lucrezia di Marchionni, Superior of the Order of the Hieronymites on said island, by the Holy Bible, by the Virgin and all that is sacred to the Catholic religion, that I have handed over into the custody of the aforementioned Alcalde Mayor all documents and statements I have solicited from any Christian whatsoever or myself written regarding all affairs whatsoever of the Antilles and other Indies that I have secretly or otherwise collected during my presence in all those dominions, and that I have neither copied nor have had copies of said documents made, nor have given copies into the hands of any other person."

The Alcalde had been thorough.

"Now sign it and date it," he said.

After Montenegro had done so the Alcalde bade me follow suit.

"Excellent," he said, "excellent," as he examined our signatures, scattering a pinch of fine sand over them to dry the ink.

He then put the signed statement with pretended casualness to the side and sat back in his chair, an ugly look of smug satisfaction on his face.

"Then we shall be going," Montenegro said unceremoniously.

"My, we are in a hurry," the Alcalde said. "Are you not at all curious as to what I am going to do with these ..." – he indicated the documents Montenegro had surrendered to him – "... libellous fictions?"

"They are not fictions," Montenegro retorted. For a moment I thought he was going to lose his composure entirely. "And well you know it, Señor."

The Alcalde looked as if he was going to contradict him but then obviously thought better of it.

"Well, I'll tell you," he said. "I shall tell you what I'm going to do with them."

"I'm all ears," Montenegro said defiantly, but the Alcalde ignored the slight.

"At first," he said, "I had it in mind show them to His Excellentissimo. But I have since changed my mind. Now, why would I do that? Why would I not show them to His Excellentissimo?"

He paused, for effect, not for a reply. Not that Montenegro, as far as I could see, had any intention of humouring him with one.

"One would think that it would be to my advantage to do so, would one not?" he resumed. But he was no longer being smug. He was being sarcastic again, but this time the target was, to my utter surprise, the Governor. "After all, His Excellentissimo would surely appreciate the efforts of his faithful servant," he continued, his tone growing more vicious, "the ever-loyal Alcalde Mayor Rudolfo Jesus de Paz, to root out all attempts to call into question the legitimacy of His Majesty's dominion over these lands and their inhabitants – and to root them out successfully. It would be a feather in my hat, as one says, would it not?"

Again, as was his manner, he paused again. That he was full of bitterness I could understand. He has been cheated of the chance of earthly happiness, in so much as any durable happiness is possible on earth, of a marriage he had set much store on, the harvest of his life's work, one could say, and most violently and suddenly so. I remember thinking as I looked at him looking at us for that brief moment of what momentary earthly happiness I myself have experienced since my arrival in this land. Two memories came fleetingly to mind: the day the sun first came out and the air filled with flocks of butterflies, and that strange surrendering peace I felt the day the earth shook.

"But it does not work like that," he continued. "No, it does not work like that at all."

"So how does it work?" Montenegro asked him with as much as he could muster.

The Alcalde shot him a venomous look.

"I shall tell you," he said. "I shall tell you how it works."

Montenegro was about to say something but the Alcalde raised his hand and said: "Don't!"

Montenegro, refraining himself, said nothing.

The Alcalde leaned forward in his chair – as if he were about to utter some aggressive and unpleasant intimacy.

"It works like this," he said, almost, but not quite, speaking through his teeth. "His Excellentissimo is a much-occupied man. Affairs of state and all that. A busy man. A man with important

things to do, reports to read, reports to write, or rather dictate –
His Excellentissimo is not a great penman – decisions to make
and so on. Important decisions. Decisions, decisions, decisions.
And being a man of vision, of course. So why disturb him with
the traitorous scribblings of some priest?" Again I thought
Montenegro would react to the provocation but he did not, and I
was thankful for it. "Well, no reason at all. But ..." – he cast me a
glance as if to make sure I was still there; during most of this
'interview' he had ignored me – "... that is not the real reason.
No, not really. The real reason is that he will not want to know.
He does not want to know what is in these documents, not really,
or rather what is alleged in these documents. And if he does know
– what is alleged, that is, which is possible; he is not a stupid
man, nor an ill-informed man – in general terms, he will not want
to know the details of it, the dirty little inconvenient bothersome
details. You see, His Excellentissimo, like most men whose duty
it is to rule over us lesser mortals, those in the upper echelons of
the pyramid of the social body, thinks of himself as a man of
vision, in the modest ways of the great and the good." That he
dared to speak so scathingly of His Excellentissimo shocked me.
He was obviously confident that neither of us would speak of it.
"After all, is not all authority justified by the claim that those who
wield it can see deeper into the nature of men and society, and
further into the future itself than us lesser mortals can? Details
muddle visions, especially dirty little details. They're bothersome.
I think, Padre, that when you get to Seville and speak of these
things to your superiors, as I'm sure you will, you will find that
many of them will not be overly happy by your burdening them
with the bothersome details alleged in these statements of yours."

"I will say it nonetheless," Montenegro said quietly.

"No doubt," the Alcalde said, looking suddenly weary, as if the
greater part of him no longer cared. "I'm sure you'd pester the
Pope of Rome himself with your obsessions if you were given
half a chance. But mark my words, Padre, the Pope of Rome
would not thank you for it."

"We shall see," Montenegro said.

"No doubt, no doubt," the Alcalde said. "But no one will ever
see these ... imaginative allegations." He indicated the documents
with a dismissive gesture. "Because I am simply going to burn
them. What's the phrase? Ah, yes, commit them to the flames ..."

The man has a perverse sense for the theatrical.

*

Fray Montenegro was in melancholic spirits when he came to our nunnery this evening, after the procession – which I and my beatas had attended. These events take place about once a month, on a Feast Day or Holy Day or at times of sickness, and are attended enthusiastically by the Castilians and the Indian inhabitants of Santo Domingo, the latter taking great pride in being allowed the privilege of carrying an image of the Virgin through the streets.

The *Incarnation* sails in two days' time and I could see that the prospect of weeks at sea was lying heavily on Montenegro's mind, along with the seeming failure of much that he has devoted himself to.

We sat together on the patio, unusually silent with each other, the night its familiar velvet black and filled with the chorus of the Haytian cicadas, a sound now familiar, but not so long ago so strange to me, and now and again the buzzing of mosquitoes. I was acutely aware that this was the last time we would sit there together – and I can only surmise that Montenegro too was aware of the finality of the occasion. We were unlikely ever to see each other again in this world. The thought of it weighed on my heart. The endings of things always bring recollections of past times. We fancy the joy that we could have had in those times – if only we had been wiser at the time, and realised the seemingly unique potential of the seemingly never-ending days of those times.

I asked him why he thought the Alcalde Mayor had expressed so much animosity towards the Governor.

"It seems he's fallen out of favour," he said.

"But why?" I asked.

"When His Excellentissimo returned from his travels, he was furious when he found out about our interdict," he explained. "He knew that when the news reached Spain he would be called on to provide some explanation. Our order is not without influence. And Fray Pedro is not without his connections. Some of the notables were not happy with the Alcalde entering into negotiations with us – or as they saw it, pandering to a crowd of newly-arrived moralistic monks – though, of course, they didn't complain about that directly. And some see him as having obtained a rank above his station and resent it. No, instead, they hinted that the Alcalde was planning to send that letter he had everyone sign directly to the Casa before His Excellentissimo returned, hoping to put himself in a good light, behind His Excellentissimo's back. I doubt if that was the case but who knows ... The irony of it is that it was most likely His

Excellentissimo whom the Alcalde wanted to impress, not the Casa, by getting us to retract, and attempting to nip the whole thing in the bud. Rudolfo Jesus de Paz is an ambitious man, but his aspirations are quite banal. He's a natural underling. Though a cunning one. I don't think he was aiming so high. I have a distinct feeling that his days of being Alcalde Mayor are drawing to a close."

"But," I said, "if he did show the statements you collected to His Excellentissimo, would that not be evidence of his loyalty?"

"Perhaps," he said, "but that could also have its risks. Rudolfo Jesus has been Alcalde Mayor for quite a few years now. A lot of what is recounted happened under his stewardship. It could be argued that he was responsible for it happening. As I said, there will be questions in Spain. His Excellentissimo might decide to be shocked ... if you see what I mean. The time might come when a scapegoat is needed and the Alcalde himself might fit that bill quite nicely. He's a commoner without any connections at the Casa or at court. But if there is no evidence, well, there is no evidence. I think Rudolfo Jesus is covering his back. He's not stupid. He knows how things work.

"The statements I collected gave names, places, dates. I was meticulous in their composition. They were not vague accounts, reports of what men had heard about or suspected. They were the freely sworn words of men who had seen horrors with their own eyes, or heard of horrors with their own ears from the mouths of those who had seen them with their own eyes. And in my own account, when I reported the testimonies of others, I had them state unmistakably the who, the when and the where. It was evidence that could not have been ignored, damning evidence. That was my intention. Their very accuracy could be a danger to the Alcalde himself. So he might actually destroy them, but then again he might not."

And with that note, my dear Balthazar, I am obliged to end this account. For Montenegro boards the *Incarnation* tomorrow.

TWENTY-NINE

Two or three days before I boarded the *Incarnation*, I summoned Felicitas to me. She had been a servant to me for many years; and, though she had been severely wrong in her dealings with the fallen nun Hildegard, she had served well in all other things. It was also principally she who had taught me what mediocre knowledge I had acquired of the tongues of Hayti, and of the customs, usages and superstitions of the Haytians, and how their warlocks held them in thrall. Without her gift of tongues, exercised on not a few occasions with the eloquence of a Haytian Cicero, during my sermons and in many other instances too numerous to list, my attempts to prise open the heathen minds of my flock and enlighten them on those things which are essential to the leading of good lives would have been more paltry than in truth they have been. Perhaps even, she is my only really true convert. Nothing in her quiet bearing and diminutive stature betrays her not inconsiderable abilities. Though there is something in her dark eyes, a peculiar perceptiveness of sorts, which makes her stand out amidst her fellows; or so it has seemed to me, at times. But then, is not how we perceive our fellow men to a greater part dependent more on the wakefulness of our own spirits than on them? The worst of us see them as means to ends, so much labour, as little more than beasts of burden, mules and oxen in human form; but the true Christian, as the Gospels teach us, should see them as our brothers and sisters, and should attempt to do so at all times. But perhaps only the saint ever succeeds in that. It was she too who, at my behest, so many months ago now, secretly borrowed and returned those pages of Sor Lucrezia's writings; and had she not succeeded in doing so adroitly, perhaps the events told here would have unfolded somewhat differently. So despite her errors in regard to the nun Hildegard, I felt that a token of my gratitude was called for, but not having a spare maravedí to my name – the little money I had, I needed for the journey - all I could offer were some fond words of farewell and a humble monk's blessing.

"I will be sorry to see you go away," she said.

"It is God's will," I told her. "We must accept it."

"And His will is mysterious," she replied.

There was despair in her voice. Rather than bitterness, though God knows she had reason enough for bitterness at my kind. It was if she were beyond bitterness.

"My people are without hope," she added.

I nearly said: "I know." But instead, I found myself taking refuge in Holy Scripture, or at least in the spirit of it.

"Hope is for the sake of the hopeless," I said. "And our only hope is a loving God. And if we do not have that hope, we have nothing. We must hope. And for that hope we must look deep into ourselves, into what we are. Only there can we find it. The times of signs and miracles are long past. Faith is needed now. Seek not to understand that you may believe, but believe that you may understand."

That those words were inspired by the writings of the Apostle Paul and Augustine she was not to know of course. Perhaps I had uttered them more to console myself.

"Nothing prepared us for your coming," she said.

"Let us pray," I said. "Come, let us pray for hope. And for faith. And that despair, the enemy of all good things, be cast out."

Then we prayed, silently.

In such quiet moments are the fates of souls decided.

I remember how, afterwards, I recalled the day when she had returned those pages of Lucrezia di Marchionni's to their hiding place and reported to me that all had gone well. Why, of all incidents, that is the one that came to mind then, as it does right now, I cannot tell. It is indeed strange what encounters and snippets of conversations with our fellows stick in our minds, sometimes most stubbornly, as if they were trying to tell us something about our inner selves or the conditions of our souls.

"She is a cruel woman," she'd said.

"Cruel?" I replied in some astonishment. Sor Lucrezia is a person who, from the very beginning, gave the impression that she was not one to be crossed lightly or contradicted without consequences (though I do not think she knows she gives this impression to others); and she has a sharp tongue (which does not come across in her own description of her conversations). But cruel? I laughed and simply said: "Oh, she's all bark, I'm sure, no bite at all."

"She whips them," she said.

"Her servants?" I said, thinking of course that was what she'd meant, about to add that as a mistress she had that right if they were wilfully disobedient or insolent and that I was sure she did so sparingly.

"No," she said, "the ones she calls her beatas. "She has a whip, a small one, with many cords. I saw it. It was blood-stained."

I asked her to describe it to me in more detail.

"It is called a scourge," I told her. "She does not whip her beatas. She whips herself."

"Herself?" she repeated, and looked at me in that peculiar way Haytians have of looking at one at times, a mixture of bewilderment and as if they are thinking that we are all utterly insane.

"It is a way of elevating the spirit," I explained. "We are both spirit and flesh. The flesh has the seeds of corruption in it. We must free ourselves from that corruption. Sor Lucrezia scourges herself. The pain she willingly inflicts upon herself is to free herself from that corruption, to purify herself. Saint Domingo took a scourge to himself every night. Clare of Assisi scourged herself for more than forty years. They say the odours from her wounds were as a heavenly incense." That, at any rate, is what our brothers the Franciscans claim. And your own people, I remember being about to say, used to inflict various tortures upon themselves; but I checked myself, the comparison would have been ridiculous.

"But," she said, for she is an intelligent woman, more familiar with doctrinal truths than many, sadly, who have been born and bred Christians in Christian countries – due to my tutelage I like to think. "Does not the flesh too rise at the end of time? Does that not make it holy?"

"It will be made holy," I said. "It will be made timeless, free of corruption, free of sin and death. But that is a mystery, something we can only meditate upon. It is pointless to try and understand it. The world is so."

I saw her once again before I boarded the *Incarnation*. She was watering some of the wondrous Haytian flowers we grow in clay pots in the shade of our modest loggia. She did not notice me observing her. As I did so, I could not help thinking how quickly all things pass.

My leave-taking of Fray Pedro was a more – I nearly wrote a more weighty event – but is not the fate of the soul of an Indian womanservant as weighty as anything? So let us say it was perhaps simply a more gravely official event.

He gave me a letter addressed to Secretary de Lillo at Saint Stephen's.

"It explains all," he said.

I nodded, knowing of course that it did not.

"The ways of the world are unpredictable," he said, "and we sometimes forget it is not just a case of one thing happening after another. Your banishment – though the injustice of it grieves me – may be for the greater good."

I asked him how that could be so.

"You will be able to put our case in person," he said, "as well as delivering the evidence you have collected. Who else could argue it with such conviction? I have told de Lillo what must be done. You will have his ear. Sermons are not enough."

Then he told me what he had decided must be done, which did not differ in its essentials from what I had argued with him many times.

I was not searched as I boarded the canoa which ferried me out to the *Incarnation* – not that there was much to search. Besides my meagre personal possessions, all I carried was the letter from Fray Pedro to Francisco de Lillo, sealed with the sign of his ring, a bag of tabaco seeds for our herbarium in Salamanca, and the chest of things Puccini had left me, which contained his guayacán bark samples, his papers and that unfinished letter to the Fugger Albrecht Schweinsteiger – and I had the Indian manuscript from tierra firme that Carlos Goya had given me. And, of course, I had the macaw with me. Puccini's collection of maps I had left with Fray Pedro.

Just after the sun – that great ball of fire that has circled the earth since the beginning of time, tuning all our lives, Castilian and Haytian, gentile and Jew, male and female, to the celestial rhythm – had set into the Antillean Sea, a small canoa rowed by two Haytians and carrying Sor Lucrezia drew up to the side of the ship. I heard her announce to the watch that she had come to bid farewell to me and ask for permission to board. I went out just as the officer in charge was ordering a rope ladder to be lowered.

On entering my cupboard she immediately fumbled in her habit and extracted a sealed envelope, containing her report, and Savonarola's letter. The latter I had given to her for safekeeping a few days earlier in case I had been searched. I had sworn to surrender all documents I had solicited from any Christian whatsoever, but Savonarola's document I had not solicited and by no stretch of the imagination could the savage be deemed to fall into the category of Christian; though in hindsight, now, I can see that perhaps he possessed, in a limited degree, more virtue than many who call themselves Christians, and a rude nobility even, in his wild and sinful way.

"Who is the influential churchman to whom I am to deliver this?" I asked." A relative?"

"No, she said. "A friend. A man I trust. His name is Balthazar di Bellisconi," she said. "He is to be found in

Rome. He is the Bishop of the Green Land."

"Of the Green Land?" I said. "But ..."

"A purely honourable, a titular position," she explained. "The see brings no benefice or rents with it. He holds it for form's sake."

I remember feeling the weight of the large envelope containing her writings. Perhaps it was even then, unbeknownst to myself, that I had secretly decided to break the seal.

"But how am I to get to Rome?" I asked. "We land at Seville or Cadiz. It would take me months to walk there. And I have no funds."

"There is an agent of my family's merchant house in Seville," she said. "I have written a letter to him. I have asked him to arrange for your transport by ship to Rome and back again. It should take no more than a few weeks. Then you can go to your motherhouse. Nobody will notice. Or are they expecting you?"

She extracted the small folded letter – this time from her sleeve – and handed it to me.

"No," I said. "No news has been sent ahead. I am carrying a letter from Fray Pedro which explains. That will be the first they hear of my return."

"Explains?" she said. "Everything?"

"No," I said. "Not everything. Fray Pedro believes that I am being expelled because of the sermons and our interdict, as an example."

"So Fray Pedro believes you still have the statements you collected, that you are travelling to Seville with them?" she said.

"Yes," I said. "He would never have allowed me to hand them over. No matter what the consequences. De Paz knew that of course. So the whole affair with Felicitas and Hildegard had to be kept secret. That was his intention by getting us to agree to keep it 'in the family'. He's a clever bugger, no doubt about it. Fray Pedro even thinks my expulsion is a blessing in disguise. He thinks it will enable me to deliver the statements in person to our motherhouse. Which is why he has not kicked up a fuss about it."

"That could be awkward for you," she said.

"It's a long voyage across the Oceanus Occidentalis," I said. "I will think of something. I will have to."

"My words will help your cause," she said, indicating the envelope containing her writings, which I still held in my hands. "Not directly. But I have reported much of what you have told me. Men of influence will read it, men with a sense of right and wrong."

"Perhaps," I said. It was my turn to be wiser in the ways of men.

"I read Savonarola's letter," she said.

"And?" I had suggested she read it.

"Do you believe he wrote the truth?" she asked.

I was not surprised by her question.

"When I first came here," I said, "I was like you. That men were faulty creatures, given over to all sorts of weaknesses and follies, even fits of raving madness and cruel crimes committed in anger – all that I could accept. But ... at first I was told things, given hints, heard crude outlandish boasts ... words upon the air, I said to myself. Men say all sorts of things and most of it is little more than wind, to be taken with a pinch of salt. A truth, and a convenient one at times. I remember the day I first saw – with my own eyes – the handiwork of our fellow Christians. It was along the coast, half a day's walk from here, to the west. Felicitas was with me. We met some soldiers on the road and a little later came across a burning pueblo. A small place, less than half a dozen caneys. There were bodies, dead bodies, all around the place, strewn about like discarded sacks of straw. One was of an old man, two were of youths, three of women in child-bearing age, and five of children. They hadn't been dead long, the flies were only settling on them."

I was trying to be matter-of-fact and, oddly, making an effort to sound grave. I almost wrote 'pretending to be' ... yet I have rarely uttered graver words.

"Heads smashed in. Bellies sliced open. Worse," I spared her the details. Perhaps I should not have. "'Castilla,' Felicitas said." I can still hear the word. She had almost whispered it, as if in a church. And as she said it, it felt as if the wind had stopped blowing, and the waves and gulls had become silent. "'Castilla.' That was all she said. All she needed to say."

"She thought that the soldiers had done it?" she said.

"She knew," I said.

"But ...," she began, but I knew what she was going to say.

"She knew," I repeated. "And for a while afterwards I thought what you are thinking now. That it could not be. That there was another explanation. That it was Canibas or some Haytian bandits. Part of me was even telling me that I had not really seen what I had really seen. As if it had all been a dream."

"A dream?" she said.

But how could I explain the stupor that such horrors numb the mind into? A state of knowing and not wanting to believe, knowing and not wanting to imagine.

"There are things we do not want to believe," I said.

She made to speak again but I had not finished.

"But gradually," I continued, "I learnt to accept that it was so. That there is such a thing as pure evil in the world, evil for the pleasure of it, for the sake of it, no matter how it's dressed up. And that it can be found in Christian hearts as easily, perhaps even with greater facility, with greater perversity, as in the hearts of warlocks and ignorant savages. And that is the terrible, unpalatable truth."

"What does that say of our Christian faith?" she asked.

"That without it, we are truly lost," I said.

But she had one other thing to give me, a letter of introduction to a Senhor Amaro Rodrigues, merchant and agent of the Marchionni on the Azores, in case the *Incarnation* stopped off there.

At that, we said our farewells. I stood at the gunwale, as the wall around the deck of a ship is called, and watched her canoa, rowed by the two Haytians, slowly disappear into the night and head for the distant lights of Santo Domingo, leaving nothing but ripples on the black mirror of the water under the moonless star-filled sky. The last I heard of her was the sound of the Haytian's oars dipping in and out of the water. Then there was silence.

The *Incarnation* sailed on the morning tide, as another day dawned over the Indies.

The grommet, a Barcelonan boy by the name of José, passed away last night. He was a lively young lad, always clambering up and down the riggings to the sails with the dexterity of a monkey. This was his second voyage, the voyage out being his first. He had been suffering from a fever for several days.

We laid him to rest in the sea this morning, just after Terce. Burials, if they can be called that, take place quickly at sea. I led the officers and crew in the prayers for his soul over his cold corpse and reminded them that we should not grieve overly, for one day, at the end of time, he, they, all of us, would rise again in glory. For is that not the central dogma of our faith: the Resurrection of the Dead.

As I prayed over poor José – a beardless youth of less than fifteen years – I tried to imagine his meat-cold flesh become warm again, expression gradually reappearing on his face, his eyes slowly opening again. And then, as I commended him to the Almighty and his corpse sank into the watery depths of the Oceanus Occidentalis, I imagined his body being consumed by crabs and all the other crawling creatures of the seafloor till there would nothing left but scattered bones which would in time become ocean sand, the dust of the sea. I tried to fancy how, at time's end, when all the acts of men are done, how all these myriad grains of sand would ... Of course, my imagination failed me. But I reminded myself that the fact that we cannot imagine something – even in our wildest reveries – does not mean that that thing cannot come to pass. What man, in his wildest imaginings, without first having experienced the world, could imagine the endless sea, the sun above us, the *Incarnation* and we who sailed upon her? Could imagine even himself? Yet these things are. And we are. And if the creation of all these things out of nothingness has taken place – and who can deny that it has taken place or that only Divinity can create being out of the utter void of nothingness? – cannot the Divine Mind also decree eternal life for all that it has created, reforming everything out of the sand and dust which all eventually becomes? For the Divine Mind, by its very nature, contains everything, remembers everything. And memorises all with such perfection that what is remembered is indistinguishable from the remembered thing itself, so that when time ends it can resurrect each individual in all his, and her, fleshly and spiritual detail.

Augustine warned us against literal-mindedness. The Holy Scriptures were written for men, men with the limited understanding of men, and ultimate truths are beyond the understanding of men, their meaning only to be vaguely discerned between and behind the words of Revelation. Holy Scripture has been given us to enable faith, to show us the way, not to give us perfect understanding of things which are beyond our understanding. It is to faith that we must hold fast, and to the way, and not distract ourselves with silly imaginings. To attempt to subject the workings and the nature of the universe to inquisition by the rules of our limited reason is full of moral pitfalls. As is any attempt to found morality on reason alone. For example, the man who cultivates a laudable indifference to his own sorrows and death might conclude that it is equally laudable to cultivate an indifference to the deaths and suffering of others, which would be a great error.

A ship's bell or two after the sad ceremony – as on land, the passing of time at sea is also marked by the ringing of bells – we finally sighted the hills of one of the Azores. The Captain says if all goes well we shall put in at Terceira tomorrow.

THIRTY

Angra do Heroísmo, Terceira, the Azores.

The *Incarnation* is in need of some repairs so we have been here for a day short of a week now. Senhor Rodrigues, a good-natured man, whom I called upon merely to pay my respects, insisted that I lodge with him for the duration in the gardened cottage where he lives overlooking the sea. It was good to feel solid land under my feet again.

The climate of these Portuguese islands is fresh and spring-like. They are not lush like the Antilles but the air is lighter and drier, or at least it is at this time of the year, and there is a purity about it. They were uninhabited until nearly two hundred years ago; and were wooded once too, Senhor Rodrigues tells me. So they have always been Christian; no heathen ghosts haunt their nights and empty places. Sugar has brought the Azores much wealth. There was never less than half a dozen caravels in the Angra do Heroísmo bay all the time I was ashore.

However, I still had a mystery to solve, a trivial one, I thought; but the meaning of that table of strange names and numbers I had found among Carlos Goya's papers had niggled at me ever since I had made a copy of it. I still tended towards the suspicion that it had not to do with some astrological or numerological theme but rather something to do with money – a sort of record of accounts, after the Venetian method, but written in a secret code of some sort, but perhaps at least partly decipherable to a man expert in the art of keeping merchants' accounts. So I decided to show it to Senhor Rodrigues.

"What do you think it means?" he asked me.

"I have heard that the Venetians," I said, voicing my theory, "have a method of counting money which involves making two entries in an account book for every transaction, for every time they sell something, and for every time they buy something."

"True," he said. "I use the method myself. It is most accurate."

"But doesn't it just mean that everything is counted twice?" I said.

"It's more complicated than that," he told me, "but at the same time elegantly simple. One entry cancels the other. If everything is correct, the sum total of all purchases and sales is zero. Then you can be sure that the account books are accurate. There is no surer way of counting money. It takes a clever Jewman to beat it. Nobody is quite sure who invented it. Some say it was Giovanni Medici. Others say it came with the Moors and their numerals. Luca Pacioli, a Franciscan, wrote a book about it about fifteen years ago. The merchants' Regiomontanus, we call him. But go on."

"You see these signs here," I continued. "And there?" I pointed out the crosses and the dashes. "The crosses look like pluses. And the dashes look like minuses. That could mean that these figures could be sums of money. But there is no indication as to what kind of money, what coinage it could be."

"Not that I can see," he agreed.

"But there must two dozen different types of coins," I went on," thalers, castellanos, gulden, ducats, florins."

"More than two dozen," he said. "Many more. And not all coins of the same denomination have the same value."

"Because some are clipped and some are not?" I suggested.

"And some have more silver in them," he explained. "Gulden minted by the Emperor Rudolf have a quarter more silver in them than those minted by Maximilian."

"But," I continued, "for any of this to make sense, it seems to me, that not only the coin that the account is being kept in should be stated, but also the value of other coins relative to it, or something like that. You merchants do it when you haggle. Such-and-such is worth such-and-such. Don't you? A cow is worth four pigs, and a pig is worth three goats and so on."

"Depends on the goats," he laughed. "And the pigs." And he continued to laugh. For a moment I thought he was just taking me for an utter fool, but finally he became more grave and said: "It's a map."

"A map?" I said totally bewildered.

"Maps are based on numbers," he explained. "Perhaps everything is. If I'm not mistaken, these are map co-ordinates. The true map is the numbers. The drawing is only an interpretation of those numbers, a flat picture of something that is in reality curved. Ptolemy's *Geographia* is numbers. It contains the longitudes and latitudes of eight thousand locations. There are no maps in it. The first time it was ever printed with maps was only fifty years ago, in the *Bologna Cosmographia*. Some scholars even doubt that there ever was an actual map, but I find that hard to imagine."

Then he took a sheet of paper, drew a series of horizontal and vertical lines in the form of a sort of grid and, glancing intermittently at Goya's table, wrote numbers along the right edge of the grid and along the bottom of it.

"Lines of latitude and longitude," he explained. "Now, if we take each of these numbers ..." – meaning the numbers on Goya's table – "... and, taking the Fortunate Isles or thereabouts as our meridian, insert them thus." For each of Goya's rows of two numbers, by measuring each one against the numbers he had written on the right edge and another against the numbers he had written on the bottom edge of the grid, he began to insert a dot for each of the strange names, one for Three Kings, one for Acamapulco and so on.

"The latitude co-ordinates are probably correct," he continued. "Anyone possessing medium skill with a quadrant can determine them. Longitude's a different story. I've seen maps of the Antilles that differ from each other to as much as ten, or even fifteen degrees. As to the exact length of a degree ... Let's just say that the cosmographers differ on the matter." He handed me the map he had drawn and continued, full of enthusiasm: "But one day they'll solve that problem. If you can put a number on it, I always say, it's within your power. Then the entire sphere of the earth will be precisely mapped, every field and manzana ..."

"... will be nailed up on crosses of latitude and longitude," I found myself saying.

There was something about his enthusiasm for precision that horrified me but I was not sure quite exactly what or why.

"... and as much as can be known about the surface of the earth will be known," he said and looked at me as if that is all there was to it, that only fools and dreamers could even think otherwise.

I looked at the map he had sketched. Rudolfo Jesus de Paz had been telling me the truth – or rather Serrano had been telling the truth when he told him about it – when he said Goya had made a map. But what it was a map of, I had no idea. It was of seven places or co-ordinates, as Senhor Rodrigues called them, at seemingly random distances from each other. They meant nothing to me.

"Kim-pecch,   Chakte-mal,   Tonala,   Pij-ija," Senhor Rodrigues read out. "Those are Indian names, I presume."

"Most probably," I said. "They have many languages. I am not familiar with them all."

"I have been told," he said, "that many are mild-mannered and meek but that others, called the Canibas, are ferocious creatures that live on human flesh."

"That is true," I said.

"What do they look like?" he asked.

"Like us," I told him, "except that they are beardless and decorate themselves in a heathen manner, with paint and feathers and tattoos. They are black-haired and have a Moorish complexion, and are ruled by warlocks."

I refrained from telling him more lest he see more differences than similarities and come to the conclusion that they are more essentially different to us than like us.

"I mean the Canibas," he said. "What do they look like?"

"I've never seen one," I replied, "in the flesh that is." Which is the truth. "But all accounts describe them as ferocious in both their appearances and manners."

Before I left, he showed me a copy of the Pharaoh's *Book of Prophecies* which he had recently obtained. I stayed up late one night reading it. In it, the Pharaoh wrote of his visions of the advent of the Antichrist and the Second Coming of our Saviour, and his own imagined role in the sacred history of the world, predicting the last days in less than a century and a half from now, no less. They say he composed it sometime after his third or fourth voyage. It's possible he was even actually writing it when I met him in the chapel of our house at Salamanca. Perhaps he was already mad then – many say he was, towards the end.

I have purchased a quire of paper, two dozen uncut sheets – things are near as expensive here as they are on Hayti – and been able to refill my ink bottle. Taking Puccini's advice, I have decided to make my case in writing and to begin immediately, though not quite as he suggested. Learned men have more influence in the world, so I will write in Latin. I have already chosen the title: *In Indorum defensionem*. Though I will take his advice regarding woodcut images. It should not be that difficult to find a draftsman or a copper engraver who can reproduce with some verisimilitude the dreadful scenes I have in my head.

The wind being good and the stars auspicious, we sail on tomorrow morning's tide.

This journey, this endless sailing across watery wastes, despite the early weeks of wretched seasickness and having to deal with Savonarola's wretched bird, has given me time to think more deeply and methodically about our plan – what Fray Pedro told me he believed must be done if there is to be any hope of an end to Spanish depredations against the innocent inhabitants of the Indian countries.

The arguments must be made clear. What they, the Spaniards, do is heresy. Men who matter must be brought

to see that this is so. All are called to God through the Holy
Roman Catholic Church, the Universal Church, the all-
embracing Church, which He founded so that all men may
find salvation. All, not the rich alone, nor the poor alone,
nor those for whom righteousness seems to come
effortlessly, but the wickedest of sinners even, all are
offered salvation. Even those who have committed murder
and sodomy and other abominable crimes, as long as they
confess and repent, are offered it. Salvation is offered to
those who have been Jews, to those who have been Moors.
To the Castilian, to the Frenchman, and to the Tartar and
the Indian. No man, or woman, remains uncalled. No man
or woman who accepts the faith can lawfully be refused
baptism. No man has the right to sort out those worthy of
salvation from those who are not. God alone elects.
Publically disputing that this is the case and tempting men
to believe otherwise – which is what many royal officials
and adventurers licensed by the Crown in the Indian
countries do, through their general demeanour and
behaviour, by treating the inhabitants of those countries as
if they were not fully men and thus not called to God, as
they themselves are – is that not heresy, by deed, if not by
word?

Furthermore, is not the excessive love of gold and other
precious things a form of idolatry – in the manner in which
the Templars worshipped the idol Baphomet – and thus,
when committed by Christians, also heresy?

And furthermore, have we not a duty to move those who
sin thus towards repentance and contrition and a
resolution to sin no more? By threat of punishment if need
be? Repentance and confession out of sincere remorse is of
course far more meritorious than repentance and
confession out of a fear of punishment. But is not the latter
also valid if the intention to sin no more that arises out of
the fear of punishment is sincere? Compulsion is not
legitimate against those who have not submitted to the
faith, only against those who have submitted and then
relapsed. The Indians may not have submitted, but those
Christians living among them have. There is only one
institution with the power to compel them to repent and
mend their ways: the Tribunal del Santo Oficio de la
Inquisición.

And that is our plan, to effect in as short a time as is
humanly possible the appointment, with full inquisitorial
and judicial powers, of inquisitors for all the Indian
countries.

In the light of all this I have been forced to pose the

following question to myself: is handing over this document
– both Sor Lucrezia's account and my additions to it - to
Balthazar di Bellisconi in Rome the best course of action to
achieve the implementation of this plan? I do not now
believe so, despite the no-doubt laudable bishop's influence
with the Monsignori of the Congregation. So I have come to
a decision. I shall not deliver, as I admittedly promised I
would, Sor Lucrezia di Marchionni's *Account of the Indian
Countries Discovered by the Admiral Don Cristóbal Colón* to
the Bishop of the Green Land. No, this document belongs in
the hands of the Tribunal del Santo Oficio – in the hands of
Fray Francisco de Lillo, the Secretary General himself. Let
him be the judge of it. Let him be the judge of all that
Lucrezia di Marchionni has written and what I have added.
Though it contains much that is unflattering, much that is
shameful, I shall not erase a word. Augustine, who when
writing his confessions, omitted not a sin he had committed
from it 'so that the sins might illuminate the virtue and
rightness of the whole', shall be my example. Knowing one's
days are numbered, no matter how vaguely, lends one a
certain courage, even ruthlessness. Fray de Lillo can decide
whether to forward it to Balthazar di Bellisconi, or not.

Ж

The following note, in another hand, is simply initialled 'FdL'. The
handwriting is so similar to that of the letter which Montenegro
included earlier from Francisco de Lillo, who seems to have held a
double office as the Secretary General to Dominicans and the
Tribunal del Santo Oficio de la Inquisición, that it would be hard
to argue that it is not by him. Thus, and given Montenegro's
confessed intention to hand over this document to de Lillo, we can
safely conclude that it is in fact by him.

*Thoughts, possible arguments against, and comments
regarding the above contentions (as advocatus diaboli) ...*
    *I. To suggest that the general demeanour and behaviour of
royal officials and adventurers licensed by the Crown is such
that it could be construed as ignoring or calling into question
the doctrine of the spiritual equality of all men before Christ –
if it were shown to be true, no easy task – and thus heresy,
while not without some merit, has no clear, if any, precedent
in canon law. However, it is a line of argument worth
investigating. Acting against the various Papal Bulls issued
on this subject is certainly a grave offence. The Borgia's* Piis
fidelium *is as clear as day on the subject. The Indians, he*

had instructed Bernaldo Boyle, were to be converted, to be instructed on how to 'walk in the commandments of the Lord' and were thus implicitly and explicitly recognised as our equals in Christ, if not in the world. But it would be difficult to argue that such a matter falls under the authority of the Office as currently defined. Many such offences would fall into the general category (permitting myself a witticism) of common and garden sin, a venial evil to be opposed by the preaching and example of the common clergy.

II. The argument that the excessive love of gold and other precious things is a form of idolatry – in the manner in which the Templars worshipped the idol Baphomet – and thus, when committed by Christians, is heresy. If so, then near all are heretics, and if near all are, then none are. Though this counterargument could hardly be stated so explicitly.

III. That we have a duty to move all those who sin thus towards repentance and contrition and so on – by threat of punishment if need be. And that all types of contrition are valid if not equally meritous. None can argue with this. But to convince princes, worldly and ecclesiastical, where their duty lies and to actually act accordingly ... another Pandora's box.

IV. Montenegro's contentions (I and II) are strictly speaking arguable; but to accept those arguments as true and right in fact and in law would have consequences which would lead, not to exaggerate, to a general chaos in Christendom and hardly serve the mission to bring all men to Christ and salvation. Thus there must be an undetected flaw in his original premises.

V. The original of Sor Lucrezia di Marchionni's account is to be forwarded to His Worship, Balthazar di Bellisconi. A diplomatic explanation of how it came into our hands should not be beyond our wits. But a copy of it is to be made for our archives.

Ж

I have many times looked at the map Senhor Rodrigues composed for me in his kindness and wondered what the fates have in store for Acamapulco, Kimpecch, Chaktemal, Tonala, Pijija and their ignorant inhabitants. But this morning I tore both documents up – both Goya's table of numbers and the map Senhor Rodrigues had sketched for me – and went to the side of the ship and discreetly let the confetti-sized pieces of paper blow away into the sea. A necessary act but of course also utterly futile. They will find the Gold Land in any case, and soon, if indeed that is what the map was of, or the seven cities or whatever the map signified. As the shreds of paper fluttered into the breeze, I wondered if, in some similar but different way, Goya, a man nominally a Christian, once a Jew, and maybe a heathen for a time – and even the savage Savonarola in his way – had thought that their mad attempt on the Governor's life had also been both necessary and futile ... I will decide later on what do with the codex Goya gave me.

Bikendi cut the macaw's tongue out this morning. To get the creature to open its beak, he had me stick a pin in one of its legs and when it squawked and opened its beak, he inserted his scissors-forceps apparatus and fastened it in place about the creature's head, trapping its tongue. Then, with a single efficient movement, he closed the handles of the device and the miniature blades, as sharp as razors, sliced through the creature's tongue at the root. The poor brute shuddered and shook violently in my hands and tried, I suppose, to scream in its bird way. It bled profusely for a moment but Bikendi's ingenious scissors-forceps apparatus held the stump of the creature's tongue in place so that he could insert a long spatula-tipped cauter, which he had preheated to an almost dull-red glow, into its mouth and cauterise the wound. The bird is now quiet, lying morosely in a small manger-like box I have made up for it. I have said a decade of the rosary that it might live, if God wills it. It was a hard thing to do, but there was nothing else that could be done. There is still a slight whiff of burning flesh in the air. The Haytians say the creatures can live up to a hundred years and more, longer than any man.

Ever since it spoke that first time I had assumed that it was Savonarola who had taught it to blaspheme. But now it occurs to me that it could in fact of have been Puccini – but I am determined not to entertain that thought.

We should reach Seville before the end of the week.

Who in future generations will believe all this?

Historical notes

This is the original postscript by the German historian Christian Neufeld as it appeared in the first English-language edition, published in London in 1939, and most probably written while he was in Paris in the second half of 1938. He signs the text 'Christian Neufeld, International Brigade, 1938'[4], but it is unlikely that he actually wrote (or rather completed) it while in Spain. When he does mention the Civil War, it is in the past tense, though perhaps this is because he believed at that stage that it was already lost – though it is also possible that he first came across the text while in Spain and began to write about it then. It is also possible he was making a political statement.

Times during which 'history' is being made – times of wars and revolutions, and these are surely such times – are rarely good times for historical research of any precision. And such has been the scale of destruction wrought by the Fascists in Spain that I fear that much of the vast, fragile, combustible and irreplaceable archive composed by the bureaucrats of the Spanish Inquisition and the Casa de la Contratación de las Indias (later the Consejo de las Indias) has been lost forever. How much of it, and other collections of documents on the so-called Conquest of the Americas, has fallen victim to Francoist and Nazi shells and bombs only time will tell. But nonetheless, as someone who has studied these matters in some degree of detail, though I am no expert, I shall endeavour to suggest some answers and possible avenues of enquiry which may shed light on the historical background to the events described in *Hayti* – in a rather haphazard order. What follows is based on the few books I have access to and conversations with scholars whose field is the so-called Conquest and related themes.

The publisher has presented *Hayti* as a 'work of fiction' and, in the strictest sense, it undoubtedly is that. It is highly implausible that a macaw could learn to recite the whole of the Lord's prayer, to say the least. There are also some 'anachronisms'. And some scenes are obviously contrived. But the strongest evidence –

---

[4] The Spanish Civil War 'officially' ended in April 1939 but the Republican International Brigade had already been disbanded in September 1938.

ironically – for its fictional nature is the fact that many of the main characters, and some of the minor ones, are obviously modelled on real personages, though many – such as Agüeybaná/Savonarola, Puccini, Jesus Rudolfo de Paz, and Sor Lucrezia di Marchionni herself (though the di Marchionni family certain existed, more or less as described) – have no *Doppelgänger* that we know of. However many questions remain. Did the original document first see the light as an actual account by Lucrezia di Marchionni? (There is no evidence that she did not actually exist, not that there could be of course.) And was it then subsequently doctored? Spiced up? Added to? Embellished for amusement or some obscure political purpose? With perhaps even Montenegro's commentary added to it at a later date?

The texts – both Lucrezia di Marchionni's and Montenegro's – contain much, as far can be gleaned from the extensive but erratic contemporary documentation of the time, which is authentic and historically true. *Hayti* is undoubtedly based on 'fact', and in numerous cases 'truthfully' relates incidents (sometimes only very lightly disguised in the telling, if at all) which we can be reasonably certain did in fact occur. The author (or authors) certainly seemed to be somebody 'who knew the facts'. Names have been changed, to be sure, but that may have been for many reasons not apparent to us today. The Dominican Bartolomé de las Casas, for example, in his *A Brief Account of the Destruction of the Indies*, is very often reluctant to give actual names. He refers, for example, and he follows the same practice on more than one occasion, to a person whom he obviously knew the identity of as "a certain officer known personally to me". And on another occasion he says he was not going to name someone because it was "a name that deserves oblivion". In other accounts from the period narrators often write of themselves in the third person.

It could be argued that when dealing with documents of this type the difference between what is fiction and what is not is at times hazy. What in one epoch might be considered a factual account of something might in another be considered pure fantasy. *Hayti* is certainly not simply 'made up' in the sense that most fiction is invented or imagined. That said, my personal and unprovable conclusion, admittedly based on intuition rather than on any painstaking scholarship, is that *Hayti* is most likely based on a real contemporary account in which names, places and dates have been disguised, but that later, another hand added much, enhanced much – and that hand was the hand of someone who knew the Spanish Americas of the period intimately and was in fact once there. Where reality ceases and the imagination commences I leave to the judgment of the reader – something which needs to be done when dealing with most 'histories' of this period in any event. Lucrezia di Marchionni and Fray Montenegro may have misunderstood many of the laws and customs of the Taíno, and some of what they relate could be said to be at odds with original sources, but then the original sources are often sparse, and often contradict each other, or seem to. As for the 'anachronisms' – the few that there are – I will discuss them below.

One last thought: *All Quiet on the Western Front* is a novel, but is it not, at a more profound level, a more truthful account of the reality of the World War than any historical tome which has since appeared?

Year in which the events described in *Hayti* are supposed to have occurred: One would imagine there would have been a date somewhere in one or other of the two narratives but there is not. This is especially curious in the case of Lucrezia di Marchionni's *Account*, as it is what one would expect in a document of this kind, even a fictional one. There may well have been a date given in the original text of course, but one certainly does not appear in the Catalan translation (of which this edition is, in turn, a translation). An oversight? Or is this deliberate? It is impossible to tell. There is also, of course, the possibility that parts of the original text are missing, or were simply omitted from the Catalan translation. However, I feel that at least some effort should be made to place the events at some point in historical time.

The tentative date which I have arrived at for the events described in the text is 1511. My main reason for reaching this conclusion is that His Excellentissimo the Governor is very clearly Diego Colón, Columbus's son. Though he is not mentioned by name, his wife, the Donna Marias de Toledo, is. He was the first Governor to bring his wife with him. Diego Colón was Governor of the Indies from 1509 to 1511, made Viceroy in 1511, remaining in that post until 1518. He is only once referred to as Viceroy in the text, during the double marriage fiesta. My reasoning is that in 1511 he had only just been appointed Viceroy but was still quite possibly being referred to as the Governor.

Other indications: The so-called Palace is obviously the El Alcázar de Colón viceregal palace and would have been under construction in 1511. It was completed around 1514. The events also seem to have taken place prior to the Burgos committee deliberations which took place in 1512, as these are not mentioned. The resulting Laws of Burgos, issued in December of that year, were aimed at reinforcing Crown power by putting the so-called Conquest on a *legal* footing and thus securing further the endless flow of gold across the Atlantic, and, to a certain extent, an attempt to rein in the ferocious brutality of the whole enterprise; the extent of Conquistador atrocities had at this stage become widely known in Europe, as witnessed by the surviving woodcuts of the period. Neither is there any mention of the infamous Requerimiento which became obligatory in 1513, a document which was henceforth to be read out to Indians (in Castilian!), informing them that the world belonged to the Catholic Church and the Pope and that if they did not submit, violence could be 'legally' used against them, their wives and children enslaved, and that "we shall confiscate your goods and do to you all the harm and damage we can, as it is lawful to do to disobedient vassals". An additional minor point which I came across by chance: the crews of the *Pinta,* the *Niña* and the *Santa María* were eventually paid in 1513 – 1,000 maravedís a month for an experienced seaman, 600 for a novice. The events described in the text also obviously takes place before the establishment of the Inquisition on Hispaniola, though that was much later, in 1523.

Hugo de Montenegro: Readers with knowledge of the period will most likely spot the similarities between Fray Montenegro and the real historical figure of Fray Hugo de Antonio Montesino. The latter also gave two well-known sermons – in 1511 – but these were delivered at Concepción, not in Santo Domingo. Bartolomé de las Casas (who himself also later became a Dominican) is supposed to have heard at least one of them first hand. Montesino arrived in Hispaniola in 1510 (Montenegro says he has been there several years) with Pedro de Cordova (see below) along with most probably the first Dominicans to go to the Americas. And like Montenegro, he was expelled back to Spain, in 1512. After Las Casas, Antonio Montesino is the best-known champion of Indian humanity known to us. He is also accredited with having written a book entitled *Informatio juridica in Indorum defensionem*; the title of Montenegro's book is *In Indorum defensionem.* The similarities between the real man and the *fictional* character of Montenegro are unmistakable.

Francisquito Guaro, or Red Francisquito as he is often referred to, seems to be based on the Taíno Indian Enriquito who organised successful resistance against the Spanish invaders from, the records say, about 1519 to 1533. He was reportedly closely related to Anacaona and his father was killed in the massacre Ovando ordered against her caciques. Enriquito's original Indian name was possibly Guarocuya, while Francisquito's is Guaro. Enriquito means 'little Enrique', just as Francisquito means 'little Francisco'. Enriquito, like Francisquito, also spent time at a Franciscan school, where he was given refuge after the massacre ordered by Ovando. His wife's name was Mencía, a mestizo granddaughter of Anacaona. Las Casas eventually negotiated a peace between Enriquito's simarons and the Spanish by which the simarons were allowed some lands and autonomy. Though Enriquito's war was later than 1511 (or so it seems) perhaps the unknown author(s) was paying him a belated surreptitious homage.

The 'teary greeting': When Sor Lucrezia di Marchionni visits the cacica Anacasabe, she writes the cacica "hugged me and shed tears – I have been told this teary greeting, as it is called, is a traditional means of welcome among them. It was a most moving gesture and more, I felt, than mere ceremony". Wasserman, in his recently published Columbus biography – unhappily available currently only in German – describes this *Tränengruß* ('teary greeting' or 'tear greeting') as being a custom among the Indians of the Caribbean but says nothing else about it. Eyewitness-chroniclers of the period also describe it, but usually interpret it (conveniently, it could be argued) as a sign of the Indians being overjoyed to meet them. Wasserman's *Christoph Columbus, der Don Quichote des Ozeans* is essential reading for anyone who wishes to gain further insight into the contradictory psychological forces that drove Columbus and his contemporaries, and formed their worldview. The only fault I can find with the book is that, to give the devil his due where it is due, Wassermann portrays the Salamanca cosmographer-theologians, with whom Columbus debated the feasibility of sailing to India across the Atlantic, as being less knowledgeable of cosmology and geography than they actually were; and, in any event, it must be admitted, they were correct. Columbus did not reach India.

Captain-General Gonzales de Esquival, or **Carnage** as he is called by the Indians, seems to be a very lightly disguised portrait of Juan de Esquival, who commanded a Spanish force that massacred 600-700 Higüeys at an Indian town called La Aleta in 1503. According to Las Casas, who describes the event, the Higüeys had rebelled against the Spanish after their cacique had been disembowelled by a war dog. The massacre described in *Hayti* seems to have taken place several years earlier and at a different location.

Carlos Goya, Pater Gerónimo Sanchez and Gonzalo Morales: The story of the shipwreck on the Yucatan coast seems to be based on a real shipwreck which took place in 1511, though the shipwreck in the text takes place several years before this (assuming of course that I am correct in my assumption that 1511 is the year in which the events described in *Hayti* took place). The caravel in question was called the *Santa María de la Barca*, not the *Trinity*, though most of the other details of the story concur with the historical record, such as it is, very closely: the ship running aground, the days spent in an open boat, the survivors eventually reaching the Yucatan, and their subsequent fate. When Cortés arrived on the Yucatan coast in 1519, two survivors from the *Santa María de la Barca* shipwreck were still alive: the Franciscan Gerónimo de Aguilar and Gonzalo Guerrero. De Aguilar joined Cortés as an interpreter, but Gonzalo Guerrero, who had married a Mayan noblewoman named Zazil Há and had children, refused to do so. He is reported to have said the following words to Gerónimo de Aguilar, who had been sent to speak to him: "Brother Aguilar, I am married and have three children, and they look on me as a cacique here, and a captain in time of war. My face is tattooed and my ears are pierced. What would the Spaniards say about me if they saw me like this? Go and God's blessing be with you, for you have seen how handsome these children of mine are."

Diego de Landa (of whom more about later), in his *Yucatan Before and After the Conquest*, has the following to say, but bear in mind he was writing half a century after the event and could only have been repeating what he had heard: "These poor fellows (the survivors) fell into the hands of a bad cacique, who sacrificed Valdivia and four others to their idols, and served them in a feast to the people. Aguilar and Guerrero and five or six others were spared in order to be fattened up. These broke out of their prison and came to another chief who was an enemy of the first, and more merciful; he made them his slaves and his successor treated them with much kindness. However, all died of grief, save only Gerónimo de Aguilar and Gonzalo Guerrero. Of these de Aguilar was a good Christian and had a breviary, by which he kept count of the feast days and finally escaped on the arrival of the Marquis Hernando Cortés in 1519. Guerrero learnt the language and went to Chectemal (Chetumal), which is Salamanca de Yucatan. He was received by a chief named Nachan Can, who placed in his charge his military affairs; in these he did well and conquered his master's enemies many times. He taught the Indians to fight, showing them how to make barricades and bastions. In this way, and by living as an Indian, he gained a great reputation and married a woman of high quality, by whom he had children, and made no attempt to escape with Aguilar. He decorated his body, let his hair grow, pierced his ears to wear rings like the Indians, and is believed to have become an idolater like them."

Pater Gerónimo Sanchez could easily be a fictionalised Gerónimo de Aguilar. How Carlos Goya relates to Gonzalo Guerrero is less clear; what they both do have in common are their tattoos and the fact that both learnt the local language. It is much more likely that it is in fact Gonzalo Morales who is a fictionalized Gonzalo Guerrero; the name indicates this and the fact that Morales, who plays a very minor role in the *Hayti* narrative, married and had children with an Indian woman. But on the other hand, Goya, like Gonzalo Guerrero, who eventually fought the Spaniards and died in battle, also revolts and turns against the Spaniards; but the former's revolt was more desperate, more hopeless and obviously suicidal from its inception.

De Landa says that Cortés had been told that there was "in the country five or six bearded men resembling us in all things".

Fray Pedro seems obviously based on Pedro de Córdoba, the leader of the Dominicans who arrived in Santo Domingo in 1510. The catechism he wrote was titled *Doctrina cristiana para instrucción e información de los Indios por manera de historia*. He became the first inquisitor appointed in the Americas, probably around in 1523, dying in Santo Domingo a couple of years later.

Nuns in the New World: The first historical mention of nuns in the Americas is several years after Cortés's conquest of the Mexica. Were there nuns on Hispaniola in and around 1511? I was unable to find any evidence, though there certainly were women from Spain on Hispaniola – and the historical record does mention two gypsy women.

The Waldseemüller map, Amerigo (Americus) Vespucci, Goya's account of seeing a ship on the Great Southern Ocean (the Pacific): The Waldseemüller map, rediscovered in an old castle library in Germany as recently as 1901, clearly shows the Pacific and its vast extent, as well as an outline of South America which any schoolboy would recognise from the world map on his classroom wall. The publication date of the Waldseemüller map is 1507 (indicated by a printer's mark in an accompanying book, written mainly by Ringmann, called the *Cosmographiae Introductio*, or the *Introduction to Cosmography*); yet, officially, Núñez de Balboa reached the Pacific in 1513, five years later, getting only a glimpse of its vastness from a hilltop. South America was only officially circumnavigated and the Pacific crossed, and its extent finally determined, by Ferdinand Magellan in 1519 – his ships (he died on the voyage) returned to Spain in 1522 – and the first account of the voyage was published in Italy in 1524 by Antonio Pigafetta, a full seventeen years after the publication of the Waldseemüller-Ringmann map. Were there earlier voyages? Voyages kept secret for political or commercial reasons? It is possible but we shall probably never know unless some definitive dusty document survives Franco and his Moors and is rediscovered. How many voyages Americus Vespucci made and how far south he sailed is not agreed upon. It is generally now accepted, after an analysis of the text by Professor Alberto Magnaghi of Milan, that at least some of the letter known as the *Four Voyages* is in fact a forgery, as is the *Mundus Novus*, also attributed to Vespucci. In the *Cosmographiae Introductio*, Waldseemüller and Ringmann say clearly that the western part of the map, what they called 'the fourth part of the world', is based on Vespucci's discoveries as laid out in the *Four Voyages*, which is actually reproduced in their *Cosmographiae Introductio*. But this only deepens the mystery of the origin of the map and as to where Waldseemüller and Ringmann got such seemingly accurate information. The distinctive ice-cream-cone shape of the South American continent: was it mere chance, a very lucky guess on the mapmaker's part?

As late as 1523 Cortes still hoped to find a central passage through to the Great Southern Ocean and sent one expedition up the Pacific side and another up the Atlantic side of North America in order to search for it. The passage continued to be depicted on later globes and maps for 25 years after the Waldseemüller map, including Johann Schöner's maps and globe (1515, 1520) and by Sebastian Münster in a map dated 1532.

Is it possible that the Portuguese carried out explorations but kept their voyages secret; because these voyages would have been in the zone of the world allocated to Spain by the Treaty of Tordesillas in 1494, when, with the blessing of the Borgia Pope Alexander VI, the two powers divided up the world between them, a sort of early version of the Congress of Berlin, in which the current masters of the world divided up Africa between them in 1884-5. Magellan insisted to his crews that he had a map from Martin Behaim – Behaim was obviously a name that carried much weight. But perhaps he was bluffing, simply attempting to reassure them as he searched for the straights through to the Pacific which today bear his name. However, Magellan did reportedly serve as a clerk from around 1495 to 1505 in the Casa de India in Lisbon. Is it possible he saw a map there, drawn or attributed to Behaim, who also worked there? Again, we shall probably never know? There are reputedly a dozen or so pre-Magellan maps and globes which show the west coast of South America but I have only been able to find solid references to and reproductions of the so-called Lenox globe, an engraved copper globe about the size of a grapefruit which is held by the New York Public Library, and which the library dates to circa 1510, about three years before Balboa's 'discovery' of the Pacific and ten years before Magellan's circumnavigation.[5] Some scholars date it to circa 1505. It is certainly the oldest post-Columbian globe in existence and accurately extends the tip of South America to 55 degrees south of the equator. It has been dated to pre-

---

[5] In 2013 an ostrich-egg globe came to light. which a has been dated to as early as 1504. It is almost an exact copy of the Lenox globe (see plates) and some scholars believe it could have been used as the cast for the copper Lenox globe.

Waldseemüller perhaps principally, but not only, on the grounds that it does not show the North American continent as a land mass but as instead a collection of islands. Alexander von Humboldt, who wrote in some depth about these matters, was of the opinion that the Portuguese explorations of South America were in fact far more extensive than is generally believed.

Magellan's voyage seems to have been financed by Cristobal de Haro – who was a Fugger agent, and who in that capacity financed both Spanish voyages and Portuguese voyages of exploration down the eastern coast of South America. The Fuggers at one stage were given the 'rights' to large areas in what is now Venezuela (as were the Welsers, another German banking family empire). The history of the role of the Fuggers and Welsers, who amassed vast quantities of capital – and what is capital but the accumulated labour of the masses of humanity? – in the bloody plunder and ruthless expropriation of the Americas, awaits to be written.

Accounts of atrocities: Montenegro's accounts of the atrocities committed by the Spaniards on Hispaniola, and indeed Castro's account, could almost have been transcribed directly from Las Casas' *A Brief History of the Destruction of the Indies*, as could many other passages describing the horrors of the Conquest.

Diego de Landa, half a century later, writing of atrocities in the Yucatan, gives the following horrifying account: "Several principal men of the province of Cupul they burned alive, and others they hung. Information being laid against the people of Yobain, a town of the Chels, they took the leading men, put them in stocks in a building and then set fire to the house, burning them alive with the greatest inhumanity in the world. I, Diego de Landa, say that I saw a great tree near the village upon the branches of which a captain had hung many women, with their infant children hung from their feet." And: "The Indians of the provinces of Cochuah and Chetumal rose, and the Spaniards so pacified them that from being the most settled and populous provinces they became the most wretched of the whole country. Unheard-of cruelties were inflicted, cutting off their noses, hands, arms and legs, and the breasts of their women; throwing them into deep water with gourds tied to their feet, thrusting the children with spears because they could not keep up with their mothers. If some of those who had been put in chains fell sick or could not keep up with the rest, they would cut off their heads among the rest rather than stop to unfasten them."

De Landa, who – as the Americans say – was no 'bleeding-heart liberal', was unlikely to have been exaggerating. His own treatment of the Indians in the Yucatan was the reason – or, to take a more cynical but perhaps more realistic interpretation – the pretext for his recall to Spain in 1562. He was accused of overstepping his jurisdiction and taking inquisitorial powers illegally upon himself and of "whipping and flogging" the Indians in his region – who, being "infants in the faith", were officially exempt from inquisitorial jurisdiction, at that particular time in any case. He also burned numerous Mayan books (see below). For this reason, I quote him rather than Las Casas, whose accounts are in any case well known.

Cannibalism: The word 'cannibalism' seems to have come from Caniba or Cariba, an island or group of islands where the so-called Canibas or Caribs or Caribals were said to have lived. These words later metamorphosised into 'Caribbean'. That ritual cannibalism was practiced in pre-Columbian America, in which the body parts of slain enemies and the victims of sacrifices were eaten for magical purposes, is pretty much undisputed, as is the existence of human sacrifice on a massive scale among the Aztecs and the Mexica, and also, though only more occasionally practiced, among other nations and ethnic groups of the Central Americas. However, there is little, if any, evidence for the type of cannibalism that inhabited the febrile imaginations of the European conquerors, in which bands of marauding Canibas went from island to island with the sole purpose of capturing other Indians to eat, sometimes after a period of 'fattening them up', because they had developed a taste for human flesh such that they "will eat no other flesh than human", as Puccini says, quoting Vespucci (from a letter which is most likely a work of fiction). It quite possible that Caribbean funerary practices, in which body parts were kept as relics, as they were in Europe and still are – the churches of Spain are full of such grisly artefacts – contributed to this belief, as did the eating of monkeys. The author(s) of *Hayti*, being a man or perhaps woman of her time, does not directly question the belief that the cannibalism practiced was of this latter sort; but he, or she, does have both Lucrezia di Marchionni and Montenegro admit to never actually seeing one of these human flesh-eating Canibas. This could be a mere incidental comment, but it may also be quite a deliberate attempt to question the conventional wisdom of the period.

Anacaona's murder: Castro's account of Anacaona's murder at the hands of Ovando is similar to Las Casas', though Las Casas does not mention Ovando by name (an omission he often practices). Las Casas did not himself take part in this expedition, though he admitted he took part in others as bloody. His account, related in his *A Brief Description of the Destruction of the Indies*, is worth quoting in full (the language in the copy I have is rather archaic): "Xaraqua is the fourth kingdom, and as it were the centre and middle of the whole island, and is not to be equalled for fluency of speech and politeness of idiom or dialect by any inhabitants of the other kingdoms, and in policy and morality transcends them all. Herein the lords and peers abounded, and the populace excelled in stature and habit of body. Their king was Behechio by name and had a sister called Anacaona; and both the brother as well as sister had loaded the Spaniards with benefits and singular acts of civility, and by delivering them from the evident and apparent danger of death, did signal services to the Castilian kings. Behechio dying, the supreme power of the kingdom fell to Anacaona. But it happened one day that the Governour of the island, attended by 60 horse and 30 foot, summoned about 300 noblemen to appear before him, and commanded the most powerful of them to be crowded into a thatched barn, to be exposed to the fury of a merciless fire, and the rest to be pierced with lances or run through with the point of the sword by his multitude of men. And Anacaona herself, because she swayed the royal sceptre, to her greater honour was hanged on a gibbet. And if it came to pass that if any person, instigated by compassion or covetousness, did entertain any Indian boys and mount them on horses, to prevent their murder, another was appointed to follow them, running them through the back or in the hinder parts, and if they chanced to escape death, and fell to the ground, they immediately cut off his legs; and those Indians that survived these barbarous massacres and betook themselves to an isle eight miles distant to escape these butcheries were captured and committed to

servitude for life." In fact, little in the text regarding the
atrocities committed against the Indians of the Caribbean
cannot also be found in Las Casas. Anacaona's murder and the
accompanying massacres are also described by Wassermann.

Savonarola's macaw: It is impossible to identify this bird with any
degree of accuracy since all Caribbean macaws are now extinct.
However, I have been informed that it is possibly the Cuban red
macaw, also referred to, but not very often, as the Hispaniolan
macaw. Some stuffed specimens are reported to exist in a few
zoological collections.

Epidemics and population decline: It is reasonably well recorded
that there was an epidemic on Hispaniola in 1493, the year of
Columbus's second voyage and his first colonising mission. A
glance at any texts written at the time can leave one in no doubt
that epidemics, major and minor, and various sicknesses among
the Indians were a frequent occurrence. It is generally thought
that the 1493 epidemic was some strain of swine flu, but I have
been told, on good authority, that it is not impossible that it could
actually have been smallpox. What is certain is that the
Hieronymite monks, who were ruling Hispaniola at the time,
reported a smallpox epidemic in January 1519. It is impossible for
us to even imagine this kind of devastation. The Black Death in
Europe, at its worst, killed off about a third of the population. The
various epidemics in the Americas killed off, by some estimates,
as much as ninety percent of the population. Not so much a *new
world* as an *end of the world*. The Spaniards too died in droves – and
one cannot help wondering what madness it was that drove them,
as it did later colonists in other parts of the world, to more or less
gamble their lives away at the same odds as the flip of a coin.
Most of the Spaniards were men in their prime, between the ages
of twenty and forty, many of them even older, and had already
been hardened by surviving who knows what diseases and germs
in the ports and ships of Europe; yet very often, in less than a
year, the chroniclers report half of them dead. The Indian
population, of course, would have had no resistance to any of the
diseases that came on the Spanish ships, and a larger proportion
of the Indian population would have been in infancy or very
young, aged, or pregnant women; so one can only come to the

conclusion that the death rate among them must have been unbelievably high.

The original population of Hispaniola is unknown. Las Casas put it at several hundred thousand, though that seems improbably high, but certainly within the bounds of the possible. He says there were 60,000 Indians living on the island when he arrived there in 1508. There can be little doubt that, when Columbus first arrived, it was as densely populated as anywhere in Europe at the time. Wassermann, in a chapter entitled *Indian Inferno*, says that by about 1520 nine-tenths of the original population had been exterminated by disease, slave labour and endless atrocities. This is the same rate of population decline that is documented for Mexico in the decades after its 'discovery' or 'conquest' – call it what one will – by Cortés in 1519.

An informal 'headcount' carried out by the colonial overlords of Hispaniola in 1508 put the Indian population at 60,000, and another one in 1514 put it at 14,000. A more rigorous census in 1548 counted the total population of the island as 3,000 Spanish, 30,000 African slaves, and a mere 500 descendants of the original Indian inhabitants.

The epidemic on the mainland described by Serrano, occurring before the Spanish invasion, is a very plausible historic event. Smallpox preceded Pizarro into Peru. De Landa, writing in 1566, has this to say about a 'plague' in the Yucatan, to which he attributes great devastation. Writing of the time before the plague he is describing, he says: "At that time they erected temples in great numbers, as is today seen everywhere; in going through the forests there can be seen in the groves the sites of houses and buildings marvellously worked." He describes it as "a pestilence, with great pustules that rotted the body, fetid in odour, and so that the members fell in pieces within four or five days". He dated this to the period before the Spanish conquest of the Yucatan, saying "since this last plague more than fifty years have now passed", which would put it prior to 1516 at the very least, so he could well have been describing the epidemic Serrano described (what the latter calls "the pox and the fevers"). De Landa finishes the chapter in which he discusses all this with the following comment: "It is a marvel that there is any of the population left."

Taíno collective suicides: Here I shall quote from Girolamo Benzoni's *La historia del mondo nuovo*, Venice, 1565 (*History of* *the New World,* Hakluyt Society edition, London, 1857). Benzoni was from Milan and went to the Americas in 1541, staying there until 1556. He travelled widely, publishing his account in 1565, several years after his return. It provides a compact and popular history from 1492 to the conquest of the Inca Empire in Peru. He was an Italian, and a Catholic – and that is partly my reason for choosing his account, as well as the fact that large parts of it were most likely related to him by eyewitnesses while he was in the Americas. Many subsequent accounts of atrocities were written by Protestants and often dismissed as the exaggerations of anti-Catholic propaganda. His book also contains woodcuts.[6] He seems to put the collective suicides in the period following Diego Colón's governorship: "... the natives, finding themselves intolerably oppressed and worked on every side, with no chance of regaining their liberty, with sighs and tears longed for death. Wherefore many went to the woods and there hung themselves, after having killed their children, saying it was far better to die than to live so miserably, serving such and so many ferocious tyrants and wicked thieves. The women, with the juice of a certain herb, dissipated their pregnancy, in order not to produce children, and then following the example of their husbands, hung themselves. Some threw themselves from high cliffs down precipices; others jumped into the sea; others again into rivers; others starved themselves to death. Sometimes they killed themselves with their flint knives; others pierced their bosoms or their sides with pointed stakes. Finally, out of the two million original inhabitants, through the numbers of suicides and other deaths, occasioned by the oppressive labour and cruelties imposed by the Spaniards, there are not a hundred and fifty now to be found: and thus has been their way of making Christians of them. What befell those poor islanders happened also to all the others around: Cuba, Jamaica, Porto Rico and other places. And although an almost infinite number of the inhabitants of the mainland have been brought to these islands as slaves, they have nearly all since died." Benzoni has been accused of 'exaggeration' and other things, among them saying little that Las Casas had not already said. But in the case of collective suicides, Las Casas does not say a great deal,

---

[6] See plates.

though he does describe quite a few individual suicides by Caribbean caciques. The only description of such a collective suicide by Indians I could find in his *Brief Description* was of such an event on Cuba: "By the ferocity of one Spanish tyrant (whom I knew) above two hundred Indians hanged themselves of their own accord; and a multitude of people perished by this kind of death." But I have not had the opportunity of reading all that he wrote. [7]

Syphilis and guayacán (guaiacum): The one disease which went the other way, from the Americas to Europe, was syphilis. One of the early 'cures' was guaiacum, the Hispaniolan Indian word *guayacán* Latinised. Later it was also called *lignum sanctum* or *holy wood* because it was believed to be the tree from which the cross on which Jesus had been crucified had been made. What Puccini says about it, the reasons for his belief in its efficacy and its origins, appears to concur with what was believed in subsequent decades. The other 'cure' for syphilis was mercury (quicksilver). The Fuggers were granted a monopoly for the importation of guaiacum and the trade in mercury, principally in return for financing the bid of Charles V (the first Hapsburg King of Spain) for the Crown of the Holy Roman Empire in 1519. The bribes required were enormous. It is more than plausible that they were also involved in the importation of guaiacum much earlier. Eventually, mercury became the preferred and fairly lethal cure for syphilis, though of course it was also in high demand for gold and silver mining.

The Inquisition in the New World: The Spanish Inquisition arrived in the Americas in the early 1520s with Fray Pedro de Córdoba's appointment as the first inquisitor, though it was only later that formal tribunals were set up. Its main objective, as in Spain and the other Spanish possessions in Europe, was to root

---

[7] The entry for Girolamo Benzoni in Wikipedia describes his history as "a book of diatribes and accusations against Spain in America" and says that "The ultra-philanthropists found Benzoni a welcome auxiliary, and foreign nations, all more or less leagued against Spain for the sake of supplanting its mastery of the Indies, adopted his extreme statements and sweeping accusations." The article is actually a reproduction of the entry for him in the *Catholic Enyclopedia* of 1917. It does however say that the London 1857 Hakluyt Society edition is the best translation of his book into English.

Ref: http://en.wikipedia.org/wiki/Girolamo_Benzoni, 16 May 2017.

out conversos who were secretly practicing Judaism. Officially, the Indians, being considered *infants in the faith*, were very often exempt from its jurisdiction. Ironically, many with converso backgrounds played a significant role in its activities. Tomás de Torquemada, the first *Inquisidor General*, and on whose prompting Sixtus IV had agreed to its establishment in Spain, was himself the grandson of a Jewess. Las Casas, who also came from a converso family – his grandfather was apparently burned at the stake for allegedly still practicing Judaism when Las Casas was seven years of age – had no compunction about enlisting the organisation on behalf of the Indians. In 1516 he convinced the Grand Inquisitor Ximenes to declare the Dominicans the *Defensor universal de los Indios*.

As for Montenegro's contention that the Spaniards in their attitude to the Indians were guilty of heresy: in 1537 a Papal Bull on the subject, *Sublimus Dei*, stated that "those who mistreat them [the Indians] serve Satan"; vindication, of sorts, in word if not in deed; the effect this had in practice seems to have been limited, to say the least.

The 'codex': There are only three surviving Maya codices, all named after the locations where they are currently stored. The Madrid Codex is 122 pages long and came to light in the 1860s. The Dresden Codex, 74 pages long, has been in Dresden since 1739. The Paris Codex is the shortest, with only 22 pages.[8] How many existed at the time of the Conquest is difficult to estimate. But what is certain is that they were all destroyed except for the three just mentioned. Even de Landa, who actually attempted to decipher the Maya script, played his part in this early *Bücherverbrennung*.[9] Just before his recall to Spain, he burned numerous Mayan books at an *auto de fé* in 1562, "ninety-nine times as much knowledge of Mayan history and sciences as is given to us in this book", as the author of the preface of the edition of the *Yucatan Before and After the Conquest* I consulted during these researches puts it. In de Landa's own words: "We found a large

---

[8] Since then another, the so-called Grolier Codex, has come to light, discovered in a cave in Tortuguero, Mexico, in the 1970s. It is only 11 pages long, and its authenticity is doubted by some scholars.

[9] Neufeld is referring here to the Nazi *Bücherverbrennung* (book burning) of Jewish and other 'degenerate literature' in front of the Berlin Opera House in Berlin in 1933.

number of books in these characters and, as they contained nothing which was not to be seen as anything other than superstition and lies of the devil, we burned them all, which they regretted to an amazing degree, and which caused them much affliction." I have been told that the last Mayan codices were destroyed as late as 1697, when the Spanish conquered Nojpeten (today in Guatemala), the last Indian city to be conquered in the Americas.

There are about 600 hieroglyphics in the pre-Columbian Mayan script. It has not yet been deciphered, a task complicated by the fact that some symbols appear to be phonetic, some syllable-based and some true hieroglyphics after the Ancient Egyptian manner, and the fact that there are over two dozen distinct Mayan dialects.[10] As for de Landa's attempt to decipher it: some scholars say his work was of value, others that it was little more than fanciful nonsense. He was the first, it seems, to develop a Latin alphabet for a Mayan dialect (the one spoken in the Yucatan) and in which modern Mayan is written today. There are reports of Spanish priests actually learning the original Mayan script, and of it still being in use into the 18th century in isolated regions. Mayan bark paper was reputedly superior to papyrus, being more durable and easier to write on.

The surviving Aztec codices, which are far more numerous, were mostly written during the Conquest or in the decades following it. The pre-Conquest documents consist of pictograms rather than a script. The post-Conquest ones also contain pictograms but are written in Nahuatl (using the Latin alphabet), in Spanish, and even with sections in Latin. Nahuatl, like Mayan, is still spoken today by many of the inhabitants of Mexico.

Dwarfs, fools and astrologers: The Spanish who plundered the Caribbean, Mexico and Peru were men of the Middle Ages, not enlightened moderns braving the seven seas to map the world and cast off geographical ignorance, their rapaciousness and religious fanaticism mere secondary traits, though this is usually the image of them that inhabits the popular imagination. The large-than-life statues of these ruthless men that stand in innumerable Spanish plazas, invariably showing them gazing

---

[10] The Mayan script, which is mainly a syllabary (the symbols represent syllables rather than actual letters), is now up to ninety percent decipherable.

sternly into the distance, sometimes with a globe or navigational instrument, though always with sword at hand, have no doubt contributed to this perception. If anything, it was the other way around: their additions to geographical knowledge were incidental – the maps of the early decades of the Spanish Conquest are incredibly inaccurate (the Portuguese were much more methodical, though they too were rapacious and fanatical). When these thugs (no other word comes to mind) held court in the Indies, they did so as 'honour' and gold-obsessed superstitious tyrants, whose mode of being was probably not that far removed from that of the Sicilian *mafia* 'bosses' in American cities today. Their courts resembled medieval courts, complete with official fools and official astrologers. Bernal Diaz, Cortés's companion in arms and eyewitness to the conquest of Mexico, tells the story of "a kind of buffoon, generally called mad Cervantes, who used to assume great liberty of speech under pretence of idiocy", and who used to run in front of Velasquez, the then Governor of Cuba, "shouting out all sorts of absurdities"; and elsewhere he mentions that Velasquez had an astrologer named Millan. The author, or authors, of *Hayti* obviously knew this and simply placed these two, presumably historical, characters in Diego Colón's court.

Columbus's *Book of Prophecies*: Like all the books mentioned in the text – with the exception of Montenegro's *In Indorum defensionem* – Columbus's *El Libro de las Profecías* is a real book. The brief description of its contents provided by Montenegro is accurate. Columbus is reported to have written elsewhere, in one of his many letters, that God had revealed to him "the messenger (referring to himself) of the new heaven and the new earth of which He spoke in the Apocalypse of St. John after having spoken of it through the mouth of Isaiah; and He showed me where to find it".

Padded cotton armour: In his *The True History of the Conquest of Mexico*, Bernal Diaz del Catillo relates how the Conquistadors wore cotton padded armour. However, it is not clear whether this was something they copied from the Mexica and the other Indians of Central America, who certainly wore cotton padded armour, or whether it was something the Conquistadors were already familiar with. If it was something they copied from the

Mexica, it would certainly have protected them from Mexica weapons, as it would have been designed to do. Columbus noted "cotton mantles and sleeveless shirts embroidered and painted in different designs" and colours "of the costliest and handsomest" type. One of the reasons for his belief that he was in India, it has been suggested.

Voodoo and Haiti (the French-speaking western part of the island; the original Indian name of *Hayti* referred to the whole island of Hispaniola) are inseparable. This religious-magical cult has its origins overwhelmingly in a synthesis of the primitive religions which the African slaves brought with them to the island and appears to consist of four or so fairly distinct but not mutually exclusive sects. However, some authorities believe that one of these sects, the Petwo or Petro sect, the sect associated with zombies (animated corpses which do the bidding of those magicians which control them, sometimes called 'the living dead'), may actually be, at least in part, of Taíno Indian origin. The word *voodoo* or *vudu* is of West African origin, and it is not impossible that it arrived in Hispaniola with the very first African slaves. The Taíno Indians certainly seem to have had a belief that the dead could wander about at night in a physical form.

The serpent that dwells in the petals of flowers: There are no poisonous snakes on Hispaniola, and one presumes there were none at the time. However, there are snakes on the mainland of Central America which would fit this description. It seems the author(s) was most probably exercising some poetic licence. However, it is also possible that at the time the Spaniards believed there were poisonous snakes on the island.

Anachronisms: The few anachronisms in the text, if that is what they are, do not really put the 'authenticity' of the text in question, if one can speak of the authenticity of a work of fiction which describes a historical epoch so faithfully. They do however seem to indicate that the texts were written perhaps up to twenty or even more years after the events described. For example, *chocol* – Mayan for 'chocolate' – is of mainland or *tierra firme* origin and became known to the Conquistadors only after the invasion of Mexico in 1519. The same is true of the word *cigar*, which is probably derived from the Mayan word *sik* or *sikar* for tobacco or rolled tobacco leaves. Similarly, the drinking of *chicha*, a beer brewed from maize, does not seem to have been a Caribbean custom, but rather a mainland one; the word itself seems to be of Nahuatl origin. A further indication that the text was possibly composed much later is the mention of voodoo or *vudu*: while it is possible that the word was used in 1511 it is far more likely that it is of a later origin, when African slaves were present in large numbers on the island – 30,000 in 1542, just thirty years after the events described, according to the census of that year. The references to tomatoes (from *tomatl*, Nahuatl) and avocadoes (from *āhuacatl*, also Nahuatl) would also indicate that it was written after the conquest of Mexico.

Early 16th-century Spanish currency: Spanish currency at the time was based on copper (maravedís), silver (reales) and gold (ducats, escudos pesos and castellanos). A maravedí was a small copper coin (though gold and silver maravedí coins had existed earlier). The 15th century was a period of monetary confusion in Spain but in 1497 the Catholic Monarchs reformed and standardised the system – in so much as was possible. Taking the maravedí as the basic currency unit at the time the events in *Hayti* occurred, the following seems to have been the case:

    1 silver real = 34 maravedís

    1 ducat = 375 maravedís

    1 peso = 450 maravedís

    1 castellano = 485 maravedís.

However, these relative 'official' values cannot be taken as fixed. Coins had both a denominational value and a 'real' value based on their metal content, and in the Americas this was complicated further by the cost and not inconsiderable risk of transporting them (particularly large quantities of maravedís) across the Atlantic before the establishment of the first mints there. Moreover, there are inconsistencies in the text. For example, the price of a slave is generally given as about 5,000 maravedís – which more or less is what one finds in contemporary documents, but in one instance the price of a slave is given as 150 ducats, which would work out at 56,000 maravedís. Crowns are also mentioned but it is not clear what they are exactly. As are thalers – however, I have been informed on good authority that they would have been extremely rare, far rarer than the frequency of their appearance in the narrative would lead one to believe. I have been unable to find out what their exchange rate to maravedís might have been. A possible reason for this confusion might have been an attempt (only partly successful) by the translator(s) of the original multi-lingual document to standardise the various currency units for the 1924 Catalan edition. Translators do at times have a tendency to try and tidy up unruly texts.

Distances: Puccini gives distances in Latin miles for the most part. He probably meant the Italian mile of the time, which is 1,238 metres. The Moorish mile he refers to is most likely the Arab mile, which is 1,830 metres.

The island of Hispaniola today is divided into two states, the Spanish-speaking Dominican Republic in the eastern part of the island, and the much smaller French-speaking Republic of Haiti on the western side. Their economies are still almost entirely based on the production of sugar for metropolitan markets. The African ancestors of the current inhabitants of Haiti were the first people ever to successfully plan and victoriously carry out a large-scale slave revolt – which they did in 1791, at the same time founding their Republic, defeating both French and British armies in the process. However, international recognition of Haiti as an independent republic only came decades later. As a precondition to recognition, France, in 1825, demanded the payment of 150 million gold francs in compensation for the lost 'property' of the previous slave-owners, a demand delivered by twelve French warships. Being a small and artificially heavily populated country, Haiti had little choice but to submit to this, or face starvation and even more utter destitution than it experiences today. The country was forced to take out loans with French banks. Her independence was finally recognised in 1835, and though this so-called 'independence debt' was reduced to 90 million gold francs later in the century, the payment of these 'reparations' has resulted in subjecting the country to a condition of poverty and destitution that is equaled in few other places in the various European capitalist-colonial empires. The debt is still being repaid today.[11]

Some final thoughts: Could any of this have been avoided? Could the discovery of the two halves of humanity of each other have

---

[11] The so-called 'independence debt' to France was eventually paid off in 1947. The total amount paid is estimated to have been €17 billion in today's values.

been even marginally happier, even an occasion of joy? Was the way it unfolded written in the stars – or, to put it in more modern terminology: was it simply the inevitable working of the subtle but iron logic of immutable laws which govern the unfolding of all great historical events, if not in their details, then in their grand sweeps? If there was ever a near unanswerable and definitive argument for deterministic historical laws – Darwinian or Marxian – surely the tragedy that befell the peoples of the pre-Conquest Americas would seem to be it.

The unfolding of this tragedy, a tragedy without precedence in the history of mankind, seems to have been overwhelmingly determined. The conjunction of cultural, economic, military, technical, psychological and biological forces that came into play, and their consequences, seems so overwhelming that any alternative scenario or outcome is difficult, if not impossible, to imagine. The diseases of the Old World were a given, as was its technological superiority in armaments, maritime capability and tactics. And add to that the fact that only the Europe of the late medieval period was in a position, and only just in that position – and thus at the particular stage of moral development it was at the time – to cross the Atlantic and gain a foothold in those lands, and initiate the subjection and devastation of their peoples. If Spain had not done it in 1492, Portugal would have done it in 1493, or France in 1494, or even England in 1495. But even if the crossing of the Atlantic – because of some chance events – had been delayed for another fifty years, say to 1542, would the outcome have been different? Hardly. Europe was a different place after the upheavals of Reformation but not different enough to make any difference to the peoples who had the misfortune to be 'discovered' by its explorers. The Tasmanians were exterminated a mere hundred years ago. It is only three-quarters of a century ago that slavery was abolished in the United States of America, a mere half a century ago that it was finally abolished in Brazil and East Africa, and it still exists in parts of Arabia; and the exploitation of the darker races continues without end. Of course, there are 'what if's'. What if, for example, the Chinese had crossed the Pacific? Or sailed down the western seaboard of North America and discovered the Mexica and the Incan Empires? A mere glance at the map is enough to enable one to imagine how such a thing could have been done, in the manner in which the Portuguese sailed to India hugging the coast of Africa. The Chinese too would have had gunpowder and compasses – they did invent them – and would have carried the same diseases the Europeans carried in their caravels, by all accounts a ship far inferior to the Chinese junk. But would the outcome have been essentially different? Difficult to imagine, I would suggest, particularly if the main agent of destruction was the lethal cocktail of old-world diseases to which the inhabitants of the Americas had no immunity. The other big 'what if' is of course: what if 'they' had discovered us? What if during the ebbs and flows of European history, at a particularly low point, say, one fine summer day in 759, a Mexica sailing ship had appeared off the coast of France, an event certainly not beyond the bounds of our imaginations? The seafarers would perhaps not have had steel or gunpowder, certainly not horses, and would probably only have borne syphilis – as opposed to the extensive arsenal of biological weapons (smallpox, measles, malaria and influenzas) that the European ships carried with them when they sailed in the opposite direction. Somehow, it is difficult to imagine that hypothetical event having the same devastating impact on us as 'we' had on 'them'. Indeed, those hypothetical Mexica explorers would even have quite possibly unwittingly carried the devastating diseases of the Old World back to their homeland on their return journey.

And yet, was there not another possibility, one that can at least be imagined? It is a possibility that can only be considered if we believe that the human being, for all his faults, has the innate potential to be a benevolent and cooperative creature; and that – if left to his own devices, free, his psychology undistorted by mechanisms of power and exploitation, and the ignorance these thrive on – he will tend to behave with generosity towards his fellows, as Kropotkin and many others believed, a vision the possibility of which has to be believed if it is to have any potential reality. That possible scenario might be as follows: that at some time, before the inevitable meeting of the Old World and the New World, a society could have arisen in Europe that was capable of seeing in the inhabitants of the Americas not half-men or soul fodder, but fellow men, and treated them accordingly; and knowing that the old-world diseases which Europeans carried would be devastating for the inhabitants of the Americas, the Europeans would have voluntarily quarantined themselves until such time as medical science had advanced to such a state that those diseases posed no greater threat to the inhabitants of the

Americas than the common cold. An idea as ridiculous as Montenegro's belief in the Resurrection of the Dead? Perhaps. But if we cannot entertain at least the thought of that having been at least possible, in some form or another, then our view of ourselves is dark and relentlessly deterministic, and without much hope. But if we do not believe that men can be essentially benevolent – or at least have the potential to be – and capable of free collective acts of will, for what then, in essence, did we fight a bloody war against Franco and his Moors? (The irony of the latter returning as Franco's henchmen – a belated racial revenge? – is not lost on me.) I have no illusions of what my fellow men are capable of, even those alongside whom I have fought, my comrades in arms. I saw the shameful outrages against the priests and monks in Barcelona (for the burned-down churches, I do not shed a thought, they were mere bricks and mortar); and while I may understand the pent-up rage of endless centuries that was the cause of it, and the desperate desire to shed at once and forever a religion that has perverted beyond any recognition the message of its founder, perhaps the very first Anarchist, and subjected the common people of Spain to the most relentless, insidious oppression and ignorance, the shedding of blood in that manner can never be right. Our belief in progress – and I do not mean the mindless progress of soulless Capital and its ideological offspring in the various Fascisms (Francoist, Italian and German racialist) – surely must have somewhere at its core a deeper belief in the potential benevolence of humanity. I am grasping at straws perhaps, but if there is nothing but straws to grasp at, then at straws we must grasp.

Christian Neufeld
International Brigade, 1938
(b. 1903, d. 1942)

Plates 4

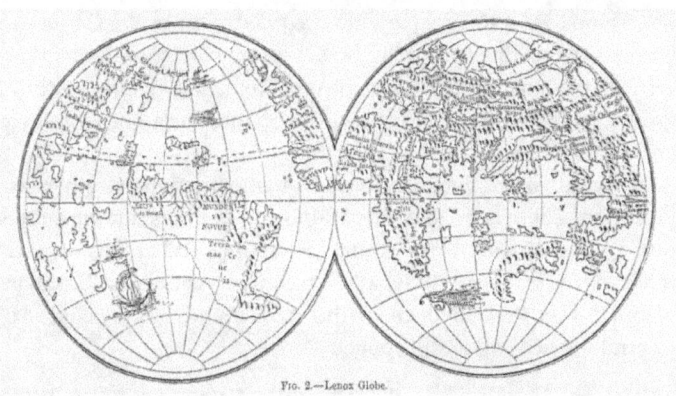

Fig. 2.—Lenox Globe.

Figure 17 *The Lenox globe held at the New York Public Library, and which the library dates to circa 1510, though some scholars date it to 1503-1507. It clearly shows South America as a separate and circumnavigable continent. Image from* Encyclopedia Britannica *1874. Source: en.wikipedia.org/wiki/Hunt-Lenox_Globe. Created by Kattigara, CC BY-SA 3.0.*

THE·LENOX·GLOBE

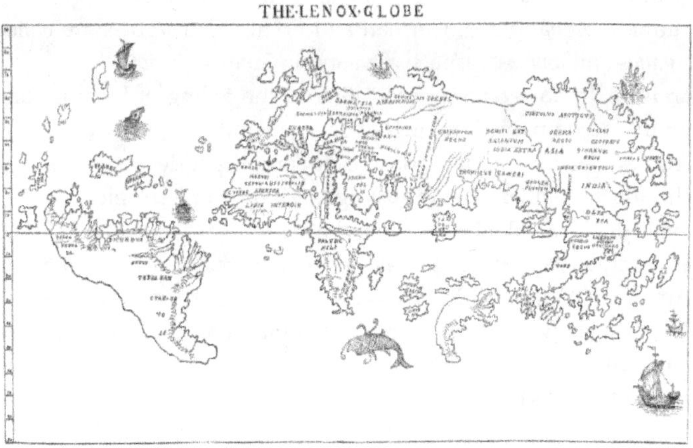

Figure 18 *World map derived from the Lenox globe by B.F. De Costa. Source: en.wikipedia.org/wiki/Hunt-Lenox_Globe. Created by Kattigara, CC BY-SA 3.0.*

Glossary of (mostly) Taíno words, place names etc. [12]

The Taínos were the people who occupied most of the Caribbean islands at the time of Columbus. Within half a century of his arrival, they had completely disappeared as a distinct cultural group, wiped out by the diseases the Spanish brought with them and as a result of Spanish depredations.

The words listed here are Taíno words, except where otherwise indicated. There is no standard Taíno, so spellings and meanings differ considerably from source to source. Where a word is referred to as Spanish, what is meant of course is Castilian. Nahuatl was the language of the Aztecs and other peoples of Central Mexico and is still spoken.

advocatus diaboli – devil's advocate, Latin; instituted as an official Vatican office in 1587, the holder of which is charged to find any possible reasons that would speak against a candidate for canonisation being officially elevated to sainthood.[13]

Alcalde and Alcalde Mayor – mayor or magistrate who presided over a town or district council, chief justice or chief magistrate, Spanish.

alcazár – fortress or castle, Spanish, of Arabic/Moorish origin.

anona – pineapple; in German and French, pineapples are called *Ananas* and *ananas*, respectively, and in Spanish *la piña*.

areíto – Taíno ceremony consisting of the telling of histories and myths, accompanied by singing and dancing.

Atabey – the goddess of the moon, the tides, springs and childbirth, mother of **Yócahu Vagua Maórocoti** (see below).

avocado – from the Nahuatl word *āhuacatl*.

axí – chilli pepper, written *ají* in modern Spanish in most South American countries, the Taíno **axí** was also used in older Spanish. The English word *chilli* comes from Nahuatl *chīlli*, *hilli* or *xilli*.

barbacoa – barbeque.

Barbudos – Barbados.

batata – sweet potato, not the common potato which originates from the Andes.

batey – ball game played by the Taíno, also called *batu*.

---

[12] This is the original glossary from the first English-language edition of *Hayti*. Additions and comments can be found in the footnotes.

[13] The office of *advocatus diaboli* was abolished in 1983 by John Paul II; an unprecedented number of canonisations and beatifications followed.

beata – pious, devout, woman who wears a religious habit, and is engaged in works of charity, but can also be used derogatorily, Spanish.

bohío – thatched rectangular house with porch, lived in by caciques and families of rank, word still used in West Indian Spanish.

bohique – shaman, also *bohuti*.

caballero – knight, Spanish.

cacica – female **cacique** (see below).

cacique – chief.

caney – thatched round house, usually lived in by commoners.

canoa – canoe.

Caniba – an island or group of islands, also called Cariba, where the so-called Canibas or Caribs or Caribals were supposed to have lived, origin of the word *cannibal*.

caoba wood – mahogany wood.

Castilla, the – Castilians, what the Taíno called the Spaniards according to the text, Spanish.

casabe – cassava.

chicha – beer brewed from maize kernels, from Nahuatl *chichiatl*.

chocol – chocolate, Yucatec Mayan.

Coaybay – the Taíno Indian afterworld, believed to be a real or dream-world island.

Casa de la Contratación de las Indias – the House of Trade for the Indies, Spanish.

cigar – from *sikar*, Yucatec Mayan, to smoke rolled tobacco leaves, **sik** meaning tobacco.[14]

Cipango – Japan.

converso – a convert to Catholicism from Judaism.

cutz – turkey, Maya.

ell – archaic English, unit of length/depth, 45 inches, a yard and a quarter.

encomienda – grant of Indian land and the labour of its Indian inhabitants to Spanish settlers by the local Spanish authorities in the name of the Spanish Crown.

falconet – a light cannon (200-400 lb. approx.), caliber 2″, also used

---

[14] Another explanation of the origin of the word *cigar* is from the Spanish word *cigarrales*, a summerhouse (near Toledo) where cigars were smoked – a *cigarrale* was so called because cicadas *(cigarrales)* could be heard in the evening when smoking, hence *cigarro*, a cigar.

to fire grapeshot, English.

fanega – Spanish, a dry measure, 55 litres approx.

Fortunate Isles – Canary Islands.

goeíza – the soul or spirit of a living person.

Giants, the – or **Islands of the Giants** – Curaçao.

guamiquina – a lord of lords, king of kings.

guanín – gold-copper alloy, but also possibly earplugs/earrings made from shells.

quinto – quintal, Spanish – a fifth, usually used in the context of a fifth of all proceeds from the Conquest due to the Spanish Crown.

guayacán – hence *guaiacum* (Latin), a plant derivative believed to cure syphilis.

guayaba – guava.

hamaca – hammock.

Hayti – Taíno word for the whole of the Island of Hispaniola, reputedly meaning 'mountainous land', the origin of *Haiti*.

hidalgo – member of the minor nobility, Spanish.

hurucan – hurricane, meaning storm but also possibly a spirit or God, some sources refer to a Mayan god of wind, storms and fire, by the name of *Hunracán* (but also *Juracán, Yuracán, Yerucán, Yorocán*).

hutia – a variety of rodent found in the Caribbean islands.[15]

iguana – iguana.

Inocentes – Innocents, Spanish.

insurrección – insurrection, Spanish.

kahwa – coffee, Arabic.

kismet – destiny, fate, Turkish, of Arabic origin.

Little Venice – Venezuela.

Lucayas, the – the Bermudas.

mahiz – maize, a similar word was used on the mainland.

manati – manatee, sea cow.

macana – wooden club.

mosque – the Spaniards habitually referred to Indian temples as mosques.

Malleus Maleficarum – *The Hammer of the Witches* or *Der Hexenhammer* (German) written by two Dominicans, Heinrich

---

[15] There were several species of hutia on Hispaniola at the time of the Conquest, only one of which still exists in small numbers in protected areas, though there have been reported sightings of another possible species/sub-species. About twenty species of Caribbean hutia have been identified, and at least a third are extinct.

Kramer and James Sprenger, in 1486; its main themes were on how to refute arguments claiming that witchcraft did not exist, to discredit those that argued it did not exist, and instruct judges on how to find and identify witches (who, according to the authors, were principally but not exclusively women).

manzana – unit of land area measurement, about 1.7 acres or a city block of houses, Spanish.

mappa mundi – world map, Latin; medieval mappa mundi were not primarily intended to be functional in the way that portolan maps or charts were, their main purpose was cosmo-theological, hence Jerusalem was invariably situated in the centre of the world.

mayohuacan – large Taíno drum made from a hollowed-out tree trunk.

mestizo – a person of Spanish and Indian origin, Spanish, from Latin *mixticius*, meaning mixed.

morisco – a Moor who had converted to Catholicism from Islam.

Mozarabic – refers to the architecture, art, religious rituals and customs of Christians living in Al-Andalus during the Muslim period in Spain.

naboria – commoner.

nitaíno – aristocrat.

Oceanus Indius Meridionalis – Indian Ocean, Latin.

Oceanus Occidentalis – Atlantic Ocean, Latin.

oikoumene – the ecumene, Greek, the Eurasian landmass, the extent of the known universe.

Opiyelguabirán – a dog-shaped god, guardian of the dead.

opía – spirit or soul of the dead.

papaw – papaya, pawpaw.

portolano – portolan chart, Spanish/English, medieval navigators' charts, showing coastlines and ports and their relative positions to one another, see also **mappa mundi**.

problema – problem, Italian/Spanish.

Pueblo Fantasma – ghost town, Spanish, used in the text as a proper name for deserted Taíno settlement.

reconciliado – one accused of heresy by the Inquisition, but who confessed and repented, and was subsequently reconciled with the Church, Spanish.

regalo – gift, Spanish.

Saint John the Baptist's Island – Puerto Rico, initially named San Juan Bautista by the Spanish, the Taíno name was *Borikén* which means Land of the Valiant Lord.

Sant-Maloù – Saint-Malo, Breton.

Schicksal – destiny, fate, fortune, German.

simarons – groups of self-emancipated slaves and Haytians, from the Taíno word *simaran* meaning flight of an arrow, origin of the English word *maroon*, also spelt *cimarrones*.[16]

Spanish Island, the – Hispaniola; Columbus named it La Isla Española and Insula Hispana (the Spanish Island), later this became Hispaniola , see also **Hayti**.

tabaco – from which the word *tobacco* is derived; it is in fact believed to have been the Taíno word for *cigar*.

Taíno – when Columbus first met the Haytians they described themselves as the Taíno, meaning good or noble.

tierra firme – solid land, dry land, Spanish.

tomatl – tomato, Nahuatl.

tributo – tribute, Spanish.

Trinity Island – Trinidad.

tuberoms and **maroxi** – archaic English words for types of sea monsters.

vara – Spanish unit of measurement equivalent to about a yard.

vudu – voodoo, the word is of Dahomey origin.

Xaymaca – Jamaica, land of hills and rivers; also *Yamaye*, land of wood and water, also *Iamiaca*.

yanqui – stranger, also possibly barbarian, possibly Nahuatl, has been tentatively suggested it is the origin of the English word *yankee*.

Yócahu Vagua Maórocoti – supreme (according to Las Casas) Taíno god who lived in the sky with his mother, the moon goddess **Atabey** (see above); according to Ramón Pané he was "invisible, for none can see him, who had no beginning, whose dwelling place and residence is heaven".

yuca – another word for **casaba** (cassava).

yucayeque – town.

zavana – savannah, Spanish, from Taíno *zabana* or *sabana*.

zemi – deity or figure of a deity, sometimes spelled *cemi*.

---

[16] Another spelling for the Taíno expression *the flight of an arrow* is *si'maran*. In Latin American Spanish a *cimarrón* (plural *cimarrones*) refers to a tamed animal which has gone feral, a fugitive, a runaway, and specifically an enslaved African who ran away from their Spanish masters. An alternative explanation of the origin of the word is that it is derived from the Spanish *cima*, meaning top or summit, hence *cimarrón*. literally *living on mountain tops*. According to tradition, the first *simaron/cimarrón/maroon* was an African slave who escaped in 1502.

A short bibliography

Readers interested in studying the history of the Spanish Conquest of the Americas might find some of the following books of interest:

Benzoni, Girolamo, *Historia del Mondo Nuovo (History of the New World)*, Venice 1565. The London 1857 Hakluyt Society edition is a very readable translation into English.

Columbus, Christopher, J. M. Cohen (Ed), *The Four Voyages*, London, 1969 – classic collection of Columbus's accounts of his voyages, excellently edited by J. M. Cohen. Available from Penguin, UK.

Columbus's *Logbook of the First Voyage*, several editions available, under different titles.

Columbus's *Book of Prophecies*, translated into English with commentary by Delno C. West and August King, University of Florida Press 1991, under the title of *The 'Libro de las Profecias' of Christopher Columbus*.

Deagan, Kathleen, and Cruxent, José María, *Columbus's Outpost among the Taínos*, Yale University Press 2002, an excellent account of the early years of the Spanish conquest of Hispaniola, based on the archaeological excavation of La Isabela.

Diaz del Catillo, Bernal *The True History of the Conquest of Mexico*, the classic eyewitness account, still in print.

Dickson, Peter W, *The Magellan Myth: Reflections on Columbus, Vespucci, and the Waldseemüller Map of 1507*, Printing Arts Press, USA, 2007.

Graves, Robert, *The Isles of Unwisdom*, a historical novel giving an account of the Spanish expedition which set off from Peru in 1595 to colonise the Solomon Islands.

Irving, Washington, *The Life and Voyages of Christopher Columbus*, first published in 1828; this is probably the first detailed biography of Columbus, and it is very detailed. Irving drew on several contemporary sources and the account Irving gives is fascinating, even if it does tend to hagiography at times and a judicious reading between the lines is called for.

Kerr, Robert (ed.), *General History and Collection of Voyages and Travels – Volume III*, includes several firsthand accounts of Spanish explorations from 1492-1520, including the first chapters of Bernal Diaz del Catillo's *The True History of the Conquest of Mexico*. Published 1824, available at http://www.gutenberg.org.

Kramer, Heinrich and Sprenger, James, *Malleus Maleficarum – The Hammer of the Witches*, first published in Germany 1486. Both authors were Dominicans. It was reprinted about thirteen times between 1486 and 1520. Despite its undoubted influence and contribution to the witch craze, the Catholic Church did not officially endorse it.

Landa Calderon, Diego de, *Yucatan Before and After the Conquest*, written around 1566. A 1937 English translation of what has survived of the original document by William Gates is available from www.forgottenbooks.org.

Lange, Werner P, *Ich war am Rande des Paradieses: Das Leben von Christoph Kolumbus*, VED FA Brockhaus Verlag, Leipzig, Germany, 1980.

Las Casas, Bartolomé de, *A Brief History of the Destruction of the Indies*, written 1542, first published in Spain in 1552 but quite possibly circulated in manuscript prior to this, numerous editions available.

Leithäuser, Joachim G, *Mappae Mundi: die geistige Eroberung der Welt*, Safari Verlag, Berlin, Germany, 1958, an excellently-illustrated history of world maps from antiquity up to the early modern period.

Lester, Toby, *The Fourth Part of the World: An Astonishing Epic of Global Discovery, Imperial Ambition, and the Birth of America*, USA, 2010, an account of the discovery of the Waldseemüller world map and its origins.

Pané, Ramón, *An Account of the Antiquities of the Indians*, Duke University Press, USA, 1999.

Rouse, Irving, *The Tainos – Rise and Decline of the People Who Greeted Columbus*, Yale University Press, USA, 1992.

Thomas, Hugh, *Rivers of Gold – The Rise of the Spanish Empire, from Columbus to Magellan*, Random House, 2003.

Tzvetan, Todorov, *The Conquest of America: The Question of the Other*, 1982, several editions available, an investigation into the origins of anthropology.

Wassermann, Jakob, *Christoph Columbus, der Don Quichote des Ozeans*, first published Berlin, Germany, 1929.

Pre-Columbus maps
http://en.wikipedia.org/wiki/Antillia – the article on Antillia gives an interesting summary of the pre-Columbus maps and the legend of the seven bishops.

Taíno Indian document
The facsimile of the Taíno Indian document on wood bark paper (Figure 9) is of unknown provenance and can be found at http://en.wikipedia.org/wiki/Haiti
and http://commons.wikimedia.org/wiki/File:Piktograf1.png